The Blue Handbag

Fiona Robyn

snowbooks

Proudly Published by Snowbooks in 2009

Snowbooks Ltd.
120 Pentonville Road
London
N1 9JN
Tel: 0790 406 2414
email: info@snowbooks.com
www.snowbooks.com

British Library Cataloguing in Publication Data
A catalogue record for this book is available from the British Library.

Library Hardback edition: 978-1-906727-05-5
Paperback edition: 978-1-905005-99-4

Printed and bound in Great Britain

Dedicated to Mum and Dad, for making me who I am.

Anything will give up its secrets if you love it enough.
George Washington Carver

Chapter 1:
A Posy of Painted Ladies

Leonard is feeding the dusty, battered suitcase into the mouth of the wheelie-bin when he catches a flash of azure blue shining from inside. He judders to a complete stop and holds himself perfectly still to give his eyes a chance to focus. There's something in there. His heart speeds up. He pulls the suitcase back out and opens the jaws of the zips wide, letting in light. It's a handbag. It must have been one of Rose's. Rose, his dear, dear wife. His body softly crumples in on itself. He presses his forehead with his left palm. It's been nearly three years now. Three years since that last migraine that wasn't a migraine at all, but a clot of blood that had detached itself from one of her arteries and travelled up to her brain. Setting off an explosion of pain, filling her with a beating, rising fear. His Rose. Three years. It seems like yesterday. It seems like a lifetime ago.

He hunkers down on the pavement, his sixty-two-year-old knees reminding him to move carefully. He lifts the handbag out, brushing away cobwebs from the material as if he were stroking his daughter's cheek. He places it on the step beside him, wiping dust from the cold bricks before he sets it down, and checks the inside of the suitcase, sliding a flat hand inside the pockets. A biro lid, a sweetie wrapper, nothing else. He pushes the suitcase back into the wheelie-bin – it just fits and the sides of it scrape the plastic. He looks around nervously to see if anyone has seen him, not knowing why it matters if they have. His heart is slowing down. He sucks in two lungfuls of late October air and turns away from the road and towards his house. He carries the handbag as if it were a baby. As if it were alive.

He's on his way to the kitchen when the phone rings and forces him back into the hall. He rests the handbag up against a green glass vase full of pink-spattered lilies on the telephone table. As he picks up the receiver, all thoughts of his wife leave him as if he's flicked a switch.

"Hello?"

All he can hear is a faint squealing noise. His daughter comes onto the line just before his second hello.

"Hi, Dad, is that you?"

"No, it's the Viscount of Prussia. How may I be of assistance to you?" he says, disguising his usual Berkshire accent with his best aristocratic voice, which despite his efforts comes out a little Welsh.

Raine makes a harrumphing noise. Leonard feels a little sad for the giggling girl in pigtails who got lost – when? When did he lose her? He used to love making her laugh. He seems to have lost the knack.

"Dad, for goodness sakes. How are you?" He can hear the familiar edge of brusqueness in her voice and guesses she's only asking from a sense of duty.

"Tickety-boo, darling. How are the twins?"

"Oh, fine, fine. Rory has a bit of a temperature. He's playing up something rotten; I can't get him to eat anything, the bugger." She breathes a quick sharp sigh. "I'm sure he'll survive. He's annoyed with me right now – I tried to force some bread and marmite down him just before I called you."

Leonard already feels a rising impatience with the conversation.

"Mh hmm," he says, to encourage her to carry on. She pauses, waiting. There's a small fluttering in his stomach.

"Is everything OK, darling?"

"Oh, yes, all fine." She pauses again. "Yes, everything's fine. I'm just tired, I suppose. Are you still coming down this weekend?"

"Yes, of course."

"Great." The squealing noise starts up in the background again – it sounds as if it's coming from a trapped animal. They both listen.

"Look, Dad, I'm sorry but Rory is making a fuss. I better go and check on him. You'd think I'd been starving him, the way he carries on. I don't know what to... well – anyway – I'll call you in a couple of days to arrange things."

"Yes darling, talk to you then. I'll let you know what train I'll be on."

"Bye Dad."

"Bye."

Just as he's pulling the phone away from his ear he hears her say 'Oh – wait! Dad?'

"I'm still here."

"I forgot – the whole reason I rang was to ask you if you liked turkey. Rory, wait a minute! I can't remember if you said something about... last time I... RORY! We're... Dad? Turkey?"

She rushes him into answering. He wonders how she ended up like this, never stopping for long enough to catch her breath. So unlike him, so unlike Rose. He slows his voice down, willing some of his calm to infuse into her, to infect her.

"Yes, that'll be lovely, darling. You're sure you're OK now? Is Ed helping you with the boys?"

"Yes, Dad. Speak soon. Bye! Oh, Ed's fine! Bye!"

By the time he gets his goodbye out she's already hung up.

He stands with the empty phone against his ear for a few seconds until his eyes catch on something blue. The handbag! The colour reminds him of Rose's wedding dress. They were so young – she was seventeen, still a child. He pictures her now, grinning at her friends from work in the congregation, her arm linked through his. The dress was plain, full-skirted and the colour of cornflowers. She told him it was a tradition in their family to wear blue rather than white. She looked so pretty with her painted lips and her dark hair cropped close to her scalp. He'd loved to run his flat fingers against the grain of her softly prickly hair. He gave it a quick skim most days, while teasing her about her temper, or when coming into a room and finding her there. She wanted sweet peas for her wedding bouquet – they'd always been her favourites. They got married in May so he grew her 'Painted Ladies', pale pink with a deep pink nose. She held them in a fat posy at her waist and ticked him off for crushing the petals when he kissed her with too much enthusiasm. He'd whispered into her ear that now they were married he'd grow her bucketfuls and bucketfuls until she was sick of them. And he had – year after year, until she really did get fed up of the sight of them. She finally spat it out one night during an argument, and it had pierced him in his chest. He didn't blame her, really. He always did go a bit over the top with things.

He leaves the handbag on his chair and goes into the kitchen to click on his shiny silver kettle. He can take his time – nothing is going anywhere. One of the advantages of living on your own – nobody will be bursting in to ask him if he can fix the Hoover or get a child a drink. He unhooks his favourite mug from the mug tree, winter-berry red on the outside and glossy green on the inside. Raine bought it for him a few Christmas ago. He readies it with a Yorkshire teabag and turns the lid off the milk. He's been drinking Yorkshire tea for twenty-five years, since a trip to a National Trust property up North. He doesn't enjoy tea at other people's houses; it always tastes insipid. He flicks his eyes around his tiny kitchen as he waits for the water to boil. There are bright crayon scribbles from the twins taped up on the fridge. According to Raine the blocks in the middle are tanks – 'They're utterly obsessed with the bloody things,' but they have bright yellow suns above them and sit on solid green grass spotted with purple flowers. There's a single glass, plate, knife and fork on the washing up drainer. He can see his face reflected, ghost-like, in the white kitchen tiles above the work surface. He notices a smear of something greasy and gets out a cloth to disappear it. He's kept the place clean since Rose died; he prides himself on that. Rose would be impressed. She always kept things neat and tidy.

As the kettle gathers steam and clicks itself off, Pickles jerks his head up and looks at Leonard, startled. He lets out a small wake-up growl. His eyes are button black and shiny, perfect rounds. He's looking scruffy again, his fur choppy as a rough sea, old mud clinging to tufts of hair on his belly. Leonard makes a mental note to tackle bathing him at the weekend. It's always a messy affair. As soon as Pickles sees there's nothing to worry about he drops his chin back onto the well-worn fur of his basket and goes back to his doggy dreams. He's always liked to sleep in the kitchen, even at their old house. Maybe he likes to stay close to his food bowl at all times just in case there are any ad-hoc doggy snacks. Leonard fills his mug and gives the bag a good squeeze, encouraging it to release its dark flavour. Rose used to say it looked like he was milking a cow in there. Finally he jolts in a small splash of milk to stop the horrible floating film that comes with black tea. 'I like it dark and sweet, just how I like my women,' he used to tease Rose – she'd always come back with, 'And I like mine weak and lukewarm, just like you, darling.' He holds the spoon under the tap to help wash away this memory so he can return to the job at hand.

He sets down his tea on the small table next to his chair, resting it on top of a rickety pile of crossword books, and lifts the handbag into his hands. It feels silky against his fingertips and reminds him of the silvery leaves of the canary clover, *Dorycnium hirsutum*. He laughs at the memory of sneaking away from his digging in the middle of the afternoon so he could crouch beside a new batch of them and stroke them. They'd have him carted off if they knew. Leonard lets his mind rest on what he's holding. One of Rose's handbags. What was it doing in their old suitcase? He can't remember ever seeing it before. Is it definitely hers? He lifts it to his face and sniffs, tentatively at first, then great, sucking-in breaths. It's only an echo now, but he remembers the original scent so well – a hint of jasmine, sandalwood, and then something underneath... what is that Indian spice called? Cardamom? The handbag was hers alright. He'll never forget that perfume until the day he dies. She must have kept one of her little bottles in here, where it spilt a golden drop or three. This scent is as familiar to him as her face is – no – more familiar. It's more of an effort now to remember exactly what she looked like, and this worries him.

But that smell. Mmm. He feels his eyes prickling and allows a single tear to escape from each one, warming his cheeks, before taking a sharp breath and blowing his nose. He's done his crying.

He studies the material close-up for a moment. It's woven, and has lots of tiny hairs like the hide of a strange blue animal. Maybe one with six legs and purple eyes and a huge mane like a lion. He places a flat palm on one side and moves it across and back, across and back. He's aware of taking his time with it, as if he's choosing the perfect chocolate from the box. The clasp is one of those old-fashioned metal ones where the metal prongs push hard against each other before finally snapping free. He un-clicks it, and then clicks it shut and un-clicks it absentmindedly a few times more before pulling it open and peering inside.

Nothing. Empty. His heart sinks – and then he laughs at himself – what exactly was he expecting to find? A new photograph of her? A bright burst of her laugh? The things she left behind are all souvenirs now – her wedding ring, the favourite cardigan he keeps in his top drawer in the bedroom. He puts his hand inside to feel the silk lining, already thinking about putting it back into the bin outside, and as he slips a thumb under the piece of silk-covered cardboard at the bottom he encounters something sharp. It's the edge of something. A small piece of paper. He checks first to make sure there's nothing else there, and then pulls it out and holds it out in front of him so he can see it properly. It's a return train ticket from Pangbourne, where Rose worked as a nurse for many years, to Didcot. It's dated the 15th of December 1998. Nearly seven years ago. On the back she's written 'decide about next Tues??? L's on hol' in blue felt tip. She'd never been to Didcot. He never went to Didcot with her. He pauses to search his memories more carefully. Did they ever go shopping there? No. To see the railway centre, or friends? No. Had she cried off when he'd suggested it, saying something about not liking the town, something about a bad memory? He can't remember. Why would she go there? What is it she needed to think about next Tuesday? Why would it make a difference that he was on holiday?

These busy thoughts fade away and he sits and points his eyes in the general direction of the window for five whole minutes, not thinking of anything in particular. He's noticed that he 'phases out' like this sometimes − if someone else were in the room they might ask him what he was thinking about. No-one asks him. He rouses himself with a shake. He used to growl like Pickles when he did this, to make Rose, and then later Raine, laugh. He does it now anyway − *grrreeowwwwWWW-HUH!* − and makes himself laugh instead. He puts the ticket back where he found it and goes outside to throw the handbag in the wheelie-bin. He comes back into the sitting room and considers rolling a cigarette. Instead he turns on a programme about ancient Rome and picks up his hot cup of tea and a crossword book. He flicks the pages, gulps his tea, and tries to ignore the ichneumon wasps who have laid their eggs inside him.

Chapter 2:
Thousands of pairs of hands

The next morning, after the usual domestic routines of a man living alone, Leonard looks into the sky and guesses rain. It's become something of an obsession, the weather, after so many years working outside – scouring the forecasts, watching the clouds... At least he's not as bad as an old boy he used to work with, who used to listen to the forecast on three different radio stations and wrote down their predictions in a little red book before he left the house every morning. Leonard used to watch him do the same at lunchtimes – he wanted to 'do a proper comparison', find out which forecast was most trustworthy. He'd written into that little book for years and never came up with any firm conclusions.

Leonard pulls on a dark green waterproof jacket, feeling the pleasant weight of the day ahead of him. He's going to tackle that holly bush today, the one that needs a serious hair-cut. He feels a short burst of gratitude at being able to do the work he loves. He's often noticed the colour draining from people's words during the traditional 'What do you do?' swap. They try their best to sound enthusiastic about their 'comfy desk-job', reassuring themselves that they 'work with some really nice people' and that they'll 'get a tidy pension'. It's not enough. He always feels pride when he says the words: 'I'm a gardener for the National Trust.' He's a lucky man. He wonders what it is about him that allows him to relish his life so much. Maybe it's how he was brought up. His parents weren't perfect – his father could be a right nasty bugger, and his mother overlooked him sometimes, got too tangled up in what other people thought. He'd believed them to be the worst parents in the world ever for a few months when he was fifteen. But all in all, they'd done a pretty good job. They'd paid attention to him, and they showed him they cared as best they could. Maybe, in the end, knowing you are loved is enough.

He throws a leg over his bicycle and climbs on, shifting about until his bottom finds the most comfortable spot before pushing off into the gloom. It's started to rain already; he can feel it dampening his face. He loves this particular variety of rain, almost as if the cool air itself has started to coagulate. He imagines absorbing it through his skin, which is leathery and creased after years of working out under the wind and sun. One of the young lads at work let on last week that he uses face cream – face cream! He said we need to look after our skin these days, that women expected it. Leonard chuckles at the thought of his bathroom cabinet, with its lonely toothbrush, shaving cream and deodorant, imagines it instead full to the brim with salves and potions with French names and scientific sounding ingredients. There are advantages to being a sixty-two-year-old widower who isn't on the market for a new wife. No fancy face creams for him.

As he cycles the familiar roads to Coburne House, he strolls around in his head, letting thoughts float up from the wilderness. Sometimes he wonders how he manages to get to work in one piece – he'll be pushing away from the house and then all at once he's wheeling his bike into the staff shed and leaning it against the wall. His thoughts hover around the ticket from the handbag as if it's a motorway accident he wants and doesn't want to look at. Why has it unsettled him so much? He also notices a fizzing of excitement in the pit of his stomach. He loves to solve puzzles. Rose used to call herself a 'crossword widow' – he's been doing them for thirty years now. They'd always been a mystery to her. He'd tried to teach her a few times but she didn't have the patience and got angry at the clues, said they were making fun of her with their cleverness. She did like the clue he'd written for her, "Got up' in a pink hue, 4 letters.' He'd presented it to her on one of her birthdays, written up neatly underneath a picture of a rose he'd found in a magazine and framed. She'd called him a silly bugger and flicked him on the cheek with the tea-towel she was carrying, so he knew she was pleased.

As he hangs up his coat, the handbag and the ticket slip away from him again. He's greeted by three of his colleagues as he walks into the chilly mess-room. His boss, Simon, is sitting at the big cluttered table in the centre of the room. He's officially Leonard's boss, but they have 'an understanding' which means Simon mostly leaves him alone to get on with whatever he wants to do. He only bugs him once a year for those ridiculous 'annual reviews' they make them fill in these days, full of words like 'proactive' and 'self-development'. One year he took a half-completed one to the pub in desperation and his friend Charlie made him read some of it out loud. He almost laughed himself off his barstool. He's referred to them as Leonard's 'annual bullshit reviews' ever since. Simon's long, angular body towers like a heron over Tommy, their new apprentice, who's short and compact with shy eyes under a shaggy fringe. He's talking Tommy through his jobs for the day, and Leonard notices the tone of frustration in his boss's voice. He wonders what Tommy is finding difficult to grasp this time. One of their long-standing volunteers, Val, is stirring one of those cups of fruit tea that smell fragrant and sweet but taste bitter and disappointing. She offers him a mug of Yorkshire, and he says thanks but no thanks. He's itching to get outside and let the green bathe his eyes.

He starts to whistle a chirpy, made-up-as-he-goes-along tune as he sets off on his usual patrol around the estate grounds. He turns left out of the garden's yard and passes through the tea-room and the shop, lifting an imaginary hat to Margie in the kitchen, to her obvious delight. He heads across the broad lawn, towards the patch of woodland, glancing left as he usually does at the big old manor. He's never been fond of it – it's dark and severe-looking, and reminds him of his rigid and unsmiling piano teacher from when he was a boy. These days it's let as a hotel and only opens for National Trust visitors once a week. He often sees taxis spitting out pale, brief-cased business people on a Monday and picking them up on a Friday. He imagines them sitting in various meetings over the week with their flipcharts and clipboards, talking about targets. Is that what they do? He hopes they give themselves some time to wander around the gardens for an hour before dinner, to catch the scent of honeysuckle on the air.

As he enters the woods he comes across a large branch on the ground that must have blown down last night – there were some pretty strong winds. He makes a mental note to come back later on one of the little tractors with a chain saw. They used to have red deer here, a long time ago, but the last owners let them get out of control. They stripped so much bark and caused such damage that they got rid of them all – a massive cull – Leonard doesn't like to think about it. The woods are still full of life. On these morning walks, an occasional Muntjac skitters away from him, and squirrels speak in semaphore with their pert tails wherever he looks. Blackbirds rustle in the undergrowth, and there are Green Woodpeckers, Goldcrests... Once he even saw a mink washing its ears like a cat, with a delicate paw.

He reaches the walled garden. It's one of their most popular attractions – people love surprises. This place is at its best in mid-July – full of garish annuals dripping with colour, 'looking like Disneyland' as Simon likes to boast. It does pack a punch, he admits – wandering in from the muted colours of the pleasure gardens and opening the plain wooden door onto such brightness... When Leonard first worked here he loved to hang around and hear the 'ooh's as the colour smacked visitors in the face, as if fireworks were going off. It all looks a bit forlorn at this time of year. He picks up a stray trowel (left by that dizzy new volunteer no doubt) and carries it with him. There are a couple of large stones on the path, and he bends and hides them near the back of the bed. There's always something to be tidied, always something that could be improved. On bad days it feels never-ending. On good days it feels the same, but he's glad of it.

He leaves the walled garden to walk along the furthest perimeter of the estate. It backs onto farmland, and he likes to stop at the gate, where he and the cows can get close to each other. He usually rips them up some long, lush grass as a breakfast treat, and lets them in on the latest goings-on in the mess-room. Today they decline to come over when he calls to them with a mixture of whistles and whoops that usually works a treat. They turn their detached gaze on him for a few seconds before continuing to crop the grass as close to the earth as they can. He wonders if they notice when they get an occasional mouthful of damp, bitter soil. Maybe they're too practised for that. He shouts cheerfully at them that he'll see them tomorrow, so they'll know that he won't hold their disinterest against them.

Completing the circle, he passes by the lake. Simon calls it the lake, anyway. He's not sure it's big enough. What is the official size at which a pond becomes a lake? It's choked with Cape Pondweed and desperately needs clearing out, but there's no money in the budget for it this year. Mending some stretches of fencing and replacing the roof in the outbuilding near the vegetable patch were seen as a bigger priority. Maybe next year.

The planting out here is looking pretty good, even if he says so himself. They don't tend to focus on all-year-round colour, being shut to the public for the colder half of the year, but here there are some glossy, red-stemmed dogwood bushes – *Cornus alba* 'Sibirica' and *Erica* 'Furzey'. He put them in a few years ago after seeing some in the Winter Garden at the Botanic Gardens in Cambridge. The new stems burn like fire from December through to April. At the right time of day, the light sparkles on the water behind them and acts as a pale, glittery backdrop. This autumn he planted a carpet of snowdrops underneath the bushes. He can't wait to see what they look like when they push their heads out into the spring sun in a few months' time.

He moves slowly through his domain, taking immense pleasure from the land. This bare rose bush, these leaves crumbling into leaf mould, these pale green buds. That line of alders on the horizon. He's looking at the results of the earth, sun and rain working together, helped along by thousands of pairs of hands through the ages. Thousands of pairs of hands, including his own. All is in order. He heads back to the mess-room for that cup of tea.

It's a satisfying day, attacking the rampant holly and bringing it into slow submission. He knows it's meant to be bad luck to cut down a holly – it's why you see them standing alone out in the countryside without their original hedge companions. He's never held much truck with superstition, unlike Rose. He used to enjoy walking underneath ladders on purpose when he was with her, just to wind her up. He'd usually fall to the ground dramatically about five paces on, writhing in agony for a few seconds and moaning 'you were right…' as she stepped over him and walked on without comment. By five o'clock he thinks a pint at The Five Bells is in order. It isn't officially his local, being in the next village but one, but he and Rose used to come here all the time when they lived in their last cottage on the estate grounds. It was Rose's favourite pub – although he suspects this was mainly because they stocked her favourite flavour of crisps, prawn cocktail. It's a brown, slightly tatty, womb-like place, all higgledy-piggledy and cluttered with random odds and sods. He's been going there for – what – thirty years now? More? He hates being able to measure time in decades.

The other locals are like a kind of family to him. They don't ever pry into each other's business, but are always ready to listen to anyone who wants to talk. Anyone except old Fred at the end of the bar, who's gnawed everyone's ears off by now and sits quietly nursing his pint, a hopeful look crossing his face when newcomers stray dangerously close to him. A few of them are drunks, he knows, but that doesn't matter – everybody has his share of problems, some are just better at hiding them than others. There hasn't been any trouble in here for a long time, not since the new landlady, Suze, took over. She's a large woman with frizzy blond hair and black roots – she wears thick make-up: dark lipstick, green eye-shadow, orangey foundation that crusts around her mouth. She greets him now and fetches his usual without asking, a pint of Tetley. He usually only has the one and drinks lemonade afterwards, or pineapple juice if he fancies a treat. They get in fresh pineapple juice especially for him now in those big cardboard cartons; it's much tastier than the thick, bitty, mucous-producing stuff in small glass bottles. He gets a bit of ribbing for the pineapple juice, but he doesn't care.

He settles into a bar chair next to his old friend Charlie, who spends more time at the Bells than anywhere else (except maybe his greenhouse).

"Alright, old man?" Leonard says, aware that his accent always changes when he speaks to Charlie – becomes even more 'local', as Raine would say.

"Alright, Leonard."

Leonard brings out his battered tobacco tin and goes about the comforting business of building a roll-up. He points it at Charlie before he starts, who holds out a flat hand and moves his head in a half-shake. He lights up. Charlie continues the conversation.

"On your bike, are you?"

"Yup. Good weather for it."

They lapse into an instant silence. Neither of them is scrabbling about for words to plug the gap – it's just that there isn't anything that needs saying. After a good ten minutes or so, when Leonard has smoked his second rollie and is a third of the way down his pint, having savoured every, warm, malty sip, Charlie speaks again.

"How're Glor and Pete doing?"

"Oh, fine, fine. Last time Glor came round, she sorted out my curtains for me, sewed them back up at the bottoms. Where do women learn these things?"

Charlie makes a grunting nose in his throat, 'Hnh,' which he uses as a substitute for a variety of words and phrases – 'Well I never,' or 'Of course I do,' or even 'I hear what you're saying, Leonard, and I know all about the complicated political situation in Outer Mongolia, but this time we'll have to agree to disagree.' This time it's, 'I know what you mean.' He cocks his head onto one side.

"She's still helping you with your bits and pieces then?"

"Yes, every other Sunday, regular as clockwork. It was hard enough to stop her from coming round every week. We had a right battle over that one."

"Cushty."

"Mmm. I've thought about – I dunno – like I ought to be able to do everything myself by now. It's been nearly three years now, you know." Charlie raises his eyebrows at this. "I cope with most things, but new jobs do crop up occasionally, even after all this time. I pay her a bit of pocket money, but it's just not been feeling… oh, I don't know."

"Hnh."

Charlie waits, but Leonard is running his fingernails over the bar, looking intently at the years of scratches and dents. Charlie rubs his grey-stubbled chin with a thumb and forefinger, and Leonard recognises the gesture and waits for his opinion.

"You'd be mad to turn her away, mate. The wife is always moaning about what she does for me. I never bring my empty glasses downstairs from the bedroom, I leave tissues in my trouser pockets, nyah nyah nyah'." He says this last bit in a high-pitched voice, a hand on one hip while he jerks his chest from side to side in a poor parody of womanhood. Leonard frowns.

"How is Marion?"

"Oh, she's alright I suppose. She was crying over some silly film last night."

"You should look after her."

His voice comes out more sternly than he intended it to. Charlie looks over at him for a moment, looks away and nods four times.

"Hnh."

They settle back into a comfortable silence until Leonard drains the last of his pint and says his goodbyes.

Amongst the bills waiting for him back at the flat is a letter addressed to 'Rose Smith' in unfamiliar handwriting. He wonders who Rose Smith is for a second before remembering his wife's maiden name. She'd been Rose Mutch for so long, he couldn't imagine her being anything else. Their old address has been crossed out and their new address written to one side in small capital letters. Who would be writing to her now? Maybe it's one of those clever advertisements where they disguise the printed address as handwriting and then bombard you with offers for loans. He has a passionate dislike for those companies, and he fake-spits at the slimy men-in-suits and their pretty assistants whenever the adverts come on the TV. Making out they're doing you a favour and getting you deeper and deeper into debt. He runs his fingers over the address – the handwriting is real; it's scored the paper. He holds it up to the light and sees more of the same large, squat handwriting through the thin paper of the envelope. He slits it open with his bone-handled letter-opener and reads it in the hall with his work bag still over one shoulder.

Dear Rose,

I'm not sure how to start... I'm not sure if I'll find you here, I found your address through the internet. My niece Meg helped me to, well, find you... she knows about these things. I hope there isn't more than one Rose Margaret Smith in Oxfordshire! Anyway, it's Lily. Lily Sorensen, from school in Cowley. I was Lily Sweet for most of my life, but I've, well, I've taken my own name back now. I hope you remember me, I'll feel dreadfully silly if you don't. We were best friends (I thought of you as my best friend anyway) for a while. I had light brown hair in two bunches, and you used to come round to my house, we used to play with dolls in the garden and pretend we were teachers or something... What a silly game! I do hope you remember me.

You probably wonder why I'm writing to you, after all this time. To be honest, Rose, I'm not really sure myself... I lost my husband last year, and it's not been easy. We didn't get on that well to be truthful, but even so... it takes a while to get used to a man-sized hole in your life after 40 years. I've been looking backwards, thinking about what I've done with my life so far, trying to work things out... I keep thinking about you, wondering where you are, what job you're doing, if you got married, what kind of house you live in... You were always kind to me, I remember that. I remember you gave me your slice of, what was it, lemon cake I think, from your lunchbox one day. Just because I said I liked it... you didn't even keep any for yourself. And so I thought, what the hell, Lily, let's see if you can find her. So here I am.

If you'd like to get in touch for a chat about old times, do write back or call me... If you don't want to drag it all up then that's fine, I'd understand, really, but just know Rose that I've never forgotten you and that I hope with all my heart that life has given you all kinds of wonderful things. You certainly deserve them.

Yours in hope,

Lily Sorenson

Leonard reads the letter twice. He lingers over the phrase at the end, 'if you don't want to drag it all up...' – drag what up? He feels sad for this woman, who doesn't seem to have considered that Rose wouldn't be alive to read her letter. He ought to write back to her, to let her know what happened. His mind flicks through all the people he's had to tell about her death, like going through a pack of cards, in order: Raine, Glor, a man he'd met in the waiting room at the hospital, Rose's friend Marjory, Charlie... Each time it was harder to find the right words, each time harder to hear them coming from his mouth.

He yawns, over-exaggerating as usual with a great long walrus sound and arms stretched over his head. He's tired of thinking about it. He puts the letter back in the envelope and slides it underneath his address book, out of sight. He goes into the kitchen to rummage through the fridge for something he can cook. As he peels and chops carrots, 'drag it all up' runs through his mind over and over, becoming more rhythmic, until it fits into a snatch of chorus from a Johnny Cash song, 'Daddy Sang Bass'. *Drag it all up... daddy sang bass...* the inside of his head sounds like a bloody train hammering over the tracks. He violently waggles his head in an impression of Pickles, trying to shake the words out. He eats as he usually does, with the plate balanced on his lap, watching television, feeling faintly guilty that he isn't using the dining room table that stands folded and pushed up against the wall. When he's cleared away the plate and turned off the television, Pickles jumps up and sits beside him, squashing himself into the warm gap between his lap and the chair-arm. Leonard tickles his ears gently and sings him a lullaby he used to sing to Raine –

> Hush-a-bye, don't you cry,
> Go to sleep-y, little Pickles.
> When you wake you shall have
> All the pretty little horses.
> Blacks and bays, dapple greys,
> Coach and six white horses.
> Hush-a-bye, don't you cry,
> Go to sleep-y, little Pickles.

Soon all Leonard can hear is the ticking of his clock and gentle, snuffled snores.

Chapter 3:
The Amazing Swinging Twins

Leonard slides a bar of fruit and nut into the bottom of his bag, just in case Raine is in the midst of another silly chocolate embargo. He's packing for a weekend with his daughter – the usual spare change of clothes, toiletries (but no fancy face cream), and (of course) a well-thumbed book of cryptic crosswords. He finds Pickles fast asleep under the spare bed and pokes him gently with a ruler so he can say a proper goodbye. It's a shame that Ed is so allergic to dogs. Leonard is always careful to explain to Pickles exactly where he's going, how long he'll be gone, and what he should do in an emergency. Pickles, as usual, doesn't seem to be paying proper attention to the different types of fire extinguishers and the number for the local police station. He drops his house keys off to Peggy-next-door, who greets him with a pink towel wrapped round her head like a turban. She loves looking after Pickles when he's away – she feeds him prime chicken breast and fusses him to death. One of these days he's convinced he'll come back to an empty house. He'll look across at her window and see a curtain twitching shut, and a paw disappearing from view...

He cycles the familiar journey to the local train station, waving so enthusiastically at the local shopkeeper out walking her dog that he almost loses his balance. The train to Reading is horribly bright and noisy on a Friday night. All those young people. He could go in his car, he supposes, but it's always such a luxury to sit back and let someone else do the driving. The train would be quieter if he waited until tomorrow, but if he stays on the Friday night he can get away with coming home late on Saturday, and have the luxury of waking up in his own bed on Sunday. He loves Raine very much, but it's always a relief to be home. Relief isn't quite the right word... it's more like how a knife must feel when you put it back into the knife rack – it's all very well going off and chopping things here there and everywhere, but there's nothing like being back in your slot. He smiles broadly at the silliness of his metaphor until a stern-looking woman standing on the platform gives him a funny look.

He manages to get a seat on the train, one next to the window, and prays that no-one with a mobile phone will sit next to him. He's lucky – it's an older woman with a book, who asks him politely if the seat is free before settling down quietly. He loves travelling by train. He loves to let his eyes skim the landscape. He mostly fixes them straight ahead so his gaze travels in parallel with the train, taking in dark shapes, covering the land with a broad brush. Occasionally they are snagged by something – a man standing at a gate with his back to the train, a tree shaped like a face, a heron. When this happens he looks at the object before his gaze pings back to where it was, like elastic. He doesn't think about anything important. Tonight he worries vaguely about the placing of the new Winter Heliotrope – it'll need a good damp piece of ground, somewhere it's not going to colonise... will it still be giving off its sweet vanilla scent when they open for visitors in April? Next he turns over a clue that he hasn't been able to solve, 'Breathing hole – it's on right and left after reorganisation'(7). Of course – Nostril. This starts him off on nostril hair, a subject he's been giving some thought to recently, having noticed his developing a life of its own. He's plucking up courage to speak to Charlie about the best way of getting rid of it, or maybe Glor... His mind skirts around the blue handbag as if it's something slightly unpleasant, like knowing he ought to book an appointment with the dentist.

After not thinking about the blue handbag he thinks about Lily's letter. He doesn't usually keep letters hanging around. He deals with them straight away and chucks them, or files them in their shiny red filing cabinet. He'd left Lily's letter tucked underneath his address book since it arrived three whole days ago. He'd finally taken himself by the scruff of the neck and sat down to write a reply. He opens the flap of his overnight bag to check it's still there, that it isn't getting creased. Yes, it's there. He'd finished it late last night after agonising over it for hours – should it be hand-written or typed with his old-fashioned type-writer? How he should address her – formally? Or would she prefer it if he acted as if she were his friend too, by association? In the end he had hand-written it with extra neat handwriting. He had gone over every word so many times he could remember exactly what he'd written. First he needed to let her know who he was.

And there it was, he couldn't work out how to avoid it. He imagines her reading that 'was' and taking a quick mouthful of air, her eyes widening. It's the only way he can break it to her.

I am sorry to say

He nearly wrote 'I regret to inform you' but decided it sounded too stiff, too formal.

that my wife died on March the 15th, 2002.

Twelve whole days after Rory and Buddy came into the world. How many times did she hold them in her arms? Did she have time to imagine their first birthday, their first day at school, their first girlfriends, did she picture herself as a part of their lives? At least it was sudden – at least she didn't have to carry that knowledge around with her. If she'd known that she was holding them for the last time...

He wasn't sure if he should write something about how she died in the letter here – it was unexpected, there was no long illness, it was an aneurism... but nothing sounded right so he left it out.

She is sorely missed.

He wants to let Lily know this. He still wants to let everyone know. Remembering his words now, he's ashamed to feel a sob rise in him. It escapes without too much noise, sounding more like a hiccup. He looks out of the corner of his eye at the woman next to him. She's still reading her book and doesn't seem to have noticed.

If there is anything further I can help you with, Lily, do feel free to get in touch. Regards, Leonard Mutch.

He hopes it's all right. There is no-one to ask. He doesn't

usually worry so much about getting things right, but this feels important. She was Rose's friend. Another new link to his wife after all this time. He can't decide if he wants Lily to get in touch with him or not. It might be nice to hear about Rose as a little girl. He doesn't know much about her past, her life before he met her. It hadn't seemed to matter when she was alive. But he feels greedy for more information about her now. Maybe he should have offered to meet with her. No, it was best to leave it up to her. She probably wouldn't want to see him anyway. It was Rose she wanted.

They're delayed arriving into Reading. Raine's husband Ed is waiting patiently for him behind the barriers, looking a bit crumpled, as usual. His dark hair is quite long on top and moves one way and then the other in rows of spikes, like a rough sea. Is it something he does to it on purpose, with some kind of gel? Raine seems to like him battered-looking. Leonard can remember her defensive reaction to an off-hand remark he'd once made about the creases in his shirt. He slides Lily's letter into a post box on the way to the car. On the fifteen-minute journey to the house, he and Ed talk about the cricket. Leonard has often felt grateful that they have this interest in common. You know where you are with cricket, Leonard feels. Ed has a friend who saw the fifth test of the Ashes at the Oval — Leonard's never been and wants to hear what he thought of the venue. They also discuss the relative merits of Harmison and Thorpe, although Leonard can never get Ed into a proper argument about anything. Leonard can't help comparing modern cricket to how he remembers the game from his youth, but is still managing to catch himself before 'in the old days' comes out of his mouth. Maybe one day he'll be too old to care about alienating young people. It's getting late, and Leonard wonders if the children will still be awake. He never can tell – they don't seem to have any kind of reliable routine. He always arrives into the middle of some new crisis. Ed pulls into the drive and turns off the engine. In those few quiet moments Leonard braces himself for the possible onslaught.

The children are asleep, and he feels equal measures of relief and disappointment. Raine greets him with an empty mug in each hand as Ed slopes off into the dark living room, the TV flickering in the corner.

"I was just about to make a cup of cocoa. Want one, Dad?"

She interrupts herself with a 'hello' and puts her arms around him, the mugs clinking heavily behind his back. The hug is quick and fierce. It is good to see her. The thought of cocoa is heavenly.

"Oh, yes please, love, that would be grand."

"How was the journey?"

"Oh, good, good – I saw a heron."

It feels good to have someone to tell. It feels good to go on a journey where someone is waiting for him at the other end. He watches her as she whizzes about her kitchen, spooning cocoa from the packet, glugging milk into a saucepan, adding a generous splash of cream. She seems to do everything extra quickly, like pressing fast forward on a video. He wonders what it feels like to live at that speed. Is she anxious all the time? Does she even notice it? Maybe it's just her normal speed. Maybe he's the one who's slow.

"Oh, that's nice," she answers.

He's not sure if she's even heard him. He notices her humouring him more often these days, as if he were the child come in from school and prattling on about sports cars or who his best friends are. It doesn't matter. He is happy to be here with her.

She finishes off the cocoa with a spiral of squirty cream from a can (what a strange invention) and some chocolate sprinkles and tiny marshmallows. He's never seen the marshmallows before – she says she'd bought them for the boys. He gets a bit carried away with the word 'marshmallow' and says it over and over in what he feels is a marshmallow-ey accent until Raine shuts him up with a growl. She sets the mug in front of him with a flourish; he gives her a round of applause. After he's taken his first sip she asks him how it tastes, anxiously. Even if it weren't, he'd tell her it was delicious, but it really is; she makes the best cocoa. He makes a small pantomime of his enjoyment for her, rolling his head from side to side.

"Mmm hmm mmmmmmhuh! Perfect, love," he croons.

She makes a dismissive gesture with a flicked hand, but he knows she's pleased; he can see her relax a little. He isn't sure how to drink it without getting cream on his nose, so he exaggerates the movement and sits drinking with a huge blob of white in the centre of his line of vision. He waits patiently for her to notice, and when she does and says 'Daaad!' in that whiny way, he wipes it with one finger and sucks it off with a loud kissing noise. They don't say much as they drink, sitting in companionable silence. When they're finished he makes his excuses and goes in to say goodnight to Ed, who's slumped in front of a programme about cars. He changes into his pyjamas at top speed and gets straight into his deliciously cool bed in the spare room, pushing his feet down between the smooth sheets. He sniffs in the daisy-fresh smell of clean linen and turns to his crosswords.

The next day passes with the usual mix of grabbed conversations with Raine, entertaining Rory and Buddy, and squeezing in five minutes of peace when he can. He's developed a toilet habit when he's at Raine's and often disappears with the paper or a crossword book for twenty minutes at a time (they have a second one downstairs, so he doesn't have to worry about small-boy toilet emergencies). Ed makes the occasional weak joke about curries or 'too much sitting on cold ground', but it's a small price to pay. The twins track him down everywhere else, and once they even started banging on the toilet door and singing 'Granddad going poopoo, Granddad going poopoo!' with great gusto until Raine came to his rescue and spirited them away.

In the morning they go to a park with a lake in the middle and an impressive playground. The boys swing on the swings for as long as the adults can bear to push them. After half an hour of continuous swinging, Leonard wonders if they would *ever* get tired of it. He sees them in his minds' eye with a huge back-up team of adult pushers to launch and re-launch them into the air twenty-four hours a day. They'll eat and drink on them, learn their times tables, sleep on them, grow out of their tiny trousers and into bigger ones and bigger ones, holding mini-TVs on their laps, chatting with friends who jump onto the swings beside them. 'The Amazing Swinging Twins!' the papers will announce, and psychologists and film-makers will come from far and wide to analyse them and film them as they swing. They'll only stop when Rory, aged seventeen, falls in love with one of his young pushers and leaps off into the air and into her arms. He'll suffer from non-swinging sickness for several weeks, but he'll visit Buddy every day, who will lose enthusiasm fast without his brother beside him. Soon afterwards Buddy will simply say, 'Enough now thank you,' and wait for the swing to come to a halt. He'll step off onto the ground and walk away, wobbling slightly. Leonard is pulled away from imagining what happens to Buddy next as the three-year-old Buddy in front of him says, 'Enough now, Granddad, enough.' He slides his bottom off the swing and runs over to the merry-go-round at full pelt where he promptly asks to be pushed again.

Later, when the boys are both sleeping in front of a Thomas the Tank Engine video, slumped on each side of a comatose Ed, Leonard tells Raine about the letter from Lily. He's always a bit wary of speaking to her about Rose – it seems to upset her. After he's told her she continues to stare at the television and a tight look comes over her face. It looks like annoyance, though he can't understand why.

"Why did you write back to her, Dad?" she asks.

"What do you mean, why?"

"Well, I don't know." She pauses and he waits for her to say something else, but she doesn't. He makes his voice sound soft, like she's still a little girl.

"I needed to let her know about your mother, otherwise she'd never have known. It was my duty to tell her, Raine. What is it?"

"Oh, I don't know, Dad." She definitely sounds angry now. "I just want to know when this whole thing will end, when we can just go back to normal again. What if this woman wants to meet you?"

"What do you mean, end?" There is an edge in his voice now; he can't keep it out. "Would you rather just forget all about your mother?"

"It's just that every time you bring it all up again…" her voice cracks and she turns away from him, eyes down, face stiff.

"Raine."

He breathes the word quietly, putting a hand on her

arm. He loves her name. Every time he says it he thinks of the gentle pattering of water onto leaves, the sudden dark spots on sandy dry earth, the coming of nourishment, the coming of life. She puts her own hand on top of his for a few seconds, pushing his hand into her arm with a sudden violence. It wrenches him in his chest. And just as suddenly she pulls it away, swipes at a single tear with the back of her hand, and takes a deep breath.

"Right!' she says, all efficiency. "Let's get those potatoes peeled for dinner. They're not going to peel themselves."

He knows the subject is closed. He offers his help, but she wants to do it herself; she needs to be useful, busy. He goes into the garden instead and makes a roll-up, staring into the sky as the end of his cigarette pierces a prick of light into the darkening afternoon.

Raine drops him off at the station at eight that evening and hugs him goodbye, apologising for not waiting with him. There's washing to be done, and she hasn't got ready for that party the twins are going to yet. As the train pulls out of the station, Leonard wonders what would happen if she just stopped. Maybe she'd fall over. He hopes she's happy. Ed's a good man, if a little un-exciting, and the children are treasures. She's got so much to be grateful for… He supposes it must be hard, though, having to work full time on top of everything else. He's not sure what she does exactly. She says it's 'marketing', but he can't get any sense from her when he asks her what she actually does – she talks about 'clients' and 'different accounts'… He imagines her going to endless meetings in her smart suit and drinking cappuccinos, but that's probably not very accurate. Maybe there's lots of pressure at work too. He's not sure if he should be doing anything differently to help her cope with it all. Rose would have known what to do. He feels a little sad, and so reassures himself by patting himself on the left shoulder, a hangover from his mother's advice to learn how to pat himself on the back. 'One of the most important things you'll ever learn to do,' she used to say. He silently mouths, 'You do your best, old man,' followed by a curt nod as he agrees with himself. He smiles and settles back into his seat.

He spends the rest of the journey under the hawthorn trees with Rose. It's the only place he can remember her telling him about from her childhood. They were on a scrap of land between her house and the rubbish tip. The branches had grown too long and drooped towards the earth so there was a kind of secret space inside, with bare mud for carpets and leaves for walls and ceiling. She called it 'Hawthorne House'. Rose would sometimes take her friends with her (was Lily there?) but she was often there alone, and the whole 'house' was her domain. She would weed the edges of the carpets where nettles came through, wrapping her hands in her skirt to protect her from the stings. She'd sweep the loose earth out with a wooden brush with a snapped handle. She'd bring in 'treasures' found at the tip or borrowed from home: a plastic teapot for plastic tea parties, a rusted bicycle wheel for a dining room table, a mouldy piece of curtain for a rug. 'There was always so much to do,' Rose would tell him, lying in his arms in the middle of the night when neither of them could sleep. When the 'work' was done she'd lie down on her back and look up at the sun shining through the leaves. Sometimes she'd sing herself a song, although she couldn't remember the words or the tune when he asked her. 'I felt safe there, safe from the whole world. Snug as a bug in a rug.' He feels safe too, remembering this place his wife had played in, remembering her telling him about it. Safe and sound.

Pickles greets him excitedly when he opens the door to his own life late on Saturday night. He still prefers his silly old owner to Peggy-next-door... phew. He grills a beef sausage and cuts it up into the dog dish just in case. It's good to have Pickles here with him, running around the kitchen or snoozing in his basket. Having the TV on provides a flickering illusion of life, but it depresses him that he has to make do with these strangers who are paid to be piped into his sitting room rather than living with a real person. Before TVs and texting and electric mowers he supposes it was rare for people to live alone. Even if they did they were probably closer to their livestock, their plants... breezes shuffling their leaves, the sun opening their petals. He leaves the TV on BBC2 mostly, and likes it most when there are nature programmes on, or travel, or cricket, of course. He's thought about getting satellite TV so he can have the nature channels, but it seems a lot of money to have plants on the TV in the background. He gets to look at the real things all day, and touch them, and sniff them.

He moves about the house in a familiar pattern – unpacking his bag, putting the washing on, changing into his blue, striped pyjamas, brushing his teeth. He thinks about Lily. She'll get his letter soon – maybe Monday or Tuesday. He imagines her reacting to the word 'was' – 'Rose was my wife.' Something occurs to him – maybe when she reads that sentence she'll just think he's divorced her. Maybe it won't sink in until she gets to the end of the next sentence, when he spells it out. He wonders how far her heart will sink. He wonders where she'll read his letter – in her hallway? At work? What does she look like? Will she cry? All these questions. He takes a new novel from the mobile library to bed, and after losing patience with the idiotic protagonist, he saves his place with a tissue and clicks off his bedside lamp.

He drifts off by imagining the twins swinging back and forth, back and forth. It comforts him, like counting sheep. He can hear the *braaaak, week! braaaak, week!* as the chains squeak against the top-bar. He can smell the boy's floral soap-powder smell when they swing towards him, their grinning faces move closer and then away, closer and then away. The train ticket appears again and flutters in the air between them. The twins spot it and reach out for it as they swing towards it, putting themselves off balance, just missing it each time. He wants to tell them to stop moving about on the swings, he tries to call to them, but there's no sound. He moves his hand to his mouth and there's nothing there, just smooth skin. He tries to open his eyes, a trick he's used before to escape from a dream that's turning into a nightmare, but they're stuck. He can only watch helplessly as the twins lean further and further towards the train ticket as it dances in the air like a moth. It's horribly inevitable. This time they both lean too far forwards and tip off into the air with their mouths shaped into huge 'oh's and their eyes wide, and they fly through the air in an arc towards Leonard. His panic rises as he stands rooted to the spot with his arms out wide but not wide enough – he won't be able to catch them both. He can't even open his mouth to make a noise.

Chapter 4:
How may I be of service?

The first thought that rises up to greet him the next morning is that Gloria is due to visit at eleven o'clock. He usually enjoys having visitors, but there's something niggling him about Gloria. He can't quite get at the feeling. It slips away from him like soap in the bath. He cranes his neck – the clock says six-thirty am. He feels comfortable and warm in his bed, as if his body had grown soft during the night, loosened, melted into the sheets. After some consideration he turns over to go back to sleep. He feels ridiculously guilty for a sixty-two-year-old man in his own bed on a Sunday morning, who doesn't have to get up for anything anyway. Will these 'oughts' and 'shoulds' ever leave him? He can blame his father for this particular self-inflicted rule. He remembers being turfed out of bed as a young boy early morning after early morning, his father muttering something about 'sin' and 'shame'. When he was old enough to resent the sneers of 'lazy-bones' at breakfast, he started getting up before the old man, even though he had to set his alarm ridiculously early. His father started setting his alarm clock earlier too, and eventually they both ended up in the cold living room, building the fire at five thirty in the morning, blinking hard, each trying to demonstrate how wide awake they were to the other. Silly testosterone games, he thinks, as he drifts back into delicious sleep. Silly buggers we were.

He's rudely woken minutes later by a bell ringing. He jumps out of bed and trips over his slippers, catching himself with a sudden hand on the wall. He's already at his wardrobe and pulling on his trousers when he realises that the bell is still ringing and that it belongs to the phone, not to the front door. He's caught between annoyance and amusement and chooses the latter when he realises he's pulling his trousers on over his pyjama bottoms. It must have rung at least six times now – how long will they wait? It better not be one of those window salesmen – he's not sure how polite he'll be. He pulls off his trousers and lurches into the hall, making clearing sounds in his throat and saying 'testing testing 1 2 3' before picking up the receiver.

'Hello, Leonard Mutch speaking?'

His mother used to laugh at him when he answered the phone like this. She thought it 'la-di-da', whatever that is. She'd put on a posh voice and ask him if she could speak to the lady of the house, or tell him that the Ming vases he'd ordered were ready for delivery. He'd picked up the habit at his first job in a bank, he'd enjoyed being asked to give his whole name to customers. It had made him feel like a proper man, the kind of man who leans nonchalantly against walls smoking Marlboros and winking at the ladies. The truth is he was a pale and pimply sixteen year old without any balls. Maybe he's still trying to inject some courage into himself, remind himself that he's a grown-up.

'Hello, is that Mr. Mutch?' The voice is quivery, gentle.

She's speaking as if she expects him to put the phone down on her at any moment.

'Yes, this is him.'

He sounds short to himself. They're going to try and sell him something, he's sure of it. He gets ready to be annoyed at his privacy being invaded. He imagines some poor girl cooped up in a windowless office all day with a stilted script in front of her and an impossible target to meet.

'Oh, hello. I'm – I was wondering if… if it would be possible to, like you said…'

As he waits for her to spit it out, he feels himself softening towards her. She sounds older than he first thought. Maybe she's got three children at home, maybe she relies on the extra money from commissions. He steps back and keeps quiet.

'Like you said. It would be good to meet up…' A pause. 'If that would be alright? I don't want to get in your way.'

She sounds pained, twisting in her embarrassment, pinned on his silence like a moth. He can't understand what she's saying. Why would they want to meet him?

'I'm sorry, I'm not interested in whatever it is you're trying to sell – thank you for calling anyway.' He prepares to put the phone down, his head still muzzy with sleep, and pauses. He's intrigued to hear what's next on this woman's script. Maybe it's her first day.

'Oh, I'm not – I didn't want to sell you anything. Oh, goodness, I haven't even told you who I am yet. You must be wondering… what a silly…'

She keeps starting new sentences and trailing unhurriedly off into silence. Her voice that reminds him of classical music.

'It's Lily, Lily Sorenson. You wrote back to me, it arrived here yesterday, when I was… the letter that is. I've just got in – I've been visiting my friend in Hampshire. It was here waiting for me, on the... I hope I haven't called too early?'

The realisation reaches him like a splash of cold water on his face. She can't have his letter already – he only posted it on Friday afternoon. He imagines a postman poised to snatch it from the red box and drive it straight to the sorting office, where it whizzes about on those conveyor belts and gets rushed into a little red van to drive it especially to Lily's house. Is it too early? He looks at his watch. It's nearly a quarter past ten. He's slept in for hours! He hears what Rose would have said: *you must have been tired, love* – her cool fingers skimming his forehead to test his temperature. Rose would have told him to *lie on in*, and offered to bring him up a nice cup of tea. The voice on the phone continues.

'I just thought I'd call you now, straight away, when I had... while I still had the nerve. I was...' Her voice changes, becomes deeper and more deliberate. 'I was so sorry to hear about Rose. So sorry.'

Leonard makes a small noise in his throat in reply.

'And here I am rabbiting on like a loony... I haven't even given you a chance to say anything.'

The flow of words stops here abruptly. He can almost hear her holding her breath, waiting for him to speak. He isn't sure what to say, scrabbles around for somewhere to start.

'Lily. I thought you were someone else.'

'That's OK, it's my fault.' He notices a faint accent to match her surname, somewhere Scandinavian, or maybe he's imagining it. He's still tying to guess her. There's a long silence and he realises she's waiting for an answer. He feels a little panicky; he wants more time to think it over. Does he want to meet her, talk about Rose with her? He has a suspicion that everyone else around him is getting tired of talking about Rose. The prospect of an interested audience is enough to decide it for him.

'Yes, I'd like to – meet up with you. I'd like that.'

'Oh, that's… I'm so relieved, I was thinking… So – shall we arrange something now? I'm not too far from you; I didn't get very far away from Cowley either, I should have tried harder…'

They arrange to meet later in the week. She offers to come to his house if it's more convenient, but he'd rather somewhere neutral. He suggests a café he knows in a small town roughly half-way between them. Before she goes, she asks him how he's coping, on his own, since Rose died. He's surprised at how directly she approaches his grief, how unafraid she seems of hearing about it. She sounds as if she wants to know the truth and so that's what he tells her – that he's still wading through, that he's through the worst of it. She says, 'You shouldn't let your sorrow come higher than your knees.' After they say their goodbyes he stands for a few minutes at the telephone table, running his fingers through his hair. That phrase about sorrow, the tune she set it to, skitters through his head like a repeating peal of bells.

He doesn't have time to take Pickles out for a walk and promises to take him out later on, talking in a loud, clear voice with plenty of hand gestures, as if speaking to a foreigner. He thinks of Rose as he does this – it had always irked her that animals weren't able to understand her, apart from one-word commands like 'walk' or 'no'. Most of all she hated taking any of their pets to the vet and not being able to explain why. After one especially difficult car journey when Rose wept more loudly than their cat caterwauled, Leonard started leaving her at home, fretting and pacing the kitchen. In later years she'd call him on their new mobile every five minutes to get updates. When he got home he'd call her a big softy and squeeze her squidgy bits. He's staring blankly at the toaster when the doorbell goes. He's jolted away from Rose's squidgy bits and checks the time again. Half past ten – it can't be Gloria yet. He isn't even out of his pyjamas! He hides behind the sofa and waits while whoever it is rings the doorbell again and then he scuttles to his bedroom, staying low, to peer out of the window and see who it is. It's only Peggy from next door, maybe coming with some more bribes for Pickles. That last cut of pork she brought was almost too good for a dog; Leonard was a whisker away from cooking it for himself with a nice dollop of apple sauce. Pickles only would have watched him eating and made him feel guilty.

As soon as Peggy is out of sight he gets on with the same morning rituals he's been carrying out for almost half a century. An unhurried visit to the toilet so he can finish another chapter of the book about boats he keeps on the bathroom shelf. Teeth brushed, with triple-striped toothpaste – he likes the way the colours come out of the tube perfectly separated, like magic. A shave using the zesty lemon and lime gel Ed bought him for his birthday. He has a close look at his face, taking in his short salt-and-peppered spiky hair, his smile-lines, his sharp cheekbones. He doesn't scrub up too badly; he reckons he could pass for fifty-five. He winks suggestively at himself in the mirror and slaps his own backside on Rose's behalf.

He's just finishing his tea when the door-bell rings again. Dead-on eleven – Gloria's always punctual. She bustles in, bringing in her usual brisk air of clean clothes and baking bread, all efficiency and slightly fake cheerfulness. She started visiting him when Rose died – she came every single day that first fortnight. He can't picture her being around the house during those first days. He can't remember much at all – staring at the switched-off TV for hours on end, dripping snot and tears onto one of Rose's skirts, walking in the woods with Pickles until his calves ached. He can remember the physical presence of his tears but it's a mystery to him how he was feeling, what he was thinking. He was vaguely aware that there were things for him to eat, that he didn't have to do any washing up, and that his clothes appeared clean and ironed in his cupboard. Glor didn't say anything about Rose or what had happened – she seemed a bit embarrassed by all of that, brushing off the things he said about Rose as if they were lint on her sleeves. He is still deeply grateful to her for keeping the machinery of his life moving onwards three years ago, for keeping him alive.

'Morning, Mr. Mutch. How may I be of service today?'

She always calls him Mr. Mutch; it's a joke they have. She likes to pretend she's his servant. Sometimes it feels uncomfortably close to the truth, but it does the trick. Leonard's noticed that people often make a joke out of things that are too difficult to say, as another way of saying them.

'Hello Gloria. How are you this beautiful morning?'

'Oh, fine, fine,' she says, dismissively, anxious that they move on to him and his wellbeing. 'So, how are you finding those curtains we re-hemmed for you last fortnight? Looking neater?'

When Gloria had first started visiting, there was always plenty to be taken care of – hand-washing, fabric softener, the right kind of fluid to use when washing windows. It shamed him that Rose had been carrying out all of these jobs without him even realising. Maybe it would have been the same if he'd died first – she wouldn't have known how to change a plug, or that she had to re-fill the window screen washer.

'Yes thanks, all tickety-boo. There isn't anything to be done today, Gloria. How about you just sit down and drink some tea with me instead?'

'Oh, there's always more to be done. What about that button I saw on your shirt last week that needed sewing? And the cushion covers?'

'Done, and done. You've taught me all I know, Gloria – I think you may have talked yourself out of a job.'

'I knew I shouldn't have given away all of my secrets. Well, I'll be off then!' she jokes, picking up her bag and pulling on her coat again.

This is a scenario they've repeated before, and at this point he usually pretends he's remembered something and says 'WAIT!' and tells her about an emergency with a dirty rug in the spare room, or a stubborn stain on the kitchen tiles. Today he feels tired of it, and besides, he can't think of anything that needs to be done anyway. She has taught him well, although it's often been a bit of a job to get it out of her. Blood out of a stone. Leonard can't think of this phrase without the accompanying visual image, of him squeezing a stone between his cupped hands so tightly that it starts to get sticky and red. So instead of joining in the usual charade he takes her bag from her and plonks it onto the sofa.

'Oh Gloria, just sit down and be quiet, and I'll bring you a cup of tea,' he says.

As Rose would have said, this takes the wind out of her sails. She drops herself onto the sofa like a bag of shopping, and he can feel her searching for some clever, sharp words to come back at him with. She settles on 'Oh, you big bully,' before sitting back with a sour face. He smiles to himself and goes to the kitchen to put more water into the kettle.

They sit awkwardly and drink their tea. Leonard makes conversation about what has been in the papers recently, the weather. She isn't responsive – it's hard work. The stone image comes to his mind again, he's squeezing and squeezing. He even does his 'Pickles chasing rabbits' impression which usually raises a smile – nothing. He wonders if she's sulking. She leaves half an hour later, muttering '…one of these days…' under her breath and giving him a perfunctory peck on the cheek. She leaves an uncomfortable atmosphere behind in the flat. His stomach comes to the rescue with a loud gurgle, like someone clearing their throat and waiting for you to notice them. He brushes the awkward feeling away by starting to think about a belated breakfast. He's got some cheese muffins in the freezer, and some real butter in the fridge…

The rest of the day passes in a pleasant blur of crosswords and pottering about with a Johnny Cash soundtrack. He puts his modest CD collection into alphabetical order, and cleans the gap between the fridge and the door, screwing up his face at miscellaneous lumps of old food. After lunch he goes on a long walk with Pickles, who disgraces himself by finding a flat, dead rat in the hedgerow. He drags it along behind him by the tail for a few minutes before Leonard spots it and makes him leave it behind.

He remembers Rose's irrational fear of mice and other little harmless mammals – he doesn't know where it came from. She used to lie awake in bed some nights and nudge him awake, asking him to listen to some tiny noise she imagined as tiny mice feet scrabbling along under the bed or in the attic. Raine looked after the school hamster Hammie one Easter, and Rose couldn't even venture in to put clean clothes on Raine's bed knowing that the hamster cage was in the same room. She got herself into quite a state once, when a rat had skittered across the path and into a bush in front of them when they were walking by a river. She flatly refused to walk any further and Leonard had to take her back along the path and walk to the car on his own to pick her up. 'Highly strung' was the phrase his mother had used to describe her. She's certainly passed on her fair share of those genes to Raine.

It feels blissful to be without people again after such a full weekend, before such a full week ahead. But there are also tinges of loneliness as he washes up his single plate and reads through the TV guide. He scolds himself out loud, calling himself a 'silly old bugger'. He looks forward all week to being alone, and when he finally gets there he doesn't want to stay for as long as he thought he did. So difficult to feel satisfied, at rest, even after sixty-two years of practise. Sometimes he imagines life as walking a tightrope – just when you think you're balanced, your body shifts over to the right and you have to make an effort to pull it back over to the left, then you need to compensate... It's like when the sun shines at full strength and you run out into the garden with your crossword book and a sun hat and before long you get too hot and have to sit in the shade where you get too cool and have to move back into the sun. Maybe that's what living is all about – the moving-towards-shade or the moving-towards-heat. If the temperature were always perfect, wouldn't we just get bored? It's getting dark. He gets up to draw his curtains and instead stands at his window and looks into a house across the street. There's a light on upstairs, and Leonard can see into the living room where a couple are sitting next to each other on the sofa. He wonders what they're saying to each other. He watches them for too long before pulling the curtains shut.

Chapter 5:
Small, diamond-shaped birthmark

Trying to teach Tommy about pruning is more difficult than teaching a cat to do the tango. This is how Leonard feels when he asks the apprentice for what feels like the tenth time when you should prune a shrub that flowers in August, and Tommy chews on his lip and says 'I know this one... it's definitely not in the winter...' It's been a frustrating day. They're sat at the mess-room table with six heavy books open in front of them. As Leonard talks, Tommy furrows his forehead and squeezes the bridge of his nose with thumb and finger as if he's staunching some bleeding. Leonard's never been very good at explaining things to other people anyway – as he told Simon when his boss asked him to spend some time with the boy. At least he's finishing early today, so he can get to his meeting with Lily in good time. He smiles encouragingly, says 'never mind', and suggests that they break for tea.

He's a good lad, really. Their working relationship took a step backwards a few weeks ago when Leonard stumbled upon him in the woods – he was meant to be checking the health of the trees. He had his personal stereo on and was holding a long fallen branch as if it were a dance partner, leaping around and moving his arms in graceful arcs. Leonard had been transfixed and had stood watching for longer than he should have before he moved towards him and tapped him in the shoulder. Tommy was struck dumb with shame. His mouth opened wide, but he couldn't get a sound out, even after Leonard had tried to make light of it with, 'May I have the next dance?'

He guesses that Tommy is still embarrassed. Leonard is impatient with things that aren't spoken about. It's always better to get awkward feelings out into the daylight so both parties can have a proper look at them. He suspects, however, that a good dose of straight talking would probably be too much for the apprentice. If Leonard brought up the dancing incident, Tommy might bolt out into the woods and he'd never see him again. He's tired of holding his tongue by the time he leaves to meet Lily. Tired of holding his tongue but amused by the image that arrives – his cut-out tongue wet and squirming in his closed fist, his hand muscles aching after hours of keeping it from leaping onto the ground and disappearing into the *Hamamelis*.

He has a tight feeling in his stomach when he parks his car along the road from the café. He's worried that the place he's chosen might be a bit too 'greasy spoon' for Lily, and also that he hasn't brushed his teeth after work and his mouth tastes of stale coffee and smoke. He strides confidently along the pavement to try to fool himself. He looks in through the café window, and a woman sitting near the front catches his eye and looks at him expectantly. She has long, smooth white hair pulled back into a kind of a twist, and a ruddy face with high, prominent cheekbones. Her eyes are a very pale blue. She's wearing a top the colour of Japanese cherry blossom. She looks too young and, for some reason, not scruffy enough to be Lily, and so he looks away and she breaks eye contact. He hovers for a second longer and when he catches her eye again, she mouths 'Leonard?' through the glass. He nods and her face changes from a question shape into a tight smile. He points at her and mouths 'Lily?' both of them exaggerating their movements like mime artists. He smiles, points to the door and makes his way inside. He realises he's looking forward to speaking to her.

As he approaches her, she stands up from the orange plastic chair and offers her hand, not her cheek as he was expecting. He takes it and she grips it hard. His father said he should never trust a woman with a firm handshake. He disagreed with most of the things his father said about women on principle. 'An educated woman is like an unexploded bomb' was another one of his classics. His mother never paid any attention to these smug pronouncements either, raising her eyebrows at Leonard behind her husband's back, and this seemed to reduce their potency. Leonard doesn't think he's been left with any residual chauvinism. He wasn't even sure that his father believed what he said either – maybe they were just a hangover from his own father, from an earlier age. Lily already has an almost-full cup of tea, so he leaves her for a minute to fetch himself one.

As he stands in the queue behind a large woman with candyfloss-like hair, he tries to order his thoughts. Why is he here? What will she want from him? What should he ask her? He's not really sure, and holds all this supposition in his head rather than formulating any questions or deciding on a direction. He's found that life unfolds more naturally that way. Wading into the river up to his chest and lifting his feet and floating off, rather than pushing against the flow of the water to get to the other side. The candy-floss woman leaves with a huge slice of cake on her tray, and he nods at the old lady in a tabard at the till. He jangles his change and brings a lint-covered tea-bag out of his pocket, explaining that of course he'll pay the normal price. The old lady raises her eye-brows and takes it by one corner without looking at Leonard. He whistles while he's waiting to pass the time.

Back at the table he steps into the chair opposite Lily. The table is too small; he feels too close to her. He pushes his chair back a bit on the floor and it makes a high-pitched screeching noise. Lily lets out a sharp 'ouch!' and moves her hands towards her ears in shock. Her face makes him laugh – it's such a perfect illustration of surprise. It's alive – very different from the frozen smile when she first shook his hand. This feels more like the Lily he spoke to on the phone. She smiles too, and her smile is looser, broader. He feels the cracking of ice. They are shifting towards each other, closing the distance between them.

She starts to talk as he's taking his first sip of tea.

'Thanks for agreeing to meet me, Leonard. I do appreciate it – I don't know what it must be like for… I don't want you to… well, you know. It's… I appreciate it, I really do.'

'It's alright – I'm happy to come. Rose never really talked about school, and it never seemed important when she was… before she died. Her history is all I've got of her now. I don't know how good it is for me, poring over it all, but… I suppose I thought maybe you'd have some new stories about her for me. I don't want you to think, it's – I'm not hanging on or anything. I have moved on with things, you know, with my life and…' He pauses and flicks his eyes to hers, which are waiting for him. He looks away and she waits for him to carry on, nodding her head slowly twice. He hadn't meant to say so much so soon and feels suddenly awkward. He tries to shift the focus onto her.

'So, how was your journey?'

'Oh, fine thanks – fine.' There's still a heavy silence after what he's said and she seems reluctant to sully it with small talk. After a few moments she notices his embarrassment and carries on speaking. He feels safe with her somehow, as if she'll carry the conversation where it needs to go.

'There was a terrible kafuffle on the way here. There's a local character… Mostly harmless, keeps himself to himself and begs a bit, you know, for a bit of money for food. Today he decided he was going to be a traffic policeman, stood in the middle of the road directing cars this way and that, the silly goose… The cars didn't know which way to… Some of the men were getting angry, you know the way men do in cars… not that all men… I didn't mean… you know. It held me up a bit – I thought I was going to be late. I'm always early for everything… except when… anyway – I'm rabbiting on again. I do rabbit on, Leonard, you have to stop me when you get tired of it.'

Leonard isn't really listening to her words. He's noticing again how her voice has a musical quality, like scales on a piano or a harp. It is as if a musician becomes intrigued with a certain tune for a while and then suddenly breaks off and starts somewhere else. A faint lilting accent, soft vowels. The sentences slip into his ears like smoke.

'I will,' he says. 'I mean I'm sure I won't… get tired of you rabbiting… and if I do I'd certainly… see, I'm doing it now as well.'

He feels colour surge into his cheeks, and is annoyed at his embarrassment – for goodness sakes Leonard, get a grip! Sometimes when he feels out of his depth with people he imagines them in their pyjamas having a bed-time story read to them. His mother taught him how to do this when he was struggling with his first boss, a silver-haired hitler called Mr. Crick. It's a variation on the usual 'sitting on the toilet' or 'naked' trick and it seems kinder somehow. He does it now with Lily, seeing her in a huge four poster with pigtails and a fluffed-up toy bunny under her arm. Her pyjamas have cartoon sheep on them. As he holds this scene in his mind's eye he notices that the quality of the silence changes. They both sit and say nothing, looking up from their tea and smiling easily at each other. There doesn't seem to be a hurry to talk about anything any more. And as often seems to happen when the urgency disappears, it feels like the perfect time to begin. Leonard puts down his cup and rests his hands on his lap, and Lily starts talking.

'So, I'm here... we're both here... because of Rose. I'm so sorry she isn't able to be here with us. Although in a way it feels like she is.' She pauses for a moment and they both nod before she continues, although Leonard is thinking, "Rubbish, she's in the All Saints cemetery down the road, under the ground."

'I'm not really sure what... I suppose I'm interested in Rose's life, after we lost touch − I'd love to hear about that. I'm not sure what I can offer you in return, Leonard. I only knew Rose until she was about eleven, when I moved to another school. You probably already know... you know... after so many years together.' He starts to protest, but she carries on over the top of him. 'Or maybe we should start by me telling you more about why I'm here... but maybe you don't care about that... I don't want to...'

It seems pointless to interrupt her. Leonard thinks she must be one of those people who think out loud, literally.

People who don't know what they want to say until they hear their own words and hold them up against what they want to communicate, trying different combinations until the words and the message matches up.

When she speaks again she sounds more decisive.

'Leonard, I'll stop dilly-dallying around. What I would really like is if you could tell me about the Rose according to... tell me about the Rose you knew. How you met her, what she did, what kind of a life she... It's up to you what you tell me and what you... I understand a lot of it is none of my... is deeply personal to you. But I'd love to have a picture in my head of her whole life, not just what I knew of her. Could you, would that be OK?'

And so he tells her about their life together. He starts at the beginning, where he feels he ought to, and describes their very first meeting. It was on a bus of all places – not at a dinner dance, not on a moonlit, starry night. Their journeys overlapped – his from his parents' house to the bank and the horrible Mr. Crick, hers from the little flat she shared with a friend to the old people's home where she worked. They both liked to sit in the same bit of the bus – not at the front, not at the back, and on the right hand side. He often ended up sitting one seat behind her and for a few weeks he gazed at her cropped hair and how it curled delicately into the nape of her pale neck. They started smiling at each other shyly in the queue, but Leonard despaired of ever gathering enough courage to speak to her. His previous record with girls wasn't exemplary. His mum's friends kept telling him he was a handsome devil and asking after his girlfriends, but whenever he tried to say anything to the fairer sex his tongue stuck to the roof of his mouth and his hands got sweaty. He gets carried away as he tells Lily now about a few of his early disastrous dates, enjoying the sound of her high-pitched hee-hee-ing laugh before remembering what he's halfway through and continuing the story.

One day there was a crisis on the bus. A middle-aged woman standing at the front took ill, and they drove straight to the hospital and waited for fifteen minutes while the woman was stretcher-ed off. This pierced the tightly-stretched 'every-day rules' and he and Lily turned to each other and talked in low voices about what was happening and whether the woman would be OK. The next time Leonard got on the bus, she caught his eye and patted the seat beside her. He was shocked at how forward she was but also eternally grateful; he would have happily walked past her without looking to save himself the trauma of untangling his tongue to speak to her. After this they sat next to each other every day. They chatted about nothing in particular – what was happening at work, how the leaves were shrivelling on the trees and a nip was stealing into the air. It took him a couple more months to find the guts to ask her to the cinema. He couldn't believe his luck when she said yes.

Leonard fast forwards past the heady early days of nervous dates and hand-holding to telling Lily about their wedding, and just how beautiful Rose looked in her cornflower blue dress. He tells her about Rose's early career – various menial jobs caring for people for little thanks, and of how proud he was of her training to be a nurse. He describes how much she enjoyed it, and repeated a few of the positive things he'd heard from old people in the village about how kind she was on the wards. His favourite was an old boy in the village who'd stopped Leonard whenever they passed for fifteen years until he died, to ask after 'that soft-handed angel of kindness'. He tells Lily about Raine, and how long it had taken for her to be conceived after they got married – 'nine long years' – just when they were giving up hope. He talks about how Rose blossomed into motherhood, and how Raine and Rose spoke to each other every day even when Raine had moved out and got married. It's a guided tour of their life together with all the landmarks pointed out. 'Over to your right, ladies and gentlemen, you'll see Rose winning a customer service award after her eleventh year of nursing. Now straight ahead, that's it, a particularly fine example of a holiday in Greece where Raine met a handsome Greek boy and they hardly saw her.'

He leaves some things out. The tens of thousands of kisses they planted on each other as they left for and returned from work over the years. The way Rose sobbed as if her heart were breaking for a solid week after Raine was born. The small diamond-shaped birthmark on Rose's left breast. The terrible argument they had about Rose being overprotective of Raine when Leonard called her a 'typical fucking woman' and she threw a plate that smashed on the wall behind him. His long illness, the way she held her hand steady on the small of his back while he vomited into a basin. A million exchanged words. A million more exchanged glances, each glance made up of another million words. A lifetime of Rose. His Rose. As he sits amidst the animal noise of the café and gathers his memories around him, he wonders if he's told Lily anything at all about his wife.

He's pulled from his reverie by the door bell jangling as a mother pushes her way inside using the pushchair containing her crying son. He notices her struggling and jumps up to hold the door open. She doesn't thank him, just looks at him briefly before continuing to tell her child off for asking for sweets. Her voice is as sharp as knives. It physically hurts him to see the way some parents treat their children. As he sits down again he returns his focus to Lily. She is smiling gently.

'Thank you, Leonard,' she says.

He feels the warmth of her words land in his stomach and sit there.

'And now, after I've fetched us some fresh tea – you've got some weird teabags in your pocket or something haven't you? Yes, after… when I'm… I wonder if there's anything you'd like to know about the Rose I knew?'

Leonard says, 'Everything. Tell me everything.'

Everything takes another three quarters of an hour. After she's run out of steam, Leonard has a strong urge to be back at home. She offers to walk with him to his car, but he says he'd rather get off quickly, making some excuse about Pickles needing his dinner. He thanks her for coming to meet him and shakes her hand firmly before leaving the café. They don't arrange to meet again.

On the drive home, his thoughts drift restlessly. He pictures the look on Lily's face when he said goodbye to her – what was it… offended that he'd left so suddenly? No – maybe more perplexed, concerned… about him? He asks his mind nicely to settle down, and imagines getting home, opening his door, moving through the hall and into the kitchen. He feels Pickle's fur under his hands, and tastes a ham and cheese toasted sandwich. By the time he pulls up at the side of the road outside the house, he's already imagining getting into bed. He feels dog tired. He has a short chat with Pickles about this, wondering whether dogs get human tired, or maybe cat tired or something else altogether, although as usual it's a mostly one-sided conversation. He knows that Pickles is listening carefully, though. Once in bed he falls quickly into a dreamless sleep. Or if not dreamless, then a sleep where the colourful tatters of dreams slip mutely away from him the moment he wakes up.

Chapter 6:
Chester the cat

The next few days are filled with preparations for the twins' birthday party at the weekend. Raine and Ed were both busy with work on their actual birthday eight months ago, and they've been getting around to arranging it ever since. Leonard is a bit concerned that the twins might get confused about the whole thing, but Raine keeps saying they're only three and assures him it won't leave any permanent scars. Better late than never, she says. There are frantic calls from Raine asking if Leonard can bring along cocktail sticks, paper napkins, food-colouring, and trips to town after work to buy cocktail sticks, paper napkins, food-colouring and some small 'post-birthday' presents for the boys. One evening he goes to a toy superstore and spends far too long browsing the remote control car section, checking out their top speeds and their manoeuvrability. He has to have a stern word with himself to stop himself from spending £200 by mistake. He's sure they'd grow tired of the car in a few weeks, even if it was a beautifully shiny red, with thick rubber wheels begging to be skidded along the tarmac.

Instead of Ed, a taxi is waiting for him at the train station on Friday evening. Nobody hears him knocking, so he lets himself in using his own key, and arrives into the middle of even more chaos than usual. He finds them in the kitchen – Ed at the table surrounded by odd-shaped balloons, trumpet-cheeked and light-headed, the twins running in and out in a pre-party-frenzy, and Raine red-faced and oven-gloved. Leonard pecks her on the cheek and she asks him if he'd mind taking the twins up to bed and reading to them. He's glad to have a job to do away from all this cooking and blowing. He says 'RIGHT!' and picks them up, slotting Rory under his left arm and Buddy under his right. He realises pretty swiftly that at three and a half they're not just heavier but longer than they used to be, with waggling arms and legs. They squeal and titter as he inelegantly bends to tip them carefully onto the lino.

'You're heavier than two barrowfuls of logs!' he says, offering a hand to each boy instead as they wriggle on the floor like maggots. As he cajoles them upstairs with help from Raine and the promise of an extra story, he wonders if he's getting too old for all of this. It is fun though.

He supervises tooth-brushing – they use a shocking pink paste that tastes of strawberries – and they laugh when Leonard eats a blob from his fingertip and then pretends to snaffle the lot, making loud scarumphing noises. When they finally get into bed, all squeezed into the bottom bunk, with Leonard flanked by a twin on each side, he asks them to close their eyes and count to twenty-seven in their heads before he starts the story. They often get muddled after twelve and so this usually buys him a bit of time. He takes a deep breath and kisses each twin gently on the very top of their heads. Their hair smells of apples. Rory hands him the book they've chosen and he opens it up.

The story is about a great big raggedy ginger tom called Chester. Leonard's only read it once or twice, but it's a firm current favourite with the boys. Raine has told him that Chester often caterwauls through the streets of her dreams. Tonight the twins are fidgeting like jumping beans when he starts reading, so he rolls right through to the end and starts again at the beginning, making his voice softer and softer as he goes. This seems to do the trick, and by three quarters of the way through they're both making little snuffling noises and Rory's thumb is drooping away from his mouth.

A few pages on, Leonard stops reading as an experiment and neither of them stirs. He sits quietly for a while and enjoys the peace of watching them sleep – their juicy looking cheeks, their mussed up thistle-down hair, the trains on their identical pyjamas. Their little fingers smell of candy-floss – he could eat them up. He wishes Rose could be here with him, downstairs chatting with Raine and Ed. He'd go down and touch her on the shoulder and they'd come back up and sit here together for a while, holding hands and enjoying the show. She's been cheated of these moments. He's been cheated of sharing them with her. But he's glad to be here; he's thankful for that. Eventually he slowly, slowly, lifts Buddy up to the top bunk and tucks them both in. Buddy says 'Chester cat!' sleepily, and Leonard says a quiet 'meow'. This seems to satisfy him – he turns over and goes back to sleep.

The next morning Leonard wakes early, noticing a small ball of excitement deep in his stomach. A party! He's always loved parties. Even everyday things like cake or music feel sunnier, more delicious, and more extravagant at parties. His usually sober father seemed to go a little bit crazy when he held parties for his son when he was small. He'd urge his wife to bake days in advance, strew paper chains and candles all through the house, and decorate paper bags so Leonard's classmates could take home a piece of cake wrapped in a paper napkin. His appetite for parties was infectious. Leonard has happy memories of the three of them and a random cast of boys from school, his mother and father singing 'Happy birthday to Len-ben' (the name they used for him when they were feeling especially affectionate). He wonders if the twins are feeling the same. When he quietly opens their door, he sees two prone lumps under the duvets. He leaves them to creep downstairs, avoiding the creak on the third stair.

It isn't yet seven and the sun is straining to have any impact on the night sky. He pulls one of Ed's big sheepskin jackets around his shoulders like a boy wearing his father's coat and unlocks the back door quietly, wanting to get out of the house before anyone wakes up and expects conversation. He claims his usual spot in the garden and smokes the first delicious roll-up of the day with great relish. He recognises the different dark shapes in the bedraggled garden. There are bushes with lots of die back, some lanky second-year pansies with ragged flowers, a stretch of fence that's fallen and needs fixing. He's offered to come round and help Raine with the fence a few times, but she reacts defensively. Maybe she thinks he's criticising her or Ed. She never seems to want any help with anything. He tries not to interfere where he isn't wanted, not like Rose. She always managed to break through Raine's wall of resistance somehow, by ignoring her protests altogether, or by coming up with a rationale Raine couldn't argue with.

When Raine was at college she'd fallen badly behind with her Maths A-level – the tutor had taken a dislike to her, and Raine started losing her confidence under the steady onslaught of criticism. Leonard had met the tutor at an open evening once, an old dragon of a woman with greasy hair and a sharp nose, full to the brim of her own opinions with no room for anyone else's. Leonard guessed she'd smelled Raine's fierce independence and felt threatened by it, decided to crush her before she became a threat. Many tears were dripped over Raine's homework books during those weeks, and Leonard's occasional attempts to help had been kicked back in his face. Only Rose was strong enough to stand her ground when Raine tried to push her away.

One particularly awful Saturday morning when Raine was thundering around the house and threatening to burn all her Maths text books, Leonard remembers his wife telling Raine she was coming shopping with her. They were gone for a couple of hours and when they came back Raine seemed different – calmer, back in control. When Leonard asked her how she was feeling she whined 'fine' as if she couldn't understand why he'd think she'd be anything else. Leonard asked Rose what she'd said to Raine, hoping he might hear some secret he could use himself another time, but all she'd say was 'We had words.' He didn't know how to break into Raine's bubble. He still doesn't have a clue, fifteen years later. And as he stands in the chill air, the dark shapes in the garden slowly gaining colour and coming into focus, he is suddenly amazed at how much he still has to learn. It seems impossibly difficult to do the simple things well – to live together with other people, to listen to them, to love them. A life-time is so short.

Someone is clattering cups in the kitchen. There's always fresh filter coffee at Raine's, a real treat. He takes a few last breaths of sweet air, stubs out his roll-up, and dives back into the raging river of the day of the twin's birthday party.

The party is a riot. It's a few days before Leonard relaxes enough for deep thoughts to swim around in his head and breach the surface of the water. He's at work one morning doing some edging when he makes a mental note to plan in over-wintering the African Lilies. The African Lilies naturally lead him to another variety – possibly Scandinavian. As he continues to be absorbed in cutting a perfectly straight line, the tool's silver edge separating the turf like sawing through a loaf of bread, he replays what Lily had told him about Rose as a young girl. He does a mental inventory of the facts she gave him. Some of these facts he knew already. She enjoyed school, especially art lessons with Mrs. Barnes. She lived in a council house on the estate nearby, although Lily was never invited there. She'd loved animals – they'd spotted a scraggy young cat crouching at the back of the playing-ground hedge one year and Rose had crouched by it for an entire lunch hour, patiently tempting it towards them so they could feed it on scraps salvaged from their lunch-boxes. Rose had been a kind friend, always thinking of other people and sometimes forgetting herself – Lily told Leonard about the time she'd spent a whole evening helping Lily with her maths homework, and then she didn't have time to do her own and got into trouble.

Lily also told him a few things that were new to him. She used to make her own way to and from school the whole time Lily knew her, whatever the weather. She was always meek and submissive in class, and noisy as a banshee in the playground. She'd worn a blue woolly hat all through the winter and late into spring. Lily had only had a vague memory of her mother – she remembers her as a 'kind lady', 'awfully shy'; she'd pick her up from Lily's house and thank Lily's mum over and over for looking after her. She only ever met her dad once, just before she left for her new school. He had burst into the classroom and had taken Rose roughly by the arm and pulled her out, to the teachers' mild protests. She can remember Rose talking about her dad as if he were her hero, telling her he'd fixed her bicycle or taken her on a special trip to the seaside.

Leonard's favourite new fact was a game they used to play at Lily's house, facing each other from opposite ends of Lily's single bed with their squirming legs under the duvet. They'd stand up their dolls (Joyce and Millie) between them and act out little lives for them. Different rooms were allocated to different coloured squares on the duvet – there was also a swimming pool (a blue scarf), a garden (a pair of knickers with flowers on them) and an endlessly shifting variety of places they could visit and things they could do. Lily said it had felt like their responsibility to give their dolls full and interesting lives – they were proud of how well they cared for them. Lily's mother brought them in biscuits or bread and butter on a plate and they'd sit there for hours, pausing the action only when one of them needed a wee or when Lily's mother told Rose it was time to go home because they were about to sit down to dinner.

As he replays Lily's words, he notices a twitching feeling in his stomach. Something isn't right. He thinks again of the train ticket to Didcot, the blue handbag. If it weren't for the ticket, maybe he'd be able to leave it alone, accept these stories as the gifts they are, put them in a back drawer in his head and leave them alone. But something isn't right... he ruminates on it all afternoon like a cow chewing on the same bit of cud. And then, when he's finished the edging and put Lily aside, as he's walking back down the path to the mess-room, the memory crashes into his head and he comes to an abrupt halt. That's it! Could he have heard Lily right? Maybe she got it wrong... He decides to give her a ring later, just to be sure.

That evening, after feeding Pickles and then himself (Pickles seemed to tuck into his cheap lumps of meat and jelly with much more enthusiasm than Leonard attacked his pale pork chops, floury boiled potatoes and tinned peas) he looks for Lily's number on her letter. He absent-mindedly writes it into his address book under 'S' before he dials. She answers after two rings, as if she's been standing and waiting for his call.

'Hello?'

'Hello, Lily? It's Leonard. From the café...' He gets ready to explain further but she interrupts him. Her voice is bright.

'Leonard! I didn't expect to hear from you again. How are you?'

'Fine thanks, fine. I'm sorry I left a bit abruptly last week. It was... well...' He tries to think of a way out of the end of the sentence, and decides to start a new one instead. 'I actually wanted to check something with you, something I think you said.'

'Mmm hmm?'

'I think you said that Rose used to sit on her hair. As if it was long. I'm not sure if I heard you right...'

'I can't remember if I said it... but yes – she did have the most beautiful hair. It was quite thick, even to the ends – I was so jealous I could spit. My hair just starts... you know... if I grow it past my shoulders, I end up looking like a scarecrow in the mornings. Still, we can't have everything we want. A lesson... Leonard, I'm rabbiting on again. I said you should stop me if I do that.'

Leonard isn't listening. Instead he's hearing his wife's voice inside his head.

'Leonard?'

He hears Lily speak his name and realises it's the second time she's said it.

'Sorry Lily. You're absolutely sure it was long?'

'Is something wrong?'

'It's just that... she said... Lily, I'm sorry, I'm getting a bit muddled. I need to... can I give you a ring another day?'

'Of course, Leonard. I hope I haven't... do let me know if... you know. If I can do anything.'

'I will. Bye.'

'Yes. Bye.'

She sounds reluctant to go. Leonard puts the phone back on the hook and sits down on the stairs. She must be mistaken. It's a silly thing. He brushes the thoughts away like flies and goes to take his damp clothes from the washing machine.

A few hours later, not able to concentrate on watching the news, Leonard admits defeat. He's tried to rearrange the facts in his head, but he can't find a way to swallow them as the truth. Rose couldn't have lied to him – she couldn't even stop herself from telling him what she'd got him for his birthdays, or that she'd had half a lager at lunchtime with her friend from work. The confessions used to tumble out of her as if she couldn't bear their weight any longer.

He rises from his chair and goes straight to the phone, finds Lily's number and dials. It's only after the fourth ring that he looks at the time and wonders if it's too late – will she be sleeping? He hovers the receiver near his ear as he decides whether he should slam it down or not. He's still hovering when she answers, sounding a little sleepy. He apologises for calling again and asks her what he needs to ask her. She agrees instantly, and they arrange the visit for the day after tomorrow, Sunday. She insists he comes to hers for afternoon tea. He puts the receiver down with a certain sense of relief – he doesn't have to think about it any more now, not until he's seen the proof. Not until it's unavoidable.

After work on Friday he drops the car off at home and jumps onto his bicycle to pop into the Five Bells. It's been a long day. He's had to faff about with some paperwork for the Trust and show three new volunteers around the estate. Sometimes there are too many people and bits of paper, and not enough plants. He swings the door open and is greeted by the familiar aroma of beer and chips, enveloping him like a duvet on a cold night. Rose used to turn her nose up, saying it smelt 'stale', but for him it's always been delicious, cosy, safe. It's always darker inside than it is outside, even at this time of year, when the light is failing. He flicks his eyes around the room – the worn, dark red carpet, the low, round tables, the garish pin-ball machine that rarely gets any use. There's old Mick with his tabloid newspaper, and a young couple he doesn't recognise, drinking their drinks and deliberately not looking at each other. And there's the pub cat, Bob, a wiry female tortoiseshell who rarely leaves the safety of the patch of carpet under corner table. Leonard has tried to coax her out a few times over the years, trying an outstretched hand and bits of ham or cheese he's brought in foil twists in his pockets. Bob's never been brave enough (or hungry enough), and why should she trust him anyway? He can't blame her for being cautious.

He recognises the square shape of Charlie at the bar and settles down next to him with their usual exchange of greetings. Suze, the landlady, is on one of her rare holidays in Ibiza with 'the girls' – Leonard hopes Spain is ready for them. A local girl is in charge, or more accurately not in charge. Leonard watches her as a couple from the village come in with their grown-up son and order three drinks. It sets her off on a frenzy of activity – going over to the till to fetch her little pad, getting the pen from the bar, going back to the till to look at the list of prices, then she's left the pen next to the till again… she pings back and forth like a game of pin-ball. Charlie is watching her too, and they glance at each other. Charlie raises an eyebrow – Leonard laughs. He realises how empty of humour he's been, and is grateful to feel his heart lighten.

The door swings open and everyone looks towards it with faint curiosity. A short, barrel-shaped man with wild white eye-brows and a yellowed, bushy moustache makes an entrance by tripping over the mat. It's Malky – an old friend of Charlie and Leonard's who moved a few years ago and changed his local. He usually turns up when he's had a larger-than-usual fight with his wife, using the Five Bells as a refuge. He greets the pair with gruff affection and pulls a bar stool towards them. He's taller when he climbs onto the stool than he is when he's standing. Leonard is pleased to see him – he's always liked Malky, a person knows where he stands with him. Old friends are often the best – at least you have a good idea of their faults.

They spend a pleasant hour or so as Charlie and Malky get into a friendly competition about who has the more impossible wife. Malky describes a Valentines Day when he and his wife agreed not to buy each other anything, as money was short. On the morning of the 14th, his wife brought him in a card and a posh cigar. Malky had looked surprised and reminded her of their agreement, and she'd said she hadn't meant she didn't want anything at all. She was furious that he hadn't even got her a card. They argued about it for weeks, Malky utterly incapable of seeing how he could be in the wrong, until he was so worn down by it he bought her some chocolates and flowers and all was forgiven. He says he'll never make that mistake again – he has added 'I don't want anything' to his translation manual along with 'How do I look?' ('Tell me I look ravishing and make it convincing.')

and 'I'm just tired.' ('I'm annoyed at something you've done, but you'll have to guess what it is and then work out how to make it up to me.').

Charlie tells a story about when his wife Marion asked him how she looked before they went out to dinner one night. He told her she looked 'very blue' – she was wearing several different shades from head to foot. She decided to take this as a terrible insult and huffed off back to her room to change, and when she re-appeared Charlie told her she looked less blue, thinking it might be the right thing to say. She shouted 'I never get anything right with you, do I?' and glared across the dinner table at him whenever the opportunity arose for the rest of the evening. Leonard was asked to judge the proceedings and pronounced Malky the winner, for a short and shocking anecdote involving a tin of beans.

By the time Malky leaves – 'to face the wrath of my marvellous wife' – Leonard is feeling a little the worse for wear. He's become caught up in rounds between the three of them and only realises quite how light-headed he feels when he gets up to go to the toilet. He giggles as he pees, trying to make figures of eights with his stream of urine. He doesn't want to go home yet and heads back to Charlie, eager to talk some more.

'Ta da!' he says, conscious of a slight stagger on his way back to the bar.

'Ta da what?'

'Oh, just ta da.'

His face falls. He lifts the nearly empty pint glass to his lips, smacking them loudly for effect. He's aware that there's something specific he wants to talk to Charlie about, but he isn't sure what. He plays for time.

'Charlie, Charlie…'

'Hnh?'

He remembers. 'I wanted to ask for your, you know, what-do-you-call-it, on something.'

'Hnh?'

'My Rose. It's my Rose, I'm… you know I went to see that woman Lily, who knew Rose when she was a kiddie? A little kiddie…little kiddie…'

'Hnh.'

Charlie looks a little drunk too. He's resting his chin in his hands and his elbows are slipping across the bar, making him look like a small boy at a dinner table.

'Well, she told me some things about Rose, Charlie. Some things that didn't… some things that weren't her. That weren't, you know. Are you understanding me? I'm not sure if I should keep… if I should dig around, try and make sense of them. Of it. Or leave it well alone. I wish I could ask her. It's…'

He's ashamed to feel his throat tighten, his voice catch. Charlie lifts his head from his hands and watches him carefully, like a dog waiting for a morsel of meat. Leonard waits a little for the emotion to pass before continuing.

'It's upsetting me. I'm upset, Charlie. I don't know why.'

There's a long silence as they both sit there considering what Leonard has said. Finally Charlie speaks.

'You should leave it, mate. No gain in digging it up. You might find something you don't want to. Let her lie in peace.'

Leonard nods slowly for almost a whole minute. He turns to Charlie and puts a hand on his shoulder and thanks him so sincerely that he only gets away with it because they're both drunk. Now he feels tired and a little queasy. He doesn't think he'll be able to ride his bicycle properly and decides to walk home. The cold air will do him good. He thanks Charlie again and turns to look at the girl behind the bar who's just called time. She looks like he feels – exhausted, utterly drained. He feels terribly sorry for her, terribly guilty for laughing at her earlier. He wants to say sorry but is afraid he'll make a fool of himself, start crying or something. Instead he catches her eye and says goodbye, reaching out his hand towards her as he does, palm up as if to shake her hand, and then making a tight fist and squeezing up his eyes. He's not sure what it means but she seems to understand and smiles back, nods. He stumbles out into the cold.

Chapter 7:
The only one without a flower

Leonard meets his dog in the hall on Sunday morning. Pickles enquires politely as to his owner's state of health with a short 'yap'. Leonard's glad to pronounce that the most terrible hangover he's had in years is finally over. He'd woken up on Saturday morning with a mouth like a dog's arse, as Charlie would have said. He drank two whole pints of water down straight, which only added to his nausea. He couldn't remember getting home at all and had to call the pub to make sure his bike was still there. He only vaguely remembered his conversation with Charlie – did he cry in front of him? He remembers telling him about Lily, and he thinks that Charlie told him to leave it alone. He's probably right.

He eats a hearty fry-up, and after washing up the breakfast things he sets off on an extra-long walk with Pickles to make up for the lack yesterday. As he walks he remembers Raine at the twin's party. She seemed even more hyped up than usual, worrying about what the parents would think of the party bags, and whether Rory would be emotionally scarred by Buddy getting the final pass-the-parcel prize. He'd thought the twins had had a great time, being in their favourite place – firmly at the dead centre of attention. They blew out their candles with such force that some of the paper plates of crusts and crushed crisps got scattered onto the floor. They were clearly delighted about this. They got in a few direct blows at other plates around the table, and a few other children had taken deep in-breaths and puffed out their cheeks, before Raine stepped in and distracted them all by asking for 'a round of applause for the birthday boys'. Leonard had heard an older girl saying, 'But it's not really their birthday…' but she'd been drowned out by the general hullabaloo.

There'd been a minor disaster with a blond child who'd stuffed his face with fairy cakes and proceeded to buzz around the room like a fly until he was sick, but he managed to do it on the kitchen floor, which was all tiled. As soon as it had been cleared up he came in and tugged on Leonard's jumper and asked if there were any more 'cakes with lovely icing'. Leonard said he'd put one in his going-home bag so he could eat it later and sent him back to the party games, which Ed was directing.

After the extra children had gone home, the three of them had worked together in the kitchen, washing glasses and cling-filming food. Leonard had tried to make Raine laugh. Even when he impersonated the puking blond boy and had Ed in stitches, she just carried on her drying up with a tight smile.

'What to make of it, eh, boy?' he asks. He lets out a slow sigh and picks up a dry stick from the road to snap into small pieces as he walks. They are nearing home again. He's actually managed to tire Pickles out and they both collapse into their beds for half an hour before lunch. After an uninspiring cheese and tomato sandwich he gets ready to drive to Lily's to settle this mystery once and for all. He's written her instructions down carefully – it's always harder to navigate without anyone sitting next to you. Although as he remembers Rose's sense of direction he revises this – it's always harder without anyone-except-Rose sitting next to you. On one never-ending journey, they had approached the same roundabout from a different direction five times.

He reads his list of instructions over and over – he usually tries to memorise the steps he needs to take, draw a mental map in his mind. He's quite good at it. He has a similar map of the estate, including which shrubs are where, when they need pruning, how old they are. He could tell you where to find the different types of soil, shade, any trouble spots prone to ground elder or getting boggy in the wet season. He wonders briefly before he sets off about the shirt he's wearing and whether it suits him. He quashes the thought as soon as it appears, calling himself a silly goose and flapping and honking as he says *au revoir* to Pickles.

It takes forty minutes to reach her village. It's a pleasant drive – he manages to avoid most of the main roads, and as usual tries to keep his eyes ahead of him but feels them drawn towards the fields and the hedgerows. There's a particularly handsome oak halfway there – balanced, stately. He can't get enough of looking at trees. He finds her house easily – she's given him pretty good instructions, for a woman. Rose would bash him on the arm for that comment. He drives the car up onto the curb and pushes in the wing-mirror to reduce the possibility of it being clipped. He wonders as he does it why he's bothering. A few extra scratches would just add more character to his already battered-looking car.

He hadn't known what to bring with him – what was the etiquette for afternoon tea? Rose would have known... So he's brought nothing, and he feels the lack of it keenly as he slams the car door and approaches her gate. He casts a quick eye over her house – semi-detached, pretty average looking, with that nasty lumpy stuff all over the front like burnt porridge. Her front garden is well-looked after – some Red Hot Pokers at the back, Busy Lizzie, Dutch irises. Nothing is blooming at the moment, but he imagines what it will look like in the Spring and in the Summer. There's nothing to catch him on fire – no *Chile Black* Pincushion Flowers, or Honeywort with fleshy whorls of blue-green leaves. But still, it looks like it's loved. He stands on her doorstep and looks himself up and down to make sure he hasn't dripped any tomato sauce down his front. The bell surprises him with a dong-ding rather than the usual ding-dong. He takes a deep breath. She opens the door, looking ruddy with health, and asks him inside.

She takes his coat and disappears off into the depths of the house, leaving him to stand there like a lemon (as Ed would say) and feel the pitch of his nerves rising. What is he even doing here? He casts his eyes around for the best place to sit. He tries to work out which seat is most likely to be hers, looking for a half-read book or an empty mug. The dusty-pink two-seater and the two armchairs arranged around a small polished coffee-table all look equally likely. He can't see a television, but he does notice a huge bookcase spilling over with books, and a kind of bin full of tangled wool with knitting needles poking out like forks from spaghetti. He also notices a large book bound in red fake leather on the side-board – that must be what he's come for. There's a wonderful smell coming from the kitchen – a cake? Biscuits? He hasn't smelt freshly-baked anything for a very long time – there's nothing like it for getting your juice buds tap-dancing. She reappears and he realises she had started talking to him a few moments ago.

'Sorry, Lily, I'm miles away.'

Her face stills itself into concern and she almost says something but decides against it. She offers him a 'cream tea' instead. He tells her he doesn't take cream in his tea, but realises as he's speaking that she means a proper cream tea with scones and jam. Mmm, freshly baked scones. She laughs at his enthusiasm, saying she hopes they'll be all right, and waves her hand across the room to indicate he should feel free to sit wherever he likes. He chooses the armchair facing towards the archway that leads to the kitchen. She talks to him from that room, her voice slightly raised, babbling prettily about her grandchildren and the state of the local park. She asks him what type of jam he'd prefer and how he takes his tea, but mostly he's not required to say anything. The armchair is comfy – soft but not too soft, all-enveloping, and he begins to settle. By the time she brings in the scones on a tray patterned with irises (they look like 'Silver Edge') he's feeling more relaxed, less self-conscious.

'Do make yourself at home Leonard, I don't like to... no point in standing on ceremony. If you want anything else you just... I won't fuss around you.'

He wouldn't mind being fussed around a little. They busy themselves with the scones – smoothing on the exact right amounts of soft yellow butter and stiff cream and dropping on soft dollops of home-made raspberry jam from a blue dish. The scones are rich and form perfect moist crumbs in his mouth when he bites into them... aaah, blissful. He finds himself making a play out of his pleasure as he does when Raine cooks for him. Lily is amused, and says she knows she must be a certain age now if her scones get a more enthusiastic reaction than her legs do. Leonard blushes but she doesn't seem to notice, or if she does she tactfully ignores it.

After the first scone she gets up and fetches the red leather album, moves his crumby plate aside and places it on the table in front of him. He feels a sinking in his stomach. She waits for a while as he sits there and looks at it.

'It's right near the front,' she says.

He takes a deep breath and lifts the weight of it into his lap. The photos are faded, and look well-worn by fingers and thumbs. He scans them quickly, waiting for a stab of recognition. The first one is of a prim-looking lady with her arm hooked into her husband's. It has a small oval stain as if it caused someone to shed a tear. There are some grinning babies, gappy-toothed and shiny-headed. And here is a page of three small square photos of school-girls in identical capes like Little Red Riding Hood. They look about seven. He's surprised that he recognises Lily instantly. Her hair is in pig-tails and she's wearing a cheeky smile. She's in the middle of all three of them, almost bursting forwards out of the photographs. On Lily's left is a taller girl with a hooked nose and big eyes. That's definitely not Rose. And the girl on the right... he holds the book away from him at arms-length to have a better look. The girl on the right has a little button nose, a slightly broad forehead. Her eyes are lowered. In the third picture she looks as if she's had enough and has turned and moved towards the edge of the frame. Her hair is tucked behind her ears and flowing down over her shoulders, getting cut off by the edges of the photo. Can it be her?

He doesn't recognise her. He squints his eyes and tries to imagine how this little girl would look when she got older, trying to match this face with the face he loved for years, the face he saw blooming and taking on character. There's something around the eyes maybe – he holds a thumb over the rest of her face to see if they becomes more recognisable. No, not really. Not really. He turns the album round so Lily can see and points at the face in the photo to double check. She nods confirmation. Lily wouldn't lie to him, would she? He has a sudden vision of the whole thing being an elaborate hoax, dreamt up by a lonely widow and designed to snare him. Maybe she never knew Rose at all? He knows he's being ridiculous, he's grasping at straws.

He is hearing his wife's voice inside his head. *A medical condition,* she'd said. *Since birth. My hair has never grown more than a few centimetres long. I hope you don't mind, Leonard. It's a medical condition; it's something in my genes.* There's nothing else for it. He has to swallow it down as the truth. Rose had lied to him. He reaches for his cup of tea and tilts it all the way up before realising the cup is empty. He looks inside the cup and as he does he notices his hand shaking. He places it back on the saucer, making a short jingling noise as china strikes china a few times.

'Are you alright, Leonard?'

Her voice is firm. She is saying it to bring him back to himself a little, not to reassure herself.

He looks at her blankly and says, 'Rose, is there any more tea?'

He's surprised at the feebleness of his voice, and is aware that he's got something wrong but he isn't sure what. She goes over and takes the album from him and looks him square in the face.

'Leonard.'

He's looking at a water-colour of a windmill on the wall, trying to decide on what he should cook himself for dinner. It feels important.

'Leonard!' She puts a hand on his shoulder. 'Leonard, I'm going to get you some more tea now. How about you come through… have a bit of fresh air, eh?'

He nods, obeying her. She leads him through the kitchen and holds the back door open for him. He sits heavily on a mildewed wooden bench and gets out his tobacco tin. He eases off the battered lid, pulls a single Rizla free from the others. A good pinch of tobacco, getting a little dry now, in need of a re-fill. A small twist of card for a filter. The final delicate lick, the paper fastened together. The familiar motions soothe him. As he stares at her back garden he's able to think without losing his footing.

Rose had lied to him about her hair for the entire time they were married. All the conversations they'd had about her mum's friends telling her off for cutting her babies' hair too short, the doctors doing tests when she was a little girl. And the sadness of being the only teenager without a flower in her hair at her last school dance. She even shed a tear when she told him about it. All the other girls were given a sweet-smelling freesia, one of their teachers stood there with hairclips and pinned them all in. Rose wasn't even given one to pin to her dress. He can picture her there now – stood at the edges of the hall, pulling gently on tufts of her hair with her thumb and fingertips as she did when she was nervous. Did she even go to her last school dance? What can he replace this memory with? How could she have lied so easily? She must have been getting it cut throughout the time of their marriage – what hairdresser did she go to? When? Was he an idiot to have believed her? He can't understand it.

He comes back into the sitting room and Lily hands him a fresh cup of tea, but he hasn't got the stomach for it. The scone is sitting heavily in him. The smell of jam from the dish on the table is sickly and overpowering, as if it's a red cloud squatting in the air. He can smell the smoke he's brought in with him, molecules of it are clinging onto his clothes and skin. He doesn't want to pollute Lily's lovely front room any more. He needs to be alone. He wants to explain it to her, but he's worried he might make more of a fool of himself. He promises her he'll meet her again when he's recovered himself and apologises for his rudeness. She's worried about his driving and makes him drink the rest of his tea before he goes. She's put lots of sugar in it, and it tastes better than he thought it would. She leaves him alone to drink it, pretends she has something to do in the kitchen, and he is grateful to her for knowing exactly what he needs without having to ask.

By the time he's finished she looks at him carefully and says the colour has returned to his cheeks. As she says goodbye to him at the door she presses her palm gently onto the outside of his wrist as it hangs down, and he wants to twist it round and take her hand.

He drives home as if he's been drinking, being careful, not quite trusting his judgement. A small, warm, furry object ambushes him at the door, darting between his ankles and nearly tripping him up. Leonard loses his temper and speaks to him in a sharp voice. There's a red light blinking on the answering machine. For months after Rose's death, whenever he got a message his brain would leap to the same silly conclusion that it was from her. This thought sneaks into his head now before he can stop it. He catches himself and says 'She'd have to be calling you from a pay-phone in heaven, you silly old goat'. He wonders if God would make her pay for the call. He doesn't believe in God anyway, or heaven. He doesn't believe in Rose being intact anywhere except inside his head, and she isn't even whole there. She's falling apart, especially as the years roll on. He can't really picture her favourite dress any more, or hear the exact noise she made when an advert she didn't like came on. Her life going on beyond her death depends on him, and he is failing her.

He forks out dog-meat for a sheepish Pickles and opens the dull mail (offers of loans, a bank statement) before he remembers the flashing light. He presses 'play'. At first he doesn't recognise the voice – it's husky, female, panicky.

'Leonard. It's me. I'm frantic, I didn't know what to do. You could be… I came round, and…'

At this precise moment he remembers. Glor! She was due to come round at two and he hadn't been there – he hadn't even thought about it all week. He listens to her voice again.

'…you weren't there, you've never not been there before. I hope something awful… ring me, Leonard, please ring. As soon as you can, whatever the time is. Umm… bye.'

She hangs up. Before he has a chance to feel guilty he's struck by how worried she sounded. Surely she realised he'd just forgotten? He has a strong urge to ignore her call and wishes he could write instead, or send her a text message the way Raine sometimes texts him. He never replies to Raine; he hasn't managed to work that bit out yet, his thumbs feel too big. He's not sure how other people can bear it – tap tap tap, all with one thumb on those tiny numbers. He's noticed how often she'll text him when she has something slightly contentious to tell him – 'cld u get takeaway on ur way' or 'rorys ill best if u dont come this weekend sorry dad love raine x'. If he understood the mechanics he could send one to Glor now – 'pickles needed vet all well now c u next week sorry leonard'. If only. He knows he'll do the right thing, he usually does. He braces himself and picks up the phone.

She picks up immediately, as if she's been poised to take his call. She sounds ridiculously relieved to hear from him.

She sounds out of breath. He's tempted to lie to soften the impact but gets a stab in his chest when he remembers Rose's hair and decides to tells her the truth – he went to Lily's, he totally forgot. Her tone changes, loses the intense relief and feels cooler. She offers to come round next Sunday instead and he says there's no need, but if she and Pete wanted to come round for a drink one evening they should set a date. This is received even more frostily. They agree she'll come in two weeks time as planned, and she seems eager to get off the phone. He hangs up feeling perplexed, but is too tired out by the afternoon to give it much serious thought.

He deletes the message and takes the phone lead out of the wall. Raine has his mobile number if anything serious happens. He shucks off his shoes and slips his tired feet into his slippers, wondering if that's how they got their name. He runs his hand against the wall as he walks into the living room as if he needs the extra support and collapses into his chair. The thought of going to work tomorrow comforts him. He'll be occupied with that patch of weeding that needs doing by the lake, he'll be out in the open air. It'll give him some time to process all of this. He picks up a new crossword book and bends the cardboard cover back so it sits flat. Pickles ambles into the room, showing signs of forgetting all about his telling off. Leonard holds up the book so Pickles can jump in underneath it, and he rests the book's spine gently on the ridge of his dog's spine. He switches on the television and sharpens his pencil.

Chapter 8:
Margery the penguin

For two nights and a day the wind blows with a fury, and Pickles crouches underneath the hall table and quivers. Leonard kneels down to speak to him in a quiet voice, but Pickles just puts his paws over his ears and carries on shaking like a blancmange. Even the tasty morsels of chicken Leonard wafts under his nose fail to tempt him away from his fear of the sky falling in.

The storm brings down a huge cedar branch in the woods at Coburne. The contractors are busy clearing debris from other people's grounds, and so on Friday Leonard, Steve and Tommy kit themselves out in full protective gear and put the whole day aside to turn the branch into firewood. Leonard hates wearing such a bulky costume, but makes the most of it by spending the first hour moving like a spaceman and talking in what he feels is an uncanny 'space accent' (Tommy suggests it sounds more like Welsh).

Leonard and Steve have their chainsaw certificates, and so put themselves in charge of cross-cutting the timber and feeding the brush through the chipping machine they've hired for the day. Tommy carts the cord back to the yard, where he stacks it up under cover to dry out. In a couple of hours they're a well-oiled timber-cutting machine. It's physically hard work, but Leonard is grateful for the distraction after the disturbing discovery at Lily's house. He also enjoys the banter between the three of them. Steve is a sarcastic old bugger, but Tommy is slowly learning to hold his own and they ping pong insults back and forth for hours on end. Steve's language is always as colourful as Azaleas in May, and the other two find themselves trying to keep up.

'Careful of your crumbly old bones, geezer, we don't want to get the fuckin' air ambulance out for you…'

'Don't run at the bleeding tree too quickly mate, your stomach will bounce you straight off again and we'll be fishing you out of the fuckin' lake.'

'You're so slow with that wheelbarrow, the bleeding wheel's going to rust up.'

Leonard rises to the challenge and feels the finest sentence of the day is 'For fuck's sake, you fuckers, shut the fucking fuck up or I'll fucking fuck you over fucking good and fucking proper.'

Sometimes Leonard has to put the chainsaw down to give himself over to the laughter. He can't remember their health and safety course covering the hazards of mixing amusing colleagues with potentially lethal power tools, and thinks it ought to be added in as a new section. Steve tells them about an American lady he overhead last Summer talking about their yew trees, saying, 'Oh, but imagine how ugly they'll look when the leaves all drop off.' Leonard copies Steve's dodgy American accent and Tommy makes him talk in it for an entire hour.

'Moove the weeeel barr-rrr rawnd oh-vr heeer, will ya?'.

Again Tommy and Steve agree it sounds more like Welsh.

They finish at four, having produced a satisfyingly large stack of logs and enough wood chippings to rejuvenate a few of their woodland pathways. Steve has kept back a log or two to give to an old boy he knows in the village – he does a little wood turning and makes exquisitely smooth wooden eggs. The cosy smoke from burning cedar is so aromatic, so sweet – Leonard can't wait for the log fires they'll have in a year or so when the wood is ready. Simon sends them home a little early, and Leonard is grateful – his body is aching everywhere, especially his back, and he's desperate to shed the protective clothing. He decides to give his usual pub visit a miss, but as he nears his house the quiet, lonely evening suddenly stretches out in front of him. He doesn't want to be alone with his thoughts. Where can he go to avoid them?

An hour later, after a quick shower and ten minutes of fuss to keep Pickles going until he gets back, his car tips him out into the faceless concrete car park attached to a big shopping complex in Reading. Coming here in the evenings is a habit he got into after Rose died. He remembers sitting in their empty house (his empty house) two weeks after her death and craving noise, colour, and people. Whenever the house got too unbearably quiet, he'd jump into his car and wander the shops for hours. They stay open until eight now at this new place. At Christmas they're open even later – ten o'clock at night – crazy. How much stuff can people need? He's not sure if mid-November is counted as Christmas yet. It gets earlier and earlier – eventually all the festivals will overlap and there'll be Easter eggs, Halloween costumes and New Year balloons all jostling for space in the aisles.

As the glass doors swish aside to let him in, he's struck again by how unnatural the place is – all artificial lights and primary colours. He turns his head from side to side as he walks, as if he's swimming. The window displays are stuffed with objects that nobody really needs, but which the shops work hard to convince the customers they want. There are all kinds of junk vying for the shoppers attention – a spearmint-green top too flimsy to provide any kind of warmth, credit card holders, white chocolate in the shape of a giraffe. *Look at me! Look at me! I'm brighter, I'm newer, I'm more fashionable. I'll make you prettier, sexier; I'll make you look richer, cleverer, more popular.* People are everywhere, like ants – ladies pushing buggies, teenage girls in small gangs. The sound-track rumbles away in the background – shoe-soles slapping on the marble, crying babies, women asking their husbands whether their bums 'look big in this'. It's about as far away from the gardens at Coburne House as you could get. It's about as far away from the quiet, uncomfortable space in his head as he can get.

He used to play little games in his mind here after Rose's death – how many women with orange lipstick could he spot in ten minutes? If he managed ten then he could stop and have a cup of coffee and an apple muffin. How many pairs of snogging teenagers? How long could he last without hearing a woman say 'really?' to her friend? Today he chooses babies in red bobble hats, and sets himself a target of five before he goes home. As he wanders along, he thinks about when he was here last – a time when he was tipping over with grief. The sight of an old couple holding hands could bring him to jagged tears. 'Crying jags', as they say in America. What a good word to describe the physical effect of bouts of tears under pressure. 'Bursting' into tears. 'Sobbing' – the sound of that word, sob. He wonders how much he really has moved on since her death. Maybe these, how should he say it... discrepancies, wouldn't be bugging him so insistently if he had truly accepted her absence? None of it matters now anyway, does it? They've had their time together. Nothing will change that – the pleasure they got from being with each other, the hours and weeks and months and years of cuddles and kind looks and shared silences. The thoughts crowd in, threaten to drown him. He needs to think of something else to do. There's only been one green bobble hat on a five year old and that doesn't count. He decides to do some dressing up and goes into Hennes. He chooses clothes from the racks that he'd never dream of wearing – trousers with straps and buckles, T-shirts with rude slogans. The young girl looks at him strangely when she checks him into the changing rooms, and he smiles at her sweetly. He tries different combinations, doing twirls for himself in the changing room mirrors, winking suggestively. He strikes the 'poses' he sees on TV with his arms out straight and his hands making the same shapes as when he cast deer shadows onto the bedroom wall for Raine. He's particularly taken by a red jacket that feels like a cross between leather and rubber, and some baggy black jeans. He imagines turning up to work in the ensemble next week, the look on Val's face. In the end he decides to buy a T-shirt that says 'shit happens'. He likes the colours, he likes the slogan. He'll wear it in bed, where no-one will see him.

What time is it? Only seven thirty. What next? The cinema, the cinema! He loves everything about the cinema – the 'papaaa papaaa' music bursting into the auditorium, the glossy adverts, the privacy of his own seat in the darkness. He feels like a kid. Rose used to despair of him when he was in this kind of a mood, preferring to be accompanied by a fellow-grown up when they took Raine to the fun-fair or to a dinosaur park. Instead she had to tell both of them to slow down and not eat too much ice cream before the rides. He walks across the bridge, crossing the river dividing the shops from the restaurants and looks at what's showing that evening. It's the usual suspects – an action thriller, a soppy romance. He's tempted by the Bollywood movie. There's also one of those new animation things – like a cartoon but all done on the computer. That's what he fancies seeing the most. The girl selling him the ticket has dark purple eye-shadow and smiles politely but vacantly when he jokes about being too old to see a cartoon.

He asks for the biggest size of popcorn – there's only fifteen pence between that and a medium, so it seems ridiculous to get a medium. He proudly asks for 'mixed' – a trick he'd learnt from Raine the last time they'd gone to the cinema together. He feels like he's in a special club knowing about it; it isn't advertised anywhere. He loves the surprise of never knowing what's going to be next – sweet or salty. He actually prefers salty and usually wonders by the end of the tub why he didn't just get that. The young Asian girl behind the till confuses him by asking if he wants 'layers' or not, and he dithers until a woman behind him in the queue tuts loudly. He settles down into his seat, draping his coat over his knees to arm himself against the air-conditioning. One of the adverts for a new kind of deodorant uses a snatch from a Johnny Cash song, 'Hey Porter', and it feels like a gift.

The film opens on a family of penguins, who live in glittering icehouses with little fires to warm their flippers when they come in from a hard day's fishing. The ice looks more like ice than real ice does, with slippery-looking curves and corners. It's packed with sudden sparkles. The story focuses on the oldest girl penguin, Margery, who feels the cold more than her brothers and sisters. She's always asking her dad to put more twigs on the fire, or begging her mum for another blanket. She has a special relationship with her Grandmother Nog, who is the only one who really understands her – she has always felt the cold too. The penguins all tell stories to each other about huge fat monsters that eat naughty children and Biggers (grown-up penguins). The only way to keep these monsters away is to be very good, and for the school children to recite their 'anti-being-eaten poem' every morning (the narrator explains that it rhymes perfectly when sung in Penguinese) –

Keep your eyes open
Look all around
If you see a strange shape
Waddle to a Bigger
If a Bigger isn't there
Find your Igg instead
Ask your Igg what you should do
And do it very quickly

One afternoon after school, her mum tells Margery that a fat monster ate her grandmother. Our heroine is devastated. She gets up in the middle of the night ever-so quietly, packs three fish and a drawing of her mother into her knapsack, and sets off into the night. She heads south, using the stars as her compass as her grandmother had taught her. As a soft blue dawn is breaking over the endless ice, she hears a quiet whimper and looks inside her knapsack to find her youngest sister, Bo, who must have crept in when she wasn't looking. After telling her off and making her cry, they find an old icehouse and eat a fish, huddling together to share their warmth. Bo sleeps curled up on top of her big sister's feet.

That night Grandmother Nog appears to Margery in a dream. Margery asks for her advice and she tells her to listen to the anti-being-eaten poem. Margery's never paid much attention to the words before, but she says it quietly to herself when she wakes up and asks herself what an Igg is. Why has she never asked anyone? There aren't any Biggers around, so she makes her own mind up – she needs to take Bo back to her parents. Of course the penguin children lose their way and get caught up in all kinds of adventures. It wouldn't have been much of a film if they didn't, Leonard thinks to himself. They narrowly escape falling into a huge crevasse, being frozen, and starving, and they get chased by a huge, vicious seal. Margery is forced to make decisions for herself as Bo is depending on her, and she wishes every day that she knew what an Igg was so she could be more sure.

Eventually they see their penguin-town in the distance. They settle in an abandoned igloo for their last night and Grandmother Nog comes to her in a dream again. She gives Margery a huge hug and says she should be proud. Margery says, 'But I didn't find my Igg!', and her grandmother smiles and says 'Have another look.' Margery looks down at her stomach, where she always imagined her Igg might be, and sees a glowing orange ball lighting up her skin and fur from inside like a stained glass window. Grandmother Nog explains that you have to grow your own Igg, and that no-one can show you how. Every decision you make by yourself feeds it, makes it burn brighter. When Margery wakes up she puts a hand on her stomach and she can feel her Igg letting out heat like a stone left in the sun.

The sweeping, aching violin music and the relief on her parent's faces when they're reunited the next morning moves Leonard terribly. He sits absolutely still in the dark while the credits roll to give himself a chance to pull himself together.

'Silly old fool,' he whispers to himself.

They play a series of 'outtakes' from the film, and he's grateful for some laughs to pull him away from a terrible ache for little Margery, out in the ice all alone. He fingers his new T-shirt in its plastic bag, feeling pleased again about buying it, and eats the last few pieces of popcorn that are mostly hard kernel. How did it all fit in his stomach – does it deflate like candyfloss? He emerges into the lobby, blinking like a mole and as a last treat before driving home he waits in a pizza restaurant for a take-away pizza – small and perfectly formed, covered in glistening pepperoni. He'll warm it in the oven when he gets home. It's been a good evening. He's glad of the freedom to go to town and stay out late if he wants to, for the privilege of being able to plant daffodil bulbs and wield a chain-saw and get paid for it. He's a lucky man. A lucky man.

The next morning he wakes a little later than usual and makes himself a bacon butty with thick white bread and butter and tomato sauce. He cooks the bacon until it's crispy and dark brown at the edges, just how he likes it. Rose was vegetarian for a few weeks in the mid-nineties, after seeing a grisly programme about the meat industry. She carried on cooking meat for Leonard and ate some kind of rubbery fake meat herself, chewing bravely and protesting it was delicious. She'd hold her nose with her fingers when the chops came out of the oven and constantly reminded him of what he was eating while he ate it. He listened to what she said, which all made perfect sense, and waited patiently. One Sunday morning he made two rounds of his special bacon sandwiches, and that was the end of that. He never said another word about it, although sometimes in the middle of arguments he was sorely tempted to use it as ammunition.

The phone rings just as he's about to leave the house with Pickles. It's Raine, sounding her usual distracted self. She says she's in the middle of a project at work, up to her eye-balls. Leonard has a fleeting visual image of her stood in a tiny office with papers piled up to the bridge of her nose. Ed needs to go to the dentist, is there any way at all... if he thinks he could cope with them... she'll be eternally grateful... And so Ed delivers the twins onto his doorstep an hour later, bundled up in navy blue woolly hats and scarves and gloves and overcoats. It takes Leonard ten minutes to unwrap them both, as if they are a pass-the-parcel. He hasn't ever babysat them during the day before. The usual routine is Raine and Ed escaping for an evening while he reads them stories and tucks them up in their own beds, surrounded by a hundred and one teddies in assorted sizes and colours. What a responsibility! He feels the start of a rising panic and gives himself a stern talking-to – pull yourself together, Leonard, they're only three. What's the worst they can do? And another visual image arrives, of the house burnt to the ground and the twins dancing in the charred remains of his kitchen, laughing manically.

As Ed is rushing off, Leonard asks him what he should do with them. Ed scratches his chin and says they like ducks and helping Raine in the kitchen. As he's driving off he screeches his brakes, winds down the window and hands Leonard a Thomas the tank engine video. Thank the heavens for Raine, Leonard thinks. Saved. He plonks them down in front of the TV to buy himself some time. They both sit cross-legged, too close to the screen, and Leonard lifts them in turn to shift them back a few feet. Their eyes don't leave the screen – it's amazing how videos can hold children's attention. He wonders if the makers have sneaked any hypnotic suggestions in between frames – buy more Thomas toys! Have screaming fits if your parents don't comply! He sits on the sofa and thinks of a recipe that would stretch to include two sets of tiny helping hands.

'Buddy, do you do stirring?'

Nothing.

'Rory. Rory!' He turns his head a few centimetres, his eyes still on the screen. 'What do you like to cook, Rory? Would you like to do some cooking with granddad?' Rory nods his head slowly and emits a single word.

'Cake.'

Fair enough. Cake it was... a recipe... he needs a recipe. He already has flour, eggs, butter... what else? Who would have a cake recipe? He'd rather not speak to Gloria after their last phone call. Maybe Lily? She made those scones; she's bound to know how to do a simple sponge. Would she mind him calling her?

She doesn't mind, and says she's just been thinking about him. She gives him the recipe and throws in a tip – that he should make mini-ones so the twins can get involved in icing them. Icing cakes is widely known by all children as 'the best bit'. She tells him some anecdotes about cooking with her grandchildren when they were younger which slightly alarm him – he makes a mental note not to do anything involving cocktail sticks or golden syrup. Before he rings off, Lily asks him if he's busy tomorrow. She's planning on trying a new walk and would appreciate some company, but understands that he's probably already busy. He says yes before really thinking about what her invitation means. Does she have something else to tell him about Rose? Can she really want more of his company after he practically walked out on her the last time they met? They agree to meet at a pub where they can leave their cars – she has one of those books with the walk all mapped out. He hears some crying from the living room and so they say their goodbyes quickly.

They'll need some more ingredients – icing sugar, little paper cake cases. They can go to the village pond on the way to the shop. It's easy enough to get Rory's teeth to detach from his brother's sleeve by mentioning ducks – the effect is immediate. They both jump up and start waddling in circles and quacking. He imagines Raine and Ed not being able to say the word in conversation, like the word 'walk' when a dog is in the room. 'I thought we could maybe have D-U-C-K for Christmas dinner this year darling,' and, 'If I hadn't D-U-C-K-ed, that ball would have hit me straight on the nose.' Leonard breaks the news to Pickles that he's leaving him at home (two small boys is responsibility enough) and he bundles his grandsons back up before they leave the house. They have to walk a little way to get to the forlorn looking village pond. Leonard wonders if Ed should have brought car seats with him, or buggies… so much paraphernalia. Irrational thoughts flick through his mind – what if he gets a really itchy nose and he has to let go of a sticky hand and then Rory runs out into the road? What if he has a heart attack? He's remembered to bring some pieces of bread with them and he helps the boys to rip it into pieces. The ducks are quack-ily appreciative and the boys squeal with satisfaction when their bits of bread get gobbled. Leonard enjoys it so much that he vows to return by himself another day.

Their next stop is the local shop. The clang of the bell lifts Mr. Harding's eyes from his paper and he greets Leonard gruffly. Harding Stores – they've been here since the beginning of time. Some of the tins of peaches have probably been here for longer than that, Leonard reckons. He manages to find everything he needs and gets some blue and red food colouring as well. Some of the stock may be a little out of date, but Mr Harding does have a knack for knowing what people in a village need when they can't be bothered to go to a supermarket. There's a minor crisis when they're nearly home when Rory suddenly cries out 'Mitten gone!' They search around the pond and retrace their steps as far as the shop – nothing. Rory gets a bit upset and says mummy will be angry, but Leonard tells him he'll talk to mummy and not to worry and gives him a little cuddle. When they reach home Leonard fumbles with the toggles on their duffel coats and catches sight of something in Rory's hood. It's the mitten. He's not sure how it got there, but Rory is much relieved.

The cake-making is fun too – like a chemical experiment. Getting the quantities right, putting in things in the right order. For some reason Buddy gets fixated by Leonard's kitchen bin – the lid lifts automatically when you open up the cupboard door. He spends most of the cooking time watching the bin appear and laughing each time at the novelty. Rory loses interest in the baking two thirds of the way through and says 'Thomas!' in a voice that is less a request and more a mandate, but Buddy leaves the joys of the bin to sit quietly and watch Leonard finishing the cake. Leonard is quite enjoying himself – he hasn't done any baking since Rose's fiftieth birthday, when he made her a surprise chocolate cake with Glor's help.

The icing is more engaging, especially as the twins join in with advice about the colouring, insisting on 'More blue! More blue!' until the icing looks like melted plastic – vile, shocking. It's a little runnier than Leonard would have liked, but he gets it wrong so many times adding more water and then more icing sugar and then more water and he garners such a surplus of blue icing that he gives up in the end. It turns out that they need a surplus of icing after all, as half of it gets tipped onto the floor 'by mistake'. (Rory later admits he wanted to see if it would make a blue puddle.)

Raine comes to pick them up in the late afternoon. They've eaten five cakes each by then (Leonard too) and are all slumped on the sofa together. Leonard has always liked having a twin for each hand when they were out walking, a twin to lean on each side of his chest when they were sitting down. There's something very satisfying about the symmetry. The twins have grudgingly agreed to watch something other than Thomas and so they are watching a neon cartoon about three punk girls. It's like something from a foreign country to Leonard, all pretend expletives and violent movement. The twins are wide awake, probably high on an overdose of blue colouring, but Leonard's eyes are drooping and the voices from the TV are sounding further and further away when the doorbell goes.

He persuades Raine to stop for a quick coffee. He puts half a teaspoon of caffeinated coffee into his mug with the decaff to wake himself up a bit – he never usually touches caffeine after midday. How naughty of him! They sit in the kitchen with 'POW's and 'ZAP's coming from the living room. He sits for a few minutes in silence, still shaking the last of the cobwebs from his head, as his mother would have said. Raine is staring out of his tiny window into the dark.

'Darling?'

'Oh, sorry Dad. I was miles away.'

'I wonder what will happen to all those sayings with all those metric-police from Europe. I was kilometres away. A kilogram of flesh. They don't have quite the same... Raine? Earth to Raine?'

'Yes. No.' She pulls her gaze away from the window. He can almost imagine the sound it makes, a sucking noise, like pulling one of those rubber soap dishes away from the bath. 'Sorry Dad. Have the boys been OK?'

'Oh, fine love, fine. They're good boys.'

'Huh — you wouldn't think so at home. I hate how children are always better behaved when they're with other people. It doesn't seem fair somehow — we put in all the hardest work — all that snot and puke and...' She trails off to take a rasping sip of coffee, fully caffeinated, two heaped teaspoons.

'I met Lily last week, the woman that went to school with mum.' Raine flicks her eyes at him and back to her coffee, startled. 'She said something about your mum that got me thinking. You know what she used to say about her hair...' He stops, noticing that the colour has leached from Raine's face. She drains the cup and starts rifling through her handbag for her car keys.

'Right. Better be off then. Sorry I can't stop any longer, Dad. I really appreciate you looking after them both, honestly I do. '

He considers pushing it but decides against it. The feeling of unease grows a little. He really wants to speak to Raine about her mother, but he's realising that she just can't manage it. He hasn't noticed before just how difficult it is for her. Has he been fooling himself? Has he been neglecting her?

'That's fine darling. I know you're busy.'

He's made his voice soft again and he tries to catch her eyes but she's all efficiency now, all movement. She won't look at him, even when he's standing in her way. She bundles the twins away, pulling Rory roughly by the arm when he refuses to leave the sofa. She won't wait for him to pack up the rest of the cakes for her and so he gives the twins one each to eat in the car. They're both crying by the time she waves from the car perfunctorily and pulls away. He sits at the kitchen table for a long time after she's gone, stroking Pickles under the table with his foot. He listens to the silence in the house and feels a terrible sadness.

Chapter 9:
Blue Heaven freesias

The next day Leonard finds himself whistling 'Sea of Heartbreak' by Don Gibson as he gets ready to go out and meet Lily for their walk. It's such a chirpy tune for the tragic lyrics. 'The lights in the harbour; Don't shine for me; I'm like a lost ship adrift on the sea...' He's determined to act a bit more normally today – if he never sees Lily again, he'd rather she were left with a better impression of him. He pulls into the pub and she's already there, sitting in her smart red Micra. She hasn't seen him and as he gets closer he can hear a 'boosh boosh' noise coming through the metal and glass. She's making strange movements with her hands as if she's directing an orchestra – small bird-like swoopings and then sharp little movements like karate chops. He imagines colours streaming from her hands – different colours from different fingers, leaving trails in the air. One of the lads at work told him once what it was like to be on LSD – that you got traces from objects like when you write your name with a sparkler. It sounded fun to Leonard, and he'd almost asked him if he could get some for him, but he knew that Rose wouldn't have approved and didn't fancy doing it behind her back.

As he watches Lily, she suddenly catches sight of him.
She's startled, and jumps in her seat. He sees colour coming
to her cheeks, and she turns down the music before winding
down the window where he's standing. It's some kind of
pop music with a screeching woman's voice. He's a country
and western man himself and he can't be doing with all that
pumping and grinding.

'Leonard! I was listening to my music... how
embarrassing. How long have you been standing there
watching me, you sneaky man?'

She gets out of the car and walks around to the boot.
He waits while she puts on her wellies – they're covered in
stiff, flaking mud. It's starting to spit, and she hovers a hand
over her umbrella on the passenger seat before deciding to
without. She says she prefers to get a bit wet rather than
hoiking that awkward thing around. Leonard guesses the
meaning of hoik; he's never heard it before. Is it even a real
word? He gets the feeling that Lily would be happy enough
making up her own words if it suited her. She's full of odd
phrases – 'walking like the cat around hot porridge', 'you
shouldn't paint the devil on the wall', something about brains
and beards... She said they were from her mother. She slams
the boot shut hard and shows him in her book which way
they're going – she seems eager to share the responsibility
with him. They set off into the gloomy afternoon.

After a few pleasantries they lapse into silence. There's
quite a long stretch of the route that follows a country lane
and there's no need to confer over directions. Leonard notices
their pace – he's walking slightly slower than he usually
would, but not frustratingly slower. She walks faster than
Rose. He enjoyed walking with Rose, but she only had one
speed and it was so slow that it did drive him mad sometimes.

He secretly longed to stride off into the distance.

He remembers one of their favourite walks along the river in the next village. They'd walked it in snow and rain, in Spring and in Autumn. They'd walked it when Rose was nearing the end of her recovery from an operation on her foot, and when Leonard had heard that very morning about his mother's death. They'd even stopped once, one crazy day, and made love in the long grass. He wonders if Lily would like to walk it with him, and feels immediately guilty for this thought. It was his and Rose's walk. How would Rose feel if she saw them walking there? As he's trying to guess, he interrupts himself. *She's dead, Leonard,* he reminds himself sternly. She doesn't feel anything. All that survives of her is my memories, and some likenesses of her stuck down onto paper with light and chemicals.

He's aware of a change in his mood – a bit of him feels somehow freed up. He becomes sharply aware of his surroundings. They're on a standard-looking English country road with bare ploughed fields on one side and gravel drives up to different shaped houses on the other. There's a misty haze ahead of them. The air – sniff! – smells of roast chicken. It must be coming from an open window – a family of strangers about to sit down to their Sunday dinner. Mmm, Sunday roast, with crispy roast potatoes and herby stuffing and thick, velvety gravy. He turns and looks at Lily. She seems lost in her own thoughts.

'Do you like Sunday roasts?'

She focuses on him, smiles.

'Where did that question come from?'

'Oh, just thinking… my mind, you know. Wandering about.'

He isn't in any hurry to speak again and they walk in silence while he waits for something else to surface. The sun moves from behind a cloud and the fine layer of water covering the road and the muddy fields flashes white for a moment before becoming dull again. He finds he wants to tell her about his work. He hesitates for a moment, not sure whether she'd be interested in hearing about it.

'Things are busy at work at the moment.'

She passes his unconscious test by saying she doesn't know much about what he does; she's always wondered what it's like to work outside for a living. They spend the next half-hour talking about life at Coburne House, in the pauses between working out whether it's right down this road or the next, and whether they should walk around the edges of a field covered in huge sods of dark earth or tramp straight through the middle. They get it completely wrong once and have to re-trace their steps after admitting defeat. She says she'd love to see the estate, and he offers to show her around one day. He loves showing people around – it's not often that people want to hear the names of plants and the best time to visit to see them in full bloom. He loves working in gardens that are open to the public. He couldn't bear to work for a private house and have the owners stroll round the garden a few times a year when they're not gallivanting around the world, staying at their third residence in the Bahamas or some other nonsense.

After they've talked about Leonard for a while, they turn to Lily and her career. She worked as some kind of researcher most of her life, something academic. It doesn't mean much to Leonard – he can't put it into any kind of context, like Raine and her marketing job. She only works part time now, 'to keep her brain from going to mush', as a librarian in the local library. She especially likes checking out books to young children and imagining all those colourful stories feeding their fresh minds and helping them grow, like a nutritious diet and plenty of exercise. She tells him a few amusing stories about her colleagues, agreeing with him that they sound like caricatures but protesting that she's not over-exaggerating anyone's character for the sake of a good story (OK then, maybe a little). There's a kind, mousey, 'never-been-loved' girl, an authoritarian manager with a nasty moustache who enjoys making his employees quake with fear, and an old battle-axe with a heart of gold. She describes them all with affection – even the manager, who, Lily says, 'makes it very difficult for people to like him'. She says that in her opinion the nastiest people are usually the ones who are the most miserable on the inside. They are the most desperate; they have been terribly let down by the people who were meant to love them and teach them how to love other people. Leonard can't imagine Lily having much truck with this manager's 'frightening' techniques.

After an hour of talking, they move back into silence. The book says they're two-thirds of the way round. Every so often one of them will see something they deem worth sharing – a blue-tit in the hedgerow, his crown the colour of the sky, or a particularly shapely holly leaf. There's so much to see, even at this time of year. Leonard sees an oak on the distant horizon, and the shape of it reminds him of the last National Trust estate he used to work at. His mind ambles around this time of his working life – in his head he bumps into his freckled boss again, and the young lady who made the cakes on whom he cultivated an innocent crush for over a year. He fondly remembers the sociable robin ('Mr. Red') who used to perch on the end of his wheelbarrow as Leonard wheeled it about. All gardeners have to know a friendly robin at some point in their career; it's in the rules. He feels safe somehow, walking with Lily, and he settles himself more and more firmly in the past. He wanders into the kitchen and eats a thick wedge of the tea-lady's best coffee cake – with coffee butter-cream and real coffee beans as decoration, best accompanied by a cup of earl grey. He puts the crumb-strewn plate down and takes the hand of the tea-lady and walks with her across the grass towards the edge of the river.

He reaches a spot where there are flat concrete steps down to the water and he sees that there's someone already sitting there, facing the water. She's wearing a navy blue top with a long cotton skirt and has pearls around her neck. Her hair is dark, cropped close. The tea lady disappears in a sudden puff of smoke and Leonard's hand is left holding empty air. It was eight years after they were married, just before Rose became pregnant with Raine. She'd come to meet him for lunch as she sometimes did. They'd sit and listen to the river, eating the sandwiches she'd made for them both – cheese and pickle, or chicken from the roast they had at the weekend as a special treat. He'd been a little worried about her for a while. She'd not been herself, and had started snapping at him for no reason. He'd been surprised by her venom. One evening he came home to find her sitting on the sofa and gazing at the wall as if she was in a trance. He'd tried asking her what was wrong but she'd just walk out of the room. He sits next to Rose on the steps by the river and the whole conversation floods back as if he's there.

'I've something to tell you, Leonard.'

He can still remember her tone of voice, the gravity, the effect it had on him.

'I've something to tell you.'

This time her voice cracks mid-way through, as if in half. The silence asks him to prepare himself, underlines the words that are coming next.

'You must leave me.'

He's horrified. He wasn't expecting that. He can't find any words. He searches her face as she stares into the water. It's as if all the life has left it. He waits for her to explain. She starts whispering something, he can hardly hear her. He asks her to speak louder, puts his ear closer to her face. She looks like someone else. She's saying it over and over, like a mantra.

'You must leave me.

You must leave me.

You must leave me.'

The emphasis on *must* – a statement of bare fact, an order. He asks her why, he asks her to explain. He says her name. She is locked in. He notices she is rocking slightly, he notices her hand is grasping the other so tightly that the knuckles are white. There are angry red spots where the blood has pooled under the skin. He touches her on the arm. He's lost her, he's utterly lost her. He begins to worry about getting her home – imagines having to hoist her over his shoulder like a sack, imagines for a horrible second her standing up and jumping into the water, going under in front of his eyes. He can't leave her on her own. He needs help. He doesn't want anyone to see her like this.

He gets her to the car somehow, coaxing her, half dragging her, and sits her in the passenger seat and straps her in. She is like a sack of compost. He wants to tell someone he is leaving but he doesn't feel able to leave her – maybe she'll get out and run, maybe she'll have some kind of fit… His heart wants to escape, his mouth is dry. When he looks at his watch he's amazed to see that he's only had ten minutes of his lunch break so far. He can phone work from home, tell them he's taken ill. He drives Rose home, and all the way she mutters 'you must leave me, you must leave me', the words starting to lose their shape, blurring into each other. It isn't a human sound. He speaks to her as they drive, 'It's OK, Rose darling, we're getting you home now', as if speaking to a child, to a hurt animal. When he pulls the car up outside their house she seems to come to, she looks around wildly. He's afraid again that she'll try to bolt – he keeps her in the car for a few minutes, carries on talking to her. They hobble in together, and when they get into the hall and he shuts the front door, she collapses onto the floor and vomits all over the carpet.

He gets her up to their bedroom and pulls the blankets up under her chin and she falls asleep instantly. He cleans up downstairs like an automaton, and wonders what else he should be doing. He doesn't once consider calling the doctor. No one else needs to know about this; it's their business. When he's finished cleaning up, he sits by her as she sleeps. He hopes she might wake up as 'herself' again, but when she does, when the sky is losing its light, she looks at him from somewhere far away. That night is the worst. She is delirious – moaning, crying, shaking off the covers, pushing him away. She says things he doesn't understand, about what a terrible person she is, about needing to keep Leonard away from her. He can hardly bear to look into her eyes. He thinks the light will never come back.

In the morning she is able to eat a little toast and shuffle to the toilet. Mid-morning between fits of sleeping she holds out her hand and said 'Leonard!' He nursed her back to health, slowly. One morning she asked for jam on her toast instead of the marmalade he'd been giving her; one afternoon she asked if he'd called her work to let them know she wasn't well. He took time off work himself and was forced to get the doctor in to write her a proper sicknote. The doctor wrote 'nerves' in neat capital letters on a bit of paper and subscribed sleeping tablets and some other pills that Leonard flushed down the toilet. Eventually he trusted her to be alone during the day. When he got home he'd go straight upstairs to see her, bringing her a few sweet-smelling 'Blue Heaven' freesias from work, stories from the day, strawberries. She got back on her feet, eventually. They never talked about it. It never happened again.

The sun pokes out from behind a cloud. It's still drizzling – there should be a rainbow. As he's searching the horizon, he catches sight of the pub in the distance – they seem to be approaching it from a different and surprising direction. He shudders to put an end to thinking about that terrible time. Lily catches his eye, and he smiles and says he was miles away, and stumbles on a dip in the road. She holds out her arm and he grasps it, steadies himself.

Back at the pub they decide to have a quick half before setting off home – a small reward for their physical efforts. Lily insists on paying for them both, leaving Leonard feeling uncomfortable but unsure of how to articulate his uneasiness. Why shouldn't she pay? They chose a table in a bay at the front of the pub so they can bathe in the weak sunshine further weakened by the thick dusty windows. The first sip of bitter is nectar. They both make 'aah!' noises at the same time as setting their glasses back on the table and sinking back into the soft red velvet seats. It feels so comfortable between them that Leonard decides it's only natural to talk to her about what is on his mind.

'Her hair had been short, really short, since I met her. She'd always told me her hair never grew, something medical – she told me stories about when she was a little girl.'

Lily doesn't have to ask who he's talking about. She just nods at him and waits for him to continue.

'I found a ticket too, in an old handbag of hers. It was

to Didcot. We'd never been there; she'd never been. I'm not sure what it all means.'

'Couldn't she have gone there shopping once, with a friend from work? Or gone with your... with your daughter and not told you?'

Leonard shakes his head. 'It wasn't like that, our marriage. We knew everything about each other. I could tell you what she'd eaten for lunch at work every day. She could tell you what colour underpants I was wearing.' He blushes a little at having mentioned his underpants by mistake. 'I knew her inside and out, Lily. Or at least I thought I did.'

They sit sipping their bitter for a while, mulling things over. He imagines Lily is going through the same thoughts he's had these past weeks – trying to think of a logical solution, a scenario that would explain why she'd felt the need to invent such elaborate lies about such a ridiculous thing. It's maddening. It reminds him of when Rose had asked him to thread a needle for her once – she'd left her reading glasses upstairs. He'd sat there for aeons, missing the tiny eye time after time with Rose dissolving into laughter behind him. He refused to let her take the needle and thread back, even once she'd gone to fetch her glasses and stood hovering over him with a hand outstretched. He was going to get that needle threaded if it took him all night. When it had finally gone through, he'd told her to never ask him to do it again, not yet ready to see the funny side.

Lily takes another sip of her drink, making a smacking noise with her lips like a man. She looks over at him.

'What are you going to do?'

'I don't know. My mate Charlie reckons I should leave it well alone, get on with my life. There's nothing good can come of digging around now she's gone. But I just can't.'

The last word comes out of his mouth with a circle of

desperation around it. He's given himself away. He lifts his own glass, grateful of something to do with his hands. He wishes he could have another, he's already thinking about the bottom of the glass. He wants to drain it in one go and order a quadruple rum and coke, sit here out of the drizzle and get happily sloshed. Instead he takes a baby sip. He reflects on what he's said to her so far. He might as well carry on.

'It's like a novel I don't know the end to. I've read the first few pages, got hooked, and now someone's hidden the book. I don't know if I even want to read it or not. I'm pretty sure it's going to be a sad ending.'

'Whatever you find out, Leonard, would it change the way you felt about her? About the years you spent... When you talk about her, I can... I can see her. I feel as if I know her. The Rose you knew... She's real already. I don't really know what I'm trying to...' She trails off, tries to find her way back. 'What I'm saying is, you can't get rid of the Rose you knew. Your wife. She'll always... She'll always be your wife. But then what do I know, really... it's not my...'

Leonard feels comforted by this, recognises the truth of what she's saying.

'I do want to try and find out,' he says. 'I don't even know if it'll be possible now; it's so long ago, I don't know if there'll be anyone left alive who'll know why... who'll be able to make some sense of it. But if I don't try, I'll always be left wondering. It's better to get to the truth, don't you think?'

'I've always believed in heading towards...' She pauses, as if searching for what she does believe. 'Worry often gives small things a big shadow. But there are different types of truth, Leonard. We never see it properly – it depends where we're looking from.' She pauses. 'If you want me to... I there's anything I can...'

He nods a 'thanks' to her. He feels ready to leave. He drains his glass and sighs, his eyes widening slightly in a 'shall we go?' gesture. As Lily hooks her handbag over her shoulder, she says as an afterthought, 'It's a shame about her mum. Seems nobody can get much sense out of her these days, now that... Such a waste...'

Leonard isn't sure he's heard her right.

'These days?'

'Yes – it's a terrible disease... my aunt was – Leonard? You did know she was ill, didn't you?'

'Rose said she was dead.'

'Oh.' She pauses, as if waiting for him to absorb the new information, and puts her handbag down again. 'I'm sorry, Leonard, I assumed you... I tracked her down first when I was looking for Rose. She lives in a home, she's got Alzheimers. She's been there for... Rose said she was dead? Maybe she couldn't cope with her any more... it's a difficult...' she breaks off as Leonard shakes his head violently.

'Rose said she died when Rose was young. Before I met her, years ago. What's going on, Lily?'

He looks into her eyes, searching for answers. All he can see is concern. She puts a hand on his arm. He drops his eyes from hers, ashamed of his need. His need for answers, his need for Rose. If she were here, he could ask her. He's suddenly angry at her. It's not fair of her to leave him with all this. He gouges chunks out of his beer mat with his car keys. He's aware of Lily's hand resting gently on him, stopping him from floating away.

'I'd like to meet her mother, to go and visit. Would that be allowed, do you think?' he asks.

'Well, I don't think there are any rules about... I suppose she's not very likely to say no. I've still got the number somewhere... We could give it a... They said she wasn't too good when I spoke to them, Leonard. It might be a waste of time.'

'That's OK. It's something to try, isn't it? Somewhere to start. If I don't do something I'll go mad.'

'Leonard, I'm happy to call them if you want me to. I'll do whatever I can to...'

'Thanks. Let me know what they say.'

He feels energised by this new approach. He's going to try to find out what's going on. He's not just going to lie down and turn it round and round in his head any more. As they're gathering themselves together to leave again, Lily remembers something.

'Oh – Leonard – I do, by the way.'

'You do?'

'Like Sunday roasts. I thought it might be a hint? Although I'm not very good at them I can never get it quite...'

He remembers his out-of-the-blue statement earlier, when they were walking. 'Oh, no, no, I didn't mean it like that!'

'Well, anyway, I'll do you one next week if you like?'

'Oh, no, really, I don't want to...' He struggles with the words, not knowing quite what he wants to say.

'It'd be a pleasure. I'll make you help me with the peeling... the chopping, the washing up.'

'OK, I'll let you know.'

'I wouldn't offer if I didn't mean it, truly. I'm not...'

'As long as you don't call me Truly anymore, we have a deal.'

It takes her a few seconds to get it, and when she does she groans loudly and fake-punches him on his arm. He pantomimes sudden pain, clutching the spot where she's touched him, clasping it with his other hand and moving backwards in slow motion with his mouth wide, his eyes scrunched up. He slumps back down onto the seat, mouth ajar, tongue hanging out. When he comes back to life, he's ready to drive home, ready to greet Pickles and find refuge in a crossword book. He might even experiment with the scone recipe Lily brought along for him.

They part in the car park, Lily leaning forward for a hug and Leonard kissing her on the cheek instead. The awkward moment is prolonged when Lily anticipates a second kiss and leans towards him to be left hanging mid-air. She laughs and tells him she's never got the hang of that silly 'mwah mwah' kissing. She suggests they start again and holds out an arm to him. How long is it since he's properly hugged anyone except his daughter? They approach each other diagonally, facing away from each other. It's a short hug, chaste, but tight – he feels her arm muscles pushing against him and squeezes back. He gets into his car and turns his music up loud.

Chapter 10:
A bag of cherries

As Leonard collects fallen leaves for Peggy's modest compost pile on a drizzly weekend afternoon, he catches a flash of orange amongst the browns and green. It's the shiny, pumpkin-coloured berries of *Iris foetidissima*, clustered in fat seedpods. There's always colour. There's always something to look at, to touch, to smell, even at the end of November. He marvels that a whole week and a half has passed since he was sat in the pub with Lily. He'll see her again in an hour's time – they've arranged to visit Rose's mum. He hates the way time seems to have speeded up the older he's got. When he was small, a year felt like an eternity – so long to wait for another birthday cake and presents, so long between fish and chips on a Wednesday and sponge pudding on a Friday night.

That morning he'd woken up with a small sinking in his stomach. He was surprised to match it up to the knowledge that Gloria was coming over. She'd ignored Leonard's suggestion that she should come round for a drink with her husband Pete instead, and had left him a message informing him she'd be there at her usual time. What would Lily think if she knew about their strange arrangement? She'd think he was taking advantage of Glor. So why did it feel like it was the other way round, as if he was somehow doing Glor a favour? He decided before he got out of bed that he'd tell her straight as soon as he saw her – that he didn't need her to come over any more. He'd spent the morning thinking about how he could put it to her without offending her, how he could explain it properly. Rose would have known what to say. It made a change to think about Gloria for a while – more straightforward. There are pitfalls now when he thinks about Rose, when he suddenly loses his footing.

In the end it had been much worse than he'd imagined. Gloria had seemed a little distant when she arrived, and Leonard almost put off saying anything, but he couldn't bear the thought of having to wait another fortnight. He tried to relax her by asking her about Pete. Leonard always had to ask about him; she never volunteered any information. She gave her usual answer, 'ticking along', and Leonard suggested again that they get together for a drink sometime, all three of them, as he hadn't seen Pete for months. She gave him a sour look, and he felt a twinge of anger.

Then he blurted it out.

'It'll be good to make sure we see each other now that – once you, you know, stop coming here. To help me out.'

In the silence that followed he tried his best to soften the impact.

'I've been meaning to say something… it's not that… I've really appreciated everything you've done for me Glor. It's just…'

He started to panic as he watched her face fall in on itself. He wanted to get out of the room and decided to offer her a cup of tea, and told her to sit down so they could talk about it properly. He waited for her to nod her assent and then disappeared into his kitchen. He heard the door slam just as he was clicking on the kettle and went out to find her gone. He'd spoken to Pickle about it for a few minutes – asked him what he could have done differently, wondered why she was so touchy. Well, at least she knew she wasn't wanted anymore now. There are more important things going on at the moment, he thinks, as he gets ready to carry another trug-full of leaves round to the compost heap. She's a grown-up – she'll get over it.

When he's finished, he pops in to tell Peggy he's off and then grabs ten minutes to sit down in his own house and read the paper before he leaves for Lily's. He'd like to catch up on what's happening with the cricket. He never goes straight from one place to another if he can help it – he likes to give his mind a chance to change gear, like going into neutral. He gets up to switch on his lamp – it's already getting dark. Pickles mistakes Leonard's lurch out of his chair for a move towards the kitchen and sits up, yapping. He's been getting extra treats recently; Leonard bought them for him when he went to Reading. Dehydrated brown lumps made from various unsavoury parts of some poor animal and smell disconcertingly of cheese – yum!

'No, Mister – you're pushing your luck…' he says, in a tone of voice that he hopes will make his message perfectly clear. 'You're always after something, aren't you, you scoundrel, you piggy doggy you, you are.' Half-way through, Leonard's sentence loses its stern timbre and deteriorates into affection accompanied by a vigorous ruffling of fur. Pickles has the look of a dog who's in no doubt about who wears the trousers. Leonard gets up and casually gets him a few treats before he leaves the house, rationalising that it's just to keep him going until his dinner. Spoilt animal.

He goes into the bathroom to splash water over his face and takes the car keys from the hook in the kitchen.

Outside Lily's house, he pulls on the hand-break with a great creak and leaves the engine running. When he beeps his horn, she pops out to tell him she'll be out in a minute and disappears back into the house. She takes ages and the frustration builds in Leonard's stomach – what can she be doing in there? She knew what time he was arriving... He starts to regret taking her with him in the first place. On the journey, his annoyance with her grows as she fails to give him proper directions – she keeps forgetting to tell him to turn off until it's almost too late, and a couple of times they miss a turning altogether. She apologises profusely each time, which seems to make it worse.

Half-way there they pass a half run-over squirrel. Lily cranes her neck as they pass, to see if she can see it moving, and makes a pained 'ooh' noise. She asks Leonard if they should go back and run it over properly to put it out of its misery. Leonard says he's sure it's already dead. He's got no patience for her today, for her fussing, for her endless chatter. After the squirrel, she sinks into a sad silence. He taps his finger-nails on the steering wheel and immediately begins to miss her endless chatter as he descends further and further into his own dark thoughts. He has a realisation that his frustration with her is probably more about his own nerves. He asks her how her day was in an attempt to start her up again like a wind-up toy, but the squirrel seems to have squashed her spirits.

He sees snapshots in his head of some of the sick or already-dead animals he's encountered in his life. Feathered or furred flat shapes hugging the road, naked and bulgy-eyed baby birds too early out of the nest. Their old cat George with laboured breathing and wide open eyes. The young thrush that bashed into their window one morning when Rose was washing up and that they nursed back to health in a cardboard box. He doesn't agree with Lily's sentimentality. It's only a squirrel; there are thousands of them out there dying all the time from disease, old age and hunger. If you spent too much of your feelings on individual animals you'd be overwhelmed. These thoughts remind him of his father, who had poisoned rats and drowned kittens without a passing nod to the life he was extinguishing. Hmm. Does he really want to model himself on that?

He does grudgingly admire the way that women can let their hearts open to include small creatures. They seem to have a greater capacity to love the lost, the weak – to feel sympathy for vile teenagers or for old men drinking their way to an early death on the streets. He remembers Rose and himself at one of Raine's parent evenings. One of the teachers, an emaciated man with hair coming from his nostrils and wrinkles eye-lids, had said some cruel things about the children in his class. He'd implied that Raine was included in his criticisms. Afterwards Rose had got a little misty-eyed. When he'd brought it up in the car on the way home Leonard had expected her to say something about how nasty he was about their daughter. Instead, she'd said, 'I can just see his mother, pushing him away from her.'

He couldn't dredge up any sympathy in himself for this total stranger. He did like to see this capacity for love in others though; it comforted him somehow. Maybe all of us are cruel sometimes, and in need of women's kindness. He flicks his eyes over to Lily. She is still sitting quietly, looking mournful. He wants to say something to let her know he understands, to let her know he is sad for the squirrel too, but he isn't sure how to put it.

'Nature is cruel,' he tries.

She looks over and smiles a watery smile, sighs, and seems to put the squirrel to rest.

'I'm hopeless with animals,' she says to herself.

She rubs a smear from her window with her sleeve and then turns her attention back to him.

'Any regrets yet? About the digging about, I mean, about...' She tails off into silence as she usually does.

'Well. No – I feel better about it all, funnily enough. Ever since I found that blasted ticket in her old handbag I've felt – well – low I suppose. It's been on my mind all the time, right at the back.' He's surprised at how easily he's confiding in her. It always seems easier when you're driving – there are fewer opportunities to look in each other's eyes, and the business of driving to keep the rest of your body busy. 'I bet this isn't quite what you expected when you sent Rose that letter.'

Lily laughs a little, shifts in her seat. She's found an empty cigarette box on the shelf underneath the dashboard – he sometimes buys a packet if he's going on a long journey and can't be bothered with all the pre-rolling. She's bending the lid back and then pushing it shut over and over. Leonard wonders if she's nervous as well.

'No, it wasn't. I wasn't really expecting to... I had a feeling that Rose would've preferred to leave me in the past where I belonged, where I... I hope she doesn't mind me being along, with you I mean. I feel a bit disloyal or something. Silly, I wouldn't have thought... What do you think? I can't really guess what she would have... Maybe you can't...'

He waits, but she's said all she's going to say. He's aware that there was a question in there somewhere, but he's not sure what it was. He offers her a roll-up instead. She laughs, tells him he'd have to roll it for her; she was always terrible at that. Unless he has one of those strange looking machines, like a mini mangle? They pass the rest of the journey more pleasantly, batting comments back and forth like children playing badminton, attempting humour and getting the punch-lines all wrong, not caring and laughing anyway.

The tension starts to build again when they realise they're nearly there. Leonard manoeuvres the car into a tight space, misjudging the angles and swearing loudly before remembering where he is and apologising. He notices his heart thumping with a little more force than usual. Before they get out of the car, Lily warns him again that they probably won't get any sense out of her, that he should prepare himself for that. He's touched by her concern, as if he's a little boy getting carried away about what might be under the Christmas tree.

The bitterly cold walk from the car to the entrance of the home feels like a long one. Lily makes a purring 'brrrrr' noise, her forehead and cheeks clenched against the wind. Leonard zips his jacket up as high as it'll go and thrusts his hands deep into his pockets, where he finds a small stick he'd stripped of bark with his fingernails a few weeks ago. The garden in front of the home is pathetic – lawn that's been mown too close and borders full of predictable, out-of-control shrubs. Leonard can spot these gardens from a mile off – low-maintenance and designed by people who don't give a fig about plants. There's an old man sat on the spot-lit bench in front of the house, wearing a tweed trilby and fingerless gloves. The creases on his face have run rampant, taking attention away from his eyes and his mouth. He's staring at a fixed point in the distance, and as they pass he glances at them and puts a hand to the rim of his hat to acknowledge them. As they walk past, a middle-aged woman approaches him and they hear her saying 'Mr. Steinberg? It's getting parky out here… let's get you back inside…' She speaks to him as if he's a child. Leonard feels a rising prickly annoyance – he hates it how old people get turned back into children again. Why do they put up with it? Is it that they don't notice? Surely they must. Is it that they don't care any more? Maybe their confidence gets slowly leached away as they're given fewer and fewer choices about how they live their lives – the deathly drip, drip, drip of institutionalisation. Leonard hopes it never happens to him. He'd rather go out as a grumpy old bugger, being patronising to anyone who spoke to him like that, and inciting the other residents to go on strike with him.

As they enter the building, Leonard wrinkles his nose at the overpowering stench of cabbage and stale urine. There's disinfectant as well, and a strong scent of artificial orange, but these sit on top of the other smells and seem to accentuate them rather than distracting from them. They approach the front desk, where a girl with bright orange hair and dark brown eyebrows is talking on the phone to a friend. She can't be any older than seventeen. What a place for a young girl to work, Leonard thinks. He remembers Rose telling him gory stories about her job on their first dates – an old man who used to cough up blood into a margarine tub, and the first time she'd caught a glimpse a dead body. The girl carries on chatting for a few seconds too long, and Lily clears her throat pointedly.

'Gotta go, Charl, speak later, yeah?' she says, and hangs up.

As she turns to them, her voice changes back to the one she uses at work. It comes out in smooth short bursts like those recorded messages on the telephone where they record a few words at a time and combine them in clusters to make sentences.

'Hello, sorry-to-keep-you-waiting, how-can-I-help?'

Lily explains who they're here to see. When the orange-haired girl gives them directions she calls Rose's mum by her first name, Mags. She cranks back into marionette-mode for her parting phrase – Leonard half expects he'd see a massive key on her back if he turned her around. If they took her out into the drizzle, her electrics would fizz and short.

'The-coffee-machine is along-the-hall, please-enjoy-your-visit.'

'Thank-you-very-much' he says, speaking in the same voice by mistake and feeling instantly embarrassed. He hopes she didn't notice. He has a habit of slipping into other people's accents. Raine used to get furious with him when he ordered Chinese on the phone or they went out to an Indian restaurant, as she was sure people would think he was taking the piss. Rose, of course, found the whole thing highly amusing.

They count the doors along the corridor. Leonard wonders about all the different residents here, one in each of these rooms, each of them with a life-time of stories. Mags' door is half open, and they can see in to a neatly made bed draped in a tartan blanket. The brown curtains are pulled half shut. Leonard knocks four times – the first knock hesitant, the last so loud it pushes the door further open. She is sitting in a straight-backed blue plush arm-chair, facing away from them. Her hair is very fine and sparse, her scalp densely dappled with liver spots. She's wearing an old pale-blue towelling dressing gown and some worn, red slippers. Her ankles are painful to look at – there are vivid blue veins and red blotches, and her very pale skin is stretched so tight over her bones that it looks like it might rip at any moment. Leonard finds himself thinking that he's grateful he never knew Rose like this. Mags doesn't turn her head, and Leonard feels nervous about seeing her face. They hover at the door, waiting. Leonard's feet feel stuck to the floor – he cranes his body and sees that her eyes are closed. Is she dead? He's planning on telling Lily he'd rather not bother after all, when she moves him out of the way so she can stand in the doorway.

'Hello, Mrs. Smith? Can we come in, please?' she says, striding into the room as she speaks.

The woman's back trembles slightly, as if from the cold, and she slowly opens her eyes. Leonard creeps into the room after Lily, as if he's tipping towards something he's afraid to touch. Mrs. Smith tilts her head onto one side but she doesn't turn to look at them – is she blind? Lily speaks again. She's speaking more loudly and more clearly than usual, but there's respect in it, not like when Mr. Steinberg was spoken to.

'My name is Lily. I've brought someone to meet you. Your daughter's husband. Rose's husband. Your daughter Rose. Mrs. Smith?'

She leaves a long pause between each statement, hoping to give her enough time to process the information, hoping to reach some part of her brain that's still working well enough. Only hearing her own name seems to bring any reaction, and the old woman screws up her face as if sucking on something sour.

'Oh… Mrs. Smith… me… Mrs. Smith… and all that… none of that… dear. Mags… None of that… Mrs. business… in the table.'

Her voice is low like a man's, and surprisingly strong. Lily gestures to Leonard that they should go and perch on the side of her single bed, where she'll be able to see them. Leonard is stupidly nervous. He holds onto the stick in his coat pocket, rubbing the smooth wood with his thumb to calm himself down. They sit, and Lily fusses about in an orange, vinyl-covered bag she's brought with her, rustling a supermarket plastic bag inside. This seems to prick Mrs. Smith's attention, and she reaches out a hand, watching Lily intently. Her nails are long and curved, dirty; her fingers are bent from arthritis. Rose used to tell Leonard about one of her elderly patients who'd refuse to have her nails cut. Rose had to bribe her with Mars bars. As Lily brings out some cherries, Mrs Smith's face contracts into a kind of grimace like a child baring its teeth for a photograph. Her remaining teeth are stained, and Leonard can't help feeling a little disgusted. She starts talking again, a stuttering stream of words. Leonard can't make sense of any of it.

'Something for... the summer window... very well... with the... how red. Red as red as red. Mags can... can have. This have... this wants to... all in the... window... Mags says... How do you... I don't know... dandy doodle? In the behind... in the war...'

While she's speaking Lily is tipping the cherries into a bowl, which she places onto Mrs. Smith's lap.

'There Mrs. Smith... Mags... some cherries,' she says.

Leonard is worried that she might not be able to feed herself properly, but she's already tucking into them, expertly spitting the stones into her right hand and dropping them into the bin beside her. She continues speaking as she eats, her jaw working, her mouth full of dark red juice and cherry pulp. Leonard wonders if they ever feed her here. After a few minutes of silence broken only by the munching of cherries, Lily tries again.

'Mrs. Smith. Mags. We've come to see you about Rose. Your daughter.'

'Red as red. Windows... in the summer... in the war. You know?'

'Your daughter, Rose.'

Lily is having to interrupt Mags, speak over her. Hope is leaking out of Leonard like water through a cracked vase. This woman doesn't know who Rose is, never mind who they are.

'Mags – Rose. ROSE.' Lily is still trying.

'Rose Rosie... red, red rose. Inside... Heaven knows... what... in the mind. In the... you know what... you know.'

Mags keeps repeating the same phrases over and over – in the war, red rose, summer window... each word clipped and emotionless, none of them linked to any of the others. Leonard wants to go home now; he wants to get away from this gloomy room, from this lost woman. Sadness washes over him as he remembers that Rose came out of that shrunken, failing body. Lily puts a hand on his arm and asks him if he's brought the photos. He doesn't think there's any point, but she says they might as well try, now that they're here. Lily shows them to Mags. They're close ups of Rose, the best ones Leonard could find. He doesn't think she'll be able to make anything out. She looks at them briefly and goes quiet. The next time she speaks, her voice is different – it contains a little more energy. She sounds more distressed.

'My face... that is... my one. Where is it... from a lady? My little. The only. Red, red... jack in the box... favourite... sweet red. Peter was... I don't know. Ouch, OUCH! OUCH!'

She seems to be getting more agitated, points a finger at Lily's face.

'Take it from... OUCH! RED ROSE! In a pickle... a pickle... in the... on... what I don't. OUCH!'

She's got one of her hands pressed against her side. Leonard wonders if she's eaten the cherries too quickly.

'Does it hurt, Mags?' says Lily. And then, 'Who's Peter?'

Mags isn't listening, or if she is, she doesn't give them

any signs of hearing. She just carries on talking, more and more words.

'Told Lester... told him. Nice man. Didn't really... in the pond... with biscuits. Rotten... Didn't really. I don't know... heaven know... real good... real person? Red Rose. Nice... she was... dirty bitch... Mrs. Smith. Mags didn't.'

As Lily takes the photo back from her she snatches at it, says 'OUCH!' again.

'Do you want it, Mags?' she says, holding it out towards her, but she's trailed off into a mumble, and they can hardly make out the words any more. Lily raises her eyebrows sadly at Leonard and hands him back the photo. She thanks Mags and tries again to leave a photo of Rose with her – she pushes it away angrily. They leave her as they found her, staring out of the window, with a tell-tale dark stain around her mouth.

On the drive home Leonard sinks into a bad mood. His back is sore and his stomach is rumbling. What is he even doing here? Lily seems thoughtful and asks him a series of questions about what Mags had said. Does he know anyone called Peter or Lester? Did any of it ring any bells? What did he think about her reaction to the photos? She keeps asking questions long after he's had enough of answering them, and she doesn't seem to notice his clipped replies. It's as if she's got a theory, but when he asks her what she's getting at, she says 'oh, nothing'. At one point she asks Leonard about their marriage, asking him if it was 'reliable'. He asks her what she means by that, and she back-tracks, conveniently trailing off in the middle of her sentence. What is she trying to imply? What does she mean, reliable? She's playing with the cigarette packet again, open-shut, open-shut, and he wants to take it from her and crumple it up, throw it out of the car window. He's intensely irritated – with her, with the other bloody useless drivers on the road, with the niggling pain at the bottom of his spine. With the whole ridiculous business. When he drops her off he politely refuses her offer of tea through gritted teeth, and as he pulls away from her house he wonders if he'll ever see her again.

Later that night, after sloping around the house and failing to find anything to satisfy his restlessness, Leonard gets the box of Rose's things out from under his bed. He'd bought this shallow plastic box with a tight-fitting lid a few months after Rose died, to keep everything clean and safe. The other flat objects he keeps under the bed – folders of his accounts, a few toys for the twins, seem to stay covered in a thick layer of dust however often he takes them out and dusts them off. He supposes it's mostly bits of himself falling down from under the mattress – flakes of skin, dried sweat, pieces of hair and nail... he thinks again of Mags and her yellowed teeth and shudders. The plastic box is a beautiful dark pink colour, the colour of the new French Lavender they developed at Kew, *Lavandula stoechas* 'Kew Red'. He'd spent ages traipsing through the shops in Reading until he'd found the perfect colour for her.

He used to open it a lot in the early days. He'd sprinkled some of her perfume on material and paper here and there so whenever he pulled off the lid with a 'crack', he'd be met with a sweet cloud of her scent. It smelt as fresh as if he were sniffing it from her neck or on the wrists of a blouse she'd left draped over a chair. The half-empty bottle of it had sat on his dressing table for nearly two years until Raine had explained how perfume 'went off'. He hadn't liked to think of it decaying and the smell going sour, so he'd thrown it away with the intention of buying a fresh bottle. He'd never quite got around to it, feeling vaguely uncomfortable about what it might imply. It was one thing to keep what was left of her smell and indulge in it every so often, but quite another to spend money on prolonging it.

As he sets the box onto his duvet and lifts the lid, he catches a memory of the scent – fainter now, fading. He bends over and dips his face into the air inside the box, like when he turns his face up to absorb the sun, or soaks his scalp in hot bath-water after a long day digging. He hasn't looked in here for, what, maybe five months? That's got to be a good sign, he thinks to himself. Then he wonders if it's really 'a good sign' to be moving further away from her. It's the kind of thing other people used to say to him all the time. He should work towards putting her in the past; he needs to look to his future. He never really understood it. Why should he? Why make an effort to forget her, to replace her, when he'd much rather keep his memories of her and live with those instead?

Here it all is – all of her bits, neatly packed away where he last left them. On one side there are piles of her papers in separate clear plastic folders with poppers. The top one contains her certificates – birth, driving license, exams she'd passed, her passport. There was no need for him to keep anything other than her birth and death certificate, but when he put the two pieces of paper into a file by themselves they looked so insubstantial that he added some paperwork from the rest of her life to bulk things out. The next folder holds the best of the letters he sent to her over her lifetime. He was ruthless when he went through them all, threw away all but the most important, the most significant. He almost knows them by heart. Here's his first letter to her, a thank-you note for their first date to the cinema to see Dr. Zhivago (Rose had quite a thing for Omar Sharif which rather put the dampeners on things for Leonard). Here's a letter he sent from his parents' house to let her know that his father was dying. Here's the first letter where he said 'I love you'. Next is a folder full of the best photos, too precious to leave in the photo album. Next the folder of Raine's drawings from school, the ones Rose had treasured all her life – a tall and smiling mummy, a brilliant butterfly.

The last folder contains the best of what Rose called her 'souvenirs'. She'd had a drawer full of them – tickets from everything they'd been to for the last twenty years, letters from her friends, birthday cards. There are even significant bus tickets (her first journey to her new job) and shopping lists (the food she bought for their 25th anniversary meal). After she died Leonard knew he'd have to sort through it all, and he put it off until everything else was dealt with. There was so much of Rose in that drawer. He'd only been able to look through it all for ten minutes at a time, timing himself with the bedroom clock, sat on the floor and surrounded by the detritus of her life. He'd walk out of the room between the ten minute sessions to wander around the house, tidy away the washing up, make himself a sandwich. He'd slept on the sofa that night, going back to the old habit that had taken him several months to break. And here it all is in a slim folder – the cream of what he'd sifted through that day. He rifles through it now. Here's the ticket to the ballet, with the memories of Rose's red silk dress and the poor girl who fell over during the second act flooding back in an instant. And here's the bill from Raine's 18th birthday meal in a posh restaurant, the best meal he'd ever tasted. Her old boyfriend Ross was there – he drank too much red wine and made a fool of himself. Maybe she was better off with Ed after all.

On the other side of the box are the objects of hers he'd allowed himself to save. There's one of her favourite silk scarves, patterned with ivory white tulips and dark green leaves. He uses his other hand to run it between his finger and thumb, relishing the smooth skim of it. There's a Victorian brooch she'd always worn on special occasions 'for luck', a dark amethyst surrounded by tiny pearls. And here's her bible – leather bound and much-thumbed. He's never been one for all that God stuff, but it was important to her. There's nothing in this box that's out of place. He knows all of it by touch, by smell, by sight. They're all relics now, he knows that – relics. Charlie's right – there's no point in digging things up. He shouldn't have listened to Lily. She's just an old busy-body – she could never hold a candle to his Rose.

Pickles is scratching at the bedroom door to be let in. Leonard opens it a crack and tells him he can sleep on the bed as a treat as long as he doesn't make a habit of it. He doesn't like to think of him in the kitchen on his own tonight. Pickles curls into a neat circle and drops off as his owner sits on his bed for a while longer, sorting through Rose's things as if he's counting his money. By the time he replaces the top on the box and slides it carefully back under the bed, placing it so it's under his head as he sleeps, he's full to the brim of Rose. Full to the brim of Rose.

Chapter 11:
The Little Matchseller

A couple of wiry teenage girls just along the platform from Leonard are making noises like exotic birds – screeches, squeals, strange purrs. One of them is sat on the other's lap and they're both looking at the screen of a mobile phone. He can't hear what they're saying, but he imagines it probably involves boys. They're wearing very tight jeans and too-small pink tops and far too much make-up for their young, fresh faces. Leonard catches himself watching them and looks away abruptly, worried that someone else on the platform will spot him and jump to the wrong conclusions.

He spares a thought for their poor fathers. He struggled with that part of fatherhood the most – losing his little girl to 'other men'. It was strange enough coming to terms with Raine's changing body – all of those new bumps and curves and the smell of hormones in her sweat. It was much worse to see the hunger in other men's eyes, when she was still too young for them to be looking at her in that way. He can sympathise with religions or cultures that have decided to cover up their women. He supposes it says something about the fathers and husbands' lack of trust in other men. And if they don't trust other men, then it follows that they can't quite trust themselves either, with other women. Whenever people get worried about someone else's behaviour, they're really worried about themselves. That's how Leonard sees it, anyway.

He enjoys the usual train journey to Reading. Being on a train always seems to clear some clutter out of his head. It works in a similar way to those routine gardening tasks he doesn't have to think about too much – potting up cuttings, edging, weeding. When he streams out of the train with the other passengers to meet Ed, he feels as if he's just getting out of a swimming pool after a long swim. He's surprised by a small bloom of warmth towards Ed when he first spots him on the concourse, struggling to take his jumper off. Leonard sidles up close to him and is standing right in front of him with his arms open in a 'ta da!' when Ed's face emerges from underneath the knitting, a shocked 'fucking hell!' bursting out of him. Ed takes Leonard's small overnight bag, and they make their way towards the car park. When Leonard puts a hand on Ed's back and asks him how he is, Ed hesitates, as if he's been caught off guard by the genuine affection in Leonard's greeting. Leonard stops walking and asks if anything is wrong. Ed says it's probably nothing, nudging an old cigarette butt along the shiny floor with the tip of one of his trainers. Leonard assumes Ed is worried about Raine, and asks Ed if he minds if they have a quick coffee before they drive back, saying he's gasping. And he'd kill for one of those honey cakes from the little Italian coffee shop. They can tell Raine the train was delayed. Ed jerks his head around as if someone might be watching, and says he does have half an hour left on the car ticket. Leonard makes it easier for him. He puts an arm around his back and steers him over to a silver table.

As Leonard stands in the coffee queue, he looks back at Ed, who's fiddling with an empty sugar stick wrapper. He feels a little sad for his daughter. Ed couldn't take charge of a cup of tea, as Rose whispered to him once as they watched him struggling to decide what birthday card to buy for Raine. They've always been fond of him, but it'd be more reassuring if Raine had picked someone a bit more... manly. Someone who could stand up to her without pulling on his top nervously, like one of the twins. Or maybe Raine should take some responsibility for that too, because she's so brittle, so likely to snap? He orders the coffees, joking with the man behind the counter about needing the extra caffeine to cope with his twin three year old grandchildren. He enjoys these small exchanges with strangers. He frequently watches other people showing their ticket to the train conductor or to Bob at the ticket booth at work without even making eye contact. He often says something foolish to the cashier at the supermarket, or asks the waitress for her opinion on what's good on the menu. They're the kind of exchanges that leave both of you a little lighter.

He arranges the cups and plate and little jugs of milk on a tray and carries it over to Ed, who's still looking gloomy. He's never been very good at balancing cups, and some of the coffee sloshes out onto the saucers. He sets the tray down, goes back to fetch some paper napkins, and then settles down to the comforting business of adding exactly the right amount of milk and stirring in sugar. He knows he'll regret this caffeine later, lying in bed with his eyes wide open at three o'clock in the morning, but right now he's feeling reckless. They sit across from one another and lift their cups in synchrony, making small slurping noises. Leonard is tempted to make a play out of the vibrato of the coffee against his lips to soften the awkwardness. He thinks of his first meeting with Lily and remembers how awkward he felt then. He wonders how she is, and feels a little ashamed about how annoyed he got with her when they visited Rose's mum. What was it that frustrated him so much? He's wondering whether he should get in touch with her again when Ed breaks the silence.

'To be honest, I'm worried, Len.'

Leonard lets this unorthodox name-shortening go. Ed's the only one who's ever gets away with it. He used to correct him but he gave up after the twentieth attempt.

'Uh huh?' he says, and waits as Ed takes another rasping sip of coffee. Leonard takes a forkful of syrupy cake to divert some of the attention from him, as if they're just having a casual coffee together.

'It's probably nothing, but…'

He dries up and slumps back in his silver seat, looking thoroughly miserable. Leonard can see that he'll need to coax it out of him. He's like a child who doesn't want to tell you that he's buried his gloves in the garden but is also desperate to confess. He decides on a direct approach.

'It's Raine, is it? The thing you're worried about?'

'Mmm.'

He's sighing again, as if there's a heaviness on his chest and he can't quite get enough air.

'It's just that she's done a couple of, you know, stuff, things, recently. It's not like her, d'you know what I mean?'

'D'you-know-what-I-mean' is a regular ending to Ed's sentences. Leonard used to reply 'yes' or 'not really' when they first knew each other, but he soon discovered that Ed wasn't expecting an answer. Leonard went through a phase of adding it on to the end of his own sentences with a little swagger, and drove Rose and Raine to distraction until Rose told him if he said it one more time she'd clock him, if he knew what SHE meant.

'What kinds of things?'

'Oh, I don't know.'

Ed seems annoyed suddenly, frustrated. He starts to rip the empty sugar wrappers into pieces, smaller and smaller, until they cover the table like snow. He runs out of paper to destroy, sighs sharply and looks up.

'Last week I found a packet of cornflakes in the fridge, and the bleach in the kitchen cupboard. When she was talking to our friends last night she called me Rory twice, without even noticing. They're little things, I know, but... there's something else. The way she's acting. I don't know if... You won't say anything to Raine, will you, Len?'

Leonard shakes his head, scrunches his forehead forwards.

'She's just so...' He stares off into space for a while, searching for the right word. 'Distant. She's just so distant. D'you know what I mean?'

Leonard does know what he means. He smiles a sad smile and nods. Both men finish their coffees in silence, each caught up in their own worlds. Leonard feels the absence of Rose so intensely that he almost feels panicky. What should he say? How can he help him? Ed holds eye-contact with him for a few seconds with a question in the air, but Leonard has nothing. He watches Ed's face close down.

'Things'll probably sort themselves out, it'll all...' Ed pauses. 'She's been like it before, and got better. I'm probably worrying about nothing. It's just the twins are such hard work at the moment, and her pressures at work... I'm sure things'll, you know'.

'You're right Ed, she'll be fine. She's got her head screwed on. It'll all be... it'll all blow over.'

They're both nodding their heads as they speak, and Leonard wonders who they're trying to fool. They're both worried, and now they've both heard the anxiety in each other's voices. But what more is there to say? Ed refuses a second cup of coffee and jangles in his pockets for the car keys. They steer the conversation onto cricket and the implications of the groupings for the next World Cup. No wonder men talk about sport so much, thinks Leonard. They tread carefully around mentioning Raine for the rest of the journey.

The evening passes in the usual fashion. Leonard peels potatoes, helps with jigsaws, listens to the boy's feverish stories about 'the snail in the garden that leaves sparkles', chops carrots, makes a round of teas and tries to watch ten minutes of the news by hiding in the upstairs study (he's found out). He's conscious of watching Raine for signs of disorder even more carefully than usual. There does seem to be a strange atmosphere in the house – tight, uneasy. She seems tired, and he can't get her to meet his eyes properly when he looks at her, but she doesn't seem much worse than usual. He decides against telling her about his meeting with Rose's mother and feels guilty about holding back, but if he isn't going to carry on with the whole thing, then there's no point, is there? He and Ed have formed a new alliance and choose safe topics for the dinner table – Ed's work at the Environment Agency, the twin's progress with learning the alphabet, more cricket. Raine seems relieved when Ed and Leonard are talking, so they keep a busy, chirpy conversation going. It's a bit of an effort, and so Leonard is pleased to volunteer to put the twins to bed. At first they refuse and 'want Mummy' but Leonard does a little clown dance that never fails to dissolve them into giggles. Afterwards he offers them a hand each and they charge up the stairs, Mummy already forgotten. She has to call them back for a good-night kiss.

The first two books go down without a yawn, but during the third, about a hedgehog who hates his spikes, they both get gradually floppier. He's persuaded by a barely-awake Buddy to read 'just one more'. Rory is already breathing slowly, with only slivers of white showing between his blond lashes. Leonard chooses a book of Hans Christian Anderson's short stories from the shelf – it still looks brand new, an unpopular present from friends, maybe. He flicks through the contents and chooses one he likes the name of – The Little Matchseller. He's familiar with several of the titles – The Ugly Duckling, The Little Mermaid, Thumbelina. As he settles back down Buddy puts his little finger into his mouth and sucks distractedly. His eyelids start to sag like Pickles' do after his dinner, sudden swoops when he blinks, coming to rest more fully each time. Leonard notes the signs and risks reading out loud without the different voices and exaggerated inflection he usually uses.

The story is about a little girl who's selling matches on a freezing New Year's Eve. She hasn't sold a single match all day and is hungry and freezing cold. In desperation, she lights one of her valuable matches and cups it in her hands. Each time she lights a match she feels a delicious warmth and sees a shimmering vision – a hot stove, a family sitting around a table laden with turkey and rich food, a huge Christmas tree. The extravagant smell of gravy and the green scent of pine needles waft through the air towards her. When each flame dies, she's left in the cold and dark again. When she strikes the next match her beloved dead grandmother appears to her, so she strikes the whole bundle of matches at once, desperate to stop her from fading away like the turkey and the Christmas tree. Her grandmother holds out her hand to the little girl, and when she reaches out to take it she finds it solid and warm. They fly up into the sky together. In the morning the matchseller's body is found, pale and smiling, still holding the blackened bundle of matches. People said that she'd burnt them to try and stay warm, but no-one could guess at the things she'd seen.

As the story unfolds Leonard is surprised at how the sadness is infecting him. He carries on reading aloud even though the twins are both snoring gently, and by the end, the tears are silently streaming down his face. He replaces the book and tiptoes onto the hall landing, calling down to Raine in a loud rasping whisper that he's going to bed. He sits on his bed and hugs his knees and cries and cries, not sure what he's crying for. It doesn't matter, he says to himself, sometimes you just need a good blubber. To clear out the waterworks, as his mother would say. He blows his nose on one of his dirty socks, not wanting to dare a trip across the hall to the bathroom in case he bumps into Ed or Raine and has to explain himself. When the tears stop, he feels tired but happy – that whole-body fatigue you get after a long day working outside in the sun.

That night he dreams he's walking in a dark forest. The leaves are all purple and blue, and there are orange birds swooping above him like bats. There are strange creatures slinking about behind the tree-trunks – like leopards, but with long curved claws on their feet that raise them above the ground, and several frizzy tails each. They seem to be baring their teeth at him, but he knows they're not really dangerous. He emerges into the sunlight and almost stumbles down the banks of a deep river that stretches away into the distance. He catches sight of what he thinks is a hummingbird in the middle of the glittering water, but when he looks closer, he recognises it as the blue handbag. He balances on the steep bank and tries to reach it with a stick, but it floats along just out of his reach. He follows it, and his soles cling to the ground as if it's made of sticky clay – he has to make an effort to pull each foot upwards with a small 'schluck' of suction. He chases along the river bank beside the purse, moving as fast as he can, but the handbag gets faster and faster, as if it's taunting him, staying just out of his reach. He falls behind, and it becomes a small blue dot in the distance before it completely disappears, and he's surprised to find himself kneeling on the ground, kissing earth.

A couple of days later Leonard is getting ready to go to Lily's house again. When he'd got back from Raine's, there'd been a message from her waiting on his answer-phone. She started the message by saying how much she hated these 'dreadful machines'. He'd listened to it twice, laughing at her several false starts and at how long and rambling it was. He called her back right away. She'd said she had a gardening question for him, hoped he didn't mind her asking; she knew how annoyed a doctor friend of hers got, forever hearing about his friends' aches and pains. She had a huge *Rosa* 'Albertine' at the back of her garden that seemed to be taking over. She wasn't sure how to cut it back properly; she'd been meaning to tackle it for ages. He'd found himself offering to do it for her, or at least show her how to get started before he left her to it. He thought to himself that he could kill two birds with one stone, and tell her when he went round there that he didn't want to investigate Rose any more. She'd promised to cook him that Sunday lunch they'd talked about on their walk in return, as a thank you.

As he's searching for the car keys (how annoying not having anyone else to blame when he puts them down in the wrong place) he remembers the last time he turned up without anything to offer her. He decides to take her an oxalis. It's an unusual plant with dark red, almost mahogany square leaves perching on thin stems like pipe-cleaners, which emerge from the pot like a fountain. It looks like butterflies tethered to the earth with string, even more so at night when the leaves close up. It fascinates Buddy; he keeps asking Leonard when 'the leaves go sleepies', imagining a fast-forward of the gently shutting. He tips the plant carefully onto his kitchen table, remembering at the last minute to cover the surface with newspaper. He separates the corms, splitting the mass into thirds and getting three for the price of one. Even after all these years, he still marvels at new growth. How amazing that plants can take in water and air and nutrients from the soil and produce foliage, fruit, wood, different colours, shapes, scents... If he really stops and thinks about it, the word 'miracle' appears in front of him again and again.

He puts the half bag of compost back in the cupboard that houses the hoover. This small collection of gardening paraphernalia – a few empty pots, plant food, a watering can with a narrow spout, is his only gesture towards being a gardener in this new house. After Rose died, he found he could no longer face tending their garden. She'd been the biggest fan of his work – always noticing new plants in the garden, and never growing tired of the bunches of fresh flowers she placed in vases around the house. After her death, he'd look out and imagine the sleeping daffodil and hyacinth bulbs in the ground, gathering their strength for the Spring, and know that Rose wouldn't be there for their big day. He couldn't see the point of growing them if she wasn't going to be there to appreciate them. The pleasure seeped out of work at Coburne House for a while as well, although it did feel more bearable there. He tried to find good homes for all of their house plants. He confided in Glor, who took most of them to distribute amongst her friends, and Charlie took a couple for his elusive wife Marion. He gave Raine a particularly handsome Parlour Palm as a 'very late birthday present'. As soon as the twins started toddling they'd head towards it to pull it over, and after a few weeks of cleaning soil from the carpet she left it out for the rubbish men to collect. A criminal waste.

Leonard's garden had started to deteriorate, to wilt under the lack of love. He let things go to ruin, reversing all the years of work he'd put into making it beautiful. He considered getting in a part-time gardener to at least maintain things as they were, but in the end, the house sale went through pretty quickly. The people who came round to look at it 'ooohed' and 'aahed' over the rose bushes, the strip of irises, the water feature in the centre. He'd chosen his current house on purpose – no dilemma about whether to tend a garden or not if there wasn't one. A strip of narrow concrete was all he had. For the first year he couldn't bear anything green in the place. Even when people sent flowers he'd give them straight to Peggy next door, guiltily pretending that he'd developed an allergy.

A year ago he'd spotted an oxalis at a local church jumble sale – he sometimes went along to look for the thick cord trousers he wore when working outside. It was such a long time since he'd seen an oxalis that he couldn't resist buying it – a bargain at 50p. He brought it into the house gingerly, half expecting prickly grief to follow it in. He felt a little sad when he looked at it on a table in the living room, but it also raised his spirits somehow, and over the next six months, other plants had started making their way back into his home. He'd become addicted to cut tulips, usually not a flower he'd give much space to, and enjoyed a blue vase of them in the hall to greet him when he returned from work. He'd started paying more attention to other people's gardens too, feeling the old machinery ticking over – that shady spot would suit a Skimmia perfectly, and he'd take out that hateful Leylandii hedge straight away and replace it with *Rosa rugosa*. And a small piece of trellis there, blocking off the view and covered in *Clematis armandii*, would work wonders. As he drives the now-familiar journey to Lily's, he checks himself – how does he feel about doing some gardening work for her? Fine – he feels fine. And he recognises a hunger for it, a rising of his energy like sap.

Lily seems more than happy to leave the pruning to him while she finishes the potatoes and prepares the veg. When he's finished she asks him to sit at the small dining table at one end of the living room and presents him with a wonderful vision. The plate is heaped with rare roast beef, crispy potatoes, carrots, peas, and a huge Yorkshire pudding that's half on the plate and half off, all covered with dark steaming gravy. She laughs a pleased laugh at the look on his face, and teases him about trying not to dribble all over her tablecloth. She clicks on Radio 4, apologising that she likes to have some background noise when she's eating, a bad habit of hers. They listen to a programme about fish reserves in the Mediterranean until the food is almost gone. Leonard emits occasional grunts, groans and exclamations of wonder, and Lily giggles as if she were still a girl.

After his last mouthful Leonard puts down his fork.

'I've decided to pack it in, Lily.'

'What, gardening?!'

'No, no, no. I can't see that ever happening – when I'm ninety-three, I'll be getting the twins to push me down the garden in my wheelchair so I can stake the tomatoes... No, it's this whole thing with Rose. I know you said you'd help me, and I'm grateful for that. It's just I don't think it's going to get me anywhere. I knew my Rose, there's, it's...'

He's expecting her to protest, but she's waving her hand at him and shaking her head, waiting until she finishes her mouthful.

'You don't need to... it's really up to... I won't say another word. You tell me if you, you know. I'd be happy to...'

'I will. I will.'

They both smile and after a respectful silence they move on to the living. Leonard gives his opinion on the best plant to put in as a backdrop to her clumps of burnt orange *Helenium* 'Moorheim Beauty' (he suggests some wispy *'Stipa arundinacea'*). They have a good-natured argument about a current political scandal – the man was caught visiting his secret children from another relationship and Leonard thought he should resign while Lily thought politicians' personal lives were none of her business. She's much feistier than Ed or Pete would be, and argues on until he concedes her point. Leonard gives her a quick overview of what Ed said about Raine, making it sound less of a crisis than it feels. After a while he feels as if he's been doing more of the talking, so starts bombarding Lily with questions about her family. She tells him a little about her children – both live abroad with families of their own – one in Canada and one back in Sweden. She tells him she had always thought that she'd be the first to leave the UK. When she was a teenager and having a hard time at school, she often blamed the 'stupid country' for all of her problems. Things would have been different in Sweden where she belonged. If only her grandfather hadn't dragged his family over here in the first place, with his bright ideas about things being better. She admits she probably picked most of this up by osmosis from her mother, who to this day is bitter about being uprooted from her life and her friends.

Lily had been close to her father, who only died a few years ago. She used to go round and play cards with him for hours on end – whist, gin rummy, four card brag. When he was getting weak from the cancer, she'd hold a fan of cards in each hand – one pointing towards her and one towards him, and he'd tell her which one he wanted to play next – 'far left' or 'second on the right'. He'd tried to get away with a playful cheat in the last hand she'd ever dealt him. Her mother was still alive and lived quite close by – they had an uneasy relationship, mostly speaking over the phone in short bursts. Lily had to brace herself before she called her, preparing herself for the litany of complaints she knew her mother would unleash. Lily was sure her mother saved them up in a notebook especially for their phone calls. 'Oh – rain again – it always rains when I want to go to the shops! Aah – this apple crumble is soggy and sour, one for the book! Lily will love to hear about this!' She imitates her mother, speaking in her usual rambling way but with a negative tone that tires Leonard out. As Lily speaks, Leonard starts to slump in his seat, his face blank, and when she notices what he's doing she carries on in an exaggerated voice until only the tip of his nose is showing over the table.

After the meal, exhaustion blankets Leonard like heat from a real log fire. He has to fight the urge to go over to her sofa, curl up and drop off. The cushions on it look so comfortable. He imagines Lily bringing over a goose-down duvet for him, and three cats to coil into circles near his ankles and purr. She could sing him a Swedish lullaby as he drifted away, and then wake him up in the morning with tea and eggs and bacon and… Instead he stretches out his arms and yawns a huge yawn and asks her if he could have a strong coffee before he thinks about driving home. She brews some proper coffee in a plunger. He makes a fuss about letting him do the plunging bit. She puts some After Eight mints on the tray and they somehow descend into a conversation about different ways to eat them. Leonard has Lily pegged as a nibbler, and he's spot on – she demonstrates the tiny bites she takes to 'make it last longer' and he teases her about her other rabbit-like behaviours – does she run out in front of cars? Enjoy lettuce? Lily guesses wrongly that Leonard is a one- or two-bite wonder – he prefers small mouthfuls and then sucking until it all dissolves into a minty, chocolaty goo. She tries to get him to demonstrate, but he's too embarrassed, and eats the last of the one he's holding behind a flat hand, swallowing it down quickly.

'Did Rose like After Eights? I was just... you know...'

She starts fiddling with her coffee cup, swivelling it by the handle, and wipes some stray sugar from the table. Leonard isn't sure why she's asked – is she jealous that he had a happy marriage? The question hangs between them and the atmosphere changes colour. Leonard becomes preoccupied with a smudge of dried mud on his trousers, scraping it off into a fine dust with his fingernails. He asks Lily if he can use her bathroom, and when he comes back she makes some small-talk, but they both know it's time for the evening to end. As they say goodbye he isn't sure what to do with his body, so stands back and holds up one hand in a stiff wave. Like the last time they met, neither of them says anything about meeting again. Some of the strange atmosphere leaks into the car with him when he opens the door, and it takes him a whole album of Johnny to shake it off. By the time he gets home he's singing 'If I Were A Carpenter' at the top of his voice.

Chapter 12:
Forty-two different varieties

It's impossible to avoid Valentine's Day. When Rose was alive, neither of them had bought into it – Rose thinking it a convenient get-out for men who didn't do anything nice for their wives any other day of the year, and Leonard seeing it as a commercial rip-off. What was the point in buying Rose flowers when he grew her sunflowers and dahlias from scratch? Where was the love in getting someone else to plant the seeds, water the seedlings, grow them on, cut them and even arrange them into a vase? But since she died, the 14th of February has taken on a new meaning for Leonard. The soppy adverts on TV, the huge bouquet that Val's flashy boyfriend sends her at work, the restaurants all pink and coupled. They all seem to be a sneering reminder of his current state of being-without-Rose. Christmas can be difficult too – another holiday that demands a full complement of happy family – but at least he still has Raine and the boys. Valentines Day is a finger pointing at his state of being alone.

This year Leonard has planned a quiet night in with Pickles, away from the kissing crowds. As he forks out rabbit in jelly for his Valentine, he decides to cook himself a special meal to go with the Western on Channel 4. He's already bought himself a small bottle of Baileys for later, a real treat. Something delicious to eat and maybe even a cigar... who needs a sweetheart? It'd be better than sitting around feeling sorry for himself, in any case. He tries to work out what he'd like to eat and pictures a plump cut of rump beef smothered in bread sauce. The roast potatoes on the side go without saying. He's cooked them a couple of times since those ones Lily gave him, but so far he hasn't come close to hers. She gave him careful instructions on the phone last week involving par-boiling and hot olive oil and he's keen to try them out. He opens the cupboard door onto three sprouting sorry-looking specimens. It's too late to have frozen chips instead – his heart is set. It's also too late for the village shop to be open, so he reluctantly gets in the car, Pickles jumping into the passenger seat. Leonard appreciates the convenience of supermarkets but hates pretty much everything else about them – the too-bright lights, the forced produce from half-way around the world, and all that wasteful packaging. He thinks nostalgically about his old vegetable patch. How wonderful it was to go out into the garden with a fork instead. There's nothing like the taste of baby Jersey potatoes fresh from the earth, boiled in their skins with a little salt and a little butter.

As he drives a straight stretch of road, he glances across at Pickles. He's staring out of the window with glazed eyes, his tongue half out of his mouth and his stumpy tail absent-mindedly waggling. What is he thinking about? Is he waiting patiently, twitcher-like, to spot a bird or two? Is he dreaming of springtime, when there'll be rabbits and longer walks? It's the middle of February already. Where does the time go? Christmas passed in a blur of mince pies and ripped wrapping paper. This year the twins were old enough to work themselves up into a frenzy of excitement previously unseen in the Wishford household. The most popular presents had been a pair of cheap yellow trucks that Ed had bought at the last minute. The more expensive gifts stayed in their packaging while the boys dragged the trucks backwards on the carpet with a click-click-clicking noise and then let out 'wheeeee's as the trucks burst forwards. There were competitions to see who could go the furthest, there was target practise using Leonard's shoes as targets – the possibilities proved endless.

Raine survived the festivities, but without any obvious signs of enjoying herself. Ed hadn't confided in Leonard again, even though Leonard asked him leading questions a couple of times when they were alone – 'so... Raine's looking well' or 'it feels like ages since we had that coffee at the station'. Raine had sat down with Leonard and a glass of red wine on Christmas Day evening, and they did have a reasonably good conversation. She and Ed had been looking into what school to send the children to, and she wanted Leonard's opinion. It had been a long time since Leonard had felt she needed him, and even though he didn't know the first thing about schooling, he answered her questions as best he could. It was a shame she couldn't have had that conversation with her mother.

The middle of February. He's surprised to still be in touch with Lily after all this time. She'd called him a week after the roast and said she was going to a Christmas market if he fancied going along. Leonard had jumped at the chance of a female opinion on his Christmas shopping. Last year Raine had seemed unimpressed with her set of wooden spoons with carved handles, despite putting on a brave face. The market was disappointing – most of the stalls were selling 'home-made crafts' that looked a little too home-made for Leonard's liking. They'd had a good time anyway, having a good (discreet) laugh about the knitted kittens and the personalised loo-roll holders. They'd met up a few times since then, and seemed to have settled into a little routine of seeing each other every fortnight. Annoyingly, Charlie has started teasing Leonard about it in the pub – having become fond of saying 'off to see Lily this weekend, are you?' with an exaggerated wink.

When the weather was bearable they'd go out – both of them preferred to be out in the fresh air. They'd tried a couple of the walks from Lily's book, and had visited a country church and wandered around the graveyard seeing who could find the oldest skeleton or the longest name. It had only rained properly once – a dark weekend in January – and they had sat in her house with mugs of cocoa and played cards instead. Leonard had taught her a game he'd learnt from the lads at work. It was called 'shit-head', and once each round started you had to get rid of all your cards in the proper order as quickly as you could. The loser had to make the tea, or at least shuffle the pack for the next round. It was fast-paced and frantic, and Lily loved it. She started every game saying that she was rubbish at cards and proceeded to thrash him into the ground.

Twenty minutes later he's in the bacon aisle trying to decide between the forty-two different varieties when someone taps him on the back.

'Leonard?'

It's Sue – one of Rose's old colleagues from the hospital. They'd worked together for years. She's a substantial lady, with three chins and glossy, dark hair. Her voice is deeper than you'd expect it to be – Leonard is sometimes reminded of her when he sees drag-queens on TV. They rarely saw her socially when Rose was alive, but Leonard used to hear all about her five children and three husbands (she left the first two, who were abusive, and the third had died on her). The last Leonard had heard, she'd been fostering children and was thriving on it. She has a small boy with her now, with curly hair and a chocolaty mouth. He's hanging onto her skirts and hiding behind her bulk. Leonard smiles.

'Leonard! My goodness... How are you? Happy Valentines Day!'

They catch up with each other's news. She tells him about her children – the two oldest have children of their own now, and she makes them call her Aunty Sue, as she can't quite face being grandma yet. She's still fostering and has three at the moment. He updates her on Raine and the twins – Sue says she misses hearing about them all, and that she misses Rose. She says she ought to be off, there are two older ones waiting at home for their tea, but if there's anything she can do to help he should let her know. He thinks for a moment. Rose used to say that there was nothing Sue loved better than helping others out, and he'd like to be able to offer her the chance. As she's turning to go, he has a thought.

'Sue? There is something... I don't know if you'll be able to help or not...'

She looks expectant.

'You didn't hear Rose ever mention Didcot for any reason, did you? I found a train ticket recently, in one of her old handbags, and I didn't think she'd ever been. I thought it might be something to do with work that she never mentioned.'

Sue thinks for a while. Leonard wonders about all the images she's having of Rose, flashing though her head one after the other.

'No, no, we've never had to go for Didcot to work. We sometimes got asked to go to meetings, training things, but not there... it's too far for...' She suddenly catches herself as a memory gathers momentum. 'You know, funnily enough she DID mention Didcot once, was it Didcot? It might have been Wantage... no I'm pretty sure... it was when she was off on one of her Tuesdays, she said she was off to Didcot. I remember it because she was always a bit mysterious about her Tuesdays and when I said 'Didcot?' she flushed bright red. She mumbled something about needing to visit one of your relatives, Leonard, but I didn't press her any further. Funny I remembered that – it must have been when I was... gosh, we were at St. Mary's, it must have been fifteen years ago! Where does the time go? I was with my second husband at the time; we were just going through... anyway, I'm sure you don't want to hear about that. Is that any help?'

'What do you mean, Sue, one of her Tuesdays?'

'You know, her afternoons off. I always admired her for that, for sticking to her guns. She always said "I don't mind what hours I do, but Tuesday afternoons have always been for me." She had to kick up quite a fuss when we had our new manager in, that awful Mr. Ritter... she almost got the sack over it. That man must have been born to a monster. She must have told you about him, Leonard...'

'Did she say anything else about them? Was it all afternoon?'

'What, her Tuesdays? Yes, she always left about half twelve and always got back to work for six o'clock, she said it made better sense that way. Just in case you decided to pick her up on a whim, so you didn't have to remember she wouldn't be there. But you already know that, of course...'

Leonard nods and smiles a fixed smile. Sue continues.

'I couldn't see the point in coming back to work again,

but it suited you both, I suppose. But something to do with work… No… I can't think of anything…'

She's trying to concentrate but the little boy is tugging on her skirt and saying 'Sue! Sue!' Leonard sweeps one of his hands through the air and frowns to gesture that she should go.

'Thank you, Sue, that's a great help. Look – I'm looking into some things at the moment, making some… well anyway, would you mind if I took a number for you, just in case I want to get in touch again?'

As he writes her mobile number on a scrap of paper the little boy starts pulling on her skirt even more energetically and shouting, 'Poo! Poo!' As she rushes off, he hears her muttering to the child that he should 'say toilet instead, remember what we said?' He moves towards the check-out, wondering what to make of this new information. It's too much to process right now. He has potatoes to par-boil. He files it in the back of his brain to get out another time, putting it in a safe-box and turning the key.

That Saturday, Lily has found a village hall sale for them to visit. She tells Leonard it's in a posh area, one of those villages on the river, so there's bound to be some quality booty. As Leonard pulls up outside Lily's house, he takes out what Sue had said from the back of his brain. He knows that Lily is probably the best person to talk to about it. He got the feeling that Charlie didn't really approve of him digging around into Rose's past before Christmas, and he wouldn't dream of speaking to Raine. He thinks he'll wait for an appropriate moment to bring it up. On the car journey they talk about pensions and then about garden pests. Lily says she's mastered dispatching slugs with the tip of her spade, which gives her a certain sense of satisfaction after the 'hostas incident'. She can't harness a similar blood-lust for snail killing, as she has a soft spot for their little antennae and their 'shy natures'. She knows that logically they're just like slugs inside their whorled shells, but even so she can't bring herself to crush them. Her current method of snail control is to throw them in a high arc over her fence and into her neighbours garden, after checking that there's no-one at the windows to see her. She asks Leonard if they're likely to survive their flights, but stops him before he answers her, as she 'couldn't bear' the thought that all her mercy throwings might have been in vain.

The village hall is larger than Leonard thought it would be, with high windows and a circle of tables around the hall. They spend a contented half hour picking through other people's unwanted belongings. Lily buys some pale blue wool (for a hat for the youngest grandchild) and a black pottery cat that Leonard thinks is a bit naff (but lies about). Leonard finds a few green-glazed pots to house new plants on his strip of concrete outside, and a home-baked cherry cake. There are chairs and tables at the back, and Leonard treats them to a pot of Earl Grey and an impressive slab of lemon drizzle cake each. He asks for a glass of water too – he's got a terrible thirst. When they're both settled down and their cake is half-guzzled, Leonard takes a deep breath.

'I bumped into one of Rose's old friends last week, in the supermarket. She told me Rose used to go off somewhere every Tuesday afternoon. She did it all the time she'd worked with her, for years and years. I didn't know anything about it, Lily.'

'Going where?'

'She didn't say; she said Rose was secretive about it. One week it slipped out that it was Didcot, just like that ticket I found in her handbag. What do you make of it?'

Lily licks sugar from her lips and puts her fork down so she can give it proper thought. Leonard is touched by how serious she suddenly looks.

'Hmm. It could have been anything, I suppose. A class she was doing that she didn't want you to know about... something medical, to do with her headaches, not wanting to worry you... or she could have been, you know, visiting someone...'

The implied suggestion squats in the air between them and Leonard allows himself consider it for the first time. He lets it enter his mind as if taking a mouthful of something bitter and swishes around carefully. Another man? Could Rose have had someone else for all that time? He holds this possibility in one hand, and everything he knew about Rose in the other. He just can't make it fit. He can't imagine it. He shakes his head and takes another forkful of cake.

'No,' he says.

Lily nods vigorously in instant agreement. He takes a gulp of his water – it tastes pure, clean, as if it's from a cold stream. The water at his house is too soft.

'The trouble is I can't make anything else fit. It could have been any of those things you said, but why wouldn't she just have told me about it?'

Lily lifts her chin and her bottom lip juts out.

'Curiouser and curiouser. What are you going to do?'

What *is* he going to do? He looks around at a couple of old ladies haggling over a flowered tea-pot. They've dug in their heels over the last 25p, and he's tempted to jump up and fish some coins from his pocket to stop the back and forth. He doesn't know what he's going to do. But he does know that it'll be harder to live with this one. He could live with the train ticket, the long hair, he could rationalise them away. There could have been a hundred innocent, every-day explanations. And maybe Rose had good reasons to pretend her mother was dead – maybe it was easier for her to leave her unhappy past where it belonged. But this? He can't just leave this one.

'I need to know, Lily. I need to know the worst.'

She nods, and puts both of her hands palm-down on the table as if ready for action.

'Right... we can try to find out... I had some thoughts last time, some ideas, when you found out about... I don't know if they'd be any... if you want to hear them?'

They all seem like sensible ideas to Leonard. They could get in touch with Rose's friends and colleagues and pretend they were writing some kind of book of remembrance for her – one of Lily's friends did one for her husband. They could look into Rose's surviving family – research her family tree, see if they could find any cousins or friends of the family who knew her when she was younger. And Leonard could do some thinking – go back through their life together and write down anything he can think of that didn't quite fit. Lily says she's read thousands of detective novels in her time, and although they're unlikely to come across any corpses in acid baths or serial killers that target one-legged women with Scottish accents, she's certainly learnt how to conduct an investigation. He notices how she relishes the word on her tongue – investigation. Lily volunteers to start looking into Rose's family tree – she knows where to start on the internet after tracking down Rose. And Leonard will do some thinking, and also make a list of all the people Rose knew. They arrange to update each other in a couple of weeks' time.

Once Lily has written this down in a little red notebook she pulls from her handbag, he's pleased to notice that he feels lighter. He finds it amusing that she had such a fully-formed plan for how the investigation should go forward. She didn't need much encouragement to go into detective-mode. As he pours their last half-cup of tea from the pot, he teases her about turning up to his house with a heavy bag full of forensic equipment, dusting the kitchen for finger-prints and questioning Pickles.

'I need to ascertain your precise whereabouts on the Tuesday in question.'

'Woof.'

'I will ask you again, Mr. Pickles, where were you on Tuesday?'

(Note for the record, suspect is licking his private regions.)

By the time they carry their purchases to the car, it's almost as if the conversation about Rose had never taken place.

Chapter 13:
Drinking lemonade with Rose

Leonard shuffles about on Pete and Glor's doorstep on Thursday evening with a ball of nerves in his stomach. He wishes there were someone there with him, to squeeze his hand and tell him everything will be fine. It's been ages since he saw Pete. He remembers the last time he saw Glor. He hasn't spoken to her since the day she walked out before the kettle was boiled. Charlie had reckoned that Leonard was best shot of her, if that was the way she was going to behave, but Leonard kept thinking about all she'd done for him when Rose died. It would be cruel of him to let her disappear so easily. Leonard had tried to get in touch with her – she hadn't returned any of his messages but he'd persevered. He'd finally got through to Pete earlier in the week. Pete had sounded pleased to hear from him and Leonard suspected that Glor hadn't told him about their falling out. Leonard suggested they get together for a drink sometime.

The four of them used to meet in 'The Green Man' – a bit out of the way for both of them, but Rose had fallen in love with their home-made chocolate fudge cake the first time they'd been there and had insisted they make it their 'Glor-and-Pete pub'. She and Glor always had a pudding before they started on their halves. This time Pete insisted that Leonard come to their house, so he could see their slides from their holiday to Portugal in September. Leonard doesn't know anyone else who actually has a full-size screen for their slide-shows. Pete had sounded proud about making a social arrangement without Glor's input, although he did say before he hung up that he'd have to 'double check with the missus'.

He takes a deep breath before he knocks. They have a huge gold knocker in the shape of a bear's head – classic Pete-and-Glor. Glor opens the door to him in full make-up – her hair is set into a smooth 'hat' which reminds him of the removable plastic hair on the twin's Lego men. She makes all the right 'ooh-ing' noises about the Belgian biscuits he's brought. Relief sweeps through him, and he feels glad to see her. He's ushered into the living room, de-coated and handed a glass of sparkling white wine by Pete, 'to keep you going until you choose what you'd like'. There is a rash of little bowls of peanuts and crisps on the tables in the front room, and he's offered his 'next drink' from a list of pretty much everything he can imagine. He's always treated like royalty at Glor and Pete's. And as always, Glor is the one who does most of the talking. She bombards him with questions about what he's been doing at work, how Pickles is, how Raine and the family are, what his Christmas was like, how he's finding the weather... He settles back into the over-soft armchair with his bitter in one hand and his wine in the other and submits.

He manages to steal a chat with Pete when Glor's out putting the last touches to the prawn cocktails (her own special recipe) and the pork with apple. There's often a slight awkwardness between them and Leonard usually makes an extra effort to find a topic of conversation that sits easily between them – how the weather is affecting Pete's fishing, or good old cricket. It reminds him of talking to Ed – neither Ed nor Pete seem to have strong opinions about anything, like a too-mild cheddar. Ed has a habit of sniggering at Leonard when he gets heated about his subject, but Pete just looks more and more earnest, as if he's thinking, 'It's what Leonard believes, so it must be the truth.' Leonard wonders if he could get him going about anything – the legalisation of prostitution, fox-hunting, child-labour in Uzbekistan... Maybe there isn't any room for opinions of your own if you live with Glor. Pete and Leonard never talk about Glor either. It's a familiar topic with other male friends – as soon as their wives are out in the kitchen, talk turns to how much hassle he's getting about visiting the pub a mere three times a week, or how she's started plastering herself with thick grey 'body cream' after baths. He's always wondered if Pete is dying to have this kind of a conversation with Leonard, but is too afraid of the consequences.

Poor Pete. He catches himself thinking this. *Is* it 'poor Pete'? Is it ever fair to feel sorry for one half of a pair? 'It takes two to tango', as his mother used to remind him (annoyingly) whenever he'd had an argument with a friend at school. Their marriage obviously suits Pete, or he wouldn't still be here. Few people are forced to stay with anyone, especially these days with divorces available on the internet. Maybe it's a relief for Pete not to need any opinions of his own. He never has to stick his neck out – Glor does that for him. And who knows what other advantages there are. Some marriages are harder to work out than others. He's never spotted any love moving between Glor and Pete, but maybe as soon as he leaves they're all over each other like randy teenagers. This mental image makes him smile at an inappropriate place in the middle of a story Pete's telling him about his new dentures. When Pete says 'what?' he has to make something up on the spot about Pete's story reminding him of his granddad leaving his dentures in the bathroom one day and his mother finding them and putting them in her mouth and pretending to bite him. It doesn't sound very funny to him but he makes some odd faces and fake-laughs and Pete finds it hilarious. Good old Pete. The food is perfectly adequate – although nothing seems to taste very strongly of anything. Leonard feels mean for thinking this – if he'd confided in Rose on the journey home she would have told him off for being so spoilt. After some fruit salad with UHT cream Pete pushes his coffee cup away and rubs his hands together as if he's trying to start a fire, which is the signal for them to retire to the living room for the slide show. He notices that Pete sits on the two-seater and leaves a space for Glor, but when she comes in she sits on the armchair instead. Does Pete look crestfallen? It's hard to tell. The slides aren't as boring as he thought they would be – Leonard has never been to Portugal and asks questions about the area that Glor is happy to answer. When they're done Leonard offers to help with the washing up – Glor protests at first but eventually concedes that he can dry if he really must. Pete goes off to potter about with his train set – there's a whole roomful of it upstairs. Usually Leonard is given a guided tour of all the new bits – a tiny white house with a painted woman at the window, or a new loop of track. As they stand side by side at the sink a silence settles on them, and Leonard can't quite get a proper taste of it – awkward? Intimate? He starts a conversation about the pork to try and shake the atmosphere off, but it persists. Maybe there's something she wants to tell him about her and Pete?

He isn't sure he wants to hear it; he hasn't had any practice at being a confidante. It might put him in an awkward position. Although he ought to be there for her, offer his friendship. After all she's done for him. He dives in.

'Is everything alright with you, Glor?'

She seems taken aback by the directness of the question.

'What do you mean, Leonard? Yes, everything is... oh, you know how it is.'

He doesn't, but nods anyway. He dries two plates and a glass before she speaks again.

'Have you ever wondered, Leonard, how things might be if they were different? If you'd gone down a different road at a point in your life, or if you'd been a different person? What's that poem, about two yellow roads in a wood?'

'What, like if we'd been born into a different family?'

'No, not really. Just if we'd made a different choice... done something... oh, different to where you are now. Don't you ever think about that?'

'Not really, Glor.'

It's the truth. As the words leave his mouth, she changes, closes off. She clatters the cutlery violently.

'No, you wouldn't. You wouldn't.'

The next time she speaks, about a film she saw last night, her voice is bright again. He's glad, and he also feels a bit guilty – he said 'not really' on purpose; he knew it would shut her back down. He doesn't want it spilling out onto him, whatever it is. He's a bad friend. And although they leave each other half an hour later with cheery assurances about how wonderful it has been and how soon they should do it again, something feels soured between them.

When he gets home there's a fidgety energy in his body, even after two slices of cheese on toast topped with grain mustard. As he's wide awake, he might as well get started on the tasks Lily has set him as part of the 'investigation'. Of course, it's not fair to say that she has 'set him tasks' – he's made up his own mind to take things further. If he's feeling guilty about being disloyal to Rose, then that's his responsibility; it's nothing to do with Lily. He doesn't have much patience with people who aren't willing to take responsibility for themselves. He probably got that from his father. Whenever Leonard complained about anything as a boy, his father would question him on what he'd done to contribute to the situation until he'd got the answers he was looking for. When his marbles got stolen, it was because he hadn't taken proper care of them during break-times. When he shouted at his mother for making him tidy his room when his friends were all going to the fair, he was really angry at himself for not doing it last week when he'd first been asked. The way his father eloquently put it was 'a clever man doesn't throw his own shit and hope it sticks on someone else' (although when his wife was listening he substituted 'mess' for the swear word).

Leonard had thought it was a load of rubbish when he was a teenager. It was only much later on, in his mid-twenties, that his father's words had come back to haunt him. He'd notice a colleague at the bank blaming his manager for everything that went wrong, or he'd moan about having no money to go to the cinema and then remember what he'd spent on a top-of-the-range garden rake. He finally acknowledged the wisdom of his father's advice and grudgingly swallowed it down. It had served him well over the years. It's certainly more onerous living this way – examining every unhappy situation with the question 'what choices have I made to get me here?' But at least he knows he's taking life on the chin – at least his father would be proud of him.

He isn't sure where to start and so spends a long time gathering his 'tools' around him, as he does when he's getting ready to do some planting out or some drastic cutting back. He fetches his gold cartridge pen and looks in his desk for a fresh notebook. He dithers between one of Rose's old ones and one Raine got him for Christmas. Rose suffered from what he supposed could be called a stationary fetish, and would have bought up half of the rainforest if he hadn't stopped her. He was just about working through the back-log now. What would she have thought if she'd known she had enough notepads, postcards and fancy pens to last for three years after her death? The present from Raine is beautiful – the stiff cover is wrapped in Chinese silk the blue-grey colour of *Hosta* 'Blue Wedgwood' leaves. He's reluctant to 'soil' it with this project somehow. But it would be too strange to use a notebook that Rose had bought herself. So he takes the one from Raine to bed, gets under the covers, and opens it up. There's nothing like a fresh page of a new book, like a first date, or a patch of turned-over earth in the garden. All the possibilities! He thinks about what he should write – a title, a name for the project. 'The Mystery of Rose'? 'The Other Life of Rose Mutch'? They both sound over-dramatic, like one of those awful detective programmes on afternoon TV full of unfamiliar actors and unlikely coincidences. He imagines Lily watches them religiously. Instead he writes the word 'Rose' in neat block capitals.

He starts a list of all the people Rose knew. He starts with her work colleagues. He's already got Sue's number – she goes down first. He also puts a note by her name – 'call her again?' Her friend Pam came up a lot in conversation – he'd only met her a couple of times, a thin wispy woman who kept fiddling with her hair. There was her good friend Linda, and – what was her name? Liz? – and the old school-

teacher Rose used to write to, Mrs... what was her name?
Would she still be alive anyway? And that other woman,
the one with the stutter... He pauses as a whole life-time's
worth of people swim into his head, jostling for space. It's
impossible! He puts the pen down, feeling a little panicky.
He puts the book down for a second and speaks kindly to
himself – come on Leonard, get a grip – it's just a place to
start. Just get them all down, all the names you can, and then
go back and look at what you've got. He picks up his pen and
it only takes fifteen minutes. Afterwards he takes a tea-break,
feeling quite a rebel to be making tea so late at night (or early
in the morning).

     He looks at his bedside clock. It's 1.03 am. He's still
wide awake, and he doesn't have anything special on at work
tomorrow. He can go in a little late and take it easy all day...
Simon is pretty relaxed about that kind of thing. It's getting
nippy. He pulls on an old navy jumper with patches on the
shoulders. He opens the curtains before climbing back under
the duvet with his note-book. It's quiet and still, the nearly-
full moon a giant eye keeping a watch on the village. A cat
yowls, caught up in its own domestic dramas – sex, territory,
violence. He remembers Lily telling him about her cat Molly,
who'd died last year at seventeen. She'd described her silky
grey-blue fur and the chunk she had missing from her left ear.
She'd told him a story about how Molly always announced
her entrance with a 'miaow' sung in the same tune as Lily's
'hello', and tears had sprung to her eyes. She'd seemed much
sadder than when she spoke about her late husband. Leonard
had been lucky, so lucky. He pulls the duvet up to his neck
and sits cross-legged against the headboard like a yogi. He
turns the notebook upside down so he can start writing on
a fresh page again, writes the date, and puts the pen down.
He takes a deep breath, pulling air into the very bottom of

his lungs so that his stomach pops out, and closes his eyes. He feels at peace. He lets the memories swim in and out, standing back from them when they appear, not wanting to scare them away.

He's mostly familiar with the memories that rise to meet him. He supposes they must symbolise something important, so his brain has preserved them nearer to the top, where they're more likely to be sparked off. Seeing daffodils usually brings back the day they stood in Dora's Field in Cumbria and held hands, their eyes skimming over a sea of daffodils the colour of egg-yolks. It was his first week of knowing that he was going to be a father, and his brain has chosen this moment to signify it – not the day after, when he'd caught stomach flu, or the day before, when they'd driven up from Oxfordshire and argued about the directions. He drags these two alternative memories up with considerable effort and then hopes they'll sink back where they came from – the daffodils are a tad more romantic than the stomach flu. And here is the moment when he comes round the corner and meets his brand new daughter, deep pink and swaddled. And here's another, when a little Raine came into their bed and was sick all over herself and both of them. 'Thanks for that one, brain,' he thinks.

He tries not to think too hard or to pull at anything. New memories slowly bump their way up from the depths. He lets them come, not asking them to stay any longer than they want to. He's forgotten all about the notebook. There are things that happened the day before memorable days like birthdays or funerals, or events in certain places or rooms. He remembers their bright kitchen in the cottage, with its cornflower blue tiles around the work-surface, and their old garden stuffed with plants. And here's their comfy old bedroom with Rose's bottles and potions all over the dressing table. He sees himself sitting outside on their expensive reclining garden chairs and drinking fresh lemonade with Rose, ice clinking in the jug. Next he's opening the door on Rose on the toilet by mistake, and laughing at the look of surprised horror on her face.

Now it's a weekday, one of their weeks off. Rose says she needs to do some 'secret shopping'; he never found out what it was. He sees himself in the kitchen, starving, with their pizza turning black in the oven while he waited for her to return. What day of the week was it? Could it have been a Tuesday? Another time, much longer ago, Raine is a toddler and Leonard is home from work with some kind of illness, a chest infection. She asks him to look after her for the afternoon. What day of the week? It was the day after his birthday; he'd been ill for that too. He could look it up later. There's a flash of a shirt he bought from an expensive shop – it was slate-grey, silky; he spilt red wine down it the second time he wore it, and they never got rid of the stain. Next is a dream Rose'd had, she'd been talking in her sleep. She'd been saying something, what was it? A name? Was it one of the names her mother had said? He made a note to ask Lily what they were. She'd also said 'don't touch', or was that a different time? She said this over and over, he's sure of it. What did it mean? He feels tightness in his chest and opens his eyes wide. There's a moment's adjustment as he finds himself back in his bedroom. He doesn't want the moon looking at him anymore and gets up to pull the curtains shut. He's exhausted. That's enough for now.

What can he think of now to wipe these uncomfortable feelings away? Lily's face swims into his head, and he pushes it to one side. Maybe some fantasy woman with long, tanned legs and a suggestive smile? No, not tonight. He decides on wandering around The Garden House in Devon, a garden that he and Rose visited often and loved. He hasn't been back there since she died – maybe Lily would be interested in a trip sometime. It has a half-wild look to it. They call it 'naturalistic planting' these days – working with nature rather than against it, using plants that would grow together in their natural habitat, and encouraging local wildlife to move in and have babies. The best examples of it have a 'scattered' look to Leonard, as if each individual plant has been sprinkled from somewhere high above and left to bed in, spread, intermingle. The snowdrops in February, the azaleas and rhododendrons, the poppies in June... there's always so much to see there. They'd visited in different seasons, mostly staying in a local B&B owned by an eccentric old man who cooked the most amazing fried breakfasts – scrambled eggs, bacon, fried tomatoes, and oh, the sausages...

The phone. The phone is ringing. He hoists his head away from his shoulder, his neck protesting, and finds himself still propped up in bed. He checks the time. 3.52 am. The time of death calls. Who's died? The person on the top of this dreaded list is Raine. He tries to still himself, takes a deep breath and makes the phone quiet. He holds it to his ear and speaks in a husky voice.

'Hello?'

'Hello, Len?'

'Yes, who is this?' He knows already – nobody else calls him Len. He wants to get all the facts right at the beginning, just in case he needs to take some action.

'It's Ed.'

Leonard waits for him to continue, but Ed pauses too long, and he can't wait.

'What's happened? Is she OK?'

'I should have waited 'til the morning...'

'Is she OK, Ed?' He can't keep the annoyance out of his voice – why won't he just tell him?

'Sorry, sorry, I'm... she's fine, well she's not fine, but it's alright, nothing's... There's been a... something's happened.'

'Yes?'

'Raine got upset tonight. We had an argument, not anything major, just a silly thing. It was about this work thing I've got to go to. I asked her if she could make some cakes or something, all the wives are bringing something along. And she flipped, Len. I don't know what... She was hysterical, I couldn't calm her down. I didn't know how to...'

He sounds like a little boy standing in the middle of an empty playground after the bullies have stolen his lunch.

'Where is she now?'

'She's sleeping upstairs. The doctor just left; she gave her some pills. They zonked her out pretty quickly. I called our GP and asked her to come out – Raine was furious with me when she got here, but I didn't know... The doctor wants us to go and see her tomorrow. The twins didn't wake up, thank fuck, I mean... they slept through the whole thing. I just wanted to, I wanted to...'

His voice cracks. He is so lost. Leonard's eyes fill with tears – not for Raine yet, but for Ed, for little Ed, who's struggling, drowning. Who doesn't know what to do. And then he cramps up with sadness for himself, as he doesn't know what to do either. Rose would know. Why isn't she here? It isn't fair. Ed is crying now, a strange hiccoughing noise. Leonard has never heard it before. He imagines him standing in his kitchen, his hair all mussed up, pinching the bridge of his nose with his finger and thumb, the way he does when he's stressed. Leonard studies the lines on the palm of his left hand while Ed cries. He waits, and a Plane tree from his last job comes into his mind. It was a huge specimen, planted long before he arrived. It was right at the back of the gardens, and so even in peak season Leonard could go there to be alone. It had a bench underneath it, facing a flimsy wire fence and the surrounding farmland. Leonard loves the edges of gardens – the fuzzy line where the formality starts seeping into nature, breaking up into forest and fields. He used to go and sit there when things got difficult – he was having a lot of problems at the time with a stubborn and fiery colleague. As soon as his bottom touched the bench, he looked up at the tree and was filled with a wonderful warm feeling, as if it were his mother towering above him, holding out her arms high up. He used to look out over the countryside, or look up through the leaves or bare branches to catch glimpses of the sky – grey or white or orange or astonishing Mediterranean blue.

Eventually Ed's crying slows, becomes more controlled. He takes a few whooshing breaths in and then sighs them out. When he speaks again his voice is thick, his nose and throat lined with mucus.

'Fuck. I'm sorry. I'm sorry.'

What can Leonard say? How can he give him some comfort? He wants to be there so he could stroke away the hair from Ed's forehead and slide a gentle thumb across his cheek. He's surprised at how tender he feels towards him, as if he's his own child. He reassures himself as he often does in these situations, speaking to himself in a kind voice, 'You can only do your best, old man.' It's the same thing Charlie said to him in the pub when Leonard was agonising over the best coffin to put Rose in. When Charlie spoke the words, it felt like he'd suddenly taken off a heavy rucksack, one he'd been carrying for miles and miles. Where would we be without other people?

'It's OK Ed. We'll get this sorted out between us. It'll all be OK. You were right to call the doctor. You were right to call me.'

This sets Ed off again, a short burst of shuddering sobs. Leonard sighs. He's so tired. He needs to get some sleep. Raine is safe for now – they can deal with this in the morning. They talk about practicalities, and it helps to push the emotion back – Ed's voice becomes steadier. Ed will call in sick and take the twins to nursery, and maybe find a friend to look after them in the afternoon. Leonard promises him he'll come over first thing tomorrow morning. He tells Ed to try to get some sleep and reassures him that they'll get through it. After hanging up, Leonard fishes the green notebook out from the gap between his bed and bedside table and puts it carefully into his top drawer. He sets his alarm and turns off the light. He feels as if he'll never be able to drop off, but the next thing he knows the alarm is beeping, and he's dragging himself up from the depths of sleep to meet the morning.

After leaving Raine's house the next day, Leonard finds himself at the pub, not wanting to face his too-quiet house. He feels faintly guilty about leaving Pickles for so long – he'll give him a treat when he gets back; there's a chicken breast in the freezer. Pickles has dined well on Leonard's guilt over the years. Pickles isn't the only one who's benefited either – Rose got chocolates whenever he stayed out at the pub too long, and his mother received a stream of small presents when he was secretly smoking. It feels good to step into the warmth. After a short conversation with Suze about her daughter's new kitten, he ask for his usual. Charlie isn't there, and there's no-one else he wants to share his silence with, so he sits alone at a table by the window, mulling things over between sips of bitter and then later sips of sweet, cold pineapple juice.

He'd been shocked by the state of Raine's house when he got there. There was a jumble of toys all over the living room floor, piles of dirty washing on the kitchen table, and washing up in the sink. Just ordinary mess, but it was so out of place in Raine's house. She didn't allow it. Ed hadn't even pulled the curtains, and the whole house was in a half-gloom. Leonard felt annoyed with Ed and wondered whether he'd even attempted to help Raine keep up with the housework. Once he'd established that Raine was still fast asleep (the doctor had warned Ed that the pills would make her sleep late) he pulled up his sleeves and told his son-in-law that they needed to get this place tidied up. His annoyance rose again when it emerged that Ed didn't even know how to use his own washing machine. As Leonard was loading it up with tiny T-shirts and socks and Ed's crumpled boxers, he remembered that until Glor, he hadn't known how to use his either, and he softened a little. He was hanging the washing out on the line when Ed popped his head out and said that Raine was awake and that he was taking her up a cup of tea. He said she seemed 'sheepish', and she was mortified that Ed had asked Leonard to come over.

Half an hour later Leonard had been summoned upstairs to sit on the end of her bed, just as he used to do when she was a child, stopping by for a bed-time chat after she was too old for stories. She looked hung over, puffy; her mouth was smiling, but her eyes were frightened. She tried to reassure him that everything was fine – it was a one-off, things had got out of hand, she could see things more clearly now it was morning. He wasn't convinced, but wasn't sure what else to do but nod and listen to her. Listen to her trying to convince herself. As they talked, he felt a backdrop of frustrated pain that he couldn't take it all away from her. Just like when she had an allergic reaction to some antibiotics and came out in itchy hives all over, just like when she got dumped by her first boyfriend, just like when she was going into labour with the twins. He'd much prefer to feel the hurt himself. Is there an operation they could do? He ended up telling her about his evening with Pete and Glor to try to make her laugh, exaggerating the lurid colour of the prawn cocktail sauce and the length of the slide show. She did chuckle a little. She slipped further and further away from him as he talked, yawning her way towards sleep. He wanted to stay and wait for her to drop off, so he could stroke her hair and plant happy dreams in her head, but she was a grown-up now and that intimacy was denied him. He kissed her on the forehead instead and told her he loved her.

He and Ed had talked for a while in the kitchen when he came downstairs. Ed had told Leonard a bit more about what had been happening, probably out of desperation. He'd told Leonard that their 'life in the bedroom, if you know what I mean' hadn't been 'functioning' since the twins were born. They hadn't been able to talk properly about anything for a while – whenever Ed tried, she'd brush him off and say she needed to get the twin's lunch ready, or get the washing in. He also mentioned that she hadn't written in her journal for a few months, and this worried Leonard most of all. She'd always had a diary, from when she was ten or eleven, and had written in them almost daily for most of her life. Sometimes it was only a sentence or two, and sometimes it was great reams – she'd lie on her belly on the carpet and scribble page after page of what Leonard could only imagine. Even when she was in hospital having the twins, he remembers her realising she hadn't packed it and asking Ed to go back home to fetch it.

Ed kept repeating that he didn't know what to do to 'sort it'. Leonard doesn't know what to do either.

He looks around the pub at the familiar pictures on the wall – a photo of the Five Bells football team from the local paper, a dusty looking cheap Monet print. The optics behind the bar, polished and shining. The musty-looking, heavy, brown curtains, permanently swagged and tied. He and Ed had decided on nothing, pinning all their hopes on the doctor, as if she might work some kind of miracle, dispensing a pot of tiny pills that would make everything better. Although he supposes there *are* pills like that – happy pills. Happy pills that have 'increased risk of suicide' as one of their many side effects, and which blunt feelings in people until they can't remember what they were sad about in the first place and want to cry but can't. He can hardly bear to look at the unhappiness inside Raine, lodged in her centre like a spiky animal, twisting and turning and utterly embedded. How can they help her to get it out? Will it just fight its own way out when it's ready, regardless of whether Raine lets it or not? As he's thinking this thought, Johnny Cash crashes onto the Five Bells' jukebox like a wounded angel. It's the song that was in the charts for a while – originally written by some punk band – what were they called, Seven Inch Nails? He'd heard another one of their records on the radio once, and its violence had shocked him. Leonard listens with all of his attention. He'll never tire of this music – the gravelly voice, the meaning that Johnny injects into every word. He's transformed this song into something tragic, something beautiful.

He sees Charlie through the yellow-tinged window, walking along the path towards the pub. He swallows his drink in one go. He doesn't want anyone to prick the meniscus of the bubble of his thoughts – he wants to keep them to himself for now. He takes his empty glass back to the bar and tells Suze to take care. He pauses to say a quick hello and goodbye to Charlie at the door before walking out into the cold air. He thinks of Pickles, and a ham and cheese sandwich. His comfortable chair, his warm bed. The black sky is studded with stars, like billowing clouds of tiny white *Crambe cordifolia* flowers floating above huge rosettes of dark green leaves.

Chapter 14:
Raspberry Pudding

Spring edges shyly closer, and Leonard makes the most of the beginnings of the tulip season. When he first bought cut flowers, after Rose died, he felt like a terrible cheat – letting someone else do all the hard work – but now he doesn't even get a pang. Why shouldn't he take a shortcut sometimes? He buys his flowers from an excellent local florist ('A Passion For Flowers') run by an ambitious woman in her thirties called Lisa Maxwell. For three weeks in a row she sells him a huge bunch of a variety called *Tulip* 'Yokohama', named after the Japanese city. They have a spring-bright, yellow bloom with slightly pointed petals, and they light up his hallway and his living room like a beacon.

Leonard first met Lisa when she had just set up the business a few years ago. She used to work in London in a high-powered job 'in IT', and she used her redundancy money to fit out the shop and set herself up. She didn't know much about flowers when she started a few years ago, but has absorbed knowledge like a sponge and her stock is getting better and better. Leonard used to give her a few pearls of wisdom whenever he visited, which she was always grateful for, but now she's started telling him things that he didn't know – that he should soak his vases in bleach overnight, as bacteria shortens the life of cut flowers, and that poppies keep longer if you singe the stems over a naked candle flame. Her shop is always bustling, and recently she's started talking about expanding. Her secret, of course, is that she loves what she does.

Yesterday Leonard asked for an extra bunch of tulips. He has arranged to meet Lily at a small National Trust garden she's never been to. He's been getting the occasional phone call from her, asking him for dates or places of birth, and she called him last week to say she had some more information to share with him. The garden isn't open to the public on Saturday mornings, so Leonard knows they'll get plenty of privacy. Lily is delighted by the flowers. At the gate Leonard flashes his card and mentions the name of the estate manager, who's a good friend of his, so Lily gets in for free as well. He enjoys this opportunity to show off about 'knowing the right people' and walks down the path with an exaggerated swagger, calling Lily 'doll' and offering his crooked arm to her. The two of them wander around the gardens with Pickles close on their heels before they get down to business. There are sheep dotted around the grounds, and as they're rounding the corner of the outbuildings they see a lone ewe cropping grass where she shouldn't be. She's 'looking pretty sheepish', as Leonard puts it. Lily stays with her, offering her freshly plucked lush grass which she politely refuses, while Leonard drags Pickles with him to fetch one of the staff, to encourage her back to where she should be.

Most of the garden isn't much to look at at this time of year. The beds are looking bedraggled. Elsewhere, except for some glossy red holly berries and pretty pink flower-clusters on some particularly fine *Viburnum tinus* 'Eve Price', there isn't much to distract from the greens and browns. Leonard surreptitiously guides Lily to a special spot he knows about. As they step around a corner, he's rewarded with her gasp of pleasure and surprise. They're in a woodland glade that's thickly carpeted with snowdrops, the yellow tips of crocuses just pushing their way up into the weak winter sun. As if on cue, the clouds move aside and the light pours down, filtering through the hazel and oak branches to fall in splashes of brilliant white on the flower heads and in small pools of honey on the undergrowth. Lily puts one of her hands out automatically and presses Leonard on the sleeve of his coat, as if she needs to be supported in the face of all this beauty. He almost puts one of his hands on top of hers, but instead he gestures to a wooden bench hidden by an ash tree. Pickles jumps up next to them and settles down for a nap.

They bathe in all that whiteness, and Leonard talks to her about snowdrops – the conditions they prefer, the terrible plague of botrytis they suffered at Coburne once. She asks him for the latin names – *Galanthus nivalis, G. caucasicus, G. ikariae* – and rolls them around in her mouth, trying to get the pronunciation exactly right. They move on to other Latin names and Leonard tells her some of his favourites – *Rosa tomentosa, Lonicera japonica, Hoheria lyallii*. She says it's like hearing poetry and asks him for more. He gets carried away then and starts showing off – trying to get her to say *Metaseqoia glyptostroboides, Paeonia mlokosewitschii, Zauschneria*. They laugh as Leonard says the names more and more slowly so she can follow him, and his voice becomes a computer-like monotone with vowels that stretch on and on and a slow-motion face which Lily watches intently, moving her own mouth into the same shapes. After some time, the sight of the snowdrops is no longer sufficient to warm them. As they get ready to walk on, their bottoms a little numb from the cold bench, Leonard realises that he is happy.

After their free carrot cake and a sausage for Pickles (the tea-lady has had a long-standing crush on Leonard, and he shamefully uses it to his full advantage) their conversation turns to Rose. Lily gets out a vivid blue folder and he puts his notebook on the table between them. They do a few rounds of 'after you, no after you', like when you meet a stranger on a narrow path, until eventually Leonard says he hasn't come up with much, so he'll get his bit over and done with. He opens his notebook and shows her the list of names, going through each one in turn – their relationship to Rose, how long they knew her for, whether he could easily get in touch with them again. When he's finished he's struck by how short the list is – a life-time of Rose's relationships with other people boiled down to one and a half pages. He wonders how it would have differed from Rose's own version – are there people he's left out who were crucially important to her? Has he included people who hardly knew her? Lily suggests that he decides on a few people to start with, so they can try to get in touch with them and see if they have any useful information.

Next he turns to the back of his notebook and shares the memories he's managed to dredge up. None of them seem very relevant, and he feels ashamed, as if he's handing in scruffy homework. He finds the note he'd written to himself and asks her for the two names Rose's mum had said, hoping one of them might match the name she shouted out in her sleep that night. She looks in her folder and says Lester and Peter. Lester... Lester... Peter... he tries both out in the hope of rekindling a dormant memory, sparking it into life, but neither sounds quite right. Peter… he thought it had ended with an 'ee' sound. Petey? Yes – maybe that was it. Petey. He's almost sure of it. He writes it in his notebook and underlines it, and she writes it on a piece of paper. Next he tells her about the times Rose disappeared for the afternoon all those years ago – he's worked out that it was a Tuesday. Lily seems pleased, and writes this down too.

He closes his notebook and they move on to what Lily's been up to. He can tell that there's something she's excited about telling him. She's been using the General Register Office website, and a few others she'd found when trying to track down Rose. She's started to draw up a simple family tree for her. She pulls it out and shows him what she'd managed to fill in so far. On her father's side, there were three brothers. One of them was called Lester! All three brothers had died – she's already ordered copies of their death certificates from the website. She's also managed to track down one of their wives – Mildred Smith – who was married to Willy. Lily wonders if it's worth them having a chat with her? She's still in her sixties, she was quite a bit younger than her husband, and Lily has found a current address for her in Nottingham. She offers to get in touch with her and set something up, and then catches herself and apologises for taking over again, for getting 'carried away'. Leonard takes the papers from her to have a look at and says he'll have a think about it. That seems like enough for now, he thinks to himself.

As Lily goes to use the ladies', Leonard feeds cake crumbs to Pickles under the table and conjures up some everyday memories of Rose. The way she'd roll over into the middle of the mattress as soon as he got out of bed, putting her arms and legs out wide and groaning with pleasure. Her favourite red lipstick, and the strange warm spicy smell of it when he leant his head on her shoulder. That special meal she cooked him one night – he can't remember what the occasion was. She'd ordered some recipe cards from TV, sending off for them weeks in advance. It was all fancy – beef Wellington with a pastry pattern on top, potatoes – what was it again? Dauphinoise? And the pudding... the most amazing pink concoction made from fresh raspberries, cream and whisky, and the crispiest, most buttery biscuits he'd ever tasted on the side to scoop up the raspberry goo. He can taste it on his tongue now – the heat of the booze, the glossy creaminess, the sharp raspberries, the crunch of those biscuits... He'd eaten three portions of it, until the pink stuff was all gone, then had polished off four more biscuits with his coffee. He'd hardly been able to move afterwards – that feeling when the skin over your stomach stretches tight like a drum. She'd glowed with pleasure. His Rose, his wonderful Rose. He imagines her looking down at him from wherever she is now and laughing, saying 'looking back through Rose-tinted glasses, are you, you big ninny. How about that Saturday when Raine was little and we argued and I stormed out and didn't come back until late? What about the way I used to get biscuit crumbs in the bed and sweep them all over to your side?' He looks up and whispers 'forgiven, love, all forgiven', just as Lily reappears from the toilets.

'What's that?' she asks, stacking the plates onto the wooden tray.

'Nothing, nothing. Thinking aloud. Let's be off then, shall we?'

Some of his curiosity returns by the time they've walked to their cars and are standing alone in the empty car-park. As he's opening the door for Pickles to jump in he asks Lily if she would mind calling Mildred Smith after all, and see if they could arrange a meeting. And would she mind coming with him? Of course she could, and of course she didn't mind coming along. It would be her pleasure.

He stops off at Lily's to look at her garden on the way home, wanting to see how her rose bushes are getting on. He's starting to feel attached to them now that he's done some work on them. He's met so many new gardens over the years – through his career, and through friends and family. At first the land is unfamiliar. He has to get to know the soil by crumbling some in his hand and by looking at which plants are already growing in it, and predict how the weather affects the exposed patch down by the lake or the borders next to the hothouse. It's an exciting time, full of promise. There's a steep learning curve and the expectation that mistakes will be made. Some gardeners like to gather as much information as they can from other people who've worked there, books and records. Leonard can see the sense in this, but he doesn't like to do it that way himself. He'd prefer to be out there under the sky, walking through the grasses, pulling aside the branches of a Forsythia here, checking on the health of a Wild Cherry there. There's no substitute for getting out there and getting your hands dirty, whatever the weather. As time goes on, the land starts to reward you – you know just the variety of Euphorbia to put next to that Globe Thistle, and the *Pulmonaria longifolia* flourish under that shady oak, their intense purple-blue flowers giving you goose-bumps.

The land even starts to talk to you – although Leonard wouldn't want to admit this to anyone. It tells you where it's suffering from black spot, and which corners are starting to look untidy. Each swathe of land has its own voice. Coburne is upper-class, male, well-spoken, old. His and Rose's last garden was a woman with a deep-throated laugh and a fondness of mischief. Lily's garden... how does it sound? He's still getting to know it, he's only walked around it a

handful of times, but he thinks maybe an adolescent boy –
eager, sincere, a little awkward. Yes – that's it. The timbre of
the voice can change too. If someone new and enthusiastic
(or foolhardy) comes in and rips everything out, then the
garden is re-born. And gardens grow up – some gathering
weight, others getting younger and more playful as time
goes on. As he walks around Lily's garden, he makes little
mental notes to himself, 'some Fritillaries would look good
there next year pushing up through the lawn', or 'those
Hostas could do with dividing'. He's getting carried away
now – who knows if he'll still be visiting Lily's garden in
the Autumn to put in those bulbs? And who's to say that Lily
would want them anyway? It's not his garden. He needs to
reign himself in a little. Maybe there's a part of him that's
getting ready to have a green space of his own again.

Later in the week he's watching a repeat of a David
Attenborough programme about polar bears and he thinks
of Raine. She loved nature programmes when she was little,
and called them her 'jungle cartoons'. She'd always been
fascinated by animals and was beside herself with joy when
they'd bought her a guinea pig for her 8th birthday. A shame
it hadn't lasted very long. There was a paddock not too far
from their cottage and they often walked there hand in hand
to watch the horses grazing or to feed them grass. Raine
was so intent on following Leonard's instruction to hold the
grass in a flat hand that her fingers bent backwards away
from her palm. As the horses chewed she watched their faces
so closely that she'd make little munching movements with
her own mouth without being conscious of it. He wonders
now why she doesn't have any pets. Then he remembers
– Ed is allergic. He has asthma and is prone to wheezing
even when they visit friends of theirs who have a rabbit in

the garden. Leonard wonders if this illness of his really is purely physical. It's not that he suspects Ed of putting it on exactly, but it does seem to take a turn for the worse when he's asked to help out around the house…

Poor Raine. Since Ed called Leonard in the middle of the night a few weeks ago, Leonard has been visiting more regularly, and calling more often. He can't stop worrying about her. It reminds him of the old days, when she couldn't leave the house without scenes of terror and destruction entering his head – there'd be a flood and she'd be washed away! There'd be an armed robbery in the post-office when she was handing over her pennies for sweets! The worst never happened. She broke her leg dare-devilling on one of those awful climbing frames built onto concrete, and she had a dangerous fever once that brought the doctor running and gave them all a scare. There were some broken hearts before Ed came along, and the trauma of exams… obstacles that no father could protect his daughter from. She'd got through it all. But it still pained him that he couldn't do more. But now there's this sadness, this nervous energy. What should he do with this? He's brought it up with Ed once or twice, snatched conversations when Raine is in the bath or reading to the twins. Ed seems to have the same level of concern that he had before, saying things still 'aren't right' and that he has a 'bad feeling'. Leonard isn't sure how seriously to take him – could he be over-exaggerating? Maybe Ed is having an emotional crisis of his own, stuck at home with a stressed wife who no longer pays him any attention and two hurricanes for children. Maybe Raine would be OK if Ed helped her out a bit more. But Leonard knows it isn't that simple. He hasn't said anything to Ed, but if the truth be told, he has a bad feeling as well. He hasn't tried to talk to Raine about it properly either. There's an invisible wall up, and Leonard knows if he touched it he'd get a hefty electric shock. All he's done so far is wait on the wrong side of the wall, standing on his tiptoes to see if he can catch a glimpse of her on the other side. Every so often he tries to shout over the top – 'I'm here, Raine!' 'Let down a ladder when you're ready!' What's going on in there? Why doesn't she want to let him in?

As he dwells on the situation, his thoughts pool and swirl. He can't concentrate on the polar bears, who are lazily scooping fish from the water with their gigantic paws. He decides to call her, to try and shake the curdled feelings away. It's about time that he told her about Lily anyway. He feels like a traitor sneaking off to see her without his daughter's knowledge. He dials too quickly the first time and gets a small girl who asks him if he'd like to speak to her mummy. He feels a bit mean saying 'no thanks' – maybe he should speak to her anyway, and ask her if she needs anything doing in her garden. It isn't the answer the little girl was expecting either – she hesitates, and after a short silence says in a quiet voice 'I'm not supposed to speak to strangers'. He tries unsuccessfully to explain that he's dialled the wrong number and eventually hangs up feeling foolish.

Ed picks up the phone the next time. He sounds as if he's been sleeping.

'Hello, Ed speaking?'

'It's Leonard. How's everything with you?'

'Oh, hi Len. Yeah, Fine. And you?'

'I'm good, very good. Are you sure it's all alright there?'

'Mmm, yes, yes. You know.' There's a note of caution in his voice. 'Would you like to speak to Raine?' As Ed asks Raine to come to the phone Leonard can hear that she's in the same room, listening in.

'Hello?'

She says this as if she can't be sure it's him, as if Ed has tricked her into speaking to someone she doesn't want to speak to. When he says 'darling?' she sounds relieved. She says she's OK, 'same same'. They chat about the weather for a while and he gets a graphic update on Rory's latest illness. He isn't sure how to broach the subject of Lily. He hesitates, wondering if it's a good idea after all.

'Raine?'

'What Dad?'

'Well, you know that friend of your mothers, Lily?'

'Yes?' It's a slow, rising yes, guarded.

'I just wanted to let you know that we're... we're still in touch.'

'In touch? How? Why?'

'We just meet up to go on walks, you know, have a chat. Different things.'

'How long has this been going on? Why have you hidden it from me?'

Her voice is already filled with outrage. He can't help but let it affect him, a sinking in his stomach. He pinches one of the yellow tulip petals between his thumb and finger, for strength.

'We've been talking about your mother a bit. There are some things that...'

At this point Raine sighs explosively, angrily. He pauses and then carries on.

'There are some things that don't make any sense, things I've found out. Your mother used to go somewhere every Tuesday afternoon, every afternoon for years as far as I can make out. What do you make of it, Raine?'

He can imagine her standing there and looking out of the window as if she isn't meeting his eye, her left hand crushing a bunch of material from her skirt and then letting it go again over and over, her foot tapping.

'Raine?'

'I'm NOT speaking to you about this. I can't believe...'

She's so angry now that she can hardly get the words out. He hears Ed in the background saying 'Raine?', the scrape of his chair as he gets up.

'You're SUSPICIOUS of her, aren't you? How could you do this? What's mum done to you, that you'd be snooping around behind her back with this, this WOMAN...'

And the line goes dead.

He stands there holding the phone against his ear and listening to the flat tone. He leans against the table and waits for the shock to fade. There's a tight, nervous feeling in his chest – he's afraid, as if she was his parent, as if he'd been told off for doing something terrible. He also feels guilty – for giving her something else to worry about, on top of everything else. For adding to her burden. And there's something else... something he'd rather not be feeling. It's anger. He isn't surprised about her reaction, not after the conversations he's already tried to have with her. But how dare she accuse him of being suspicious of Rose? She doesn't know the first thing about how he feels about his wife. He's the one who's lost his lifelong partner. He's the one who's been grieving for her. The way she spoke about their investigation, saying he was 'snooping around behind her back'... Rose is dead for god's sake! It's about time that Raine got used to it. It's been three years now! So what should he do next? Where does he go from here?

Ten minutes later he's topping up the water in the vase of tulips when the phone rings again. It can't be Raine – he can't remember her ever backing down from an argument in her life. It's Ed. He's talking quickly, wheezing as if he can't suck in enough air. He tells Leonard how Raine screamed out a string of swear-words before grabbing her coat and shoes and storming out of the house and into the night. He ran out onto the drive after her, shouting for her to stay as she slammed the car door shut, but she just wound down the window and swore at him again before screeching off. 'She was like a mad person', he says. Leonard can hear the fear in Ed's voice and recognises it from all those years of living with Raine. The thump of dread when she used to tell him she didn't care about him, or that he didn't understand her. And yes, he recognises it from living with Rose too. Rose had that same power, he'd almost forgotten. Once when he missed their wedding anniversary she didn't speak to him for two whole weeks. Two weeks! And there was the time she misunderstood something he said about her cooking. She took all the food and drinks out of the cupboards, even the custard powder, and dumped it all in bin bags. She left it out on the road in front of their house – the neighbours were peeking out from behind their curtains. Leonard was so ashamed. It isn't fair that Raine has this power over people. That's just not the way it works. He can't spend his whole life pussy-footing around her. It's time for her to stop it, this ridiculous acting up. He isn't playing any more. He checks that the twins are OK. He tells Ed firmly that she's an adult, that she can look after herself. He adds that they'll have a proper chat about it when Raine has calmed down. And then he wants to be off the phone, away from all this fuss and bother. He catches sight of her photo on the way back to the living room and feels nothing.

Chapter 15:
Like being slapped with a fish

Leonard manages to put Raine out of his mind altogether for a few days, but the worry and guilt build again before long. Whenever the feelings bloom, he reassures himself that he'll have a proper look at them when he sees Lily next, and this helps settle them down again. This means that when does see her next, on their trip to see Rose's aunt, and when she asks him how Raine is on the journey there, he finds the feelings all bubbling up at once. She flicks her eyes away from the road towards him and notices his mouth twisting to one side.

'What's up, doc?', she asks.

He hesitates, wondering if speaking with Lily about Raine is a further 'betrayal' of Rose. If he can't speak to her mother about her, should he speak to anyone else? Lily is waiting quietly. Since they've got to know each other better, she's less prone to running on and on – it must be her brand of nervousness, filling all the spaces with words without checking whether or not they're the right ones. She's actually a pretty good listener.

'I'm worried about my daughter.'

This is how he begins. These words act like a champagne cork, and are followed by a torrent of other words, sentences, paragraphs. He tells Lily about the way Raine used to manipulate him when she was a little girl, and his complicit surrender to her charm. There's the anger he felt at Rose for siding with Raine, because she was too scared to stand up to her, or recognised too much of herself in her daughter. And the 'odd man out' feeling he got whenever the three of them were together. The awkwardness that existed between him and Raine after Rose died – the way they'd floundered without her. Leonard's frustration with Ed, who lets Raine get away with too much, like everyone does. He spoke of his anger at Raine's reaction to the fact that he was still seeing Lily. He's amazed at how much he has to say. Finally he speaks about how horrible it is to know she's unhappy, despite everything he's said, and that he's stopped himself from calling her a hundred times.

'It's unbearable for you, not to be… to not reach out to her,' Lily says gently.

Tears spring to his eyes – quickly, almost violently. He is struck dumb and turns his head to look out of the window and concentrate on the passing houses and trees.

When he's recovered himself, he turns back to face forwards, slowly nods his head four times and sighs a long sigh. He's done it now; he's showed her another hidden corner of his insides. He feels better, as if he's siphoned a portion of the worry out, but still feels desperate for some kind of solution. What does she think he should do? But when he asks her, she'll only say 'it's difficult', and pats his knee.

They travel in silence for the rest of the journey. Leonard is in the middle of thinking about the best varieties of climber for Lily's garden when he's called into service as map-reader for the final leg. The approach to Mildred's town is run-down and grey. They pass a faceless red brick shopping centre, a vandalised phone box, and Lily manoeuvres the car around a thousand roundabouts. Mildred lives in a sheltered housing complex on the outskirts – self-contained flats where residents can come and go as they please. Leonard could just about bear to live somewhere like this, with 24-hour warden cover for emergencies and a small communal garden out the back where he could potter about. He'd rather die than be stuck in a boxy room with a mean single bed, only able to go out if someone took pity on him and propped him up in his wheelchair and wheeled him out. Rose could have wheeled him around all day long – that was always their plan – but not any more. He snaps himself out of such morbid thoughts and steels himself for the conversation they're about to have. He makes a play of being nervous, chattering his teeth and shaking his hands as she puts on the hand-brake. They sit in the car for a few minutes to discuss their strategy. Lily wants to check the family tree with Mildred and ask her what family she's still in touch with. They'll both try to encourage her to talk about herself, and ask her to talk about Rose's childhood – anything she can remember. They argue about who is going to be the good cop – they both quite fancy having a go at bad cop. Leonard says he should have brought a false moustache along so he could twirl it and look mysterious, but Lily says he's out of date; detectives these days are more likely to have goatees and wear combat trousers. Leonard isn't even sure what combat trousers are. He slams the car door with too much force and they climb the steps to the third floor, giving the odoriferous lift a miss.

Mildred opens the door to them with a toothy grin and a 'ta-da!' Leonard is worried she might be a bit doollally, and exchanges a surreptitious glance with Lily. Her flat smells of steak and kidney pie. They walk in to a riot of colour, like those council bedding displays Leonard has no time for, all tarty Begonias and brash pansies, more like a carnival than a flower bed. Different patterned materials are all shouting for attention – a blue and white flowered throw over half of the brown sofa, fussy pink and orange curtains, a beige carpet with dark red circles. Mildred herself is wearing a bright pink cardigan over a lime green T-shirt, and red trousers made of that cheap shiny material that's nasty to touch. She has a couple of thick hairs sprouting from her chin, and bosoms that start from her breastbones and ski-slope downwards to join with her stomach in a continuous curve. It's the kind of body you don't want to imagine naked, thinks Leonard, as a mental image appears despite himself. That always happens when he asks himself not to imagine something.

Her flat looks well-kept – clean, tidy, with none of the piles of newspapers or boxes of junk that Leonard might have imagined finding in a place like this. There's a series of shelves on either side of the electric fire filled to bursting with china ornaments, from cheap-looking things that look as if they've come out of a cracker, to a hideous pink grinning rabbit standing as big as a pint glass. Enough to give anyone nightmares, as Lily says later on the drive home. Mildred shepherds them over to the sofa and toddles off to get some tea and biscuits, leaving them squinting in the brightness. Leonard feels too close to the floor – the sofa is squishy and his knees are too high. He makes a play of patting all his pockets – when Lily asks what he's looking for he says 'I'm sure I brought my sunglasses along…' After ten minutes of clattering and banging noises, she brings in a tray with a teapot (bright red with orange spots) and a plate of bourbon biscuits. Leonard takes one but it gives too easily against his teeth, so he puts it into Lily's handbag when neither of the women are looking, making a mental note to tell her about it later before she discovers it for herself.

After a few sips, all of them grinning stupidly at each other, Mildred speaks.

'So! You're my little Rose's husband. Are you two married now, then?'

It's an embarrassing start, and both of them scramble to put her right. Leonard feels hot and bothered, and he notices the colour on Lily's cheeks.

'Just friends,' Lily says, and Mildred nods in an understanding way, making a 'mm, mm, mm' noise, a short murmur from low in her throat, repeated three times. Again it makes her seem a little crazy – Leonard wonders where she might sit on the 'sane' to 'certifiable' scale. They begin to talk about Rose. Lily sets the scene for her – they've been asked to write Rose's biography by a local publishing company, who are interested in the life of an 'average village woman' who spent her life looking after others. She makes it sound pretty convincing and even gives the name of the publishers – Leonard is perturbed by how easily she lies. Once they've made it all sound reasonable, Lily starts the questions. They've agreed that Leonard will make notes – he's always been good at that.

Lily gets Mildred warmed up by getting her to talk about herself. She's certainly skilled at loosening people's tongues, thinks Leonard, remembering how much he spilled during their journey here. They are already starting at an advantage – Mildred seems to be one of those elderly persons living alone, who is starving for an attentive audience. Lily's questions uncork a seemingly never-ending stream of stories and observations. Leonard and Lily hear all about Mildred's terrible time as a factory worker during the war, and her children who are 'good kids' and visit 'three times a year like clockwork – you could set your watch to them, mm, mm, mm'. She hints that her own marriage wasn't a terribly happy one, and Leonard wonders if she might have said more if he weren't there. Lily gradually guides her onto what they are here for and asks about Rose.

She starts by apologising and saying that she probably won't be much use to them. She never heard from Rose after she left home – none of the family did. She can remember Rose's father making attempts to keep in touch and then trying to track her down after she'd moved, but her mother just said, 'If she wants to stay lost, then we'll let her stay lost.' Mildred had always wondered what had happened to her. Almost mid-sentence she stands up, walks over to her ornaments, and moves one of them a centimetre to the right. She seems satisfied by this and settles back down into her chair. She looks up into the corner of the ceiling as she remembers.

She tells them about her first memory of Rose. She and her family lived only a short distance from Rose's parents. Mildred was ten years old when she first saw Rose, only a few weeks old and swaddled in a cream blanket, fast asleep in her crib. She talks about a few times when Rose had come along on their family days out – once to the sea-side, which had been a real treat. Lily lets her talk, and although Leonard is interested, he wonders how any of this could help them out. Next Lily asks Mildred about Rose's family. The change in her face is almost frightening. She narrows her eyes and turns her head away from them.

'Oh, I'm sure you don't want to put any of that business

in your book. Mm, mm, mm. People won't want to read about that.'

This time she is shaking her head with the 'mm's.

Lily nods reassuringly. 'Yes, Mildred, we know it was… the whole thing was just… Rose talked to you about it all the time, didn't she Leonard?' She turns to confirm it with him, more lies. 'But the publishers are keen to show how, you know, how Rose managed to rise above her difficult beginnings, turn her life into… They said it would help the readers to sympathise with her, if they knew some of the… if they could read about what really went on.'

It's an impressive speech and it has the intended effect. Leonard wonders if Mildred is secretly dying to speak about 'that business' anyway, and pleased to have been given permission. She talks with renewed enthusiasm.

'Well, it's got to be hard growing up in a household like that. My Willy wasn't a model husband, as you can imagine, but Rose's father… mm, mm, mm… you only had to look at him and you'd feel the back of his hand across your cheek. His skin was always so chilly… it was like being slapped with a fish. And her mother… mm… so sad when women let themselves go like that, not lady-like – you know? I heard her calling to little Rose from her bed once, yelling, "Mummy needs her special drink," as if it was medicine, getting Rose to fetch it for her. It weren't right. If it weren't for her little habit, she'd never have been able to put up with him. I don't know if Rose would have been better off if Mags had left him. Are you better off with one lummox parent or two? What do you reckon, love?'

Lily shrugs and smiles. There's a silence as Mildred fiddles with her top and hesitates before speaking decisively.

'There isn't anything else. That's your lot, mm, mm, mm.'

Lily and Leonard exchange a glance. There's something she isn't telling them.

'Are you sure there isn't anything…' Lily starts, but Mildred interrupts her forcefully.

'I can't see how writing this down is going to make any of it better. I don't feel right talking about it, I don't. You could be anyone, walked in off the street, and here I am showing you the family skeletons. No disrespect. It was a hard life for her. That's all I'm going to say – you can quote me on that.'

Leonard scribbles this down and puts quotation marks around it, forgetting for a moment that they're only playing at writing a book. Lily makes a final effort to get more out of her and asks if she knew a Peter, or a Lester. Mildred thinks for a while.

'I don't know no Peter. Lester was Willy's brother. He was the good 'un. The best of a bad lot. He was a real charmer, mm, mm, mm. I wish I'd have chosen Lester instead of my Willy. Life would've been so different… He was a good influence on that girl, went round the house regular, bought her good shoes for school. He didn't have any nippers of his own; his wife wasn't, you know, she couldn't. He treated Rose just like his own daughter. Maybe he put some of his goodness into her. Some of her kindness. God knows where else she would've got it from.'

She heaves herself out of her chair again, and after swapping a china turtle over with a china cat, she offers to get some family photos out for them to look at. They sit for another twenty minutes making the appropriate noises. Most of the photos are filled with people Leonard had never heard of until Lily's research – Mildred looking proud and thin in her wedding dress next to a dark-faced man, twelve near-identical photos of the same baby looking ugly in the way that only other people's new babies can, anonymous people in unfamiliar surroundings. Mildred names everyone in every photo, and Lily writes it all down – drawing a sketch of where everyone fitted in. There are only two of Rose, and they are so blurred he can't make out her face properly. He wants to study them for hours. There are a few of Lester, and he does look charming, baring his teeth at them, with his hair brylcreemed back. Did he take her out on trips to the seaside when her mother was having a bad day? Did he ever step in front of his brother and stop him from striking his daughter? Leonard feels a wave of gratitude towards him. What had it been like for his Rose to live in a household like that? And why had she never shared any of it with him, her own husband? He'd known every little thing about her – her hatred of radishes, what she said to God in her prayers, the way the stubble itched after she'd shaved her pubic hair into shape. She missed so much out – what good can it have done to keep it all inside of her? So many questions, so many questions.

Mildred is reluctant to let them go. She's offered them a nice bit of cheese on toast, some Battenberg, some cut up apple and a quick omelette before Lily firmly interrupts and tells her that they have another appointment to get to. At the door Mildred squeezes Leonard into a too-long hug, and he can't help focussing on the sensation of her bosom pressed up against his stomach. Once they get into the carpark he does a strange dance, waggling his arms and legs, as if he's Pickles shaking water from his fur. She's harmless enough, but Leonard hopes he'll never have to return. They don't talk about what she's said on the way home. They have a good-natured argument about pop music instead (Lily for, Leonard against) and soon Leonard's head is feeling heavy. He gives in to gravity and rests his cheek up against the seatbelt for a few seconds. He comes to an hour later, disoriented and fuzzy-headed. He asks Lily to drop him off at the Five Bells but doesn't invite her in with him. He wants to give his shaken-up thoughts a chance to settle, like one of those plastic snowstorm bubbles. The pub feels like a huge incubation tank sometimes. When he's inside, the problems of the world don't penetrate, as if the walls contain a magic substance that bends them back out again. For some of the regulars here, it's the haze of alcohol that keeps the problems away. But Leonard has never really been a big drinker. Who knows how it works?

Charlie is occupying his usual position at the bar – 'a part of the furniture' as he proudly says, 'I came free with the bar-stool, a special offer.' They nod to each other and Leonard settles his bottom onto the stool next to him and asks Suze for his usual. They speak about events in the 'outside world' for a while – the fuel crisis, the earthquake in Sumatra. Leonard can see why politicians and newsreaders and media people are comfortable inhabiting this world. Discussing the terrible things going on 'out there' and what can be done about them has the amazing effect of taking attention away from the things going on closer to home. Even a wayward son, a depressed wife or a dying mother-in-law can lose their potency if you compare them to global warming or to the next general election. His conversation with Charlie comforts him in this way until he feels ready enough to talk about his afternoon.

'Charlie?'

'Hnh?'

'I've been doing some investigating. About Rose.'

'Hnh?'

'You know I was saying before, last year, that some things had turned up that didn't make any sense. Well, I know you said I should leave it alone. But I couldn't, I tried. They kept eating away at me, like bloody wasp larvae. I had to do something. Lily's been helping me out.'

'Hnh.'

'We met an old dear up near Nottingham today, an aunt of Rose's. You should have seen her house, so many different colours and patterns, like a pile of sick.' Charlie chuckles at this – Leonard is tuned in to his sense of humour and put that one in especially for him. 'Rose had a terrible time of it when she was small, from what this woman was saying. Her mother drank, and her dad was a violent bastard. She had a terrible time. I had no idea.'

As he speaks this last sentence he hears the incredulity in his voice and realises for the first time just what a shock it all is.

'It makes more sense, now I know. That she wouldn't have wanted anything to do with them. How stupid could I have been, not realising for all those years. What an idiot.'

He's almost talking to himself and is surprised when Charlie speaks.

'We don't hear what we're not ready for.'

How wise Charlie is. He sits at this bar day after day, soaking in what people say to him, mulling it all over, and giving out little nuggets like that.

'Am I ready to hear it now, though? That's the question. There's more to find out, I'm sure of it. There's something we haven't come across yet, something... Maybe it's from her past, maybe not. Am I ready to know it? How do you know, Charlie?'

'Hnh. You just know, mate. If you're not, you'll stop your ears up, or you'll not quite catch it. Like me not knowing about Patrick, you know? I heard it eventually, even though it'd been staring me in the face for years.'

Leonard nods. Patrick is Charlie's son. He'd lived on his own for years and Charlie had often spoken about him in the pub, worrying about when he was going to settle down and give him a handful of grand-children to add to those his daughter had already produced. One day Charlie walked into the pub looking ashen and told Leonard that he'd finally worked it out – his son was 'one of those'. He'd talked to Leonard about 'them' before, with some mysterious theories about how they were a disaster for this country's economy. Leonard knew about Charlie's 'traditional values' – he'd admitted one night that they'd been drummed into him, quite often literally, by his strict father. For months Charlie had struggled with his revelation like a fish on a hook. Months and months. He'd talked it over with Leonard sometimes, dipping into the subject like a toe into too-hot water, the conversations ending with a kind of 'ouch' and a screwed up face. It took time, but it got easier. Leonard remembers the day he brought Patrick into the pub, a hand on his back, beaming, proud. He introduced him to people and dropped into the conversation that 'Patrick's partner is a doctor, you know, a doctor.' He worked his way up to approaching it directly, his son squirming a little in anticipation. Finally he seized the moment, when Leonard was talking about Rose's feet and how they were playing her up. 'You should ask Doug about that. That's Patrick's partner, the doctor. Shouldn't he, Patrick?' He remembers the shine that came to Patrick's eyes. He remembers Charlie noticing, and blustering that he needed a whiz, banging his son on the back so hard that he almost choked on his drink. He made a quick exit for what Leonard suspects was a little cry of his own in the toilets.

Leonard smiles. Nods. He'll know when he's ready. He catches Suze's eye and asks her for a packet of salt and vinegar crisps, which he tears down the sides and lays flat so Charlie can help himself. He's happy to be here, licking salt and vinegar from his fingers and listening in on other people's conversations. He's happy to be here with his mate. They lapse back into silence until time is called.

Chapter 16:
Flesh-coloured stockings

Leonard traces his usual morning circle around the grounds of Coburne, the soles of his shoes pressing on thousands of previous footsteps. He imagines leaving a layer of something shimmery on the ground behind him, like a snail's trail – different pastel colours for different days, gradually building up into a rainbow of glitter. He goes out of his way to visit the small *Magnolia stellata* near the lake. It's studded with broad but delicate-looking star-shaped white flowers, the petals ever-so faintly flushed with pink. He leans in to breathe the sweet, heady scent. He notices that the sun is picking up strength and thinks of one of Lily's sayings, delighting at how perfectly it matches his mood. 'The morning hour has gold in its mouth.' Things are coming alive again.

The quickening in his blood reminds him of how he felt a year after Rose died. He hadn't noticed how shrivelled and closed down he'd become until he started noticing spring. He can remember a day he went walking with Raine along the river, the sleeping twins being bumped along the path beside him in their broad buggy. The ducks were chatting away to each other. The green shoots of bulbs were emerging from the grass behind them, and an ice-cream van's tune chimed in the distance. He felt something shift inside him, as if light was getting in for the first time since that awful dark day. A single ray, slipping between heavy curtains and turning the specks of dust into bright dots.

It was a real turning point for him. He wanted to tell Raine at the time, but he wasn't sure she'd understand. She didn't seem to have even stepped into her own dark place yet. She was still outside the door, shuffling from foot to foot, just like she was in the hospital corridor that last night. She wouldn't come in, she wouldn't say goodbye. After Rose had said, 'I can't go first,' and closed her eyes for the last time, after Leonard had spent half an hour with her body, trying to memorise every last line on her face, the angle of her cheek-bones, the exact colour of her hair, knowing that someone would be taking her away from him soon, when he felt ready and stepped outside of the room, Raine was still on her plastic chair holding onto a cup of cold coffee. When he told her she'd simply nodded and said, 'I thought so.' There were tears, later, the kind of tears that slip out of you silently without you really wanting them to, and he saw her with red eyes and mussed-up hair a few times. But there was never any sobbing. Maybe she did get upset, when he wasn't there – maybe she thought she was protecting him. He was careful that she never saw him in a total mess – he was the parent after all. But it was her job, as his child, to lean on him. And she hadn't. He can't imagine her leaning on Ed either, not from what Leonard knows of him. He sighs and bends to pull a weed from a bed of peonies. Leonard has felt more distant than ever from her since that angry phone-call. They've spoken, but it's felt even more scripted than usual. This is where we ask each other how we are. This is where we tell each other we're fine. This is where we tell a couple of harmless anecdotes about our week. He hasn't spoken properly to Ed either. Leonard has made sure that there haven't been any opportunities. The truth is that he's still angry with her. Partly as a hangover of the power she wielded over him when she was younger, and partly because she refuses so steadfastly to speak about her mother.

His eyes catch on some winter jasmine. He could cut back their stems today, make sure that they produce a fresh batch of flowering wands for next year's show. His thoughts have wandered into uncomfortable territory, but that's what happens when you give yourself time and space. Things come up. It reminds him of the newly-retired businessmen and the smart young mothers who often visit Coburne. He learns a lot from standing on the side-lines, sweeping the leaves and keeping one ear open. No wonder young people these days fill every second of their time with things to do and places to go. Ballet lessons for the children, dinner parties, salsa classes, skiing holidays… It's easier than having to get in touch with the messy stuff that rises up inside them. They complain about the busy pace of life, the things they're expected to do, and seem utterly unaware that they're actually making that choice for themselves every day. It's a choice that protects them from having to face who-knows-what.

They've had some of the casualties here as volunteers – grey, broken-looking men and women from high powered jobs that Leonard can only imagine. Some of them manage to catch themselves before they de-rail altogether – going into work one day and demanding every Thursday off, not caring if their colleagues whisper about them behind their backs. Others have to reach breaking point before anything changes. They rely too much on the role they perform at work – they need to see themselves as someone who copes, someone who's powerful, invulnerable. These men and women usually keep going and keep going, making more and more mistakes at work and getting their secretaries and colleagues to cover up for them. Their spouses and squash partners grow more and more worried. Finally, one morning they wake up and discover that they physically can't get out of their beds. They panic, thinking they might be paralysed. The doctor is called. And he diagnoses a panic attack, something that has always happened to other people. Their whole lives collapse around them.

Leonard remembers one man in particular – Gordon Mackenzie. He was high up in some oil company before he ended up at Coburne. He was a large man, with orange hair and a bluish tint to his skin. After his breakdown an old family friend on the National Trust board suggested a gardening placement for four short days a week. The first time Leonard met him he tried on some of his old behaviour, making himself big and shaking Leonard's hand with a tight grip. He spoke down to Leonard, asking patronising questions about his career history and asking whether the job 'kept him intellectually challenged'. Leonard could smell the fear behind the arrogance, and held back from disliking him until they'd spent a little more time together. Gordon had kept up his pretence for a few days, and then one day Leonard had walked in on him in one of the greenhouses. He was sat like a collapsed puppet on a tiny stool with tears streaming down his cheeks. Leonard hadn't known what to do and had said he'd be back in ten minutes to give him a chance to gather himself together.

Gordon had been quiet that day, and the next. He'd started opening up a little, telling Leonard about the long hours he'd worked for so many years, and how there hadn't been any time to ask himself how he felt about his life. The crisis point came when his father had a sudden aneurism and died before he'd had a chance to use any of the money he'd spent his whole life saving. The luxurious holiday plans for their retirement, the grandchildren he'd been promising to spend more time with – it all turned to dust. Gordon couldn't escape the parallels with his own life, and it had been 'downhill from there'. He'd sat in his usual meetings and tried to concentrate, but he couldn't help noticing how meaningless it all was. He had to stop himself from laughing at the corporate speak: 'pro-activity', 'headcount benchmarks' and 'let's talk off-line about the blue-sky vision'. Whenever he'd felt stressed or disillusioned before, he'd gone out and booked his family an exotic holiday, but even after their trip to Ecuador he couldn't work up any enthusiasm for his sales targets. He'd quietly started to sabotage himself. The thing that most disturbed him, he told Leonard, was how long it had taken for anyone to notice. 'Was I really that expendable?' he asked. 'I hadn't made a single phone call or replied to an email for five weeks by the time they caught up with me. I'd played Patience on the computer pretty solidly for the past fortnight.' Coburne was Gordon's saviour. He'd stayed for seven months, and the last Leonard had heard, he was running a successful mail order business selling fair-trade chocolates from home, and spending more time with his wife and three dogs.

Leonard guesses that the same thing is happening to Raine. Her life is 'too busy' because she needs it to be. How can you help someone like that? Leonard can hear Charlie telling him the answer. You can't help them. Not until they're ready to hear it, not until they're ready to listen to themselves. It's infuriating. All you can do is wait on the sidelines, ready to catch them if and when they fall. If they want you to catch them, that is. If only it were as easy as that teenager in *Catcher in the Rye*, who dreamed of standing in tall rye grass at the edge of a cliff and catching children when they strayed too close to the edge. Sometimes it's too painful to be caught – it's easier to run off the cliff. He can imagine the little children swerving away from him as he tries to grab them, their faces calm and determined. He imagines catching one every so often and holding it, squealing, in his arms, and not being sure what to do with it next. How long can you hold on to someone before you let them go again to carry on heading where they're heading? What can you whisper in their ears to make them change their minds?

He notices that he's almost back at the staff room again. He meets Val on the path. She's just arrived and is wearing a smock-like, shocking pink coat. Leonard supposes it must be a fashion thing. They chat about the weather and walk the final ten yards to the staff-room together. As he opens the door, he's greeted by a strong whiff of bacon. He imagines taking bites of the air and tasting it. His stomach shoos away the last of the difficult, tangled thoughts, and he focuses on the easier dilemma of brown bread or white, brown sauce or tomato.

Later that week, he's at home, quietly watching a comedy sitcom on television, when there's a knock on the door. The knocking comes right in the middle of a hilarious scene involving a donkey and a bath, and he feels a shiver of annoyance. He drags his eyes away from the screen to look at the clock – it's 9.17pm. Who would be here at this time of night? Before he reaches the door, there's another spate of knocking, more frantic. He looks through his peep-hole and sees Glor standing on the doorstep. Glor? He looks behind her, but Pete isn't there. He opens the door and stands there for a few seconds before remembering his manners and stepping aside to let her come inside. He asks her if everything is alright, and she says 'not really'. She doesn't look upset, just a little flustered, maybe – there are bright red dots on her cheek, and her hands are fluttering around her like moths. He asks her to have a seat and offers her a hot drink. She asks if he's got anything stronger. He's got an old half-bottle of whisky somewhere and the tins and jars in the cupboard clink as he rummages around for it. He pours a little for each of them, imagining she might be embarrassed to be drinking alone, being a woman. Although those kinds of rules don't seem to apply any more these days. They sit there for a few minutes sipping whisky diluted in lemonade. It actually tastes pretty good – Leonard is enjoying the warm rub of it on his tongue when she finally speaks.

'I need to talk to you.' As she speaks, she fiddles with her necklace, twirling one of the orange beads around and around. Leonard sits back in his chair.

'OK, Glor, I'm listening.'

After such a confident start, she seems unsure of what to say next. Leonard wonders if he should try and help her out, give her a prompt, but he has no idea what she's about to say. She might be ill? Could it be something about her children? But why is she here? She opens her mouth several times, shuts it, and finally settles on a word to start with.

'Leonard.' It's a statement, not a question.

'Glor?'

'We go back a long way now... we... me and Pete. You see, me and Pete, we're...' It's a tortuous process. She changes gear again, and her next words are another statement, something she can be sure about.

'Me and Pete don't get on.'

They've had a terrible argument, Leonard thinks. She's going to ask me for my advice. He remembers flicking through an article in a magazine at Lily's house a few weeks ago – 'Ten secrets to a happy marriage' – and he starts racking his brain for what they were. One of them involved financial matters, and maybe something about never shaving your legs in front of your husband…

'Sorry to hear that, Glor, I didn't realise things were like that at the moment.'

'It's not at the moment, Leonard. We don't get on, period. We never have really. It's like we – it's like we both made an agreement to pretend, years ago, before we even got married. The others were all pairing up, and we didn't feel as if we had much time left. We were getting older. We both found ourselves in the same, you know… it seemed churlish to want 'love' as well, to expect that we'd have feelings for each other. Maybe we thought it'd grow, the way you hear about it growing in these Asian marriages, you know, what do you call them.'

She pronounces Asian as 'Hasian'.

'Arranged?' Leonard offers.

'Yes, those. But it never did. If anything, it just got worse, the soft feelings we had for each other in the first place just… it got more… complicated. It didn't come natural to either of us. It was OK, we've both lived with it all this time. We didn't know any different.' She stops, sighs. 'But then we got to know you and Rose. We watched you when you were out together. I saw something on her face that I'd never seen on mine, a feeling I'd never felt. That she was loved. That she was loved.'

Leonard feels a small wave of sadness, for himself, and for her.

'And then… and now…'

She seems to be approaching a peak of uncomfortable-ness. She sits on the edge of her chair with a straight back, poised. Then she suddenly stands up and lunges forwards. Leonard thinks maybe she's feeling ill, but she moves in towards him, fast, crouches beside him and puts a heavy hand on his shoulder. Her face is diving in towards his, and he realises what is happening and pulls away just in time – her mouth catches him on the ear, squashing it, and he feels a warm wetness. He lifts himself up out of the sofa and moves away from her, and she falls into the gap he's left, awkwardly, her skirt riding up and revealing the top of her stockings, flesh coloured and too tight. She makes a noise as she falls, 'aiieee', a mournful sound, as if she's in pain. He stands awkwardly in the middle of the room – he isn't sure what to do with himself. He wants to walk out of the door; he wants to wipe the saliva from his ear. He expects her to bolt at any second, but she just lies there on the sofa, one foot in the air, not looking at him. They both hold their bodies still, as if they're waiting for the music to start again. The embarrassment is so thick in the room that he imagines he would hardly see his own hand in front of his face. He crosses his arms tightly across his chest.

'Gloria, are you alright?'

He speaks so quietly, he wonders if she can hear him. He doesn't move towards her. Her eyes are shut, and her whole neck is a deep pink. She's breathing more quickly, in little gasps. She pulls her legs in towards her, foetus-like, and cups a palm tightly over her eyes. And then she starts to cry. It's mostly silent, her body shaking to a syncopated, unpredictable rhythm – There. Wait… there. There. It's almost like she's having convulsions. He's still standing there, his body still bent sideways from the movement that took him away from her.

Pickles chooses this moment to lift his head from sleep and yap at Leonard, a question yap, 'are you there?' He's curled up on a carefully folded blanket next to the television. Pickles often changes his favourite snoozing-spots, and Leonard has been known to lift him and slide a doggy bed or blankets underneath him to make him more comfortable. Spoilt dog. Leonard glances over at him, and this is all the encouragement Pickles needs – he bounds over to stand at his feet, looking up at him lovingly. Leonard wants to laugh. He remembers when he and Rose had made love for the first time and afterwards they had looked over to see their cat George in the doorway, watching the proceedings with an extremely serious expression on his face. It was if he were saying, 'I really don't approve of this, you know.' They'd giggled and giggled. He catches this thought and throws it back to where it came from – there are more important matters at hand. He stays where he is and calls to her again, asking her if she'd like some more whisky. She says no, angrily, through her tears. She starts speaking in between the spasms, the sudden intakes of breath. He can hardly understand her.

'I shouldn't have been... uhh, such... uhh, an idiot... uhh, uhh, ... why would ... you... want uhh, me... it's... just...'

She carries on as if she's talking to herself. Maybe she is. Leonard feels his back aching from the position he's holding – he imagines himself in some kind of modern dance troupe, or doing some life modelling for a circle of students. He eases himself down into the chair she'd been sitting in before she... well, before she pounced on him. He rubs his ear vigorously with the back of his hand, as if scratching one of those unbearably itchy itches inside your nose. How does he get himself into these situations? How dare you have left me, Rose, he thinks for the millionth time. It's all very well for you to stand up there laughing. It's not very funny down here.

After a while, Glor's breathing seems to slow down, and eventually her body seems to ask her to move position, and she slowly manoeuvres herself round and props herself up on one arm, looking puffy and squinty-eyed. She glances up at Leonard, covers her face with both hands and cries a little more. She takes a deep, slow breath.

'I told him I was leaving him.'

Her voice is thick, choked. And before he's worked out a response to this, his phone goes. It's all too much – he just wants to go up to bed with his crossword book and a chocolate biscuit. He goes out to the hall and picks it up.

'She's there, isn't she?' a male voice says. 'Tell her I'm coming over. I won't be long.'

Pete has finished his sentence and hung up before Leonard places his voice. He sighs, puts the phone down and goes back to the living room.

'It was him, wasn't it? Is he coming over?' she asks.

Leonard nods and sits back down in his chair again feeling weary. None of this has anything to do with him. Their stupid marriage... and Glor is trying again now, one last chance – asking him if there's any way he could ever, if there's anything she could do to... Her voice is whiny, pathetic. He doesn't want to see her ever again. He even briefly considers throwing her out, just opening the front door and asking her to leave. Lordy, lordy. That's what Rose used to say, when things got really bad. When she went into labour, and when they got caught speeding because they didn't want their fish and chips to go cold. He doesn't know where she got it from – it sounds more like something a traditionally built African woman might say. Lordy, lordy. He mouths it a few times to himself before noticing that Glor is waiting for an answer.

'No, sorry, Glor. There isn't any chance'.

He doesn't soften it with any excuses – he needs to be clear. He watches Glor's face go blank, and she sinks down into murkier waters, coming to rest in a deeper level of sadness. They sit in silence. He preferred it when she was crying.

When Pete gets there, it's all very civilised. He shakes Leonard's hand at the door and Leonard is a little sad to notice how Pete has taken it for granted that nothing has happened between him and his wife. He's certain that Leonard has rejected her. Pete walks into the living room without looking at her and asks her to get her things together. She does this without a fuss, looking like a told-off child, all the anger and desperation melted away. Glor doesn't meet Leonard's eyes as they leave, and Pete shakes his hand again, squeezing hard and saying 'thanks, mate'. Leonard can't remember him ever calling him mate before. As they drive off into the darkness, Leonard sees Glor turning to her head sideways to look out of the window. Will they say anything to each other during the journey? What will happen when they get home? Will there be violence? Tenderness? A terrible silence?

'There but for the grace of God, Mister P. There but for the grace of God,' Leonard says to his dog, and Pickles agrees entirely.

Leonard prepares them a small snack each – a few cubes of cheese for Pickles, and a packet of instant noodles, 'beef' flavour, for himself. As he's pottering about in the kitchen he discusses the evening's events with Pickles. They both agree that it must have been brewing in Glor for some time – her strange moods of late are making a bit more sense. He asks Pickles whether he thinks he could be accused of leading Glor on in any way. The rascal keeps quiet about this one, but does suggest that Leonard focuses on getting a good night's sleep before thinking about it in the morning. He's always right, just like Charlie. He goes back to the easy comfort of the television, and forgets all about it. The next morning he can't quite believe the whole thing really happened, until he finds Gloria's poppy-red lipstick on the floor.

Chapter 17:
The cat ran and the tail swung

As March becomes April and April becomes May, the plants do their usual seasonal shuffle. The daffodils die out, and the Wisteria start to drip their gorgeous, blowsy petals. The new bed Leonard planted out last autumn starts gaining bulk like a blossoming teenage girl. The visitors start arriving in a broader stream, and Leonard is pleased to see them back. He loves to hear them marvel at what he and his colleagues have helped to create. He gets particular pleasure from watching the older ones (and some of the younger ones) who've learnt to slow down and really look at things – the ones who aren't more concerned about how long it's going to take them to drive home through the traffic on the M4.

He doesn't hear anything from Pete and Glor for a fortnight, and then a postcard drops through his front door, full of the usual meaningless postcard phrases – 'good food' and "lots of sunshine' and 'hope it's not raining back at home'. It's a few seconds before he realises it was posted from Portugal, before Glor jumped on him – it must have got lost in the post somewhere. Communication begins to get easier with Raine again – she seems to have perked up at the prospect of a new position coming up at work. She thinks it'll be less stressful and is planning on applying for it. Ed seems happier too – when Leonard's been round there he's noticed little looks passing between him and Raine, and last weekend they held hands on the sofa. Leonard is hugely relieved – he isn't sure what's causing the change, but as long as she's happy, then he's happy.

He still hasn't spoken to Raine about the investigation he's carrying out with Lily. This has been pottering along. Lily and Leonard have started to work their way down his list of the people in Rose's life. They'd met up with a few of them, and had phone conversations with a few more. Lily has managed to track down a couple more relatives – a niece and a second cousin. The niece was rude on the phone and said she wanted nothing more to do with 'that family'. They met her second cousin at a service station with her bullish looking husband. She was in her mid-forties and had her first child on the way, saying it was 'better late than never'. She was so huge, Leonard was afraid she might go into labour before the end of their coffee. Although she was very keen to be helpful, she didn't tell them anything they didn't already know. She said that the Smiths were known as a 'troubled family'. She remembers her mum referring to Rose as 'that poor child'. Her mum had often told the second cousin that Rose's parents didn't deserve her. Apart from a 'silly phase' when she was younger, when she refused to go to school for a while, Rose had been 'good as gold'. No-one in the family had heard anything from her after she was old enough to leave home.

One ex-colleague, Margot, told them a story about a patient Rose had developed a special relationship with. She was a young anorexic girl, and Rose had spent as much time as she could spare by her bedside. They 'whispered into each other's ears' as if they were hatching a plot. Rose had brought in novels for her, and home-baked cakes to try and tempt her more successfully than the tasteless hospital food. Margot said that there was something about their relationship that 'gave her the creeps', before she apologised to Leonard for 'speaking out of turn'. When this girl had finally inexorably starved herself to death, Rose had broken down in front of everyone, saying she should have tried harder to keep her alive, that it was her fault. Margot said it was 'most unlike her'. She'd gone to the girl's funeral, and she refused to nurse anyone in the same bed for months afterwards. Margot was surprised that Rose hadn't spoken to Leonard about her. Another old work colleague confirmed that Rose used to take Thursday mornings off work, every week as long as they'd worked together, and another colleague from later on remembered the rough date that the Thursdays had changed to Tuesdays. The reasons Rose gave for this time off were mostly similar – to have some time for herself, to catch up on things, it was simply 'a rule she had for herself'.

They had a long conversation with one of Rose's good friends, Linda Scoles, over a cup of tea. Leonard enjoyed chatting her so much that they left with promises to keep in touch. Leonard had told her the truth about the situation, and as a result she'd trusted him with information the others might not have shared, for fear of being disloyal to Rose. She said that Rose sometimes did have funny moods. She was usually so kind and giving, but when she got into what they referred to in the staff-room as one of her 'huffs', it was best to stay away. Once she'd even made one of the new girls cry by being short with her about something or other. Lily asked Linda if she'd ever said anything about a Peter. Linda thought for a while and said 'Peter March'. She explained how she'd been sitting watching TV with Rose one day, and they'd said the name 'Peter March' on the news. It was a local news item about someone who'd been mugged and beaten up in the park. She'd heard Rose catch her breath and when she'd looked over at her she'd gone 'as pale as a sheet'. Rose had mouthed 'Peter March' once, and when Linda had said 'what's wrong?' she'd been shushed until the end of the news report. When she'd asked Rose about it afterwards, Rose said she'd made a mistake, she'd thought it was a different name. Linda said she still seemed pretty shaken up.

Leonard and Lily had received new snippets of information like this every week or so – more facts to add to Lily's bulging folder. Leonard knows they'll have to put it all together soon, to see if they can come to any conclusions. He's been putting it off.

That weekend, Leonard has agreed to have the twins for the day again. He wants to take them out somewhere, but he doesn't have the confidence to cope with both of them on his own. So he ropes in Lily – she responded to his request with fake fear by rolling her eyes and fanning herself with a magazine. They decide on swimming. The twins don't get to do much of this, as Ed is a bit of a wimp around water (he has a horror of 'getting it in his ears') and Raine is unnecessarily paranoid about how she looks in a swimsuit. Lily suggests a pool she's been to a couple of times with her own grandchildren. They set off with a car-full of air bands and rubber rings and goggles and towels and various bits of kit that Raine had left them with 'just in case' – the twins favourite plastic beakers, some story books, potties... It's all very exciting for a day-trip, thinks Leonard, but thank goodness he only has himself to be responsible for, these days.

During the journey, Lily teaches the twins to sing a Swedish nursery rhyme, 'the cat and its tail'. The three of them sing it together – the twins mouthing most of it at first, being sure of only the last word on each line. They build up their confidence and get faster and louder and by what feels like the hundredth time they're word perfect.

> I'll sing a little song
> about the little cat:
> he was to chase his own tail,
> but wouldn't catch it.
> The cat ran and the tail swung,
> the cat ran and the tail swung.
> This story isn't long,
> we can sing it once again.

By the time they reach the car-park they've reached an excruciating pitch of excitement and Leonard has to ask them to sit quietly for a minute before they get out of the car. Lily recommends that before they get changed into their things, they go through to the restaurant on the second floor, to look down at the pool from the viewing panels. The twins press their button noses up against the glass and are quieter than they've been all day. There's a large pirate ship in the middle of the pool, which is surrounded by smaller pools, waves, fake rain, plastic boats...: it's a Technicolor, plastic-and-chlorine heaven for children. Lily offers to take the children with her into the changing room, and Leonard gives her a large fake kiss on her forehead and calls her a marvellous woman.

Leonard chooses the least soggy-looking changing room and struggles into his old navy trunks. He spends some time examining his body in the full-length mirror, looking at himself from different angles and trying to work out what kind of shape he's in for his age. He's not very tanned yet – it's not the right time of year – in a few months time he'll be the colour of a hazelnut. Flesh always looks a little more attractive when it's been baked like that, even if they are saying now that it's bad for you. His muscles are still visible under his skin, although they don't quite bulge as they used to. They've become more sinewy as he's got older, like tight elastic bands. There's a little reservoir of fat at his stomach which is almost folding over the band of his swimming trunks. He can blame that on Lily, he reckons, and the perfect roast potatoes recipe he can't stop cooking for himself. He turns from side to side and flexes his arms... it's a long time since he's looked this closely at his body. He feels a little guilty about neglecting it for so long – there could have been a lump growing somewhere, or a mole changing colour.

'Sorry, old chap,' he says to his body. 'I'll try and keep a better eye on you.'

He waves goodbye to his reflection and braces himself to tackle the lockers. He spends some time fiddling with the coin slot and key before he gives in and asks a small boy to help him.

He splashes through the shallow water troughs and steps into the warm chemical-laden atmosphere of the pool. It's like exiting a plane into tropical heat. Lily is already at the edge of the water with the twins, who are dipping in one toe at a time and squealing with excitement and pretend cold. Lily looks around and he puts up a hand, feeling a little self-conscious with so much of his flesh on show. Her costume in Himalayan Poppy blue – it covers her top like a T-shirt and ends in a kind of frilly skirt thing. It's not fair that women are allowed to be so covered up, and it's an unfair advantage to have that elastic material to keep all her bits in place. His next thought is that he's overstepped a mark by thinking about her bits. He flushes a little and starts to do a little hopping dance to distract himself. The twins are happy to see him and start shouting 'Gran-da! Gran-da!' and he feels a wave of pride pass through him. These children wouldn't be here if it wasn't for him. They're packed with his fine genetic material – a Smith Wishford hybrid, Smithsonia x Wishfordia.

All four of them have a great time horsing around in the water. There's a lot of mild splashing, and the boys only have to be reigned in a couple of times when they get water into a little girl's eye, and when they start running on the side of the pool and Leonard can see a nasty accident unfolding in his mind. The boys invent a game involving the rain jets, and as far as he can gather, it involves seeing how long you can stand underneath the fine drops of water without making a sound, and then swapping over. They call it the 'umbrella game'. Leonard loves how children become so utterly absorbed in their play, in fantasy. We forget how to do it as adults, he thinks. As he expects, the grown-ups get tired of the water before the twins do, and Lily gives them two ten-minute warnings before they drag them out. They head off a crying fit with the promise of something nice to eat upstairs where they can look at the people swimming from 'up in the sky'. Lily volunteers to get them dry and dressed as well. Leonard's amazed when once again he finds them waiting for him in the corridor when he emerges. Lily and Leonard happily sit and drink their tea while the twins munch on their various chemically-coloured, flavoured and scented foods. Leonard enjoys watching a baby and her mother in the pool. She's got the baby in her arms and is dipping her into the water and then scooping her out again, looking directly into her face and sharing everything. The baby's eyes are wide and she's beaming and chuckling.

Leonard volunteers to drive home and before long not just the twins, but Lily are totally out for the count. The car smells of chlorine and clean bodies. The tune of 'The Cat and His Tail' goes round and round in his mind, just like the poor dizzy cat. He listens to the three of them breathing and another of Lily's expressions comes to his mind. He's 'floating on small clouds'.

When they get home, he rouses Lily, and between them they carry the dead weight of the sleeping twins onto the sofa. Buddy wakes up asking for 'doggie', but when Leonard deposits Pickles onto his lap, he looks most disappointed and says 'no, DOGgie'. Leonard says 'this IS the doggie', but before things deteriorate further Lily interrupts by bringing in the video they'd brought with them about a plasticine dog called, imaginatively, 'Doggie'. They put on the video, and Leonard gives Pickles some extra fussing to compensate for his hurt feelings. Leonard asks Lily to wait until Raine has collected the twins before she gets out her blue folder, feeling a little guilty about involving her in his deception. He meets Raine from the car and warns her that Lily is inside, to give her a chance to compose her face. She brings noise and fast jerky movement into the house with her – the children spin around her like tiny dervishes. She shakes Lily's hand curtly and looks into her broadly smiling face for only a fraction of a second before apologising and turning away to tend to the twins. Then she busies herself with gathering the twins' things up and putting them into bags, answering Lily's polite questions about the twin's beautiful jumpers with small clots of words – forced, short. She shakes off Leonard's offer of coffee, and when Leonard presses her, she refuses with something approaching annoyance. There's a horrible moment of silence after all the bustle, when the twins are safely strapped in and Raine is sat with the engine running and her window wound down. Leonard breaks it by bending down to kiss her on the forehead, tenderly. Raine nods curtly at Lily once more before almost screeching away from the kerb.

They both stand there on the pavement, as if she's left a cloud of dust behind and they're watching it settle. They fold up their arms against the cold. Leonard makes a growling noise in his throat, and turns to apologise to Lily for his daughter's behaviour. Lily puts up her hand towards him, palm forward, and he stops – he doesn't need to explain. They unfold their arms and head back inside.

Leonard feels a bit flummoxed as to how they might draw some conclusions from what they've got so far. He can't decide if some of the little things they've got written down are even relevant. Rose had refused to ever wear a watch – was it just because she didn't like the feel of metal against her wrist? Or is it the crucial bit of information that everything else hinges from? Lily says she's been giving it some thought. She reminds him of the thousands of detective novels she's read in her time. She suggests that they make a simple list of all the things they've found out about Rose that are 'new' to Leonard. A way of 'pulling the pearls out of the pile of straw', she says. He isn't sure if this is another Swedish proverb or one of Lily's own. So that's what they do – starting with two fresh pieces of paper – one for the things they can think of no logical explanations for, and one with the facts that are potentially irrelevant to their investigation. There's a lot of debate about what should go on the second sheet rather than the first. They end up with a short list of the unexplainable facts:

Taking Tuesday afternoons (or Thursdays) off every week

Her mother is still alive after all

She could have grown her hair if she'd wanted to

The second page is almost full, and much less neat. Lily writes it almost as a flow of consciousness, with little questions and lines and arrows to join various facts together. It looks like Leonard's brain feels. It starts:

Violent father, alcoholic mother

Always wanted to sit on the front carriage in trains, didn't say why

The blue handbag – train ticket to Didcot

Friends with anorexic girl

Peter March?

Summer window, Peter etc (from Rose's mum)

Had a funny phobia about earwigs

As Leonard reads the second list he realises just how much he's shared with Lily. She probably knows more about Rose than anyone else, except for him of course. They spread the lists on the kitchen table between them and Lily announces a need for caffeine. She pushes her chair back and busies herself brewing them a fresh pot. She uses the plunger she bought him for Christmas; she'd told him she couldn't bear his 'instant cat's piss' any more. She rummages around in his cupboard and makes an 'aha!' noise when she falls upon some jammy dodgers, waving them in front of him and tearing them open. She sits back down and they both let their eyes rest on the pieces of paper – thinking, munching and sipping. Eventually Leonard thinks he may as well say it out loud. He takes a deep breath.

'There's still only one explanation I can think of, Lily. It's what you said before, when I shot you down. That she was having an affair all those years.'

They sit absorbing the impact of this, and Leonard notices how much of a relief it's been to shape his worst fears into this sentence. He breathes a long slow stream of air in and then out of his lungs. It's not really a sigh of sadness, more a letting go of the tension. He continues.

'I don't want to believe it of her. It doesn't fit with the Rose I knew. But at least if we found out... Maybe she had her reasons. With a past like that – maybe it helped her to keep it back, a way of – looking after – of making sure she didn't damage our life together. I'm not sure how to say it. Do you know what I mean?'

'It could've been a kind of... a sort of survival mechanism for her?'

'Yes, something like that, I suppose.'

They are quiet for a while, and again Leonard decides to put his thoughts into words, where he can get a better look at them.

'The question I'm asking myself now, is... well, do I want to know for sure? I could stop here, put this stuff all away, knowing that Rose had another side to her, a different part of her that I'll never know about. I could learn to live with the possibility. But do I want to know for sure that she had someone else all these years? That's the question I'm asking myself.'

'Hmm. I can't help you there, Leonard... I don't want you to think I'm taking over on ... it's your thing to do or not do, just because I'm getting carried away doesn't mean... It's a tricky one. You won't know until you get there, I suppose. If only we could...'

As she talks, stringing together more words than is strictly necessary, Leonard tunes her out. He imagines having the same conversation with Rose. What would she have wanted him to do? It still seems an important question to consider, even though she's gone. It's her memory he's honouring somehow – not just what's left of her in his own head, but what's left of her in the rest of the world: her essence. What would he say to her if she was sitting across from him now, dunking her jammy dodgers in her coffee? He'd want to tell her that he's able to accept it – whatever it is she did behind his back. And so he has his answer. He wants to know everything, so he can accept it, swallow it down – however difficult that is, however much it sticks in his throat. Lily finally notices that he's lost in his own thoughts and stops talking. When he looks over to her she's ready, waiting, a question on her face. He nods decisively, and she understands.

'Right,' she says. 'Let's go as far as we... lets go to the end with this.'

They both agree that the most promising place to start is the name that keeps cropping up, now that they have a surname as well. Peter March. They'll start in Didcot and move outwards from there. They have a look in the phone book straight away. There are four P Marches listed, and Lily tries the numbers while Leonard sits on the stairs. She reaches two answer machines belonging to a Paul and a Patrick, and speaks directly to another Paul and a Patricia. Leonard 'isn't a part of the 21st Century yet' as Lily puts it, and doesn't have a computer, so she says she'll have a look on the sites she's been using for the family tree. When it's all been decided, there doesn't seem to be much else to do except put the folder away and wash up the coffee cups. Lily wipes the crumbs from the table with a flat hand and challenges

Leonard to a game of shit-head before she goes. He gets out the pack of cards and deals onto the kitchen table. As usual their competitive streaks rise to the challenge and Leonard has to tell Lily to quieten down or he'll have complaints from the neighbours. Eventually Leonard 'lets her win'.

Chapter 18:
A Magnificent Moustache

Later that week, Pete calls Leonard and asks him in a grave voice if he can meet him in the pub to 'discuss something'. Leonard tries to get more detail out of him but Pete says he'd rather wait until he can see 'the whites of his eyes'. It'll only be him, no Gloria. He wonders if Leonard would mind coming out this evening, if he isn't too busy? The only item on Leonard's schedule that evening is a repeat of Time Team he thinks he's already seen, so he agrees to meet Pete in an hour. While he's getting ready to go out, he wonders if Pete is planning on having a go at him, maybe accuse him of leading Glor on. The visual image that accompanies the thought is so unlikely that he dismisses it with a curl of amusement. He asks Pickles what he thinks it might be all about, but Pickles has even less of an idea than he does, or at least if he does know, he isn't saying. Leonard doesn't like walking into situations where he doesn't know what to expect. It reminds him of when Rose used to tell him over breakfast that she 'wanted a word with him' after work. He'd imagine all kinds of terrible things all day – illness, accusations – and it would turn out she'd had enough of him not changing the empty toilet-roll, or wanted some money for some new curtains. He's grateful that Pete suggests they meet at the Five Bells – at least he'll be on home ground. He feels more comfortable there than he does anywhere else.

When Leonard gets to the Bells, Pete is already sitting at the table furthest away from the bar with an empty pint glass in front of him. He's wearing a shirt and a spotted tie, as if he's waiting for a business associate. He stands up and nervously wipes his palms on the sides of his trousers before holding out a hand. As they shake and nod murmured 'alright's, Leonard has a strong urge to twirl Pete's hand over his head and sweep him into a pirouette. He's never been much good at keeping a straight face in situations that require one. There's something perverse in him that wants to do a little jig or pull a face. He remembers an embarrassing incident at one of Rose's colleague's funerals, when he told the widower an inappropriate joke about a dead rabbit. The poor man had managed a weak smile, but Rose had glared daggers at him and given him an earful on the way home.

Leonard leaves Pete to fetch them a drink, saying a brief hello to Charlie's 'hnh'. There's no need to explain to him why they're not coming to sit with him – sometimes it's appropriate to share their space, and sometimes it's not. Leonard sits back down on the sagging seat and sets down a pint in front of each of them. Pete wipes his hands on his trousers again before he takes hold of his glass, catching Leonard's eye guiltily before looking down again. He takes a jerky sip and a little escapes down his chin. He rolls his eyes at his clumsiness and his cheeks colour. It's painful for Leonard to watch him squirm, and he smiles and looks away. He pretends to be interested in a young lad playing the pinball machine as Pete wipes his chin and shifts about on his seat. Eventually he seems to settle down, and he clears his throat theatrically.

'I need some advice, Leonard.'

This isn't how Leonard had expected the conversation to start. Pete continues.

'I'm not sure if I can speak to you in confidence, that is, if you'd... if you wouldn't mind?'

'Of course, Pete.'

'It's just that I know you know Glor better than you know me, really. I don't know if it's right for me to be asking you. But I didn't know who else to talk to. You're the only one who knows... who knows how bad things are. I'm assuming she told you about what goes on in our marriage.'

'She said you were having some problems, Pete, she did say that.'

Pete rolls his eyes at this, sighs.

'Some problems. Yes, that's one way of putting it, eh?'

Pete pauses and examines his nails, with his palm facing him and his fingers curled forward like a woman. He makes a tutting noise and asks if he can take a match from Leonard's box on the table between them. He sits for a minute or two, scraping specks of grey dirt from the neatly clipped half-moons. Leonard watches, entranced. Pete hesitates about whether to put the match back in the box when he's finished, and decides on putting it in his pocket. He lifts his head up from where it's been bowed for the conversation so far and looks Leonard in the eyes.

'I do love her, you know.'

He waits for a response, needing Leonard to believe him. It's a surprising thing for Leonard to hear him say, but he can see that Pete's sincere and so he nods his affirmation.

'Despite all her faults. I do love her. And she loves me too, in her own way, I'm sure of it. If she'd let herself, if I was able to...'

His head droops again, a snowdrop on its stalk. He's speaking so quietly that Leonard can hardly hear him. What is Pete expecting from him? He tries to stop his attention floating off as Pete starts to speak again.

'It was never the best start to a marriage. Neither of us were, well, overenthusiastic about it. It suited us – it got us both out of a hole, I suppose. Not like you and Rose, eh? Not quite Romeo and Juliet, no, not that.' He sounds sad as he says this. 'But we got on alright. It was like we'd made a pact – "we've got each other now, make the most of it." "Count yourself lucky." And I did feel lucky, to have someone... Glor's got her fair share of faults, I'll give you that, but who doesn't, and she can be awful kind. Some of the things she's done for me over the years... you'd be surprised, Leonard, you really would.'

He looks off into the distance, remembering these small kindnesses.

'And God knows, I'm no perfect catch myself. That's the truth, it really is.'

Leonard nods at this before he realises what he's doing and shakes his head instead, holding up his hand. Pete chuckles – it lets some of the tension out of the conversation like air out of a football. Then he frowns and takes a slow breath in, as if gathering force to put behind the difficult words coming next.

'I've never been very good at it, you see, letting her know how I feel. About her, I mean. I've never... I've never even said...'

His voice cracks a little. He puts his head on one side as if nudging something, makes a 'you know' expression with his face. I love you. He's never even said he loves her. Poor old Pete. Poor Glor. Leonard nods his understanding.

'She said it, to start with. All the time. But there's only so many times you can say it into fresh air. That's what she

said, when she stopped. I can't even say she looks nice, stuff
like that, that normal husbands do. She got a raw deal with
me, Leonard, she really did.'

Leonard has never heard Pete say so much at once
before. He wonders if he's had more than one pint. He thinks
it might be time for him to say something and scrabbles
around for something wise in response to what he's been
told. He opens his mouth but Pete hasn't finished.

'I don't know. I know what you're going to say to me.
That I should just bite the bullet. Start saying it, to make up
for all those lost years. Buy her flowers, that kind of stuff
that women like. But I'm scared, Leonard. I'm scared that
she won't want me any more. Maybe she never did, eh? What
should I do?'

Leonard waits a bit, as an experiment, hopeful. Finally
he says 'Well...', not sure how he's going to end the sentence.
And once again Pete interrupts him.

'There's no easy way out of this one, is there? If I
don't take that risk... It's all shrivelled up at the moment,
our marriage is. Like an old nectarine, all tiny and wrinkled.
I need to put some water onto it, to give it a chance to come
back to life. I've nothing to lose, have I? It's not worth saving,
this dried up thing we've got right now. Not worth saving.'

He's almost talking to himself and shaking his head.
When Leonard lifts up his glass, Pete looks up suddenly, as
if surprised to see him still there. He smiles a watery smile
and looks at his own pint, twisting his mouth in a brief show
of disgust and pushing it away from him.

'Thank you, mate, you've been a real help. I know what
I've got to do. I'm glad I called you, I wasn't sure if... I'm not
sure how things will... I'm not sure what...' He sighs. 'But
I'll give it my best shot, eh? All there is for it. Eh?'

Leonard nods and puts a hand on Pete's upper arm. He

tries to will some strength into him, imagines it pulsing into Pete like electricity. When he pulls his hand away, he feels tired. Pete seems ready to go, and they stand up to shake hands goodbye. After the bell on the door rings, Leonard sits at the table for a few minutes to mull things over. What was it he'd said to Pete that was so useful? He must be better at giving advice than he thought he was. He drains his drink and approaches the bar. A pineapple juice is in order, and some good-natured arguing with Charlie about whatever comes into their heads.

He hears from Lily the following week, as the Rock Roses at work are beginning their silvery-pink show. She tells him she's managed to track down several Peter Marches living in or around Didcot. She'd weeded out anyone who'd died more than five years ago – she said they could always look at them later on if they ran out of leads. Finally the twenty year old Peter March and the two Peter Marches who died more recently, one at 93 and the other at a home for people with learning disabilities, didn't have much potential as Rose's secret amours. That left her with one Peter March – a man a few years older than Rose. He's ex-directory, but she's managed to get his address – he lives quite close to the station. They have a conversation about how they should approach him. Leonard is keen to tell the truth, but Lily says he's not likely to be honest if he'd been having an affair with Rose all those years and is faced with her widowed husband. Lily tells him she'll think something up, and they plan a visit for the following evening.

In the car on the journey there, the atmosphere is strained. Leonard has insisted they bring Pickles, and he begins to regret it as the hot dog ricochets between the two half-open back windows, sticking his head out as far as it'll go and panting. He only runs to one mood in the car – excitable. Lily tries to make conversation, talking about her grandchildren and then a woman down her road who's having an art exhibition, but it falls on barren ground. Leonard smokes three pre-rolled roll-ups, one after the other. When they arrive, Leonard promises Pickles they won't be long and leaves him with a silver dish of water and all the windows open a crack. Lily takes his arm as they walk along the pavement, dodging 'dogs' doings' as Rose used to call them. They count the house numbers and stop in front of a small terrace painted a dark shade of grey. One of the upstairs windows is boarded up. There's no front garden, just dirty gravel on concrete with weeds sprouting up at the edges. Could this be the place? Did Rose arrive here every week, knocking on the door and waiting with as much anticipation as he has in his stomach right now? It's a long time before the door opens, and when it does it only opens a crack. A pair of green eyes peer at them suspiciously.

'Mr. March?' Lily asks.

'Who's asking?' His voice is rasping and high pitched.

'We're from the regional department of environmental welfare. I'm Lily Sorenson and this is my colleague, Mr. Leonard Mutch.'

She flashes him her library card and then pulls out a pen and notebook.

'It's just a very brief matter, we'll need to come inside. We won't need much of your time.'

'You'd better come in then, I suppose,' he mutters, and opens the door wider.

They're faced with an old man with a white moustache and thick smeary glasses, in tracksuit bottoms and an oversized faded T-shirt saying 'Speedway Extravaganza 1989'. Lily and Leonard exchange a quick glance – could this be him? Surely not. Maybe twenty years ago... but the ticket in Rose's handbag was only dated a few months before she died. Would she have carried on seeing him for charity? For old time's sake? They move past him into the house, and without being asked, Lily sits down on his sagging sofa. His plain living room smells disconcertingly of cheap sausages. He sits opposite them, unsmiling.

'So what's all this about, then?'

They both hesitate, and Leonard speaks. 'Mr. March, I'm afraid we've... we're actually here to ask you about something personal. Something that's important to me, from my past. We want to know if...'

His words are having an alarming effect on the old man, who's getting up out of his seat and reaching for his walking stick. He interrupts Leonard.

'You're not from the council, then? Think you're going to rip me off, think I'm too old to fight you? I'll have you. I'll have you both, I'll knock your heads off.'

He starts to jump about the room in little hops. It might have been comical, if it weren't for the brutal metal tip of his walking stick, which passes dangerously close to Lily's face. Leonard stands up and moves in front of her. He holds both of his hands up palm forward and tries to reassure the man.

'Mr. March. We haven't come to steal anything, we just wanted to speak to you about...'

Mr. March isn't listening. He's stepping forward with jabbing movements – there's a crazy pleasure in his eyes. Leonard goes straight to the point.

'Rose Mutch. We're here about Rose Mutch.'

'Rose mush? What's rose mush? You won't be getting any from me, I'll have you I will, I'll crush you into a pulp.'

'Rose Mutch. She came to see you on Tuesday afternoons. Your girlfriend, Rose.'

He's almost shouting it, wanting to make absolutely sure that he can trust the flood of relief washing through him. This man hasn't got a clue what he's talking about. They make a hasty exit – Leonard shielding Lily from the whirlwind of the man and his stick. As they back out of the front door he's still making little stabs at them as if he's fencing.

'Girlfriend! I never! My wife would turn in her grave! I told you I'd have you! You won't mess with me again, oh no. Go on with you! You won't mess with Pete March again in a hurry!'

When Leonard gets back later that day, Peggy Margoyles has been waiting for the sound of his car. She pops her head out of her front door and beckons him and Pickles over. She tells him that Raine had dropped in today to say hello; she was on the way back from seeing a friend. She'd seen Peggy and asked her to let Leonard know she'd called by. Peggy had told her he was out 'seeing some gentleman in Didcot with his lady friend.' Leonard hadn't told her where they were going – she must have overheard Lily saying something. Peggy guesses by the look on his face that she might have done something wrong. She hopes she hasn't said anything out of turn. Leonard curses her inwardly and reassures her that it's fine and says thank you. He politely fends off her hundreds of questions about how the trip went, and who exactly the gentleman was. It's not her fault – she's just a lonely woman with too much time on her hands. It's too late now; the damage has been done.

Pickles says (insistently) that car journeys always make him ravenous, so Leonard is pressured into forking out some meat for him before he thinks about his own rumbling tummy. Why do the animals in his household always get to eat first? It doesn't seem right somehow. He feels let down by his pub lunch with Lily on the way back from Didcot, soggy steak and kidney pie and carrots from a tin, and feels he deserves something really yummy to make up for it. He's never enjoyed eating purely to plug hunger, and would almost rather go without, if it's not good food. Rose seemed satisfied by less-than-wonderful food – her restaurant meal would arrive bland or overcooked and she'd still shovel it down happily, saying it was 'filling a hole'. As he potters about the kitchen, gathering ingredients, he finds a tin of olives and remembers a restaurant in Greece he and Rose frequented one holiday. The 'Aiolos Taverna'. It was their first trip away without Raine, who'd recently moved in with Ed. The restaurant was next to the sea, and they sat at a table near the edge of the balcony so they could look down at the waves. They had delicious, cheap wine, and the food was simple and tasty – goats cheese, fresh bread, olives, sardines. They'd returned night after night and had become friendly with the owner, Nikos, a short, stout man with a magnificent moustache. On their last night he'd explained that Aiolos was an ancient king who Zeus had set up as 'boss of the winds'. It was too much for Leonard to resist. He smiles as he remembers the prim, elderly women at the next table trying their hardest to ignore Leonard's pretend-farting, and Rose laughing so much that she almost slipped off her chair.

What a holiday that had been. Their sex life had been up and down over the years of their marriage, as is to be expected. But after Raine hit teenager-dom, it had been erratic to say the least. Leonard had started to count the gaps between instances in months rather than weeks or days. On the first night of the holiday they'd felt a little tipsy from the red wine and from the long-forgotten buzz of being away without someone else to consider. They'd walked along the beach before they'd gone back to their apartment, and Rose had slipped her hand into his, something she hadn't done for a long time. They'd talked as they walked – easy conversations about what it was like now Raine was gone, and about what they wanted to do with their future. They congratulated themselves on how well they were doing, thirty years down the line and holding hands and happy in each other's company. When they'd got back, Leonard had challenged her to a game they hadn't played for years – who could get undressed and into bed first. They pulled off their clothes in a giggling frenzy and dived under the sheet, Leonard winning as usual – Rose always complained that she had more things to take off, and that her bra should earn her a four-second head start. They'd both lay there for a while, not touching, waiting for their fast breathing to slow down, and then they turned towards each other, so they could look into each other's eyes. Leonard whispered her name to her like a prayer – 'My Rose Margaret Mutch. My Rose Margaret Mutch'. He could feel the tension building up, imagining her generous belly, her squishy breasts – just over there – if he wanted he could reach out and touch them. But they'd lain still for even longer, listening to each other's breathing as it sped up again.

Eventually Leonard had reached out a hand, slowly, and when he came into contact with Rose's bare skin, she let out a low hum and shut her eyes. He shut his eyes too and concentrated on what was under his fingertips – walking them over her whole body, noticing where it was silky smooth, where it was creased, pressing into the soft bits, gently, gently, tracing tiny figures-of-eight on her breasts, rubbing the back of his hand down her waist. Rose let out sounds that reminded him of the sea or the wind. When they moved towards each other and touched with the full lengths of their bodies, he wanted to carry on pressing into her, joining with her into one amorphous mass. They kissed for longer than usual – gentle kisses, looking into each others eyes every so often and smiling. Rose started to cry, and this set him off as well, it was too much, there was too much love. Leonard gripped her upper arms hard and they channelled their love into a different kind of energy, an urgency. They made love more violently than they had for years, since they were first together, but somehow their love-making reached down into the ground further, had deeper roots. And violence is the wrong word, thinks Leonard, it has too many negative connotations. It was the opposite of violence – it was fierce love – strong, hungry. Spaghetti Bolognese. That's what he'll make for himself, with lots of garlic and fresh tomatoes. He rummages about for an old pot of parmesan in the cupboard, and bends to take some frozen mince from the freezer.

Chapter 19:
Three big dock-leaves

It's late Sunday night, and Leonard is reading a novel that Lily has lent him. She seems to know so much about books. This one's about a small boy who ends up on a raft with a lion and who has all kinds of adventures. It's exactly the kind of book Leonard loves – why write about ordinary things when you can invent something fabulous and strange? Although it's really about some of the most ordinary things there are – survival, relationships, and faith. Leonard relishes and is repelled by the gory parts – the book doesn't flinch away from the ferocity of life, as so many do. The boy is just about to climb off the raft and onto a mysterious island when the phone rings. His first thought is annoyance – he hates to be interrupted when he's in the middle of a good bit. He glances at the alarm clock and sees that it's after one in the morning, and quickly realises that this is another one of those dreaded middle-of-the-night calls. This time his first assumption is that Lily has taken ill. He stumbles downstairs without putting on any clothes and lifts the receiver to Ed's panicky voice.

'It's happening again, Len... I couldn't stop her from crying. The doctor wouldn't come out, she just said to keep her calm and wait until the morning. I don't know what to do... the twins are awake, they're worried. Can I bring her over to you? I can't seem to... I can't... The twins are crying, they're in their bedroom, they're wide awake. I didn't know what to say to them. I'm... it's...'

'What do you mean, bring her over? Here? Now?'

'I'm sorry, you probably don't... I don't know what to do, I can't do it. She's been worse again. It's been building for a few days, she's losing it. She hasn't been to work. I didn't want to tell you, was worried about... what shall I do Len?'

Leonard stands there with the phone against his ear and tries to think. The twins are the main priority – he doesn't like to think of them in a chaotic house. Maybe she could come and stay with him for a while, to give her a break. But would she want to? And would Ed cope on his own?

'Where is she now?'

'She's in the bedroom. She's just been ill in the toilet – too much crying. She's slowed down a bit. Maybe she'll go to sleep now. I don't know what...'

'Do you think you could wait until the morning? So the twins don't have to come out with you in the middle of the night?'

'I suppose so... would you be happy to have her?'

'She's my daughter, Ed, of course I am.'

'Sorry. I should be... I'm her husband. I'm not...'

'Listen, why don't you go up there now. Take her a cup of tea or something and tell her she can stay with me for a few days, just to have a break from the children. You'll arrange for someone to look after them, won't you? Don't ask her if she wants to come. Tell her that's what we've decided. OK?'

'OK. Yes, yes, I will do that.' He takes a breath. 'Will you stay on the phone for five minutes, while I check?'

'Of course, Ed. I'll stay right here.'

He waits, rearranging the jobs he has planned at work over the next few days and rehearsing the phone-call he'll make to Simon. How much of the truth should he tell him? He could say that his daughter isn't well, that he's needed to help look after her. Or maybe Raine would be alright in his house on her own – she could watch TV, and he could leave meals for her in the fridge. He realises he's looking forward to it in a way. He hopes she'll agree to come. Maybe he can get to the bottom of all this. His daughter is coming home, for a little while at least. After ten minutes, he guesses that Ed had forgotten all about him, and he hangs up, gently. Pickles has come downstairs with him and has been sitting on the second step patiently. Leonard reassures him that everything will be OK and they both go up to try and get some sleep.

Raine doesn't look too bad when Ed drops her off the next morning. She's wearing pale brown lipstick and manages a weak smile through the car window. But when she climbs out of the car, Leonard can see the emptiness behind the careful make-up. While Ed gets her suitcase out of the boot, she stands on the pavement with a hold-all in her hand and looks like a little lost girl in a big cold station. Or Paddington Bear. 'Could someone please look after this bear?' Leonard steps towards her and opens his arms to her, and she almost collapses into them. She feels thin under her clothes. She only allows herself a second of being held before she takes a deep breath and goes to help Ed with the suitcase. Ed shakes Leonard's hand and says 'thanks, mate' under his breath. Leonard checks that the twins are all right, and Ed says they're fine, everything is arranged until the end of the week. She can stay with Leonard until Sunday. As Ed says goodbye to his wife, Leonard notices how rigid she goes when he tries to hug her.

And now he's alone with his daughter. His poor, sad daughter. She disappears upstairs to the spare room with her suitcase and comes down when called for a cup of tea. They talk about practicalities first – he's taken the day off work, and says it's up to her if she wants him around for the rest of the week. She says no, he should go in, it'll be good for her to be on her own for a while. She says she's told the twins she's going on a 'mummy holiday', and that she'll speak to them every night. She has an appointment with her doctor later that day, would it be OK if he drove her in? The pills she's on obviously aren't working... Leonard didn't know she was on any pills and tries not to look surprised. He feels disappointed in her, but he's not sure why. She warns him, too – that she just can't stop crying, and as she says this, the tears start dripping onto her lap and into her tea. She says more angrily that he shouldn't expect her to snap out of it; she's been trying, she's really been trying. She weeps a little more, her shoulders shaking, her head bent forward, her long hair moving in waves. Leonard wants to go over to her but also thinks that if he hugs her, she might think he wants her to stop. He sits and listens to her cry.

The days pass, and they get into a kind of routine. Raine is prescribed some different pills by her doctor – apparently they can take four to six weeks to kick in, so she was told to monitor how she was feeling and to come in every couple of weeks. It doesn't seem like much to Leonard, some pills and an appointment in two weeks' time. But then, what else could the doctor, or anyone else, be expected to do? Raine doesn't get up until after Leonard has left for work, and he gives her a quick ring at lunchtime just to make sure she's OK. She tells him she spends most of the day in her bathrobe, crying. She tries to make a joke out of it, saying she'll scare off the Jehovah's Witnesses for him or that she's getting her mid-life crisis over and done with, but Leonard can't bring himself to laugh. When he comes home, he prepares them a simple meal, and they eat together. She isn't eating much, but he doesn't want to force her. He leaves lots of little bars of chocolate and fruit around the house in the hope that she'll take something while he's out. They talk a little about his day – Raine likes to hear about the jobs he's been doing – progress in the vegetable garden, Val's ongoing boyfriend traumas. It's neutral talk, nothing that might be difficult for her. She calls home and speaks briefly to the twins at 6.30 every night, just before their bath, and asks them what they've been doing at nursery and what bedtime story Daddy is going to read to them. They chatter away at her, and she smiles a sad smile.

Thursday is a particularly bad day. She doesn't come down from the spare bedroom all evening. Leonard takes up a meal on a tray and leaves it outside her door. He picks it up later, practically untouched. She has a bath late that night and he lies in bed and imagines her weeping into the bathwater. Lily rings one evening and Leonard asks if he could call her back on Sunday evening. He calls out to Raine that it was a window salesman, feeling a little guilty at his lie and smiling to himself as he remembers his first phone-call from Lily. He can't see any improvement at all by Friday evening and thinks about taking some more drastic action. He knows that nothing will shift until she starts talking to someone properly – him or Ed, he doesn't care which. She needs to start letting out whatever it is. He's starting to feel a little trapped, too – she's brought her sadness into the house with her, and it hangs in the rooms in a grey fog. But instead of reaching out to her, he sits on his armchair a foot away from her and doesn't say a word all night. They watch terrible Friday evening TV – invented for people who are too old or too lonely to be out and about, all bright colours and fake smiles. He realises that although he could lean over and touch her on her arm if he shifted in his seat, he feels further away from her than he's ever been before.

He's glad to leave the house on Saturday morning to drop his car off for its MOT. He'd booked it in weeks ago with a local mechanic. Raine insisted he should still go, almost pushing him out of the house. The mechanic, Marvin, is much in demand – he's one of the rare old-fashioned types who insist on creating good relationships with their customers. You don't get that in the towns and cities these days, just three greasy young men who can't wait to get off work and go and 'pull girls', or whatever it is they call it these days. He smiles at how out of touch he is. When Raine was at school, he used to ask her to teach him all the latest slang words like 'sad' or 'trendy'. There are no young people around him now, nobody he can interrogate to give himself the illusion of being 'with the youth'. Do they say 'with the youth' any more? He'll have to make up a few of his own instead – start a new fashion. He imagines dropping his new words into conversations with young people at supermarket check-outs and at work. 'That's a really bonging T-shirt you're wearing there,' and, 'I got so pashed last night, I could hardly stand up'. His cool new slang would sweep the country – he might even get a mention in the dictionary!

He drops off the car, exchanging pleasantries with the girl in the office, as usual. She's a pretty little thing, with very dark hair, and freckles scattered over her pale skin. He realises that if he were to make a comment to anyone about how lovely she is, he'd be seen as a dirty old pervert. He's reached the age where he isn't allowed to appreciate younger women any more, even if he'd never dream of approaching them. Do older women still lust after young men? He'll have to ask Lily. He's never heard them talking about it. Maybe they're just better at keeping those things secret. He walks to a nearby café as planned, to wait the couple of hours the MOT will take. He can always get a taxi home if there's more wrong with its innards than he thinks there is. He orders a hot chocolate and a tea-cake. He asks for real butter, not wanting any of that margarine crap. 'Crap' – is that out of date too now? He's brought a trusty crossword book with him. It's amazing how such a small bundle of paper covered in black and white squares can provide him with so many hours of entertainment and education. He'd never have known what jalopies are or what farctate means if it weren't for crosswords. He loves words. His favourite ever is 'zenzizenzizenzic', which means the eighth power of a number. He'd driven Rose mad when he'd first discovered it, as he couldn't stop telling people about it wherever they went. He'd been known to beckon over complete strangers at the pub and bring it out as if it were a bunch of flowers. It's been one of his life's ambitions to use it in conversation, but he hasn't managed it yet.

He swipes the crumbs left behind by previous customers off the thick plastic-covered table-cloth and flattens the book open in front of him. His eyes are getting worryingly blurry. Last time he visited the optician, they told him he really ought to get some glasses, but he persuaded them that he was still on the cusp, and that he could survive for just a few months longer. He's been putting off returning, cancelling his appointment with a new excuse each time, knowing that he won't be able to convince them next time. He could memorise the letters on the poster beforehand and cheat... although even he can see the nonsense of paying for an eye test and then not getting them properly tested. What he really dreads is having to wear glasses to see plants properly close-up. He's noticed a fuzziness around the edges at Coburne recently. He can't quite see the fine hairs on the silver sage, or the individual star-shapes on the lollipop-like Alliums. Squinting helps a little, but his face is lined enough already, especially around the eyes. He's been too happy over the years, that's his problem. Old Bob at work is as smooth as a baby around his eyes, and Leonard has never seen him crack a smile. Maybe he should get some of that botox stuff.

He reins in his thoughts before they get too silly and looks at the grid. It's a fresh one – no ticked off clues, no circles of letters to help him with the anagrams. The only thing more satisfying than starting a new puzzle is writing in the final solution. He gets five across straight away – 'secret'. He pencils it in, thinking as he does about the meaning of the word. Secret... Knowing something that someone else doesn't? But that would apply to what Lily has for lunch every day, and he doesn't see that as a secret. What does his little pocket dictionary say? 'Kept hidden or separate from the knowledge of others'. No, that doesn't do it for him either. What the dictionary has left out is the quality of what is kept hidden. It needs to be able to shock, to disappoint, to make someone happy (Leonard remembers Raine waiting until she was three months pregnant before she told him and Rose). The knowledge has to have some kind of emotional impact on the other person, even if it's a guessed emotional impact. Even if the secret lands more gently than the secret-holder imagines. We are all full of secrets, Leonard thinks, we all contain knowledge that has power against the people we love. All of us keep hundreds of small bits of information back – she called her boyfriend a 'skinflint' when talking to a friend, he broke that favourite mug in anger rather than through clumsiness. And most of us have a bigger secret, a secret that sometimes threatens to choke us. She has a deep horror of her mother. She didn't (and still doesn't) want her third child. He hides whisky in his bathroom. He has fallen in love with his best friend. These secrets push at us from the inside, insistent, wanting to be out.

Leonard's next question to himself is – how should we handle secrets? Are they sometimes justified, like a 'just war'? What if he'd never found that blue handbag, what if he'd never replied to the letter from Lily? Would his life be better, or worse? What's the harm in ignorant bliss? Are there different types of secrets, some that are best revealed, and some that are best kept hidden? How can you tell the difference, by holding them up to the light? It's too knotty. But none of that matters now anyway. He hasn't got the luxury of deciding whether or not to acknowledge Rose's secret. It's too late for that. The only choice he has is whether to unwrap it or not. Leonard almost sloshes his hot chocolate as some tinny music crashes into the café. It's a woman at the next table – her mobile is going off. She answers it with an enthusiastic 'alright my lovely!' and proceeds to have a loud conversation about her date last night. Leonard hears her say how well it went until the man admitted over coffee that the 'girl' he'd just been on holiday with to Bali was actually his wife. Leonard's tea-cake has been reduced to crumbs and his hot chocolate is half gone. There's still only a single word in his crossword grid – he focuses his attention back onto the list of clues until it's time to pick up the car.

When he gets home, Raine is sitting on the sofa, watching TV with three empty mugs on the coffee table beside her. She's still in her pyjamas, and her dressing gown and her hair is all mussed up. He tells her to get dressed, that they're going out for a walk. He has a plan for pulling her secrets out of her, like teeth. Pickles doesn't need any persuading and is up from his basket and ready to go in two seconds flat. Raine is more reluctant and starts to protest, but he brings out his old 'daddy' voice and says 'Raine' threateningly. To his great surprise it works, and she grudgingly drags herself up from the sofa like a teenager and carries the mugs through to the kitchen.

They don't say much to each other in the car, and Leonard thinks about how stubborn Raine was even as a young child. He remembers the one time she backed down from an argument. She was only about nine years old, and she'd taken her frustration with her school work out on him one day, calling him a boring old fart. It wasn't the most cutting insult in the world, but she'd said it with real venom, and he'd been genuinely hurt. Rose told her to apologise to her father at once, but she refused and didn't speak to him for the rest of that day or the next. The atmosphere in the house was thick – it was almost like a lovers' tiff. If Raine needed him to pass the mashed potato, she'd ask Rose to ask him, and he just pretended she wasn't there at all. It was horrible. Eventually he'd gone into the garden for a smoke one evening and had heard her crying upstairs through her open window. He'd gone up and opened the door, and she'd said sorry, sorry, running at him and hugging him. It had felt so good to have her back.

Leonard is planning on taking her on the same walk that he and Lily did just after he first met her. They can have a lemonade in the pub afterwards, and maybe some food if they're hungry. Leonard aims the car at a parking space and chuckles at the memory of Lily's thumping music. He says 'nothing' when Raine asks him what's funny. Leonard goes round to open the door for Raine like a chauffer, but Pickles spoils the effect by leap-frogging over her and out into the fresh air in a flurry of excited fur. It's a very different day to when he and Lily were here last. Crisp sunshine is lighting up the tops of the hedgerows and catching fly-away strands of hair in Raine's fringe. He remembers the hair-styles she's had over her life-time – short and spiky as a teenager, and all poufed up in her twenties with some kind of sticky gunk. The hours and hours she's spent over it. It must be a sign of growing up – no longer caring about your hair, seeing it as an inconvenience that has to be cut every so often, washed, brushed. She catches him looking at her and touches her hair self-consciously.

'What are you looking at?' she asks, scowling.

He touches her cheek with the back of his hand and smiles.

'Dad!' she says, in a whine, brushing him away and shrinking back as if she's still twelve and he's embarrassed her in front of her friends. She calls Pickles over to her and makes a fuss of him instead, calling him a 'good, good dog' and rubbing the fur on his forehead.

They settle into a good regular pace. Pickles goes on ahead to make sure that everything is safe for them, zig-zagging between the best smells and the most interesting objects. Leonard compares Raine with Lily as they walk – she's a bit brisker, and she doesn't seem to be looking around her as much as Lily does. He wonders why he chose to bring her here. It's as if he feels reassured by the ghost of Lily's presence, left behind her on these roads like a snail-trail. Lily is more 'here' than Rose, he supposes. At least he can talk to her about it afterwards if he needs to. She has an unfair advantage over Rose. But then Rose has an unfair advantage over Lily too, because in death no-one can touch her. Rose would have given Leonard the perfect advice about how to help Raine, she would have supported him in exactly the right way. Lily will let him down, over and over, by not quite saying the right thing, by not doing what he expects her to do. He looks over at Raine. They're approaching a pretty trellis covered in clematis that he remembers from last time – it's good to see it in bloom. They're about a third of the way round. If he starts the difficult conversation now, it'll be more difficult for her to escape.

'Raine, darling?'

She turns and looks at him suspiciously.

'Yes?' It's one of her long, "what now?" yeses.

'Raine – we need to talk.'

What a bad start. He sounds like a character from a dodgy American sitcom. He catches a glimmer of a smile, and tries to pry it open a little wider by repeating what he's said in his best worst American accent. She rolls her eyes and looks ahead. She's not going to help him out here – that's OK. He pushes on.

'I've been thinking about some things. I know you're not happy. But you're not talking to me, to anyone. I want to – I know I can't force you but – I think it'd be good for you to just tell me what's going on in that head of yours. I can't imagine that...'

He dries up, and looks over at her. She's looking straight ahead, and her face is hardening. He takes a deep breath.

'I know you don't like it when I ask you about this stuff, but I can't help thinking, love, that it's got something to do with your mother.'

He leaves this word hanging in the air. It's a few minutes before she talks.

'I don't think there's anything to discuss.'

'Well, there obviously is, or you wouldn't get so angry whenever I mention it.'

'I don't get angry!' she says, furious.

'Darling.'

She sighs. They walk some more. Leonard stops his daughter and Pickles to show them some **mousetail** in the hedge and tell them how rare it is. Raine looks and nods, as if humouring a child. Pickles seems more impressed than she is and jumps up to have a better sniff. Leonard fumbles around with some words in his head and tries again.

'I'm sorry, Raine, I'm not going to leave this. I'm worried about you. I'm not doing it to make you angry. I love you, munchkin.'

He hasn't called her munchkin for years. She started getting embarrassed at twelve and banned it. And now she's crying, silently, wiping the tears away from her cheeks with quick sharp swipes. Angry tears, frustrated tears. What does he have to do to get it out of her? He has a mental image of torturing it out of her with a feather, or by denying her chocolate for weeks. He waits. They walk on, and the crying dies down. She's sniffing now, great ugly snorts, and he wishes he was the kind of person who had tissues in his handbag. Even a handbag would be a start. How clever of women to carry round all those bits and bobs to make themselves more comfortable – aspirins, mirrors, lipsticks, mints... why don't men do it? Why aren't they more prepared? He stops near the hedgerow, catches her by the arm to stop her from storming on ahead, and picks her three big dock-leaves. He hands them to her. She hesitates, turns her mouth up at the corners and takes them. She tells him to turn away as she blows her nose messily, and then bends to drop the leaves deep into the hedge, as if someone might find them on the verge and know it was her. They set off again and finally, finally, she starts to speak.

'I didn't want you to know about it.'

'Know about what, darling?'

'Mum's… her… you know.'

She's squirming. What does she know? He waits.

'That she had a… another… the way she…'

He can't bear to see her dangling on a hook like a fresh grub any more.

'That she had another man?' he asks, and looks at her.

She nods, mute. His stomach swoops. He didn't know; he still doesn't know. Could it really be true? He recovers sufficiently to look back at Raine, who's tight-lipped and hard-faced.

'What do you know? How do you know?'

She tells him the story. When she was fourteen, she had bad period pains and came home early from school one day. She let herself in with the key from under the plant pot, and came in to find her mum in the living room writing a birthday card. She thought she'd surprise her. When she crept over and peered over her shoulder she saw the name in the card – 'Peter' – and five kisses. Raine touched her mum gently on the shoulder and her mum jumped out of her seat and started shouting at her. She accused Raine of sneaking up on her, asked her what the bloody hell she thought she was doing, told her to go up to her bloody room NOW. Raine couldn't understand it. There was a look in mum's eyes, she says, she'd never seen it before. It was like a dog snarling. She'd run upstairs and slammed her bedroom door, and when she realised that Rose wasn't coming up to say she was sorry, she grew angry at the injustice of it and came downstairs.

She sidled over to her mum and said, 'Who's Peter, anyway?' Rose looked over in her direction as if she weren't there, and then walked straight out of the house and down the road. She was wearing her slippers and an old baggy T-shirt she wore around the house and said she'd 'never be seen dead in'.

Her mum came back just before Leonard got home and acted normally over dinner. Raine went up to bed early to read. Rose followed her up the stairs and into her bedroom, and shut the door behind her. She'd sat on Raine's bed, leaned up close to her face and spoke in a voice that had 'made her bones go cold'. She held up a finger as she spoke, and Raine couldn't take her eyes away from it, it was shaking with rage. Rose had said that if Raine ever, EVER said anything about this to her father, his heart would break, and Rose would kill herself – she'd slit her wrists in the bath and the water would go red. Raine would be responsible for her death. Raine started crying and Rose put her hand over her daughter's mouth, and repeated what she'd said and asked her if she understood. The next morning her mum had acted as if nothing had happened.

She'd kept this incident a secret for years – this terrible heavy knowledge that had the power to break her father's heart and to kill her mother. When Lily had started 'poking her nose in', encouraging him to dig around, she'd been terrified that he might find out. She knows Rose can't kill herself now, but maybe… and here she breaks down again and stops dead in the road. She holds her hand to her mouth and sobs in little spasms, trying to get the words out in between. Leonard holds her – she won't stop shaking, like a wet kitten. She tells him she'd brought the whole thing up with her mum again, a few weeks before Rose had died. They'd been sitting alone in Raine's house, Raine balancing a box of chocolate on her huge bump – Ed was out 'making the most of his last days of freedom'. Someone had mentioned a Peter on TV. She'd sat there for another hour with the question growing inside her before it burst out. 'Who was Peter, mum?' Rose had looked daggers at her, piercing into her with her eyes, and then got up and walked a few steps towards her. Raine flinched and the chocolates tipped onto the floor. As she sat there holding her stomach, Rose froze above her, her face a mask of shock, and then turned and left the room. She was almost staggering – she knocked a vase off the table in the hall. Raine heard her slam the front door and drive off.

Raine is spitting out the words between her sobs. Leonard is crying too, rubbing his eyes as if he's got something in them. She blinks hard and looks straight at him.

'And then... she died. I... killed her... Dad, I killed... her. And... now... I'm breaking... your heart.'

Chapter 20:
Charlie's best tomatoes

The gardens at Coburne are in full bloom. Leonard has a fondness for all the seasons – the bronze and rose colours of autumn, frost-laced sycamore leaves, the first daffodil socking you in the eye. Even so, it's difficult not to love this time of year most of all. All of this colour everywhere – like rows and rows of can-can girls, all frilly skirts and flirting. Today it's the perfect weather for ice-cream. It's no wonder that this old couple are holding hands as they amble along the path, and that this woman is sitting on a bench with her legs stretched forwards and her eyes shut, wearing a satisfied, sleepy smile. This morning the sneezeweed is at the absolute peak of its power, and Leonard lingers over the deadheading he's doing nearby so he can stop, look up, and marvel afresh at the rich, dark copper-red.

Raine went back to Ed and the twins a few weeks ago now. Leonard still misses her, especially when he's making a sandwich or out buying a cream cake – it's back to one of everything. Since their walk he's felt as if some rocks have been cut out of the hems of his trousers. After Raine had finally coughed up what had been bothering her, they'd talked and talked. They'd sat in the car until Raine's face had 'stopped looking red and crumply', then gone into the pub to hungrily devour a ploughman's lunch and a spotted dick and custard each. Raine had told him what it had been like to carry Rose's secret around with her for all those years. It had got bigger and uglier as time went by, as Raine had imagined more and more details to fill in the gaps. She used to imagine Rose talking to Peter about her family, and laughing about what a fool Leonard was to not guess anything. Whenever Raine did something her mother disapproved of, she guessed that Rose would tell her boyfriend about it later. She found herself starting to really care about what this mystery Peter thought of her and her dad, and felt it extremely unfair that he only ever got Rose's side of the story.

She was also terrified about the possibility that Rose might leave them both for Peter. If she were stroppy a little too often, or if Leonard weren't kind enough to her, maybe Rose would be pushed to a final decision that she'd be better off without them. Maybe this Peter had a better job, more money... maybe he made Rose cups of tea more often or told her she looked beautiful. It was difficult to compete when she knew nothing about the competition. And the hardest thing of all was that she felt complicit in her mum's deception, and she enjoyed it. It was as if they had a special alliance against Leonard – they both knew something that could tear him apart. It was a horrible thing to admit to herself, and it took her years to make sense of it, but she felt a certain pleasure in holding this power. She knew something that her father didn't, and if she chose to, she could turn the whole family upside-down.

It was difficult for Leonard to listen to her. All this had been happening under his nose and he hadn't had a clue. He wondered if Rose knew what an impact she'd had on her daughter, over all those years. How could she have been so irresponsible? Once Raine had talked herself out, she'd moved on to other subjects – how claustrophobic she'd felt with the twins recently, how guilty she felt for not loving them as much as she should, and how she'd been shutting poor Ed out for months and months. Leonard leant forward on his seat as it all poured out of her in a continuous stream. When he'd taken the last cold sip of their second coffee, he looked at his watch and was shocked to see that they'd been there for three hours. Raine had yawned a long, luxurious, end-of-the-day yawn. He'd taken her back to his house and put her to bed as if she were still a girl, tucking her in and kissing her on her forehead.

He's hardly started to think about how he feels about what Raine told him just over a week ago. A stubborn corner of him is still resisting the neat explanation of Rose seeing another man. Occasionally his mind rests on the new knowledge, like a mosquito touching down on a bare arm, but he swats it away as soon as he notices. He hasn't even said anything to Lily yet. He mentioned it to Charlie a few days ago in the pub, making it clear that it wasn't yet available for discussion. He can trust Charlie not to hurry him. It doesn't make any sense, anyway. It suits him to focus on Raine for now, to go over and over in his head what she said that afternoon, how he can best support her. He'll start thinking about how he feels when he's satisfied that she's going to be OK. He's interrupted from his thoughts as the second visitor of the morning approaches him to ask for the name of the sneezeweed. He straightens up and gets ready to answer their questions.

After work he's unblocking the sink and has his head stuck deep in the cupboard's innards when the phone rings. He almost leaves it, but after the fourteenth ring, he gives up and pulls out his head. As he rushes to catch it, he almost trips over Pickles, who's waiting patiently with his head cocked, just in case Leonard might find something interesting in the pipes, like a juicy bone. It's Lily. She sounds flustered, and he asks her what's wrong. She tells him that she's just got home and has had some news. She doesn't want to tell him over the phone. Can he come over? He tells her not to worry, he'll be there soon.

On the drive over there his imagination runs riot. They've found a lump and done a scan and its spread to her lymph nodes. Her daughter's been killed in a car crash. She's been hiding terrible debts from him and they're repossessing her house. Or maybe she's met someone, a man – maybe this man is jealous and has asked her to stop spending time with Leonard. Eventually he forces himself to think about something else to stop the butterflies in his stomach from multiplying any further. They're going to run out of space – start squeezing their way out of his ears and nose, and fill up the car with their frantic fluttering. It'll be difficult for him to see the road.

Instead he imagines starting a second career at the age of sixty two as a clown. He'll go to children's parties and twist balloons into the shapes of flowers and sausage dogs. He could wear a huge green wig, a green nose, he could call himself... what do clowns call themselves these days? Loony Leonard, that would do. Loony Leonard. He imagines attending clown school, all of the students sat in a classroom wearing full make-up and looking serious as the tutor instructs them in funny walks and how to operate a button-hole that squirts people with water. He imagines graduation day, with great black flat hats to fit over their wigs, and doing their best funny walks as they collect their certificate from the head of department.

He so successfully distracts himself that he's shocked to see Lily waiting outside her house for him. He looks at her and the clowns disappear when he sees that she's been crying. She comes over and hugs him before he locks the car as if she can't wait any longer. He realises instantly that the news is for him. She's found something out.

'What is it, Lily?' he asks.

'Come inside.'

He has a sudden urge to get back into his car and drive off so he never has to hear whatever it is. Instead she holds on to him, and they walk into the house slowly with their arms linked, as if she's helping a weak-limbed invalid fresh from hospital. She sits him down on the sofa and perches on the edge of the chair opposite him. There's a funny smell in the air, as if something's been burnt. The front curtain is drawn, and it's darker than usual. There's a piece of A4 paper on the table between them, face down. She leans forward and puts her hands on his. He looks at the red stains around her eyes like watermarks, or Rorschach ink blots.

'I got some paperwork through today. I wanted to do this properly, make sure we weren't missing anything that could... I wasn't sure that there was any point, but proper detectives need to get a full picture of things, even when, you know, from my books... I didn't tell you, but I ordered copies of birth certificates for those three Peter Marches in Didcot, a while ago. The one that had learning disabilities, Leonard. The one that died. This is his birth certificate.'

She holds it out and he takes it. He scans it. Peter Michael March. Born 1962. Didcot Hospital. Father – unregistered. Mother – Rose Margaret Smith. He reads that bit again. Rose Margaret Smith. Mother. Rose Margaret Smith. He looks up at her, his eyes wild.

'I'm so sorry, Leonard. I wanted to be sure about this.

I called Rose's aunt again, you know, Mildred, just before I called you. She didn't want to say anything at first but... I confronted her with it; I said we already knew. Told her we were only looking for confirmation. Rose was only fourteen. Her mum took her out of school, locked her away in the house. Mildred said nobody knew what... where it went. The baby. They thought it might have died.'

She's started to cry a little, and Leonard isn't sure who she's crying for. Him? Rose? Herself? He doesn't feel anything. She dabs at her eyes and carries on.

'It must have been... it was who she was visiting, all those years. Every Tuesday afternoon. I'm so sorry. Rose was... I don't know what to...'

Leonard smiles brightly, shakes his head briskly.

'You've made a mistake, Lily. You were right – Rose was having an affair after all. Raine told me – she'd... I was going to tell you, when I... it was taking me a while to get it into my head. She saw a card, that her mother was writing. A birthday card. Her mother told her... it was...'

He starts to falter. Lily looks confused, continues to look at him, cocks her head to one side.

'It was another man, Lily, it wasn't... Raine told me that...'

He absent-mindedly touches the top of his head with his left hand, and when he speaks next his voice is flat.

'It was her son's birthday.'

Lily turns the corners of her mouth upwards, her eyebrows raised. They sit there for a while listening to the ticking of Lily's grandfather clock. Leonard realises he's holding on to the birth certificate too tightly and loosens his grip. His eyes have become fixed. He can still smell the burning – maybe she's lit a candle, or maybe she burnt something in the oven earlier. He'd like to open the curtains

at the front, to let in some more light. He'd like to go into the
garden and have a smoke. Rose had a baby. Rose had a son.
The words repeat on him and he tries to mutate them into
something else. Rose had a maybe. Moses had a son. They
keep changing back, despite his best efforts. He needs to get
it right, find a new sentence that will stick. Eventually Lily
slides one of her hands out half-way across the table, palm
up. He's busy trying to concentrate. He looks at it as if it's
an alien object, full of creases and strangely shiny as if made
of plastic. He looks at it and doesn't take it. She tries to catch
his eye, but he doesn't look at her. He clears his throat.

'I think I want to be on my own now,' he says.

Lily takes her hand away and folds her arms tight. 'Oh.'
She looks pained, she's narrowing her eyes and frowning. 'I
hope I haven't… I just wanted to…'

'I do appreciate all you've done for me. That's it, now.'

She looks at him, wide-eyed.

'I'm a stupid… thinking that you might… and all along
she's not been…' She's thinking out loud. 'Rose didn't… it
wasn't what we… after all of that. It's not…'

There's a note of what sounds like desperation or panic
in her voice. He drags his attention away from the words in
his head and looks at her properly.

'Lily?'

'I can't… I really can't… it's not…'

She looks towards the kitchen. She's breathing more
shallowly. She clasps her mouth with one of her hands
and whimpers, as if she's had a sudden stab of pain in her
stomach. He's not thinking about Rose any more. He can't
get Lily to look at him.

'Lily, what is it? Are you ill?' he asks again, putting a
hand on her arm.

She pulls away from him and makes a strange noise, a

high-pitched hard-edged 'uh'. She turns her body away from him and crunches her body forward, hiding her eyes with her hand. She rocks forward and back from her waist. When she speaks to him again, she sounds like a little girl.

'Can you go away now, please?'

'What is it? What have I said?'

'Go away. I want you to go away!'

'But I don't understand what…'

'Go! NOW! GO!'

He backs away from her, looking around as if he might find some explanation for what is happening. He makes his voice calm.

'OK, OK. I'll call you later, OK?'

'Leonard, please go now. Please. Please.' She's pleading, desperate.

He leaves her where she's sitting and fetches his jacket from the cupboard under the stairs. Outside, the sun is shining hard, and he has to shade his eyes to see his way to the gate. He lingers on her path for a few seconds, as if she might call out after him and ask him back inside, until he sees a hand emerging around the edge of the front curtains and pulling them completely shut.

Leonard drives straight to the Five Bells in a kind of daze. He's not sure what else to do, where to go. His head is full. During the journey, he pushes Rose's son away again and instead runs through what he said to Lily. He tries to work out what offended her. He can't remember saying much at all – she'd done all the talking. Maybe she could have misinterpreted something? But such an extreme reaction… He'd refused her hand, and said he wanted some time on his own – did she feel he was being ungrateful after everything she'd done? This train of thought leads him to something that's been niggling at him – why was she so keen to help him out at the beginning? He can understand it now – they've got to know each other, they enjoy each other's company. She's helping him out as she would any friend. But what about when she didn't know him from Adam? Why did she make herself so available?

There's an empty space at the bar where Charlie usually sits. Leonard stands for a few moments in the doorway, wondering what he should do.

'Are you going to come in or would you rather stand there and gawp?' Suze asks him.

'No Charlie?'

'No, not tonight. Shall I bring your usual over to you?'

'Could I borrow your phone, Suze?'

'Help yourself, darling.'

She pulls the phone up from behind the bar and stretches the extension lead across between the optics and the pumps.

Leonard gets Charlie's number from an old boy at the bar, and his wife Marion picks up. Marion says Charlie's not going to the Bells tonight – he's 'faffing about in his greenhouse instead'. Leonard hesitates and she asks him, with that wonderful sixth sense that women have, whether he'd like to come over and have a word with him. Leonard says it doesn't really matter, but Marion insists, saying it will be lovely to see him. He's only been to Charlie's house once before in however many years they've known each other, although when Rose was alive, the four of them used to meet up at the pub a few times a year for a catch-up. Marion reminds him of their address and the directions. He thanks Suze for use of the phone and gets back into his car.

Marion meets him at the door wearing rubber gloves covered in dollops of washing-up-liquid foam. She kisses him on the cheek and gets a glob of it on his T-shirt. When she tries to wipe it away she only makes matters worse. She asks after Raine and takes him through the house and out into their large garden. Once she's pointed out the dark Charlie-shaped shadow in the greenhouse at the bottom of the lawn she leaves him to 'go back to the suds'. He walks across the neatly-clipped grass and cranes his head around the greenhouse door.

'Charlie.'

'Leonard.'

'I'm sorry for bothering you at home, I just…'

Charlie looks at him sternly. 'Put your arse down there and let me get on with my pricking out.'

They are quiet for a few minutes as Leonard perches on an upturned crate and acclimatises himself to his surroundings. It's warm and humid, and the sweet compost and fecund, intoxicating tomato aromas help him to feel at home. It's a pretty large greenhouse for a domestic garden, and is full to the brim of bushy tomato plants, glossy green pepper plants, a few cucumbers, and God knows what else. Leonard spots some particularly fine chilli peppers – he knows that Charlie grows these for his son-in-law, as Charlie and Marion can't bear spicy food. He's often ranted in the pub about the pointlessness of putting nice flavours into cooking and then masking the whole lot with something that makes your eyes water and your throat seize up. Everything is neat and tidy – Leonard can see under the benches from where he's sitting, and even the hundreds of spare plant pots are neatly stacked up and arranged into rows in order of size. Charlie's busy dividing up some healthy-looking Kale seedlings from a large tray and plugging them gently into individual pots. Leonard gets out his tobacco to roll one for the way home and starts talking.

'I've just come from Lily's house. She went all weird on me. I don't know what happened to her... She told me that, that Rose...'

Leonard allows the words back into his head like letting in an unwelcome visitor. Rose had a baby.

'She wasn't having an affair, like we thought, Charlie. Like Raine told me. She had a baby. A baby I didn't know about.'

Charlie stops what he's doing for a second. He looks round and raises an eye-brow before turning back to his task.

'A baby, eh?'

'She had it when she was fourteen. Had him – he's called Peter.' He remembers something. 'He was called Peter. He died, a while ago I think. He had something wrong with him, lived in one of those residential places. That's where Rose had been going.'

'Hnh. A son.'

'A half-brother for Raine. I suppose you could call him my step-son.' These new thoughts hit him just before he speaks them out loud.

'No affair then, eh?'

'No, it wasn't an affair. It wasn't an affair! My Rose, I knew she wouldn't have... but what should I do, Charlie?'

'Do?'

'I ought to do something. I ought to...'

He trails off. Marion appears at the door and asks Leonard if he'd like a nice cup of tea.

'Can't you see we're busy, woman?' Charlie says.

'Oh, shut up, you big lug. I'm not talking to you, anyway.' She turns to Leonard, peering round a particularly bushy tomato plant to catch his eye. 'Milk-no-sugar, Leonard?'

'I could murder a cup of tea, thank you, Marion.'

She returns five minutes later with two mugs and sets

one in front of her husband, who tuts loudly. Leonard sees
him snaking a sneaky hand onto her bottom and giving her
an affectionate tweak as she turns to leave the greenhouse.

'Mind you don't listen to anything he says, the great
sod,' she warns Leonard as she goes.

Charlie finishes the pricking out and clears away the
left-over pots and compost. Leonard sips his tea gratefully.
He lets the liquid warm him from the inside, and the
concentrated sunlight warm him from the outside. He
looks at the hairs on his bare shins and wonders what his
legs would look like if he shaved it all off. They sit for ten
minutes or more, the silence broken only by the sound of
Charlie seeing to his tomatoes. He carefully measures out
tomato feed into a battered-looking metal watering can and
fills it to the brim with water. He tips it onto the soil around
the base of the plants, the rose of the can dividing the water
into thin sparkling threads. When he's finished watering,
he starts removing any yellowed leaves he finds and starts
pinching out the tips.

Leonard sets down his empty mug.

'I don't know.' He takes a slow breath. 'I suppose I don't
need to do anything. I know now, don't I? It's all finished.
That's all there is to it. What else is there to say?'

'It'll need some time to soak in, Leonard.'

'I know, Charlie, I know. I'll have to think about telling
Raine. And this business with Lily – she practically chucked
me out of her house. Who knows what's going through
that woman's head.' He shakes his head and runs his fingers
through his hair. 'Maybe the best thing to do next is to go
home and have some dinner.'

'Hnh. Some dinner'd be good. Marion's probably
cooking me up one of her unique creations right now. You
be grateful you can cook for yourself'.

'The poor woman, it's a wonder she puts up with you.'

'Hnh.' This 'hnh' is accompanied by raised eye-brows and nodding. 'I'll see you down the Bells then?'

'Yeah. Thanks, Charlie, for – you know.'

Charlie pushes his mouth forward into a frown and makes a flapping motion with one of his hands. As Leonard gets up to leave, Charlie beckons him over to show him a particularly fine looking specimen covered in bunches and bunches of green rounds.

'These here, see? These are going to be my best tomatoes yet. I'll bring you some when they're ready. You'll never have tasted anything like them.'

Leonard takes the empty mugs back to Marion in the kitchen. The washing machine is rumbling away in the background, and their cat is winding about Marion's legs. The reassuring sounds of everyday domesticity. She asks him pointedly if everything is alright now, and he says yes, thanks, it will be. He chats with her for a few minutes as she chops onions and wipes the earth from eight bright radishes. He likes Marion. They talk about the fine weather they've been having and agree that there's nothing like home-grown vegetables. Leonard remembers the first carrots he ever grew with his father, and this reminds Marion of a story about a gardening friend of hers. This friend wanted to encourage green fingers in her young children as early as she could. One day she put them in their little Wellington boots, and they'd all gone out to sow carrot seed in neat rows. The next morning before breakfast her children rushed into the garden to see if the carrots had appeared. Their mother explained how long they would take, but their young minds couldn't quite imagine beyond 'tomorrow'. By the fifth morning Marion's friend couldn't bear their disappointed faces. She sneaked out and went to the local market where she bought a bunch of young carrots with the leafy tops still attached. That night she planted them under the moonlight.

Chapter 21:
The blond waitress, etc.

When Leonard gets back from Charlie's house, he feeds Pickles and promptly falls asleep on the sofa. When he wakes up, with a thick red line imprinted on his cheek, Rose's baby is the first thing he thinks about. He spends the rest of the evening with the TV switched off, imagining Rose sat on the sofa next to him with a tiny baby boy in her arms. He looks at them and considers the implications. He guesses how Rose might have felt when she discovered something growing inside her at fourteen. He wonders how she felt about him when he was born. He tries out the words 'step-son', and 'half-sister'. He doesn't really feel very much – maybe the feelings will come later. Or maybe they won't come at all. His dreams that night are of a never-ending hotel with miles and miles of twisted corridor – he knows that Rose is there somewhere but however many doors he flings open he just can't find her.

He doesn't remember Lily until the next morning. He tries her and gets her cheerful answer-phone message, 'Lily isn't free to take your call, DO leave a message and she'll get back to you as soon she can.' It goes straight to the message all day – he wonders if she's left the phone off the hook by mistake. By the second day he has to acknowledge that she's screening her calls. He forces himself to leave her a message. He hates those bloody machines and always seems to end up sounding like an idiot. This time is no different. He gives up waiting for the beep and starts speaking, and then it suddenly interrupts him. This throws him and he gets all muddled, and while he's trying to correct himself he gets cut off by the end of the tape. After ten minutes he rings back again and says 'please ignore my last message, just give me a call when you get this.' Later on he realises he didn't actually tell her who was calling, but he hopes Lily will recognise his voice by now, or at least his lack of skill at leaving messages.

During the week Leonard had called Raine and asked her if she could get away from the twins for a couple of hours at the weekend. He said he had something to tell her. Ed had obliged without a murmur. Ever since he'd single-handedly looked after the boys for the week when Raine was with Leonard, he's had a new appreciation of the sheer volume of work involved. He's even started a new habit of bathing the boys on Monday, Wednesdays and Fridays, and last week – shock horror – he offered to hang the washing out for her. Raine had suggested they meet at one of those shiny new coffee places in Reading. She's already there when he arrives, and has bagsied a table near the window with comfy armchairs. She's always been skilled at getting good tables, just like Rose. Leonard is far too polite – if one becomes free he hovers about to make absolutely sure no-one else wants it, until someone brushes past him and plonks themselves down without even noticing him. Raine kisses him on the cheek and says she'll have a cappuccino. He goes up to order, and after he's had to look at it from his place in the queue for five minutes he can't resist a huge cinnamon and apple pastry dripping with icing. He's feeling a little anxious about telling Raine the news – he can't predict how she'll react. When he gets back to the table, she's fiddling with her tiny new mobile phone, one of those models that folds in two. Leonard thinks it's quite pretty – the pale pink, shimmery coating reminds him of mother-of-pearl.

'Here you go, darling.'

'Thanks, Dad. So what bomb-shell do you have to drop on me today?'

He finishes putting the coffees and the pastry on the small round table and takes the tray back. And then he tells her. As he talks, she bends her phone closed and then opens it up repeatedly, and then rubs her thumb against the smooth glass of the screen. He can see a photo of the twins behind her thumb as he talks, their mouths close to the camera and grinning widely. She seems to take the news calmly. She sits with the new information for the time it takes him to demolish his pastry, refusing his offer of half. He sits back in his seat and groans, holding his stomach.

'What a stupid idiot she was', she says. 'For not trusting us with Peter. It's such a waste.'

'She must have had her reasons, love. Maybe she was ashamed of getting pregnant so young. You know what she was like about those young single mothers.'

'Yes, but she was still a silly idiot, don't you think?'

Leonard agrees by tilting his chin upwards, twice.

'I suppose you have to admire her though, don't you? For sticking with her responsibility towards this... man – her son – for keeping in touch year after year. Just like her, don't you think?'

Again Leonard agrees. Raine sighs, and pouts a little.

'It's a relief. I can feel it in my stomach, sort of... calmer now, knowing it was all different. She wasn't going behind your back, Dad, or not in the way I thought she was. It's better this way, don't you think? It makes much more sense this way.'

'I suppose it does, darling. I've not really got round to thinking it all through yet.'

A small boy at another table starts shouting 'choccie! choccie!' and they both watch his mother as she fusses around and tries to shut him up. She gets angrier and angrier at him and eventually hisses something into his ear that makes him cry.

'So what was wrong with this Peter, Dad? Did anyone else know about where she went every week? It can't have been possible for her to keep it absolutely to herself, could it?' She leans forward as more thoughts come to her in a rush. 'Who was the father? How did Peter die?'

They are all sensible questions. Leonard hasn't asked them himself yet.

'I don't know, love, but I'll try and find out for you if I can. I can ask...'

He hesitates, and then brings up the subject of Lily. He tells Raine about her odd outburst, and complains that she's being selfish having a tantrum considering everything he's going through at the moment. Raine actually sticks up for her, and suggests he shouldn't make any judgements until he knows what's going on. She also apologises to him for being rude when she first met her, and admits that she's finding it difficult to think about her dad being with anyone else. When she says this Leonard puts his cup back on his saucer with a loud clattering noise. He protests that they're just good friends, but annoyingly Raine isn't convinced, and just smiles wryly as he continues to explain. He digs himself even deeper with a Freudian slip, saying he only pops round every so often to 'have breakfast with her, I mean dinner. Dinner!' Raine folds up with laughter.

Before they go their separate ways they talk about a party that Raine is planning for Ed's birthday. A friend of Raine's has offered to take the twins for the night, and Raine is thinking about having a Buddy Holly theme. She knows a bakery that will print any photo you want onto the icing of a cake, and she asks Leonard if he could help her by tracking down one of those stand-up cardboard figures. She can already picture the look on his face when he meets Buddy Holly in the living room and then all of his friends pour out of the kitchen. They don't speak any more about Rose, about Peter. Leonard considers bringing it up again, but Raine seems happy to leave it – maybe she needs time for it to sink in. He knows he does. After Leonard kisses her goodbye and watches her walking away down the street he thinks to himself that saying breakfast by mistake was definitely worth it. It was so good to hear that unfamiliar sound again – the tune of his daughter's laughter.

By the following Friday, Leonard has had enough of getting Lily's answer-phone. He's also growing increasingly worried about her. He decides to drop in uninvited and see what's going on. He leaves Pickles at home, just in case there's any friction – Pickles is a sensitive soul and retreats to quiver under the nearest table at the first sign of any shouting. He puts on Radio 2 in the car and sings along to 'Ghost Town'. He especially enjoys the 'ah, la la, la la la la la...' bits and gets so carried away he almost drives over a broken bottle in the road. He's starting to regret drinking a whole pint of water just before he left the house as the pressure on his bladder slowly increases. He almost pulls over in a lay-by near a suitable looking hedge but decides to hold on, he's always worried about being caught by the police with his trousers down and it makes it difficult for him to 'go'. When he pulls up at Lily's house, he's alarmed to notice that her front curtains are still shut. He has a sudden image of her dead on the sofa with empty pill bottles all over the floor. He knocks on her door and turns his head to see the curtains twitching. He waits a little longer and then pushes her letter-box open.

'I know you're in there, Lily. I'm not going anywhere until you let me in.'

After a few more minutes he knocks again.

'I'm worried about you in there. I'll need to call the police if you don't come out – just open the door and let me see you're OK. And anyway, I really need a wee.'

This does the trick. She shouts 'OK, OK, give me a minute,' and opens the door so he can see her. She doesn't move aside to let him in. She looks tired, and her eyes look sore.

'Leonard. What are you doing here?'

'Are you going to let me in, then?'

'I don't think… I'm not in the best… I didn't think that you wanted to…'

'Lily, let me in. I'm dying for a wee.' He jumps around a little on the path to illustrate.

She reluctantly steps aside. When he returns from the toilet, he looks around her front room. It smells musty and is in a state of disarray. There are three open books face down on the sofa, and a stack of unopened mail on floor next to the mat. He can see through to the kitchen, where there's a pile of clothes on the floor near the washing machine, as if she hasn't had the energy to put them inside. Lily is wearing a long dressing gown with some raggedy cotton trousers. She doesn't look like she's been to work today.

'Can I make you a cup of tea?' he asks.

'That should be my job, Leonard. But yes, I would like a cup of tea.'

When he brings it in to her, she's sitting facing the switched-off television and staring just to the right of it. She takes the tea without looking at him and forces her mouth into a smile. He settles down on an armchair opposite her and waits.

'I'm sorry.'

She's already taking a screwed-up piece of tissue from her dressing gown pocket, ready for the tears.

'I'm so embarrassed. You're probably wondering... all of this out of the blue... I don't know why you're here. When you said you never wanted to see me again, Leonard -'

'That I never wanted to... I never said that! I said I wanted to be on my own, Lily. It was all a bit of a shock.'

'Oh.' She screws up her face and dabs at her eyes, and immediately becomes angry at herself. 'I wish I could stop this ridiculous crying... bloody waterworks... it's so... I thought you'd meant there was no point in seeing me any more, after...' She trails off and rubs her forehead.

'What's up, Lily?'

She presses her tissue hard into the corners of her eyes and puts it back into her pocket.

'I'll tell you, Leonard, but you might not want to know me any more, once... I'm not a nice person, you see. Not a nice person at all.'

He nods. 'Go on.'

'OK. I've been... I was... Well, I wished that Rose had had an affair. Behind your back, all along. I wanted you find out the worst, that she wasn't who you thought she was... I wanted to help you find it out. When I found out about Peter I was... Oh, Leonard. I was disappointed.'

She lets her tea go cold while she explains. Her husband

Roy had cheated on her, throughout their marriage. The first time she caught him was on their honeymoon, when she came back from powdering her nose and found him slipping his telephone number to a blond waitress. She didn't want to be the one to spoil their holiday – they'd saved up for so long – so she pretended she hadn't seen anything. That night, after he'd made love to her and fallen asleep, she'd gone onto the balcony in her nighty to cry. The next time she knew about was two months later, when they'd settled into their two-bed semi. She found lipstick on his collar, as if she was starring in a bad movie. It was bright red, and she only wore pink. She hadn't known what to do, and had gone to her mother for advice. Her mother was of the opinion that she should count her blessings that she had a man at all. She said it was typical of Lily to moan about something so 'inconsequential'. So Lily stopped up her mouth, and concentrated on being a good wife as well as a good daughter.

The affairs had continued over the years – 'one silly tart after another'. Roy would stay out late after work most days, and he sometimes he went away for 'business weekends' and came back attentive and loving. Whenever he 'touched her', she imagined him with his other women – buying them fancy chocolates with their grocery money, or putting his hairy hands on their backsides as they walked along the beach. He even invited a couple of them around for dinner – the 'secretary', the 'daughter of a friend who's in town on her own' – and Lily mashed potatoes for them while they played footsie underneath the table.

She never spoke to her mother about it again, and only ever confided in one other person, a good friend called Betty. Betty was outraged and told Lily she should leave him. The thought of being on her own terrified her, and she spent the next few weeks listing all of his better qualities in her head – he did buy her those earrings for Christmas, and he sometimes complimented her on her cooking. He did still make an effort to hide his indiscretions – giving her long descriptions of 'boring business meetings' and hiding their phone numbers in a red book in a shoebox at the back of his cupboard. He did love her, in his way. When Betty asked her about it again, Lily lied. She said she'd confronted him and he'd promised to stop, and the friends never spoke about it again.

Most of the time, it didn't affect her everyday life, but she started automatically looking for fault-lines in other couple's relationships. Contented couples made her feel uncomfortable, as if they were taunting her with their happiness. She'd notice this wife's patronising tone towards her husband, and this husband's fishing obsession that left his wife alone and lonely. She sought out friends who were miserable in their marriages too, and they colluded with each other, saying how lucky they were to have a man bringing in a good wage, someone who didn't treat them unkindly or beat them. Maybe that's partly what she was hoping to find when she started looking for Rose – Leonard could be one last example of a kind person with a failing relationship – some kind of final proof that there's no such thing as a happy marriage.

When she'd met Leonard for the first time in that café and he'd talked about Rose, she'd felt the familiar tensing in her stomach. She knew her reaction didn't make sense, she said – Roy was long dead, and there was no reason to defend against her decision to not leave the marriage any longer. But if it really were possible that Leonard and Rose had been as happy as he'd said they were, then… then she'd wasted her life. Wasted it. And so when Leonard had told her about the handbag, she'd grown hopeful – here was a hint of a different side to Rose, evidence that they must have damaged each other somehow…

As time had gone on she'd got to know Leonard better, and she enjoyed his company. It didn't matter so much that he'd had a happy marriage, and she'd even found herself hoping that Rose hadn't been having an affair. The investigation had evolved into a good excuse to keep seeing Leonard. She couldn't believe that he'd want to stay in touch with her 'for the sake of it', and was expecting him to stop calling her once she'd outlived her usefulness. But when she'd found out about Peter, her reaction had floored her.

'I must have been secretly hoping to… hoping that you'd like me anyway,' she says. 'Despite myself. Some long, long, long squashed hope that… that I'm enough, just the way I am.'

She stops, lifts her shoulders up towards her ears and lets them drop.

'What a silly goose,' she says, quietly. 'Daring to think that I'm enough, the way I am… after all those years of proof that… As if, forty years later, I still haven't quite got the message.'

Leonard listens to her carefully without interrupting and notes his reactions. Here's a new layer of Lily. Here's something different to what he's seen of her so far – something raw, ugly. He's shocked at what she's saying, but another part of him isn't surprised. It makes more sense now – her eagerness to help him out, and her sudden flashes of insecurity. He moves his gaze from a photo of her grandchildren on the table and looks at her. Her eyes are swollen, and there's mascara smeared across one of her cheeks. A small part of him is repelled.

'I'm so sorry, Leonard. I'm so sorry. I know you won't want to… that after today…'

Does he want to see her again? What does all of this mean? He needs longer to process what she's said – there's so little space in his head as it is. He thinks about having a roll-up in the garden. He puts his hand in his pocket and brings out his tobacco tin. He reads the word on it. 'Swan'. His mother told him once that a swan's wings are powerful enough to break your arm. He doesn't know whether it's true or not. Ever since, whenever he's heard the throb of their wings waou, waou waou-ing above him, or a protective male has jerked towards him across the water, those words have arrived in his head unasked for. 'A swan could break your arm.' Could. Could. He opens his tin and pinches out a wad of tobacco.

'It'll take more than that to get rid of me, Lily.'

'But I can't let you… it's not right, I can't…'

'I didn't say I was going to let you off scot free. I'll be making a list – several roasts, letting me win at cards for three months, ten lifts back from the pub…'

He counts them off on his fingers. She covers one of her eyes with a hand and smiles weakly.

'And it's going to take a bit of getting used to, Lily,' he says, more softly. 'I'm not sure quite how I… there's a lot to… Maybe we could talk about it again another day. When my head is reeling a bit less from all this other stuff.'

'Yes, of course. I'm sorry the timing is so… I'd be glad to do that. I'm sure I don't deserve it, but I'm very grateful.'

'We all deserve it, Lily. We're all as bad as each other, you know, once you really get down to it. We all have secrets.'

Before Leonard leaves, Lily says there's something she didn't manage to tell him the last time he was here. There's one more person he could visit if he wants to find out more about Peter. She'd called the care home where Peter lived when he died – Missleden House – and asked to speak to the longest-serving member of staff. This was a support worker called Iris, who happened to be on duty and was upstairs changing bed linen when Lily called. She came to the phone and confirmed that Peter had had a lady visitor every week. She'd only talked to the visitor in passing but she remembered the old Service Manager, Winnie Cox, getting on quite well with her. Winne had worked there for seventeen years before retiring last year. The person in charge of the house had said it wasn't their policy to release any member of staff's telephone numbers, but she'd offered to call Winnie and pass on Lily's details.

Winnie had called Lily a few days later and said she'd be very happy to speak to Leonard. She said that Rose had told her a lot about him. If Leonard would like her to, Lily says to him now, she could set up a meeting between them. It could be the final piece of his investigation. Leonard takes her up on her offer. He isn't sure how curious he is about Peter, but Winnie might know the answers to Raine's questions. He carries the tea things back into her kitchen before he leaves, washes them up, and then stands in her garden to smoke his roll-up. He watches Lily through the kitchen window, straightening up after putting her clothes into the machine and yawning a long, luxurious yawn. He catches it from her and holds his lit cigarette between two fingers so he can surrender himself to it more completely. As she moves across to the sink, he sees her mouth 'right then, Lily' before she tackles the rest of the washing up, and he feels a small frisson of affection for her. He lets out a perfect circle of smoke. It floats towards the early moon, which sits like a sliver of apple on dark blue. The smoke-ring lazily twists and loosens before melting into the evening.

Chapter 22:
Peeling potatoes at Missleden

Winnie Cox lives in a nondescript red brick house on a modern housing estate. The roads all have twee names like 'Rosemary Way' and 'Oregano Walk'. Leonard turns the car into 'Marjoram Close' and Lily reads the house numbers out loud as they crawl along. He drives up onto the pavement at the bottom of the cul-de-sac. This is the end of the road, he supposes. They get out and Lily takes his hand as they walk towards No. 34. He's glad of the momentary distraction, and notices the way her hand fits into his, how surprisingly soft her skin is. He wonders if she can feel the rough edges around the pads of his fingertips, his palm, hardened from a lifetime of pulling things up, separating things, making space in the earth. A lifetime of helping things grow. On the doorstep they smile at each other before they knock, and this time Leonard can't mistake it – something is growing between them. Something deep inside him is thinking about germinating. They could almost kiss, he thinks, if they weren't here. If they weren't so close to the memory of Rose.

The door is opened by a slender man with a deeply lined face. Leonard thinks of the word 'sprightly' – he's moving more fluidly than you might expect for his age.

'Lily? You are happy for me to call you Lily?' he says, looking towards her. Maybe he can't remember Leonard's name.

'Yes, and this is Leonard.'

'Aah, yes. Yes. Good to meet you both.' His handshake is firm. 'My wife is expecting you – she thought you might like to sit in the garden, seeing as it's such a beautiful evening. Would you like to come through? Our daughter is staying with us, so apologies for all the grandchildren rampaging around the living room'.

He ushers them quickly through the busy house and into the quiet of the garden. There's a fat, grinning toddler on a woman's lap on the sofa, and two older children playing on one of those game consoles attached to the TV. Leonard notices how his gut feels about this house, this family. He already likes them. This house feels honest, generous of spirit – as if the people here have cooked their children good dinners, and been very careful when brushing out the tangles in their hair before they sent them to school.

The garden is bigger than he expected from the front of the house. It's full of soft shadows and half-lit shrubs and flowers. There's lavender, alliums, a fine tree peony. Winnie's husband points to a green metal garden table and chairs in the shade of an oak. An older woman is sitting there alone, smiling broadly at them. She's in her late sixties, maybe older; it's difficult to see under the broad cream hat she's wearing. Her face is softer than her husband's, more fleshy. She stands up, and the chair scrapes on the decking underneath the table. Her husband introduces them, forgetting Leonard's name again, but Winnie already knows it. She doesn't hold out a hand, just nods her head, and when she speaks, Leonard is surprised by her strong Scottish accent. Her husband takes their order for tea – Winnie says she'll have peppermint, and

Lily says she'll have the same. They speak for a few minutes about the garden. Winnie knows he's a gardener, and says, 'Rose spoke of you often.' She says she feels like she knows him already. Her husband brings out the tea and retreats back into the house. As he opens the sliding doors, Leonard can hear a burst of children's laughter. The smell of mint is strong in the air – it reminds Leonard of Raine's chewing gum phase when she was fifteen. She carried a minty aura around with her for a whole year. Leonard tries a sip of Lily's and makes a face, and the women both laugh at him. After Winnie has blown on her tea a few times, she puts down her cup. She presses her hands together as if she's a Buddhist, then touches her finger-tips to her lips before addressing Leonard.

'Lily said on the phone that you've only just found out about Peter. She said you don't know anything about him, or much about Rose's childhood either.'

'Yes – we thought... I thought she was having an affair at first. I found a train ticket in an old handbag of hers, last year. We had a very happy marriage, me and Rose...'

He flicks his eyes over to Lily to check her reaction. She nods to encourage him to continue.

'It only came together slowly. We only found out about Peter a couple of weeks ago – from his birth certificate. My daughter had some questions. I... it would be good to know a little more, but I don't know how much you...'

He tapers off. There's a blackbird up in one of the trees, and its song holds the silence together until Winnie speaks again. She smiles a tight smile and looks slightly pained.

'I know a bit. From what Rose said, I'm the only one who does. It's been a heavy story to carry round all this time. I must say, Leonard, I'm grateful for the opportunity to share it. I never thought I'd be sitting here in front of you. The only reason Rose… confided in me, is that I was cut off from everyone else in her life.'

She gazes out at the butterflies on the buddleia, who are trying to decide which of the clusters of lilac blossoms are promising the sweetest nectar. Leonard spots a Painted Lady and a couple of Meadow Browns amongst the throngs of Cabbage Whites. Winnie takes a sip of her pale green tea and continues.

'So. Here we are. I need to ask you, Leonard, before I start. Are you sure you want to hear what I've got to say? It's not pretty, and I'm not going to gussy it up for you. I'm happy to keep hold of it for you if you decide not to hear it.'

Leonard looks away from her and stares out into the garden. The lilac is budding, getting ready to burst into colour. He thinks he recognises it as 'Katherine Havemeyer', and would like to go over and have a closer look to be sure. How can he answer her? How can he decide whether he wants to hear something before he knows what it is? Can't he choose afterwards? Lily says his name softly and he looks back to her. She's still there, calm, quiet – she's been there all along. He shifts his gaze to Winnie and raises his shoulders slightly, then nods. She nods back and leans forward in her chair.

'OK. I'm not sure where to start... I first met Rose – well, first saw her anyway, not long after I moved to the job at Missleden, Missleden House. We'd moved areas so my husband Edward could start at his new company. I was still getting to know Peter – you don't know anything about him yet, do you? He had what we used to call a 'severe learning disability'. They might call it something different now – the labels change all the time. A silly race for political correctness, as if changing the words might change people's attitudes… He had a rare, well, a syndrome – it affected the way he looked, he was quite short, had a kind of pointy nose. It affects different people in different ways, you know? Peter had a bad heart as well. He was pretty independent, really – could get himself dressed, make himself beans on toast, go out on his own to post a letter or walk into town. He was a happy chap, really. He was pretty close to one of the older ladies who lived there – they used to spend a lot of time together, always whispering about something, plotting some mischief.'

She smiles as she talks and looks up and to the right. Leonard keeps forgetting she's talking about his wife's son. He tries to hold the knowledge in his mind, but it keeps slipping out, like an eel.

'Rose used to come in on a Tuesday afternoon. They'd do all kinds of different things together – sometimes she'd take him out shopping, or to a film, or bowling – he loved that. Sometimes they'd just stay in the house and play board games in the living room – she enjoyed chatting with the other residents, involving them all. Most of them looked forward to her visit every week. We had quite a palaver with one young lady who got too attached and had a hissy-fit every time they decided to go out instead.

'Rose was regular as clockwork. She didn't speak with the staff much, apart from passing the time of day, but one week she came and Peter was ill with a cold; he was a bit of a hypochondriac really. He was tucked up in bed and kept dozing off. She came and sat in the kitchen with me – I was making dinner, and she asked if she could help by peeling the potatoes. I had this feeling about her... that I had to be careful with her – she was tight as a bud. After that afternoon she used to stop in on the way out and talk to me about Peter – was he happy? How was he after she left? I had the feeling she'd never talked to anyone about him before, you know?

She was so eager to hear what I had to say, she soaked it up. I think she was grateful that I talked about him like he was a human being. Some of the staff in those places... it's dreadful, but...

'Anyway, at one time Peter had swimming late on Tuesday afternoons; he was gone in the mini-bus before she had to leave, and she got into the habit of staying and helping me get their dinner ready. She said it felt good to be making a contribution, that when Peter ate his dinner, he could think of her. I always made sure I told them all she'd helped, that Peter's mum had helped to cook the crumble, or whatever it was, and they got a real kick out of that, especially Peter. We got talking while we cooked. It was usually quiet in the house – most of the clients were out doing one thing or another at the sports centre. She didn't tell me anything about herself for months. We talked about Coronation Street instead, or about the best recipe for custard.

'I never pushed her for any information, that's not my way. I think that helped her loosen up. The first thing she told me, and I remember this clearly, Leonard, was that her husband had the flu that week, and was laid up in bed. I remember thinking to myself – glory be – she's starting to trust me at last. I was careful with the little pieces of information she gave me, held onto them tight. She'd already watched me with bits of gossip that other people had given me. I've always been good at keeping my mouth shut. It might not seem like it now... but it feels like, well...'

She falters as she becomes aware of her contradiction. Leonard tries to reassure her.

'Rose is long gone now, Winnie, and so is Peter. We already know the worst of it, anyway.'

'Yes, yes, I suppose you're right. I still feel that... So, anyway. I found out about you, Leonard, and your daughter

Raine – how is she, by the way; was everything OK with the baby?'

'Yes, she got two for the price of one. Rory and Buddy.'

'Twins? Oh, how wonderful. You must be… I'd love to hear about them later, or another time. What a shame Rose couldn't have had more time to enjoy them. So. Then. Slowly, ever so slowly, over the years, I started building up a picture of what had happened. She told me that Peter was a secret, and that she didn't want to mix up her 'old life' with her 'new life'. She said they'd 'curdle'. She was very young when she had Peter. Her parents kept it from everyone, even from her friends, from her school. Maybe you already know that? Her mother sounded like a sad, damaged woman. Her father… she told me about some lovely things he'd done for her. When she spoke about him you could tell they'd adored each other. She said she might not have managed a 'normal relationship' with you, Leonard, if it hadn't been for her dad. But he could also be, well, frightening really. Not often, but she could never quite predict it. She never knew what she was going to come home to – a doting father who'd give her a big hug and ask her all about her day, or a monster who'd ask her to make him a cup of tea and then smash it on the floor when she didn't put in exactly the right amount of sugar.

'As she told me more, I started getting a feeling in the pit of my stomach, you know? When you're talking to someone about, oh – whatever, and you just know there's something else… you know it's there waiting to be said. I didn't think she'd ever tell me, and that was fine – sometimes it's better for people that things stay where they're under control, manageable, you know?'

A bee buzzes close to her ear and she swipes at it absent-mindedly. There are more of them bumbling around inside the foxgloves nearby, drinking their pollen, keeping the plants alive. The foxgloves are white, and their throats are spattered with crimson splashes. Leonard can't remember the variety, but knows that they come true from seed. He thinks about using some in Lily's garden – they'd look good scattered around the shady corner by her shed. He focuses his attention back on Winnie as she starts to talk again.

'So, it must have been at least a year after I've met her, that she had this fight with Peter. They never argued about anything, it was a surprise really. It started over something silly I think, she accused him of cheating at Ludo and he had a temper tantrum, and then a bit later when they were still annoyed with each other, something was on the television about single mothers. I came in after it happened but one of the other residents told me that Peter had said he wanted a father. He said that other people had one, that it wasn't fair. He could be a real pain if the spirit struck him. Rose had got angry at him, maybe she wanted to shut him up, I don't know, but it ended up with her slapping him on his arm – he ran upstairs and slammed his door. I knew we wouldn't see him again until he got hungry for his dinner, but she was outside the door for nearly an hour, pleading with him.

'Eventually I couldn't bear to see her like it any more. I took her out the back; we sat on the steps in the sunshine. She was all worn out from the emotion, as if she'd been through a mangle. She started talking in a very quiet voice, baby-like. She said Peter's father didn't deserve to know he'd got Peter. That's why she'd not used his surname for him. Peter was full of light, she said, and his father put her through years of darkness. And just then I knew, just before she told me.'

She pauses and puts both of her hands palm down on the table in front of her. She studies them, and when she looks up again into Leonard's eyes his heart is thumping.

'Rose had been interfered with. When she was a child. I've seen it in others. She'd been interfered with for years, Leonard. It was her uncle Lester. Peter was Lester's baby.'

Leonard is aware of a wave of feeling rising up in him. It's so strong that all he can do to begin with is contain it, is to stop it from spilling out of his mouth or his eyes. He sits quite still for several moments and hopes that nobody will touch him, especially Lily. He couldn't bear her kindness; he couldn't bear the pain of her tenderness. The objects and people around him are out of focus, as if he's looking through thick smeared glass. There's nothing holding him down, nothing anchoring him, the feelings inside him are pushing outwards as if his skin were the skin of a balloon. The first thing he's able to hold onto properly is his tea cup. It's still in his hand, half-way between his mouth and the table. He brings it closer to his mouth before realising that he's moving it the wrong way and puts it clumsily back on the table, lukewarm tea sloshing into the saucer. The sight of it sickens him.

What is he feeling? It's almost as if he's full of some kind of substance. The feelings are so solid, so choking. They're like a kind of wadding, like loft insulation – the same nasty yellow colour. He'd like to vomit it out. Instead he swallows, hard, and finds himself lifting his chest and letting in air. He's not been breathing properly, and his body is asking him to put in more oxygen, put in more oxygen. It gives him comfort, that whatever happens, his lungs will carry on doing their job, his heart will keep on pumping, his nervous system will keep on telling his body to sit upright in this chair.

It's grief. That's what he's feeling. The exact way he felt when he realised for the first time that Rose wasn't coming back. It was a few days after her death. He was stood in the kitchen, thinking about making a sandwich, and he called out to her, to ask her if she wanted one as well. There was a long silence, after he called out. An infinite silence. It's pure, unadulterated grief. He's feeling the loss of her as if she'd just gone. And he's grieving for himself – for aren't we always grieving for ourselves? Because he can't do what he wants to do right now, which is to go to her and say 'I know'. To crush her in his arms. To hold her close and let the knowledge pass between them, to help her to carry it. A single tear escapes. He doesn't wipe it away. Lily and Winnie are sitting quietly. The children's muted laughter drifts towards him across the lawn, carried on eddies of the breeze. A thrush joins in, clear and fluting, repeating the same phrase over and over, as if it's fallen in love with the sound of its own voice. He listens to the singing and the weight of the grief eases a little, like when you swap a heavy carrier bag between hands and can carry it a little further.

A thought comes to him.

'Did she ever say anything about her hair?'

Winnie looks confused, shakes her head.

What did he do to her hair? What did he do to her beautiful, long hair? The bastard. And suddenly Leonard is filled with a fury so strong that it almost knocks him off his seat. He clenches his fists and imagines wringing this man's neck, or pushing a blade through his face. Kicking him with hard boots until his bones crack and splinter. Obliterating him.

He puts a hand to his forehead and rubs his eyes. He wants to go home now, he wants to go to bed. He speaks to Winnie without looking at her.

'How did Peter die?'

'We never knew what had happened to Rose. I was afraid something terrible might have... She never gave me your phone number, Leonard, or your address; it was too risky for her. I don't think she was expecting to die so suddenly – I suppose none of us do. It wasn't like her not to make sure things would be taken care of. Peter took it very badly. Very badly. She'd only missed a handful of Tuesdays before, and she'd always called ahead. That first Tuesday, he moped around the house, looking woebegone... The next Tuesday he was angry. And the one after that... it scared me, seeing him like that. He was beside himself. He sat in his bed saying 'Mum gone. Mum gone.' There was a finality to the way he said it, as if he knew. I know he can't have known... not really... but... He caught some kind of virus the next day. It caused complications, because of his condition. He went quickly. He'd only just been admitted to hospital. I wasn't there, Leonard.'

Soon Winnie kisses them both goodbye, pressing her cheek up hard against theirs in turn and clasping their hands. Lily negotiates their passage back through the house and into the night outside. She clicks the front door shut and leaves them alone in the silent cul-de-sac. Leonard stands on the pavement and watches the bright spots of insects swerving in and out of the halo of a street-lamp. There's a bitter taste in his mouth. He hopes the moths won't scorch their wings. As Lily takes his arm, he looks around himself and wonders where he is.

Chapter 23:
Give my love to Rose

Mrs. Money-spider has decided, for reasons of her own, to go for a quick swim in Leonard's tea. Leonard puts in a careful finger-tip and fishes her out without hurting her, so she can eat more nasty aphids. He holds his finger out in front of him and blows on her gently to dry her off, before holding her out towards Lily.

'Would you like to spin her around you head?'

They're both in Lily's garden, reclining in her threadbare, multi-coloured striped deckchairs. Lily is drinking mint tea – she's been hooked on it since they visited Winnie a few weeks ago. Pickles is lying in the shade of the house, panting and keeping his beady eye on something moving about in the grass.

'What are you talking about now, you strange man?'

'You know – if you lasso it three times around your head, clockwise I think, you'll come into money before long.'

'I haven't heard that one. And anyway, what would I want with any more money? I have my tea, my beautiful garden, fine company… I'm including you in that, of course,

Pickles,' she says, turning towards Pickles, who glances up at her before returning to his insect vigil. 'What more could a girl want?'

They sit and gaze at the garden. Lily's brilliant red bergamots are looking perfect in their shagginess, and the bees are showing their appreciation. Of all the additions Leonard has made, he's particularly proud of the clump of *Rudbeckia* 'Goldsturm' – their daisy-like petals and dark centres hold up a torch of vivid yellow against Lily's collection of ornamental grasses. Leonard puts down his lemonade and leans forward slightly, as if he's about to heave himself up out of his chair.

'I must go and pull out those weeds behind the shed. They'll be scattering their seed across the lawn if we're not careful.'

'Oh, just lie back and shut up and enjoy the sunshine. We'll need to get going soon anyway. And you know what they say, Leonard. "Love is like dew that falls on both nettles and lilies." We have to leave a little bit of room for the nettles.'

He leans back, grateful to have been given permission to take it easy.

'No, I didn't know they said that. Love is like dew... is that why your mum called you Lily?'

She frowns a confused frown until she lights up in amusement as she realises what he means.

'Ha! That's an idea... that my mother would've... that she could've been capable of an affectionate gesture like that. I'll ask her next time we... just for a laugh.'

Leonard sighs a relaxed sigh and makes the most of doing nothing. They've made plans to visit Peter's grave later on. It was Lily's suggestion. They've had a few conversations about Peter and Rose. One evening Leonard talked about how distant he feels from the idea of Peter as a real person. Lily thought it might be helpful if he could do something practical, so his body can encourage his mind to grapple with the truth. She said she's always believed in rituals, in symbolic gestures. She thought that if they could visit the place where he's buried, then it might make Peter more real for him. Leonard thinks it's worth a try, but he's not really convinced. He shakes his glass of lemonade to hear the high, tinkling clink of his ice-cubes and enjoys the warmth of the sun on his closed eyelids.

The weeks since they visited Winnie have passed slowly for him. When he got back from seeing her that first evening, he hadn't known what to do with himself. After the first shock of grief in her garden, the sadness had come in waves. Sometimes it swallowed him up and he'd had to go to bed in the middle of the evening, to curl up under his duvet and try and sleep. Once at work the tears started flowing from him without warning, and he had to go and walk in the woods for an hour until he could calm himself down. It feels like it's wearing off now, but it's difficult to predict.

It's helped his muddled head to say the facts out loud to other people. He spoke to Raine first, when he went round to help her get ready for Ed's party, propping Buddy Holly up in the car so he was looking out of the passenger seat. He's thinking about getting one for himself – a Johnny Cash to look out of his top bedroom window, or a Darth Vader taped to the back of the toilet door to scare his guests. He told Raine what he knew as they assembled canapés in the kitchen, layering anchovies and strips of pepper in pastry cases and whizzing up fresh liver pate to spread on tiny crackers. They'd talked for a little while about what it might have been like for Rose, trying to guess her reasons for keeping it all separate, until Raine started shrinking back and then changed the subject. It's still hard for her to talk about, Leonard knows that. She needs to take things at her own pace – she's doing the best she can.

He told Charlie over shepherd's pie with Lily and Marion. The women got on like a house on fire, but Charlie had seemed reluctant to give up his pub/greenhouse time. Leonard couldn't even get any 'hnhs' out of him. Thankfully, the alcohol started flowing a little more freely as the evening went on, and by pudding he was leaning conspiratorially towards Lily and telling her all about his son and his doctor boyfriend. Marion got so drunk that Charlie had to take her up to bed at eleven thirty, laughing his head off as he helped her stagger up the stairs.

The last people he told were Pete and Glor. He met them in the Bells. It was the first time he'd seen Glor, and things still felt a little awkward between them – he kept getting a mental image of her on his sofa with her legs in the air. He's sure it'll pass. Pete told him they were planning an extended holiday, 'the cruise of a life-time' as he kept proudly calling it. When Pete went to the toilet, Glor thanked Leonard for meeting up with Pete that day and giving him 'the benefit of his wisdom'. Whatever Leonard had said to him, she said, it had 'worked wonders'.

It's been more difficult to accommodate the new information within himself. For the first few days it had felt as if there literally weren't any room for it – the memories he had of Rose were so complete that the new knowledge just kept slipping out. His brain kept rejecting the truth of it – how could his wife have kept a whole person from him? How could she not have trusted him with it? But the information wouldn't soak away into the floor either – it followed him along wherever he went, trying to get inside him. Eventually it squirmed into the middle of the section labelled 'memories of Rose' and lodged there. Connections started growing between it and the other things he remembered. The hysterical tears after Raine had been born. The strange migraines. That time she went a little mad, telling him he should leave her. Her lies about her mother. Her blue wedding dress – not white, not virginal. Her last words – 'I can't go first.' She wasn't talking about Leonard. It even shed new light on things that hadn't been a part of their investigation. Her strong reluctance to move away from the area, her protests that she felt 'rooted' where they were. Her fondness for her friend's little boy who had Downs – she always made a special fuss of him and told him how proud she was of him. He'd thought that she just felt sorry for him. The new knowledge got so tangled up with the old that he knew he'd never be able to cut it out.

Leonard takes another sip of his lemonade and looks over at Lily, whose book is resting face down on her stomach. Her head is slumped to one side, and she seems to be quietly snoring. Pickles is stretched out like a cat in the sun, also fast asleep, his leg twitching. They're both missing the show. The garden is laid out before them and everything is changing right now, while they're sleeping. The slow pace of growing has steadied Leonard so many times in his life. In these impatient times, it's easy to forget how slowly things really change – how difficult it really is to move from one feeling to another, deep down. He knows how growing works – that some of the best plants, the ones that offer the biggest rewards, take their time. You might not wait a single season for the best flowers, the thickest display of leaves, but ten seasons. That's how it is for him, inside. He's not going to process this new information about Rose straight away, and he doesn't expect himself to. This first year will be the most dramatic – there'll be new growth, he might have to move some things around inside himself, re-plant them somewhere else. Some roots will get shifted. But there's no hurry. It'll percolate through him slowly, like sprinkling fish bone and blood onto the soil. There might be rough weather ahead, the winds will blow, he might lose some of his prize specimens. But he can grow them again, if he wants to. Or maybe he'll try something new in their place.

By the time Lily wakes up with a not-very-ladylike snort, the sky is beginning to cloud over. They fold up the deck-chairs and put them back in the shed, although Leonard isn't convinced a spot of rain could do much more to hasten the already imminent end of their lives. They decide to take Leonard's car – Lily's has apparently started making 'strange rumbling noises in its belly'. Leonard straps himself in and thinks about all the other journeys he's made with Lily over the last seven months – to visit Rose's mum, to see her aunt Mildred and the cousin, the final trip to meet Winnie. He'll be glad when this journey is over. Or maybe he'll make it again? Does he want this dead person to be a part of his life now? He isn't sure. It's too early to know.

They pass a field full of pigs on the way, and Pickles leans out of the window to sniff the exciting piggy whiffs carried on the breeze. They're roaming free and each has a corrugated iron-topped 'house' of their own. Most of them are out and about despite the fine rain, grubbing around in the mud for their tasty food pellets, but Leonard likes to think of a few of them tucked up in their warm straw beds out of the rain, dreaming of a worldwide ban on bacon.

It's still spitting when they arrive, and the temperature has dropped dramatically. Lily asks him to wait while she puts on her jumper, stretching her arms out awkwardly in the enclosed space of the car. She also puts on some lipstick – pink and fake-looking, and he teases her about being paranoid about how she looks even when the men are already dead. It's a dismal place, even when he tries to imagine the sun shining on it. From anywhere in the graveyard, there's a view of the local business park, all concrete and plastic signs. The 'garden' is full of ivy and weeds. A lot of the graveyard looks 'too new' – there are headstones from ten years ago that look like they were engraved last week, and nasty grey and white gravel sprinkled everywhere. They walk slowly alongside the rows of mounds, Pickles trampling over grave after grave as if he's deliberately disrespecting the dead. Lily has taken Leonard's arm again, and they have to unlink to walk single file down a narrow stretch of the path. He misses the solid feeling of her bones and flesh against his, and holds his elbow out towards her when there's enough space again. She smiles and feeds her hand through like threading a huge needle.

It takes them fifteen minutes to find Peter's headstone. It is so small and grey – Leonard supposes it must be standard government issue.

'Here lies Peter March, 1962 – 2002'.

That's all it says. Nothing more. If Rose had waited a little longer, if Peter had died first, there would have been a stone angel with a loving inscription, or at least some flowers. Lily has thought to bring some along today – a generous bunch of peach-coloured roses and snapdragons. She gives herself a final waft of their perfume and almost points them towards Leonard so he can do the same before she remembers where she is and decides against it. She kneels to poke each stem into a hole in the small vase-like receptacle near the base of the headstone. They stand there for a while and Leonard reads the epitaph over and over. He isn't sure what he's meant to be doing. Should he feel sad? He never knew this man. Did he really live a happy life, like Winnie said? Did he know anything about Leonard at all? Had he lived in different institutions since he was a child? He lived a whole lifetime without Leonard knowing about his existence – from being born to a frightened teenager, to dying alone and abandoned. Who was he?

He doesn't feel anything apart from cold. After what he guesses is a reasonably respectable amount of time, he pulls on Lily's arm. He asks her if she fancies a drink, and she nods gratefully. They call to Pickles, who's invented a fun game which involves pulling at a piece of ivy, running around in a circle and then going back to have another go at it, and all three of them pick their way back to the car. Lily is still holding onto a rose that didn't fit into the vase and every so often she lifts it to her nose. Leonard can feel an awkward silence – not really between him and Lily, but in the air. It's as if there's something that should have been done or said or felt, and it hasn't been. The rain strengthens and they break into a run – Lily putting an ineffectual arm over her head.

They dive into the car, laughing, and Lily gets her handbag tangled up on the gear stick. Leonard holds his door open from inside and encourages Pickles, who's fallen behind and is now running towards the car as fast as his little legs can carry him. He leap-frogs over his owner, leaving a generous gift of water and mud and sticks on Leonard's trousers, and spreads a little more over the back seat as Leonard slams the door shut. He feels strangely empty. The quiet in the car is oppressive, so he leans across Lily to rummage in the glove compartment for a Johnny Cash album. As he hovers over her he catches her scent and lingers for a while, even after he's put his hand onto the CD. It's not her perfume, it's coming directly from her skin – it smells of… what is it? Sweet peas? Lily-of-the-valley? He hasn't heard the whole of this Cash album yet. It's a present from Ed for 'being the man, d'you know what I mean?' Ed isn't known for his thoughtful gestures, and Leonard was touched. It's the last one Johnny recorded before he died, and it's mostly covers of other people's songs. He slides it into his CD player and is glad to start the car and pull away from the gloomy place. His heating is broken, and he notices Lily shiver. After asking Pickles if he'd mind, he pulls a blanket from the back seat and offers it to her. He warns her it's a bit 'eau de doggy', but she falls on it gratefully and wraps herself up like a baby.

They're driving along a narrow country lane when the fourth song comes on. The narrator is singing about a man who's just been let out of prison after serving his ten year sentence. He's trying to get back to Louisiana, so he can see his wife and get to know his son. The narrator finds the man dying on the railroad track between San Francisco and home. Johnny sings:

> Give my love to Rose, please won't you, mister
> Take her all my money, tell her to buy some pretty clothes
> Tell my boy his daddy's so proud of him
> And don't forget to give my love to Rose

Hearing Rose's name unlocks something inside of him. His foundations shift, tectonic plates pushing up against each other. He feels the sobs rising up like marbles in his chest. He doesn't care anymore, he doesn't care about holding it in. He pulls the car over, carefully, so he can give himself over to what's coming. He unclicks his seat belt and lets out a shuddered whimper. Lily holds out her arms to him and he leans his body over towards her, letting himself be swallowed up by her warmth, her layers of soft clothes, burrowing down towards her sweet scent. His stomach tenses up and the pain pushes its way out of him in waves. He lets out a sound with each wave through clenched teeth and bared lips – a rasping 'shhhh' like water through pebbles. After each wave, he enters a clear space of balm before the next one builds. He empties himself into her. The salty water spills onto his cheeks and drips onto the doggy blanket. Lily is saying 'it's OK, it's OK', and stroking his hair with a calm hand. She's saying his name.

And then the song comes to an end, and he's had enough of crying. But he doesn't want to move, and he leans against her for longer, until his back starts to stiffen up. He knows he'll have to move. Rather than moving away, he manoeuvres himself up closer and brings his face up towards hers. He kisses her, her eyes wide with surprise. The first kiss is chaste – the kind you'd get from a small child, or plant on a spouse when leaving for work. He notices the give of her lips against his, the layer of grease where he imagines the pink coming off onto his own lips. She's still looking at him, wide-eyed. And then she relaxes her face a little. Closes her eyes. Waits for him to come towards her again. And he does, and they kiss again, properly, their mouths moving as if they are saying something important to each other. And they are.

Acknowledgements

Thanks to all at Snowbooks, for all their hard work.

Thanks to Steve Biggins, Jonathan Kellett, Sarah Brown, Dave Wallace, Chris Heron, and Susan Hill and Rory Stuart (via Reflections from a Garden) for generously sharing their love of the land with me.

Thanks to Wendy Hall, Hazel Cook, Claire King, Peter Biddlecombe and Mike Brogan for important details.

Thanks to Jo Brogan for wanting to get to the end.

Thanks to Esther Morgan, Heather Butler, Nicola Weller, Jacqui Lofthouse, Susan Utting and Alex Valy for being friends of my writing and friends with me.

Thanks to the readers of 'a small stone' and 'Planting Words'.

Thanks to Steve, for IT support and for all the rest.

About the Author

Fiona Robyn was born in 1974 in Surrey and grew up in Sarawak. Her website is at www.fionarobyn.com. She currently lives in rural Hampshire with her partner and her vegetable patch.

Next from Fiona Robyn...

Thaw

Coming Early 2010

Monday 1st March

These hands are ninety-three years old. They belong to Charlotte Marie Bradley Miller. She was so frail her grand-daughter had to carry her onto the set to take this photo. It's a close-up. Her bony arms emerge from the top corners of the photo and the background is black, maybe velvet, as if we're being protected from seeing the strings. One wrist rests on the other and her fingers hang loose, close together, a pair of folded wings. And you can see her insides. Her knuckle bones bulge out of her skin, which sags like plastic that has melted in the sun and is dripping off her, wrinkling and folding. Her veins look stuck onto the outside of her hands. They're a colour that's difficult to describe – blue, but also silver, green – her blood runs through them, close to the surface. The book says she died shortly after they took this picture. Did she even get to see it? Maybe it was the last beautiful thing she left in the world.

I'm trying to decide whether or not I want to carry on living. I'm giving myself three months of this journal to decide. You might think that sounds melodramatic, but I don't think I'm alone in wondering whether it's all worth it. I've seen the look in people's eyes. Stiff suits travelling to work morning after morning on the cramped and humid tube. Tarted-up girls and gangs of boys reeking of aftershave, reeling on the pavements on a Friday night, trying to mop up the dreariness of their week with one desperate, fake-happy night. I've heard the weary grief in my dad's voice.

So where do I start with all this? What do you want to know about me? I'm Ruth White, thirty two years old, going on a hundred. I live alone with no boyfriend and no cat in a tiny flat in central London. In fact I had a non-relationship with a man at work, Dan, for seven years. I'm sitting in my bedroom-cum-living room right now, looking up every so often at the thin rain slanting across a flat grey sky. I work in a city hospital lab as a microbiologist. My dad is an accountant and lives with his sensible second wife Julie in a sensible second home. Mother finished dying when I was fourteen, three years after her first diagnosis. What else? What else is there?

Charlotte Marie Bradley Miller. I looked at her hands for twelve minutes. It was odd describing what I was seeing in words. Usually the picture just sits inside my head and I swish it around like tasting wine. I have huge books all over my flat – books you have to take in both hands to lift. I've had the photo habit for years. Mother bought me my first book, black and white landscapes by Ansel Adams. When she got really ill I used to take it to bed with me and look at it for hours, concentrating on the huge trees, the still water, the never-ending skies. I suppose it helped me to think about something other than what was happening. I learned to focus on one photo at a time rather than flicking from scene to scene in search of something to hold me. If I concentrate then everything stands still. Although I use them to escape the world, I also think they bring me closer to it. I've still got that book. When I take it out I handle the pages as if they might flake into dust.

Mother used to write a journal. When I was small I sat by her bed in the early mornings on a hard chair and looked at her face as her pen spat out sentences in short bursts. I imagined what she might have been writing about – princesses dressed in star-patterned silk, talking horses, adventures with pirates. More likely she was writing about what she was going to cook for dinner and how irritating dad's snoring was.

I've always wanted to write my own journal and this is my chance. Maybe my last chance. The idea is that every night for three months I'll take one of these heavy sheets of pure white paper, rough under my fingertips, and fill it up on both sides. If my suicide note is nearly a hundred pages long then no-one can accuse me of not thinking it through. No-one can say 'it makes no sense, she was a polite, cheerful girl, had everything to live for', before adding that I did keep myself to myself. It'll all be here. I'm using a silver fountain pen with purple ink. A bit flamboyant for me, I know. I need these idiosyncratic rituals, they hold things in place. Like the way I make tea, squeezing the tea-bag three times, the exact amount of milk, seven stirs. My writing is small and neat, I'm striping the paper. I'm near the bottom of the page now. Only ninety-one more days to go before I'm allowed to make my decision. That's it for today. It's begun.

Tuesday 2nd March

What an exciting life I lead. Alarm set for 7.35. Pull on a dressing gown, even though no-one can see into my flat.

I hear my grandma's voice: 'what if there's a fire!' Crappy morning TV. Breakfast of branflakes, semi-skimmed milk, a glass of orange juice (supermarket own). Freshly squeezed is too expensive. Dad's drilled it into me, save money! I'm not sure what I'm saving it for. Shower, get dressed (a white shirt, a black pair of trousers, smart shoes that hurt when I walk). Mascara. I see myself in the mirror and notice that the lines around my eyes stay visible even when I uncrease my face. I look back at my grey-blue eyes – they're asking me a question but I can't quite hear what they're saying. Pale mushroom skin. Long, straight black hair that always reminds me of those evil- looking ravens, pulled back into a neat pony-tail. There's nothing about my face that should make me ugly, nothing unusual, but I don't quite pull off looking pretty.

Make sandwiches for lunch. Fetch my boring black handbag with its exciting contents – a packet of tissues, my purse, a small first-aid kit, a mirror. Lock the front door and join the river of commuters at the tube, we're always in such a hurry – for what? Get to work, clock in. Say hi to the others – Maggie, John, Khalid, using my best pretend-happy voice. Button up my lab coat, start work. Collect Petri dishes from the hot room. Collect patient report forms. Match them up. Look at what's grown. Look down my microscope. Look at more Petri dishes. Look down my microscope again. Repeat one hundred times.

10.45 tea break. 12.30 lunch, usually spent in Hyde park, alone with my sandwiches. Back to work. 15.30 tea break. Work. 17.30 home. Stop falling asleep at the back there, this is my life. 17.50 get home and open my exciting mail, bills and junk. 18.00 cook dinner, crap telly. 21.30 choose a photo to look at before I go to sleep. I often toss and turn in the middle of the night so it's good to get into bed early, and what would I be staying up for anyway? Up at 7.35. Pull on my dressing gown. You get the idea. Nothing that makes any difference to the world.

I thought about mother this evening. It's what dad always called her, 'your mother'. 'Ask your mother if she wants a cup of coffee.' 'Fetch a knife for your mother.' Even now when he talks about her to other people he calls her 'Ruth's mother' or 'my late wife'. I've never heard him say her name. Morden. A beautiful word, it didn't get used enough. I don't even know if it's a real name. Her mother Aggie liked to do things differently, and I can imagine her noticing it on the map one day and liking the sound of it. To me it sounds medieval, mysterious. I was thinking about her dying, like always. About the three things that happened, the three things I witnessed that I'll never forget. They taunted me as they usually do, threatening to take up the space behind my eyes. They spin like a merry-go-round and I only catch a glimpse of each one before the next appears. If I'm not careful they'll swing into focus. Maybe if I could look at them full on, stare them out, they'd lose some of their power. I will write them down – I'll tell you about them as soon as I feel strong enough. But not yet. Not yet.

Last night I dreamt up her voice, complaining. I was sat in my bedroom in our old house in Maida Vale as a grown-up, doing a jigsaw with a picture on it that I couldn't make out. There were feathers and fur and teeth on different pieces. It sounded like she was just outside my door. She was saying 'Ruthie! Can't you remember some good days? What about when we went to the circus, or when we made fairy cakes? When I was healthy, before I started to shrink! I'm sick of seeing myself like that in your head Ruthie, sick of it!' It went on and on. I wanted her to shut up, I wanted to get my jigsaw finished. Her voice held me frozen to the spot, squirming.

I've been thinking about getting a special present for dad, just in case, and wondered about having my portrait painted. I saw an advert in the local paper a couple of weeks ago – I remember reading it and thinking it odd. I rummaged about in the pile of papers waiting to be recycled and found it. It said 'Portraits. Want to know how others see you? Come and be painted.' Then it had the word 'Red' (was that her name?) and a contact number. I'll give her a ring tomorrow, see what she says. I'm not sure I want to know how others see me.

Wednesday 3rd March

I'm still not sure what to do with this big white space. It's silly, but before I start writing my heart speeds up. What should I write about? If I'm stuck on the third day then what are my hopes for getting this finished? I can write about what's outside me, about the pictures I look at, the people I see on the way to work. But I'm meant to be writing about me. Rummaging about in my head, pulling out what I think will be useful for you to see. Hand over hand – a thread of words that comes out like a string of knotted handkerchiefs from a magician's sleeve. I can't find anything to get a grip on. It feels like there's nothing there. Maybe there isn't anything, maybe my soul just rattles around inside me, a pea-sized lump of grey that gets me out of bed, into my clothes, into work, back home. That puts food into my mouth, chews and swallows. That flicks the TV from channel to channel, that speaks pretend words with a pretend voice. How dead am I already? Where did I go? When did it happen?

An Afro-Caribbean girl called Mary started at work

today. She's spending some time on the main swabs section with me before she goes to our training officer Tony for some 'proper' training. She's tiny, with matchstick arms and legs, short afro hair and a nervous, toothy smile. The training portfolio they have to fill in now was almost bigger than she was. She seems so young, straight out of university and in her first job – she couldn't even look me in the eye when I talked to her. I tried to put her at ease by telling her about my scary first day when I dropped a tray of agar plates all over the floor. Today I showed her round the whole lab and explained things as I went – the prep room, the TB cabinet, the blood culture room… she was anxious to commit everything I said to memory. I suppose I'm responsible for her for the time being. I felt sorry for her. I wasn't sure what to say to make it any easier for her.

I called the portrait painter from the advert this evening. When a man answered I asked if I could speak to Red and he said 'This is Red.' His accent was strong, Russian or Eastern European, his voice deep. I'd written down a list of questions so I didn't get flustered and he answered them all quite brusquely – he didn't seem bothered about persuading me to hire him. He charges two hundred pounds for a painting, and he needs you to sit for him twice a week for six or seven sessions. That's quite a lot of time and the price sounded reasonable to me. He works from his house near Hyde Park and has an afternoon slot free at two on Tuesdays and Thursdays. My line manager at work should be OK about that. He wanted me to see some of his paintings before I came round and gave me two internet addresses. I'm seeing him for an initial meeting next Tuesday. When I'd put the phone down I felt a short bloom of excitement – I don't usually do things like that. It pushed aside the usual background sadness for a while, the sadness that I'm so used to I hardly notice any more. Like looking through dirty windows – it's only when a fly lands on the glass that you notice how filthy they are, how much they're obscuring your view.

Speaking to Red reminded me of a book of photos I have of Russia. I looked at a frozen Lake Baikal tonight. The water reaches more than halfway up the page where it meets a thin strip of land hung with mist, and above is the sky, full of fluffy white and blue-grey clouds that look as if they're made out of something you could touch – marshmallow or whipped cream. The book said that this lake is four hundred miles long and holds twenty percent of the world's fresh water. Three hundred and thirty six rivers flow into it. In the middle of the picture are a few blocks of ice, crumbled onto the water like lumps of icing sugar, balancing the whiteness of the clouds above. In the foreground you can see pieces of ice floating on the surface in the shape of those scissor-shells I remember picking up from the beach as a child. Underneath the water are big rocks, mostly hidden by the sunlight colouring the surface silver. Further off is a blanket of ice, keeping everything underneath it safe. I'd like to take off my clothes and paddle, feeling the large stones against the soles of my feet. Just before I'm out of my depth I'd take a last, deep breath and submerge – swimming under the ice, my eyes shut and my hair flowing back, feeling the strength of the water as I push past. My skin would tingle as glittering scales pushed up through it and my legs would join together into a strong flat muscle designed for moving fast through water. I'd like to find a home for myself under that ice-covering.

Thursday 4th March

I suppose I'd better start on the story of my life. But where do I begin? I'd rather not start at all – I don't want to drag it all up again (as dad would say). I'll start with Abbie, my aunt. I can talk about her – it'll get me warmed up. Abbie is mother's sister. I only met her a couple of times when I was small. There was some kind of squabble between them and they hadn't spoken for years. Mother told me she lived 'in the country', and as far as I knew everyone in the country had a farm. I imagined her feeding the chickens and cows every morning like in a picture book my dad read to me over and over. I remember being fascinated by the tea she brought to drink – it was light green with no milk and smelt funny. When she let me take a sip I thought it tasted of grass and I could even see strands of it floating about at the bottom of the mug. I thought she might have been teasing me but was far too polite to say anything. Whenever I drink green tea it takes me back to her dark auburn hair with glints of gold in a thick rope plait, and her crinkly green eyes. It takes me back to her steady, musical voice, which soothed me.

When mother got really ill Abbie started coming round again. She used to disappear into mother's bedroom for hours on end and come out looking grey and drawn. Her clothes were always colourful – patchwork and velvet with tiny stitched-in mirrors – I thought she looked like a hippy. She tried to talk to me in the hallway, trying different conversations openers – 'how was school today?' or 'what kind of music do you like?' or 'how are you doing?' I answered in polite monosyllables and eventually she got the message. I didn't want to talk to anyone by then, it was nothing personal. Afterwards I stayed with her for a few weeks while dad tried to gather the pieces of himself together. She didn't have cows or chickens but she did have a huge tortoise-shell cat, Oscar, who took a liking to me right away and jumped onto my lap whenever I sat down. We'd never had pets at home and I was a bit wary of him at first – he had massive paws and I saw his spiked claws come out when he puddened on a cushion. When he washed himself I was amazed at the loudness of the noises he made – sucking and squelching, quite obscene. Abbie respected my privacy, always offering to spend time with me, and not looking offended when I turned her down (which I always did). She gave me space like a gift. As I write tears are pricking at my eyes, I'm surprised, I didn't realise how grateful I was. And Oscar became my confidante – I talked to him quietly so no-one else could hear. He was a good listener, except the times when he suddenly decided he'd had enough and wandered outside to stalk the autumn leaves. I couldn't blame him for that. He never answered back. He didn't expect anything from me. And he kept everything that I said to him a secret. In a way Oscar was more real to me than Abbie during those first few weeks.

I loved her house too – a wonderful lived-in house full of books and mugs with dregs in and lengths of Indian material and small piles of pine cones she was collecting for god knows what. There was a real fire in the living room and one night we cooked chestnuts in the embers. The garden was tangled with weeds and was full of places to crouch in, to hide. I stubbed my toe on a stone fairy once, hidden in the undergrowth. I called her Lila and made a little shrine for her in the broken shed. I surrounded her with fresh flowers, shiny stones and empty snail shells. I talked to her too, when Oscar was busy with other things. I was sorry to leave her behind. Towards the end of my stay I thought I might be ready to speak to Abbie as well, but then dad came to take me home. The strength of her goodbye hug nearly winded me, and after a few startled moments I became terrified that I'd start crying and wouldn't know how to stop. Thankfully she let go just in time, told me to 'go well', and that was that. I didn't go there again – dad told me that she reminded him of my mother too much, and I was fiercely loyal to him – who else was there to be loyal to?

She lives twenty three miles away from me now, and I haven't seen her for eighteen years. You think that's odd? It's not that I don't want to see her. It just feels easier to let her slip into the past, with mother. I haven't even thought about Abbie for ages. Although that's not strictly true. Whenever I see a woman with dark auburn hair my stomach does a little flip. I can never decide if I should cross the street to see if it's her, or hide my face and hurry past. It's never been her.